Justine Lewis wr[...]
contemporary rom[...]
with her hero hus[...]
outgoing puppy. When she isn't writing she
loves to walk her dog in the bush near her house,
attempt to keep her garden alive and search for the
perfect frock. She loves hearing from readers and
you can visit her at justinelewis.com.

Scarlett Clarke's interest in romance can be
traced back to her love of Nancy Drew books,
when she tried to solve the mysteries of her
favourite detective while rereading the romantic
chapters with Ned Nickerson. She's thrilled now
to be writing romances of her own. Scarlett lives
in, and loves, her hometown of Kansas City. By
day she works in public relations and wrangles
two toddlers, two cats and a dog. By night she
writes romance and tries to steal a few moments
with her firefighter hubby.

Also by Justine Lewis

Swipe Right for Mr Perfect

Invitation from Bali miniseries

Breaking the Best Friend Rule
The Billionaire's Plus-One Deal

Princesses' Night Out miniseries

How To Win Back a Royal

Also by Scarlett Clarke

Royal Encounters miniseries

The Prince She Kissed in Paris
Royally Forbidden to the Boss

Discover more at millsandboon.co.uk.

DATING GAME WITH HER ENEMY

JUSTINE LEWIS

THE BILLIONAIRE SHE LOVES TO HATE

SCARLETT CLARKE

MILLS & BOON

All rights reserved including the right of reproduction in whole or in part in any form. This edition is published by arrangement with Harlequin Enterprises ULC.

This is a work of fiction. Names, characters, places, locations and incidents are purely fictional and bear no relationship to any real life individuals, living or dead, or to any actual places, business establishments, locations, events or incidents. Any resemblance is entirely coincidental.

This book is sold subject to the condition that it shall not, by way of trade or otherwise, be lent, resold, hired out or otherwise circulated without the prior consent of the publisher in any form of binding or cover other than that in which it is published and without a similar condition including this condition being imposed on the subsequent purchaser.

® and TM are trademarks owned and used by the trademark owner and/or its licensee. Trademarks marked with ® are registered with the United Kingdom Patent Office and/or the Office for Harmonisation in the Internal Market and in other countries.

First published in Great Britain 2025
by Mills & Boon, an imprint of HarperCollins*Publishers* Ltd,
1 London Bridge Street, London, SE1 9GF

www.harpercollins.co.uk

HarperCollins*Publishers*, Macken House, 39/40 Mayor Street Upper, Dublin 1, D01 C9W8, Ireland

Dating Game with Her Enemy © 2025 Justine Lewis

The Billionaire She Loves to Hate © 2025 Scarlett Clarke

ISBN: 978-0-263-39679-9

05/25

This book contains FSC™ certified paper
and other controlled sources to ensure responsible forest management.

For more information visit www.harpercollins.co.uk/green.

Printed and Bound in the UK using 100% Renewable Electricity
at CPI Group (UK) Ltd, Croydon, CR0 4YY

DATING GAME WITH HER ENEMY

JUSTINE LEWIS

MILLS & BOON

For the best café in the world, Tilley's, for your
red carpet, cosy wooden booths and sustaining coffees.

I've seen some of my favourite gigs,
had countless life-changing conversations and
sought sanctuary there many times over the years.

Most of all, I've written so many words.

Thank you. xx

CHAPTER ONE

As usual, the function to launch and celebrate the latest Evermore resort was somewhere low-key and understated, yet in a gorgeous location. The rowing club in Manly faced the harbour and the ferry terminal. It was old, full of character and right on the water, with a view of the sun setting over the silver spires of the city.

They were a long way from the new resort, which was in northern New South Wales, but a company known for its stance on sustainability was hardly going to fly everyone up north for a party. Instead they had gathered everyone who had worked on the project, along with select influencers and PR types, to hype the launch of their new eco resort. There were photos and an interactive display for guests to look at as they mingled and enjoyed the wine and canapés.

Meg felt the stress slipping from her shoulders with each sip of champagne. This was one of the most ambitious projects she'd worked on and now it was complete. Following a successful soft launch, the resort was now officially open and, thankfully, fully booked for the next month. She was proud of her team and to have been a part of such a worthwhile project.

Meg's tights rubbed at just the wrong place on her inner thigh. She glanced around the room and, seeing no one was watching, turned towards the wall, adjusted her tights and smoothed down her dress. She looked back up as she turned and caught the eye of Daniel Fairweather, her colleague and sworn enemy. She groaned softly. Daniel made every occasion slightly worse and every day just that little bit more annoying. And now he'd seen her pull her tights out from her crotch. Everything was an opportunity for him to mock her; he had a gift for managing to notice her at her most vulnerable and she hated that.

She wasn't vulnerable, she was strong, independent and successful, and Daniel was just an arrogant pain in the backside. An arrogant pain who was now walking towards her.

Why? Neither of them spoke to one another any more than was absolutely necessary. There were a hundred other people here who would be happy to talk to him. Yet, he was coming her way.

Meg loved her job as Chief Financial Officer at Evermore. But to say she loathed her colleague Dan would be an understatement. If this had been any other company she would have left years ago, but she believed strongly in their business and making it as successful as possible. When anyone asked what the business did, she answered, 'We build eco resorts.' The answer was far more complex but usually her prepared answer told the other person all they needed to know. In reality, Evermore designed and built self-sustainable and regenerative yet luxurious hotels, resorts and camps. They owned and managed some of them, but devolved others back to the local communities, with which they always worked in partnership.

Dan was a thorn in her side, but the work was rewarding. Besides, Meg wasn't going to be the first to leave the company. She wasn't going to give Dan that satisfaction.

He stopped next to her, far too close in Meg's opinion. And he looked at her far too closely as well. That wasn't normal. Usually the pair of them avoided eye contact with one another as much as possible.

'Are you okay?'

'Yes. Why wouldn't I be?'

He grinned. 'Good, just checking.'

Insufferable. Intolerable. Insolent. She could go on. Many unflattering words could describe the man now standing next to her with a silly smirk on his too-handsome face.

His hair was flecked with grey, though still impressively thick for a man in his late fifties. His face was creased with some wrinkles, but she had to concede that his boyish good looks were still apparent. Which, of course, wasn't fair, because he had the personality of a toad.

Dan wiped the side of his mouth with his fingers and raised his eyebrows as he indicated towards her with a nod. Great, now he was making faces at her. How did he still have a job? How did he have friends? Why did people still speak so highly of him when he was so irritating?

'What is your problem?' she spat.

'You've got something on your chin. Sauce, I think. That's what I came to tell you.'

She wiped her finger where he'd indicated and sure enough found a smudge of sauce on her index finger. Great. She'd eaten that prawn cocktail ten minutes ago and had been walking around like this ever since.

A little part of her died inside. She wouldn't have minded if anyone else had pointed that out, but why did it have to be Dan?

Which was ridiculous. She was fifty-three, not thirteen. And Dan was a grown man, older than she was. They had both been around the sun enough times not to find this sort of thing unusual or even embarrassing.

But when it came to Daniel Fairweather her body seemed to work separately from her brain. Things that usually made sense stopped making sense around him. Her logical thoughts became frozen and the old, emotional part of her brain tried to take over. Meg would have none of it. She stepped back from him just as Dan reached for a napkin from a passing waiter and handed it to her. She wiped her chin.

'Thanks,' she mumbled, her mouth hating having to say those words to him.

'No problem,' he said, with a bounce in his voice.

'It's a good turnout.' She looked around the room. The guests were clustered around the VR goggles and the large screens playing videos of the resort. The room was filled with the unmistakable hum of excitement. 'It was a great project, well-delivered. And it'll be well run also.'

'Thank you,' he said, smiling.

'It was a good job by the team.' She stressed the final word as hard as she could without spelling it out. Did he actually think she was giving him credit for the whole project?

'Yes, but I designed it.'

'You drafted the first design.'

'Yes, so it wouldn't have happened without me.'

She laughed. The man was delusional.

'What's so funny?'

'Your first design was so impractical it would have bankrupted us.'

'My first design was beautiful and if the penny pinchers hadn't been so pedantic we might be opening that beautiful resort now.'

His words were pointed at her.

'Penny pinchers? Are you serious? It looked more like a cathedral than an eco resort.'

'Of course I'm serious. I'm tired of having my visions shot down by people unwilling to take risks.'

'I'm not unwilling to take risks. I'm just unwilling to take unnecessary ones.'

'It wouldn't kill you to loosen the purse strings a little every now and then, you know.'

Meg downed the last of her glass. *Don't bite. Don't bite. He's not worth it.*

Except he was so wrong! Daniel Fairweather might have been Chief Architect at Evermore, but his head was in the clouds. It was easy to come up with fanciful ideas if you weren't responsible for paying for them. Which Meg was.

'And I should let the company go bust? Then where would we all be?'

'I'm not saying we should risk going bust, but we don't need to be so…'

Don't say it. Don't you dare say it.

'Tight,' he said.

Meg grabbed a glass from a nearby waiter. Contemplated throwing it at Daniel but realised it would be a waste of perfectly good wine.

'If it weren't for me and my team's attention to detail, the company would've collapsed years ago. Not to mention your salary would be a fraction of what it is.'

That stopped him in his tracks. It always did. As the CFO she knew Dan's salary, but he did not know hers. And he hated that.

And Meg loved that he hated that.

'If it weren't for my vision and creativity, we wouldn't have so many people here now drooling over this new resort.'

'Don't be ridiculous. I've saved you from overstretching and over-investing so many times I've lost count.'

'If it weren't for me—' he began but a couple moved in their direction to look at the nearby display. Meg stepped back into the corner to make way, but the couple kept coming. Dan moved in the same direction as Meg to give them room. He was now right next to her, a mere foot away. If she'd gesticulated emphatically she would have bumped him so she kept very still. Meg and Dan listened in silent agreement at what the couple were saying.

'It's beautiful. Truly stunning. I can't wait to see it in person,' the woman said.

Meg flicked a glance in Dan's direction. He was trying to keep his expression neutral but his ego couldn't help the smile twitching the corner of his mouth.

'It's too expensive though. The prices they're charging...' the man said.

Meg felt Dan's gaze on hers and despite her wishing otherwise her cheeks tingled. 'It is not!' she wanted to retort. A sustainable, regenerative resort was more expensive to begin with, but that was simply because it had to reflect the true cost of the building and the works and the costs to offset environmental damage! Luckily, the woman came to Meg's defence.

'Don't be ridiculous. It simply reflects the real costs of sustainable tourism, the impact on the environment and the local community. Not to mention fair labour costs.'

Meg silently cheered. She glanced at Dan and gave him a smirk back. Ha!

Just as Meg was making to slip away to enjoy her small victory in peace, the first couple were joined by another and, rather than being able to leave, she was pushed further back towards the wall.

Dan attempted to stay at the front, but the tide of people pushed him back as well. He tried to move to the opposite corner from Meg, but a tall man beat him to it. Before either of them had a chance to prepare themselves for what was happening, Dan was in the corner, right next to Meg, his body straight and taut and held firmly away from her. Meg pushed herself as far as she could away. If they touched who knew what might happen? A rupture of the space-time continuum? Certainly nothing good.

She supposed they could have excused themselves, but eavesdropping on the unguarded conversation was too good an opportunity to pass up. Dan obviously thought so too because he stayed, squished in the small space with her, holding himself as far away from her as possible.

'I love what they've done with the common spaces,' one of the new women said.

'The design is quite something. A spectacular use of the environment, perfectly with the site.'

Meg cleared her throat, but Dan wasn't about to move, not when he was being lavished with praise by strangers.

'George Moreau is a genius,' another man said and Dan glanced back at Meg. His eyebrow twitched with another suppressed smile.

'So successful, yes. And apparently a lovely man. My niece's neighbour works for them and says they are a wonderful company to work for.'

Meg didn't even try to hide her smile when she next met Dan's eye. She managed the corporate division and took that compliment as her own.

Their boss, George Moreau, had had the idea for Evermore about two decades ago and had built it from the ground up, slowly at first but gradually taking on more employees and projects over the years. Their offices were in a converted warehouse a block from the rowing club and three blocks from South Steyne, the main Manly beach. They were lucky to be based where they were: in an iconic location that felt like a seaside resort but was a hop, skip and a ferry ride from the centre of Sydney.

Meg was fortunate to have a job she loved and to live in such a place. Dan Fairweather was one of the only downsides in her life.

'Excuse me,' said a woman and the crowd rearranged itself to let her move, resulting in, momentarily at least, Meg and Dan being forced back even further, Meg's back literally up against the wall. The physical distance between their bodies was now theoretical only. She shifted her body slightly to save as much space as possible, resulting in her standing flush with Dan, her eyes level with his shoulder. She felt the fabric of his jacket against her bare arms, and his cologne ticked her nose. Her face was so close to his shoulder she could see the weave of the fabric in his suit. Then she heard him. He inhaled, deeply, through his nose.

Did he just smell my hair?

No. He breathed in and her head happened to be in the way. That was all.

And yet she could see out of the corner of her eye that his eyes were closed.

Thankfully at that moment the crowd rearranged itself enough that Meg could slip to one side and she took three quick steps away from the display and the corner of doom.

She exhaled loudly and then breathed in fresh, Dan-free air.

But somehow he was still next to her.

'That was an illuminating conversation,' he said.

'I trust your ego feels satisfactorily boosted.'

'Indeed. And vindicated.'

'What do you mean?'

'Expensive? Overpriced?'

Of course that would be the detail he remembered.

'First, that guy has no idea how much it costs to build a resort like this. Second of all, if we'd gone with your original design we'd be charging guests twice as much to pay for it.'

When would this guy get it? They'd been having this argument for nigh on fifteen years. It didn't seem likely he'd catch on any time soon.

'I'm going to mingle,' she said.

Before he could retort with some smug remark about running away, she turned and left. Her hands shook. All her excitement, every last ounce of pride, had been smashed by that man.

Daniel Fairweather. The most annoying man in the world.

Even, perhaps, more annoying than her ex-husband.

Certainly more infuriating than her flawed father.

Yes, she calculated, he faced some serious competition, but Daniel Fairweather was the worst man she'd ever met.

'George is here to see you,' Meg's executive assistant, Gabby, said when she arrived at her office the next morning. 'He's waiting in your office.'

George Moreau, the CEO and founder of Evermore, was one of Meg's favourite people in the world. Inspiring, driven and just about the best boss a person could hope for. He had headhunted Meg when she'd been a newly divorced, single mother to a ten-year-old. She'd been reluctant to move from her safe and established position at a large construction company to work for what was essentially an untested start-up. Her worries about juggling her job, her daughter and providing them both with financial security had been front and centre of her mind, but when she'd met George, he'd easily gained her trust.

She'd told him she loved the sound of his business but had confided her situation and worries. George had offered her more than the salary she was then earning, and had provided her with all the flexibility she'd ever needed to care for her daughter, Olive, letting her work from home decades before that was commonplace, and letting Olive come into the office when that wasn't possible.

George was making himself comfortable as usual. Other bosses she'd had would summon you to their own office if they wanted to talk, whereas George floated around the warehouse that was the headquarters of Evermore and dropped in on his employees for formal or informal talks where it was most convenient for them.

Meg greeted him with a broad smile. 'How are you this morning? Last night seemed to go well.'

'Indeed it did. Do you have a moment for a chat?'

'Of course.' Meg took a seat.

'I've already seen a few reviews that will go out shortly and the bookings have been far in excess of what we'd hoped.'

Meg's chest warmed. This was exactly what a CFO wanted to hear. It looked as though this latest project would be a success.

'So now it's been launched, we're looking for our next project.'

'So soon?'

'Of course.'

Meg put on her best smile, but it didn't fool George.

'You were hoping for a bit of a break first?'

'Well, I guess, yes.' Building and launching a new resort was a lot of work, along with managing the dozen they still owned. 'I was hoping to have a week or so off before diving into something else.'

'I think what I have in mind will serve both purposes.'

'Oh?'

'As you know, the board are keen to expand into the South Pacific.'

Meg nodded.

'And an opportunity appears to have come up in French Polynesia.'

'Tahiti?' Meg asked.

'Not precisely. A small island near to it, called Isle St Jean.'

'I haven't heard of it,' Meg admitted.

'It's small, volcanic. Gorgeous, apparently. Amazing diving. There are only a couple of other small resorts there and a well-established town.'

Meg nodded. This was good. Evermore tried to rely on existing infrastructure as much as possible, to keep their footprint as small as possible.

'Sounds promising.'

'And we have a site in mind. The owner seems keen to work with us but obviously we won't know if it's feasible until you check it out.'

'Me?'

'Yes. And you'll get that break you wanted as well.'

Meg did some quick calculations. A trip to French Polynesia, have a meeting or two with the owner and potential partner, check out the property by sight. Most of the legwork would be done online, so maybe it would be a chance for a break.

'And you're coming too?'

George frowned. 'I can't this time.'

'What?'

This was George's main job: to visit potential sites, make all the preliminary assessments about what was and wasn't possible. Carry the negotiations.

'But I can't…not on my own. I've picked up a lot of things over the years, but…' There were many aspects of George's job she'd been trained to do, many she'd learnt on the way. You didn't set up several dozen resorts over the years without learning the things to look for, but she'd never done it alone.

'While I think you are more than capable of doing the preliminary scoping on your own, you won't be going by yourself.'

Meg thought about her assistant, Gabby. She'd been shadowing Meg for some time but she wouldn't be able to fill the gaps in Meg's knowledge.

'Dan will go with you.'

Meg thought she mustn't have heard correctly. 'Pardon?'

'Daniel will go with you.'

No. No!

'Is that necessary…? I mean, I guess, like you said, I probably could manage on my own.'

George laughed.

'Relax. I know the pair of you don't always see eye to eye. I'm not blind. But you're my most senior employees and I know you will both be...professional.'

Something about the way he said the last word made Meg's stomach flip.

Did he know?

Meg shook her head. There was nothing to know. They had always been professional.

Mostly.

It was a fine line, wasn't it, between professionalism and something else? A line they had spent much of their relationship learning not to cross, in one way or another. Ever since the night they had crossed the line and then some. But the less she thought about That Night, the better.

'You know more than both of us. Wouldn't it make more sense for you to come and just take one of us?' That had always been how they had done things in the past.

'I wish I could, I really do. But...' George rubbed his chin and looked around the office. 'Doctor's orders, I'm afraid.'

Meg's heart fell. 'Oh, I'm sorry to hear that.'

George had undergone a heart bypass the year before. He'd been trying to work less since then but in the lead-up to the latest launch he'd been working harder than ever. Meg had assumed he'd been well enough, but now it seemed she might have assumed incorrectly.

'It isn't far, and you'd have a rest too. Jenny could come.'

'I'm sure my wife would love that, but no. I have to sit this one out. I will...' He looked Meg in the eyes. 'I haven't said anything to the board yet, and I won't, but you should probably know that I'm going to start stepping back. Probably within the next few months.'

'Stepping back? What does that mean?' George had founded Evermore, built it into the highly successful and regarded company it was, launched it on the stock exchange. He *was* Evermore.

'It means I won't be the CEO for ever.'

The questions stuck in Meg's throat: When? How? But most importantly of all, *who* would replace him?

Me, said the tiny voice at the back of her mind. *It has to be me.*

She was the CFO, she had the most management experience, she'd led the public launch and the board all trusted her. This was what George was hinting at.

Suddenly it was clear what she had to do—go to French Polynesia, seal this deal and build the most successful resort they'd ever created.

This was her chance to really prove herself.

CEO of Evermore? It was hers for the taking.

CHAPTER TWO

'No. Absolutely not.'

'You know she has to go with you.'

Dan crossed his arms and glared at George. He knew he was being belligerent, but with Megan Granger that was pretty much his default setting.

'We want to land this deal, not reject it at the first hurdle. And you know as well as I do that she'll find absolutely everything she can wrong with this site.'

And she'll spend the whole time telling me what's wrong with me.

'That's her job. To make our ideas workable, financially feasible.'

Dan grunted.

George raised an eyebrow that said, *Watch it*.

Dan would watch it, but only because this was the last time he'd have to work with her.

When Dan became the CEO of Evermore, Megan Granger would have to do exactly what he said.

Or leave.

Dan smiled. That was a happy thought, Megan Granger being out of his life. He'd easily find another CFO, one who wasn't so obstructive. One who didn't loathe him. One who didn't make his body shift just by entering a room, or make his blood pressure spike when she spoke.

Not that anyone else knew that George was planning on

stepping down from his CEO role. Dan was the only person he'd told so far, and Dan wasn't about to broadcast the news. It was something he'd been thinking on, quietly to himself, for the past few days.

CEO of Evermore. It was George's company, he'd had the vision, built it into the business it was today, but it was natural that Dan, as the creative mind behind the enterprise, would be the one to take it over.

The thought filled him with excitement at the things he would achieve. He was going to take an amazing business and make it brilliant. Do all the things he'd been wanting to for years. Build all the things, make the world a better place. Without worrying about spending a couple of dollars over budget.

'Fine,' Dan said and George stood.

'Good. We'll make the arrangements.'

Dan stood as well to show George out. As he walked to the door he glanced out of the window at the sparkling harbour. But it wasn't the water that caught his eye this time, it was the photographs of his two sons on the credenza. Rufus and Jake. A photo of them on Christmas morning when they were both toddlers, another in Paris as teenagers posing stiffly. Two photos with his ex-wife and him bookending them on two graduation days, and now, Rufus in London where he was pursuing an acting career and Jake in Antarctica, pursuing his scientific studies.

Both were bright, ambitious and living their best lives. Despite his best efforts they were more likely to call their mother if they needed anything and they seemed increasingly too busy to spare time for him. Dan knew, logically, that was what happened when children became adults, but guilt still woke him in the early hours of the morning. He'd tried his best to be a good father, yet he felt as though he'd failed them at every turn.

Dan was on polite, if stilted, terms with their mother, his ex-wife, Astrid. He and Astrid had been childhood sweethearts and he'd thought they would spend their lives together. Astrid had had other ideas.

They had been together since they were fifteen years old and Dan had cherished the fact that they had grown up with one another, but their expectations about how their lives would work were too different. Astrid didn't understand Dan's drive to work, and Dan had only been trying to provide for his wife and sons and it had frustrated him that Astrid didn't see that.

The photo reminded him of all the things he'd given up getting to this place. All the things he'd sacrificed, knowingly and accidentally. Dan had been raised by his mother alone when his own father had walked out, and, aged eight, Dan had sworn he wouldn't do the same to his family: that his boys would want for nothing and that he would never leave them.

Best laid plans and all that. Some people managed to find the balance between financially supporting your family and being physically and emotionally present, but Dan had never been able to. He consoled himself with the fact that, while after the spilt he'd only seen them every second weekend and school holidays, he had been able to financially support them.

His career had been his life. It hadn't always been his intention, but it was what it was. He had a good job. A great job. He got to use his imagination, his skills, and he got to make a difference. He believed in this job, perhaps more than anything else in his life. George was such a part of Evermore that him leaving was almost unthinkable, but if he was then Dan was willing to fill his shoes to keep the company going.

So he'd go to French Polynesia, but did he really have to take Meg?

'What about Gabby? She's pretty good.'

'Gabby's great, but she's still learning. It has to be Meg.'

'She's spent the last fifteen years telling me everything that's wrong with all of my great ideas.' It was hardly a state secret that he and Meg didn't get along.

'She's also spent the last fifteen years saving you from bad deals, and from overextending. She saved us from ourselves more times than either of us could count. Without her, we might've gone belly up years ago.'

Dan sighed. 'You don't really think that, do you?'

George nodded.

Evermore's long-term CFO was cautious in the extreme, obstructive, and just generally disapproving of every idea Dan had. Because she was generally disapproving of *him*.

While he recognised that someone like that was valuable in this business—everyone needed someone who gave them honest advice—that didn't mean he had to like it. Or her.

Luckily, Meg's and his enmity was mutual, or it would've been awkward.

'I'd rather do this deal on my own.'

'You need to take someone. This'll be a big deal and I need both of you on it.'

'Are you sure you can't come?'

'You know I can't.'

'Is there no one else?' They employed more than a hundred people, for crying out loud.

'I'm sure there are dozens, but you need *her*. You need her financial advice, but you also need her pragmatism. I know you don't always like what she has to say, but you know she's always right.'

Meg was not always right. She was right some of the time.

Maybe ninety-five per cent of the time. Which was hardly all of the time.

'She won't agree to come.'

'Why would you say that?'

Because Meg hated him. Loathed him. Most of all, she

avoided him. That was why she worked two floors away in the office furthest away from his. Why she had a spark in her eye every time she pointed out an error or a problem with one of his new ideas. She loved proving him wrong. It was her one true passion.

It had been fifteen years since That Night. Why couldn't she get over it?

Dan reached for the door but George touched his wrist gently.

'There is one more thing.'

The serious look in George's eyes made Dan tense. George was going to announce his retirement already. George was going to recommend Dan for the role.

'The resort you're staying at on Isle St Jean is one of only a few hotels on the island.'

Dan nodded. He knew this much. Isle St Jean was fairly underdeveloped, which was why it was such a great opportunity for them.

'There are no other large businesses based on the island, so there's no real reason for you to be visiting the island except for tourism.'

'I don't understand what you're getting at.'

'I've asked Marie to book you one villa to share. You can't be there together in separate villas.'

'Why on earth not?'

'It'll look suspicious.'

'No, it won't. We'll look like two people who don't want to share a room.'

'They'll ask what you're doing on the island. They can't know *why* you're there. It could blow the whole deal.'

George wasn't wrong and yet…

'So, we'll tell them we're friends.'

'Friends who won't even share a villa? There are two bedrooms. I'm not asking you to share a bed.'

Dan's mouth went dry. A memory he tried his best to suppress every day rose to the surface. A bed. Tangled sheets and silky skin. The taste of red wine. One of the silliest mistakes of his life. Before he'd finally figured out that relationships were impossible and happy endings a fantasy created by people who just wanted to sell you something.

George could not be serious.

'Two bedrooms. But I thought you should know.'

Dan's office felt warm. Maybe it was the afternoon sun. It couldn't be anything else.

'I get it, I do. But has Meg really agreed?'

'She's going. I spoke to her this morning.'

'But have you told her about sharing a villa?'

'Not yet. I'm choosing my moment.'

Dan bit back a smile. George was a smart man, but when it came to Megan Granger, he had blinkers on.

That was the really irritating thing about Meg: everybody else adored her. They all spoke about her in glowing terms. People went out of their way to tell him how lucky the company was to have her.

What did they see that he had missed? She was clever, that wasn't in doubt. She had a sharp sense of humour. Not one he always appreciated, particularly when it was focused in his direction. She was kind, thoughtful, charming, and could convince the board to do almost anything. And, yes, she was beautiful.

He'd liked her when he'd first met her as well. Meg was calm and self-assured. He had liked that she'd always looked him in the eye. He'd liked that he needed to be on his toes around her. And yes, the fact that she was stunning hadn't escaped his notice either. Blonde hair that swished around her shoulders. Long limbs and the bluest eyes he'd ever seen.

But then he'd got to know her, and everything had changed.

She was not as easy-going and open-minded as he'd first thought. She was uptight and, most of all, judgemental.

He wasn't blameless in the whole mess, he could admit as much. When it came to relationships he hardly had a blemish-free track record, which was why from That Night on he'd decided to give serious relationships a very wide berth. But Meg hadn't needed to overreact the way she had, then, or at every other opportunity she'd had since.

She won't agree to go. The thought buoyed him and he smiled. There was no way on this green and blue earth that Meg would agree to go to French Polynesia if it meant sharing a villa with him.

Meg looked out of her window at the gorgeous harbour, verdant brush punctuated by white beaches and sandstone cliffs, stretching off to the horizon and the Sydney CBD. Her office, literally, had million-dollar views and she knew this because she'd seen the balance sheets.

Outside her open door the office buzzed with happy, productive sounds. Ringing phones, fingers on keyboards and occasional laughter. It was wonderful to work with a tight team of like-minded people who were all propelled by the same goals she was, building this industry.

Travel was a luxury, but it wasn't a pointless one. Tourism fuelled economies, travel broadened minds and broke down barriers. From the first time she'd gone overseas as an eighteen-year-old backpacker she'd loved the way travel made the world smaller and brought people together.

But tourism could also be an environmental nightmare, which was where enterprises like Evermore came in: establishing sustainable, ecologically friendly resorts that supported local communities and remunerated them fairly.

She didn't want to lose any of it. What if there was someone out there with more qualifications than she had to take over the business? What if a new CEO's plans for the business were not as George thought? What if a new CEO didn't like her?

Impossible. Everyone liked her.

Almost everyone.

Dan Fairweather had everyone fooled, but not her. Oh, sure, at first she'd thought he was wonderful as well. Until she'd figured him out.

Meg had been at one of the lowest points in her life when she'd first met Dan. Which was probably why it had all happened as it had. Her divorce from her ex-husband, Paul, had been less than a year old, but Paul had already remarried and the week before she had learnt—accidentally via Olive—that Paul and his new wife were expecting a baby.

She'd felt on the verge of throwing up ever since, and on top of that had recently resigned from her safe and stable job to take up the position with George. Instead of feeling excited, she had been nervous and on edge.

And then she'd met Dan.

Evermore had been much smaller at that time, George and Dan and maybe a dozen other employees.

What have I done? I've left a billion-dollar company to come and work in a tin shed, she'd thought when she'd placed her handbag on her new desk. Not even in an office. They hadn't even moved into the warehouse at that stage but had been based in a literal shed at the back of George's house.

But she'd looked up and there was Dan. Smiling at her.

He'd worn a boyish, cheeky grin and a sparkle in his eye. A lock of his dark hair had fallen into his eye and she'd fought back the urge to brush it away. A bubble of lightness and longing had risen up inside her, the first time it had happened since she'd discovered Paul's affair. Until that point, she'd never expected to have that feeling again, one bubble becoming many rising and then expanding in her chest. This man was lovely!

He'd taken her out for coffee, explained the lie of the land at Evermore and all the office gossip.

'Why are you telling me all of this?' she'd asked.

'Because you and I have to be allies. After George, it's you and me. We'll do a better job of managing everyone else if we're a united front.'

'Right,' she'd replied. It was business only.

'And I could tell right away that we'd get along.' He'd smiled at her and her heart had sung.

And he'd been right. They had got along.

They'd established a routine of meeting for coffee each morning where they'd got to know one another. Dan had come from a large architectural firm where they hadn't truly supported all the ideas he had for sustainable and regenerative buildings. He had also casually let it slip that he was single, sending more bubbles fizzing through Meg. At the end of the first week, Dan and George had taken her out for a drink and she'd felt, for the first time in a long time, that things were turning around for her. The company was good, her colleagues were great. She'd made the right decision to change jobs.

Meg had also begun to wonder if she'd had men all wrong. If her husband had simply been a bad apple. If she might be able to trust a man again.

If her new colleague could be even more than a good friend.

That was the thing about Dan, he was instantly charming, could put even the prickliest customer at ease. People smiled when he walked into a room and sat up straight.

But she'd soon realised it was like all other overly charming men. Like Paul. Like her father. Untrustworthy.

Which was why being alone with Dan for a day or two, with no one else as a buffer, was not something she was keen to do. Meg made two lists in her head, and tapped one finger on her desk with each item, just as she did each time she faced a problem.

The 'cons' side of the ledger went as follows:

Spending time with Dan
Spending time alone with Dan

The 'pros' side of the ledger went:

Landing a great deal
Becoming the CEO of Evermore
Having Daniel Fairweather having to do exactly as I say and not flinch every time I enter a room or speak
Or better yet having him finally leave and let us all continue our jobs and happy existence in peace

That was why she was doing this. Weren't a few days alone with Dan a small price to pay for eternal freedom?

Out of the corner of her eye she saw her screen flash with an incoming email from George's personal assistant. Her itinerary. She clicked on it immediately.

Meg stopped. Blinked. Then she stood and marched down to George's office. His assistant, Marie, was at her desk outside their boss's office.

'Marie, I think there's been a mistake.'

Marie looked from Meg and into George's office and back again.

'Come in, Meg. Don't worry, Marie.'

Meg's heart dropped. It wasn't a mistake. George waved Meg into his office and she shut his door behind her.

'Marie only booked one villa. We need two.'

'I was planning on talking to you about it. I asked her specifically to book a single villa.'

Meg paused. Let that news sink in.

'It's because...'

Meg nodded. She should have anticipated this. She and George usually shared a suite when they travelled together for new projects; they told anyone who asked that they were old friends. It sometimes didn't even feel like a lie since they got on so well. They never wanted to alert other hotels or accommodation businesses to the fact that they were considering building some competition.

But she liked George. She didn't like Dan.

'She booked the biggest suite they have. Two bedrooms and bathrooms.'

That was something.

'It's okay, I know why you did it.' Isle St Jean was tiny. They needed to be particularly careful not to let anyone know what they were doing on the island before anything had been settled.

'Will you be okay with it?' George asked.

No.

'I do understand. And it's only for a couple of days,' she said.

They might be sharing a suite, but she didn't have to leave her room.

'Good, I was going to come and talk to you, because, well, I do want to make sure that you're okay with it in particular.'

'Because I don't like Dan?'

'Yes, well, that, and you know. The other thing.'

The other thing?

Did George know about That Night?

No. He couldn't. They'd been so discreet. And it had been so long ago.

'What other thing?' Meg's heart beat a little too quickly for comfort.

George took a few deep breaths, as though he was struggling to figure out how to say whatever he needed to say.

'Just tell me. I promise I can handle it.'

'The fact that he likes you.'

Meg's mouth fell and she lost the power of speech. Her brain stalled and caught on George's last, strange, incomprehensible words.

'I'm sorry, I don't think I heard you.'

George nodded. 'You heard me well enough. He has feelings for you.'

Meg laughed, a hard, loud bark. 'Don't be ridiculous.' It was mid-May. The first of April was weeks ago.

'I'm not having you on. It's true.'

Meg shook her head. 'If this is a joke, it's not funny.' Her chest was tight and her skin began to bloom with sweat.

'It's not a joke.' George leant forward and whispered, 'We all thought you'd figure it out.'

'All?'

George pulled another face.

'Who exactly is all?'

'Some of the staff.'

'Who?'

'Almost everyone. You honestly didn't know?'

Meg shook her head again but even as she did, even as she protested, there came a memory, an old, faded one. One she hadn't thought of in years. About a night out, at a bar. After everyone else went home. Of laughing, smiling, flirting. With Dan.

And of what came next.

But no one knew about That Night and Dan certainly didn't feel the same way about her after that. Meg's temples felt as though they were closing in on her skull. She rubbed them. She shook her head. They all had it wrong. Dan did not like her.

'Look, forget I said anything now. Just go on as you always have. I'm probably wrong.'

George was rarely wrong. And besides, it wasn't just him. It was 'everyone'.

What was she going to do?

Nothing. Absolutely nothing. Unless...

'Why mention it now?'

'Because you're about to spend a lot of time alone together. And this deal is important.'

That seemed like the absolute worst time to say anything. She certainly wouldn't want to work day after day, year after year with someone she was attracted to. Hopefully once she was the CEO Dan would decide to leave and move on to somewhere else.

'I thought it was best that you knew now. Before it's too late.'

'Too late for what?' The sushi Meg had eaten for lunch suddenly threatened to make a reappearance.

George sighed loudly. 'Oh, I don't know really. It just seems like this might be a turning point. With me looking to step back. Look, Meg, I'm sorry I said anything. You know I don't like gossiping. I was only trying to help. Truly. It's worried me all this time that you may not be aware.'

Meg shook her head. She hadn't been aware.

How could she have known? He was always so belligerent, so prickly. So defensive.

George's words made sense logically and yet they didn't make sense at all.

Dan couldn't have feelings for her. They'd bickered at the party, just last night.

But he'd smelt her hair. Inhaled her scent.

Meg shivered.

Damn.

'I thought it might help you.'

'How?' Meg rubbed her throbbing temples. She didn't need to know this, not now. It would distract her when her focus was meant to be on securing a deal that would propel her into the CEO role.

'So there are no misunderstandings between you.'

Meg laughed. 'There will always be misunderstandings between us. We just don't get along. We're too different.' *He's an arrogant, untrustworthy man. I'm a reasonable female.*

'Maybe you're too similar?'

Meg scoffed. Any similarities they had were on the surface only. Hard-working, dedicated, passionate about their jobs. That was all. And those adjectives described lots of people.

Besides, differences, similarities, it didn't matter because they hated one another.

No, you hate him. Apparently he *has a crush on you.*

How was it possible for two people to have such wildly different opinions of one another? At least he hadn't made his feelings clear to her. At least he hadn't made any declarations or acted on his feelings. Her stomach churned at even the idea.

George stood, signalling she should leave. 'If you want to talk, you know where to find me.'

Meg nodded and stood. But she wouldn't be talking about this. She'd be filing this information about Dan away. Possibly to use against him. Or, hopefully, to forget about for ever.

CHAPTER THREE

But as hard as she tried, Meg couldn't forget about the conversation with George. It kept bubbling back up into her consciousness like a fly she couldn't swat. Buzzing, irritating and always there.

Every time she tried to tell herself that George must be mistaken, she remembered the sound of Dan breathing in as they stood next to one another at the launch. Or worse, she remembered that other time. But that had been fifteen years ago. Surely so much had happened since then.

Her stomach churned with another feeling, something she couldn't pin down at first, but as she finished her workday, gathered up her things, it came to her.

Pity.

No matter what else he was, or what he had done, he was a person with feelings. Strange and very misguided ones, but feelings nonetheless. She'd been awful to him over the years. Granted, she'd done nothing overly rude, but she'd never been warm. She'd never been kind.

It wouldn't have taken much to have thought for even a moment of his feelings. She might have moved on from that night, and she'd believed he had too, but, clearly, he hadn't.

He tricked you, betrayed you, remember? Wasn't that reason enough to be cold to him? Yes, it was, but then, it had also been a decade and a half ago. She groaned and tried to finish her work for the day.

With all the distraction, Meg was the last on her floor to leave the office. Most of the lights were out as she made her way to the elevator down to the basement car park. The lift doors opened and Meg only just held back the urge to curse under her breath, because standing in the lift with his head down looking at his phone was Dan.

The breath that was going to be a curse came out of her mouth as a sort of managed sigh. He looked up. A lock of his hair, one dark, now streaked with silver, fell across his forehead. His eyes, once brilliant azure now a subtler blue, narrowed as he regarded her.

He'd removed his tie since she'd seen him that morning and the top button of his shirt was undone, leaving a glimpse of collarbone and sending her mouth dry.

She stared for a second too long, then blinked.

Her heart was suddenly racing and she took a breath to steady it but inhaled only him. He smelt of warmth, the Evermore offices and a trace of his sharp aftershave.

This morning she would have interpreted the expression on his face as disgust. But now? Had he been using this impolite facade to protect himself?

Usually if they were ever in one of these awkward situations they would just look at their phones, pretend to be strangers. It suited them both better than the agony of making the small talk neither of them wanted to bother with.

'How was your day?' she asked before she could overthink it.

Dan looked back up, tipped his head to one side.

'Fine.' His voice lifted at the end of the word. Surprised she had engaged him in conversation.

But it was the right thing to do. Show him that she could be the bigger person.

'Are you all set for the trip?' She wanted to cringe at the question. Of course he was and he wouldn't tell her if he wasn't.

This was why they didn't do polite small talk—their relationship was too far gone to bother with pleasantries and superficialities.

'Physically or emotionally?' he joked and she laughed.

But, after, her cheeks flushed. Was he talking about going on the trip alone with her?

'I guess we'll know when you get there,' she said, hoping to make light of it. To fill the silence.

'I guess so.'

What was taking this lift so long? She should report it to building services.

After a few more excruciating seconds the lift finally stopped at the basement. Meg went first but turned after Dan had exited.

'Have a good night,' she said.

He gave her another puzzled look, as well he might.

'You too,' he said and tilted his head.

She turned left to her car space and he turned right to his.

The entire office knows we hate one another. They even organised the parking layout around us. No. They know you don't like him and have arranged things so you don't have to see him.

The news about Dan was too much to process. She got into her car and stared at her phone, waiting for him to drive out, but he didn't leave. She looked for a podcast to listen to on her drive home, but still Dan didn't drive by. Finally, she started the ignition and began to reverse, only to see him round the corner in his black car just as she did. They both braked hard.

She drove back into her space to give way to him, but still he didn't move. So, of course, Meg reversed again just at the moment Dan drove forward. They both braked again.

Dan honked his horn and Meg wound down her window. 'I'm letting you go,' she yelled.

'I'm letting you go!' he yelled back.

'You have right of way!'

He shook his head and she dropped her forehead to the steering wheel, gently tapping it with her head.

She was fifty-three years old, for goodness' sake! She'd given birth, divorced, buried both her parents and was second in command at a publicly listed company. This thing with Dan should not be rattling her.

The squeal of tyres on concrete finally indicated Dan was driving away. Meg counted to twenty, then reversed her car again.

Arriving home at her small house not too far from her office, she was surprised to see her daughter's car in the driveway. Olive still technically lived with her; her mail was still delivered to the house, but a week could go by without Meg seeing her daughter. Olive stayed with her boyfriend, worked late and occasionally stayed the night with her father, stepmother and half-siblings. Meg was in no hurry for this to change. She loved it when their paths happened to cross like this.

Even more happily, when Meg walked in the front door she smelt frying garlic and heard the sound of music and Olive's off-key singing coming from the kitchen. She sighed and, for the first time all day, everything was right in the world.

Olive greeted her with a quick kiss and waved her hand to an already open bottle of red. 'I hope it's okay if I cook?'

'I'm not sure why you're even asking that.'

Meg had split from her daughter's father when Olive was nine. The end of her marriage had hit Meg like a tsunami: brutal and with very little warning. With hindsight, Meg should have seen the signs—Paul had seemed a little distracted in the months leading up to it, a little tired even. But Meg had been busy juggling Olive and work and had assumed Paul's tiredness had been caused by the same thing.

But no. While Meg had been distracted and worn out raising a child and building a career, Paul had only been distracted and worn out by Sophie.

Meg still seethed a little when she thought of it. The intensity of her feelings might have faded with time, but she still smarted if she let herself dwell on it. Paul had broken her heart, but, even worse than that, he'd let her down. He'd promised her a lifetime, he'd promised to raise their daughter together and then he'd changed his mind. And he'd done all that even knowing about Meg's father, and how he'd hurt her.

She wasn't still in love with Paul, but no one wanted their marriage to fail. She was content on her own and yet still felt foolish that she'd somehow fallen for a man just like her own father, despite desperately trying to do otherwise. The longer she'd been single, the older she got, the less likely it seemed that another man would be prepared to commit to her. She had friends, colleagues and family, but it would have been nice to have her own person.

'You're not going out tonight?'

'I have a presentation tomorrow. I needed a night in.'

Meg just nodded. Olive had recently graduated and had started work as a lawyer.

Olive presented Meg with a big bowl of fresh pasta and they chatted about Olive's new job, whether she should buy a new car or save for a trip to Europe.

Olive poured Meg a second glass of wine and then asked her mother about her day.

'It was...' Strange. Unbelievable? Funny? 'It was a little odd.'

'How so?'

How to even begin to explain? Olive wasn't a baby any longer and, while Meg had made a conscious decision to never discuss her relationship with Paul in front of Olive, a resolution that hadn't always been easy to keep, this wasn't about Paul or his failings as a husband. This was completely different.

'What would you do if you found out that someone had a crush on you?' she asked.

'Depends entirely on who it is. Anyone I know?'

'You know of him.' Meg had spoken about Dan over the years, of her frustrations and problems with him.

'It's Dan, isn't it?'

For the second time that day, Meg's jaw dropped. 'Why would you say that?'

'It is, isn't it?' Olive grinned.

Olive had met Dan a few times, but years ago. When Meg was juggling school holidays and sickness as a single mother Olive would occasionally spend the day in the office, sitting by her mother with a book.

'Again, why? Why, of all the people in the world, was he the first person you thought of?'

'He's been crushing on you for years, hasn't he? I knew all that animosity was just a disguise for pent-up sexual tension.'

'What are you talking about?' Meg's face burnt. Maybe her daughter wasn't the best person to be having this conversation with after all.

Olive giggled, but she was wrong; there was no pent-up anything. It was simply anger and annoyance that neither of them tried very hard to hide. Despite what everyone might think, she didn't hate Dan. That would imply too much emotion. No, she loathed him. He brought out the worst in her. Something about him made her want to argue. Something about him ignited something in her.

And it wasn't the sort of thing her daughter was suggesting. It was determination. Competition. The need to win.

'How did you find out? Has he declared his love?' Olive asked.

'No, thank goodness.' The mere thought of that made Meg recoil. 'George told me.'

Olive rubbed her hands. 'Why?'

'Because...' Meg looked at her wide-eyed daughter and groaned. She'd have to tell her everything. 'Because we have to go away together. To French Polynesia. And we have to share a villa.'

Olive squealed. 'He invited you to go away with him? He has it bad.'

'For *work*. George is making us go together.'

'He's hot.'

Meg paused at the sink. 'He's not.'

'Open your eyes! Of course he's good-looking. Like Hugh Grant and Colin Firth had a love child.'

Even though there was some truth in that comment, Meg still shook her head and said, 'You're being ridiculous.' She'd spent the past decade and a half trying not to notice how attractive Dan was. How his eyes, when he actually smiled at you, could draw you straight in like a warm hug. How they crinkled around the edges when he laughed. How he was one of the few people in the world who made her heart skip when she saw them.

But your heart skips out of annoyance, not attraction!

'You're totally missing the point,' Meg said.

'What are you going to do?' Olive leant forward over the table.

'Nothing, of course.'

Olive shrugged, but still grinned.

'I'm glad you find my distress so funny.'

'Oh, come on, Mum. It is funny. He's secretly been in love with you all these years!'

'Is George having me on?'

'You think it could be a joke?' Olive asked.

But the thing was, Meg did believe George was telling the truth. She had been there. It had happened.

One night. Drinks after work. Olive had been at her father's...

Meg shook her head.

'I don't think George is lying, I just think he must be mistaken,' Meg said.

'Why is it so hard to believe? Because you don't think anyone can love you?'

Meg scoffed, but there was a hint of truth in Olive's jibe. No man had loved her, at least not for very long. And not for a long time.

'You're amazing, everyone knows that. Dad was a fool. Everyone knows that too. Even Sophie. But he's too old now so she's stuck with him.'

Meg's heart warmed. No matter what else she'd achieved in her life, she'd raised an incredible daughter.

'Don't say that about your father,' Meg said, but smiled so it was clear she was kidding.

'Everyone else seems to like Dan.' Meg shrugged. But that was because he was the light touch in the office, the sociable one, the one that promised office parties and generous perks. The one who didn't have to figure out how to pay for it all.

'Not me,' said her ever loyal daughter. 'I think he's a pain in the neck.'

'You've mostly only heard about him through me. I've probably coloured your point of view.'

Olive's expression turned serious. 'I've met him, Mum. He was nice to me. He let me watch the television in the boardroom that time I was sick. And the time I was there for school holidays he brought me doughnuts every morning.'

'What doughnuts?' This was news to Meg.

Olive shrugged. 'He'd often bring me snacks if I was in the office with you.'

That familiar irritation again rose up in Meg. How dare he do that behind her back? Bribe her daughter with sugar? Without her permission! Dan was one stealthy, underhanded...

'Relax, Mum, it was nice of him.'

'You do like him?'

'No, I didn't say that. He's obviously a complex character, as most people are. But he is nice to other people, he does have a kind side. But the fact that you don't like him is enough for me.'

Why did no one else seem to see the side of Dan that she did? George thought he was terrific. All his clients, all his staff, everyone thought he was great. Even Olive had a soft spot for him.

Because no one else was with him That Night.

Did everything in their relationship have to come back to that one horrible moment?

Yes. Maybe it did.

Dan looked back at his itinerary for the trip to Isle St Jean. Then back at George, who was standing across his desk, looking expectant. Almost, he suspected, trying not to laugh.

'I just came to check again that you're okay with everything.'

Dan wasn't, but he'd get past it. He had to if he was going to produce the most beautiful resort design he'd ever produced, secure this deal and the CEO role.

He couldn't have been alone in thinking that sharing a villa with Meg was a bad idea. He was certain Meg was dreading the whole thing as much as he was.

Although...

Yesterday had been strange. The encounter at the launch party had been awkward yet on brand for them. It was the other time, on the way home in the evening, that had really rattled him.

She'd been civil. No, more than civil. She'd almost been polite. Kind. She'd asked him how his day had been. As if they were both normal people who had a normal professional relationship. Instead of two people who brought out the absolute worst in one another. Two people who...

George glanced around the office, closed the door and sat. He shifted awkwardly, as if his suit didn't fit properly.

'Good to hear. But there's something else.'

'What?' What could be worse than being stuck for a few days with grumpy, self-righteous Meg?

Dan had known for a few days that George was thinking about stepping back from the company. Redefining his role. He'd made a good recovery from his operation, but it had shifted his priorities. He wanted to spend more time with his wife and grandchildren and that was a sensible decision.

Dan knew all too well what happened when you put work ahead of your family and he didn't want that for George. Dan didn't have a wife. Or children who needed him for more than a phone call once or twice a week. He was ready to devote himself fully to the business. As its new CEO.

It would be a natural progression for him as the creative mind supporting the business. His heart beat a little faster at the prospect. He loved the company, and loved the thought of what he could do if he were the one ultimately making the decisions. If he were CEO his decisions could overrule the CFO's and he'd finally be able to create the type of buildings he'd always dreamed of—sustainable, functional and, most of all, beautiful. He smiled. George was about to give him more details about his departure and Dan's succession to the role of CEO.

'Look, I've debated whether to tell you this or not, but I think, considering you're about to spend a few days alone with her, there's something I should explain to you about Meg.'

'What about Meg?' Was she planning on leaving the company as well? That would certainly make things smoother for Dan.

George looked around the office as though looking for an escape route. Waiting for someone to come and get his attention urgently on something.

Dan leant back in his chair and crossed his arms.

Finally George said, 'It's just that Meg...well, I thought you knew, but I've realised lately that you don't and what with me and my plans... It's something you should be aware of if you're going to go away with her.'

Dan held up his hand. 'She hates me with the heat of a thousand burning suns? Don't worry, I know.'

'See, that's the thing. She doesn't.'

'She doesn't hate me with the intensity of a thousand burning suns? Just a couple of hundred?'

'It's the hate part really.'

'She doesn't like me. I don't like her. It's our thing. But we're stuck together because you like us both too much and you pay us both too well.'

'I don't think she's just stayed because of the money.'

'George, please stop talking in riddles.' Dan had a horrible feeling he wasn't going to like what George had to say one little bit, but he didn't want it sugar-coated. He didn't want any ambiguity to remain. He wanted, as Meg would say, *cold, hard figures*.

'I think she likes you.'

'Likes? Are we in primary school?'

'I don't know exactly how she would define her feelings, but she has feelings. Positive feelings. *Passionate* feelings for you.'

Dan shook his head. The idea of using Meg and passionate in the same sentence made a strange, unwelcome sensation rise up inside him. 'No, she doesn't. Is this something you've just dreamt up?'

'Nope, not me. Everyone knows.'

'Everyone?'

'Well, just the whole office.'

How was there something the whole office knew that Dan didn't? He prided himself on knowing all the staff and what was going on, particularly now he was getting ready to take it over.

'How did I not know?'

George shook his head. 'I honestly don't know. It's been obvious to everyone else for years.'

No.

Dan shook his head.

That Meg hated him was his North Star. And if that wasn't true?

'She chose the office at the opposite end of the building from me. That's not the action of someone who likes someone.'

'Or it's the action of someone who wants to put some distance there, for professional and personal reasons. Maybe when you see someone as little as possible, you miss things.'

How had he missed this?

And what was he going to do about it?

The first was easy. Meg was clearly trying to hide her true feelings with sharp remarks and cutting rebukes, so it was no wonder he'd taken her words and actions at face value. She'd intended him to believe she didn't have feelings for him. It wasn't his fault he hadn't realised.

And the second question? That was easy—nothing. He'd do nothing. Ignore the whole thing. Pretend this conversation had never happened.

George sighed. 'You don't have to believe me, but I thought you would want to know. Before you spend all this time together.'

'I don't believe you.'

Even as he said the words he knew they were a lie.

He did believe George because once upon a time he'd believed it himself.

Dan stopped with his mouth wide open. He tried his best not to think about That Night, wished his brain would block it from his mind. But it hadn't. The memory always seemed to surface at the worst possible times, if she was challenging him in a meeting. Or when she was standing right next to him at the launch.

That's why you both hate one another, he thought. *Or at least why she pretends to. That Night.*

Dan had been exhilarated when he'd first met Meg. They'd seemed to have so much to talk about and both loved the business they had both recently come to work for. They'd shared a mutual excitement about working for George, establishing the company and all the things they thought they could do. He'd thought he might even have found someone he would finally click with, both professionally and personally.

His ex, Astrid, hadn't fully understood his passion for work, hadn't understood why he didn't want to walk out through the office door at five p.m. each night. She hadn't understood that he'd wanted to support his family financially in the way his father hadn't. He'd felt torn; he hadn't seemed able to earn money and make sure they were financially secure, and be home when she'd wanted him to be, at the same time. As much as he'd loved Astrid, they'd struggled to make it work. His absences from home with two young children had made her angry, and her lack of understanding that he'd been working so hard because he loved them and had wanted to provide for them had made him frustrated.

When Meg had come to work for the company, his marriage had just ended. Shell-shocked, Dan had still been living in the spare room while they'd worked out future arrangements.

Meg had been a revelation. She understood the ambition that propelled him. In hindsight, they'd taken things too fast. Misjudged one another terribly. He'd made assumptions and she certainly had too.

The weeks of getting to know one another had led to that moment, in the bar on the water. George had joined them for after-work drinks but had left early. They'd both lost track of time and the number of glasses of pinot consumed. Much of the night was a blur in his mind after all these years but the memory of his feelings lingered in his bones. Feeling right. Feeling that, no matter what obstacles they had to face, they understood one another to make things right.

The feeling that Meg was the answer to everything that had ever been missing from his life.

But then had come the other feelings. Need. Desire that had swirled around them like a lasso, pulling them closer and closer to one another as the night had progressed. The kisses they had shared in a booth at the back of a bar he hadn't set foot in since.

'I need you. I need more,' she'd gasped through the kisses he couldn't stop giving her. His hand under her blouse, her body soft and quickening beneath his fingers.

'I need you, too,' he'd said and at the time he'd meant every word. They were going fast, but he'd been helpless to stop. What he'd been feeling for Meg had overridden everything else. The fact that she was his colleague, the fact he was still drowning in guilt over his failed marriage. The fact that he hadn't yet told her about Astrid and the boys. All those thoughts had evaporated when he'd kissed her.

The cab ride to her house had been a blur of hands and tongues. First times were often awkward, but not with Meg. Time and self-preservation had caused him to forget or deliberately block out most of what had happened between them but the one memory he never seemed to be able to shake was one moment of perfect clarity as he'd held her. Three words that had blinded his mind in the semi-darkness of her room with their brightness: *This is it*.

They'd dozed, made love again and somewhere in the early hours he'd pulled her to him for a last kiss.

'I need to get going.'

'It's the middle of the night.'

'I should be home by morning.' It had been his morning to get the boys ready for school.

She'd pulled away then, quickly, decisively.

'Oh, my goodness, are you married?'

'Only technically.'

'Technically? What does that mean?'

'Separated. But we still live together.'

Meg had scrambled to pull the sheets around herself and swatted at him to get off the bed.

'You told me you were single! What kind of fool do you think I am?'

'I don't think you're a fool at all. Meg, we're separated, it's my morning to get the boys off to school…'

'Married?' she'd gasped.

'Separated.'

'No. No. This was a mistake.'

He hadn't done anything wrong. He had been single. Yes, technically married, but they had been in the process of separating. They had agreed their relationship was over.

They had been separated though he had still been suffocated by grief and guilt. Which was why those moments with Meg had been so exhilarating, why he hadn't told her about Astrid. With Meg he wasn't a failure, and he hadn't wanted her to know how hopeless he really was. 'I'm not trying to trick you—my marriage is over.'

'Same old excuse.'

'It's not an excuse.'

'You men are all the same.'

All men? Like his father? He'd tried his whole life not to be like his father. Tried and failed, it seemed.

Something had tripped something inside him and he'd blurted, 'Oh, I get it. All men are unreliable, selfish bastards. Am I right?'

She'd blinked.

'Not all. But most.'

'Yeah, I agree, this was a mistake. I didn't realise you were a raging man-hater.'

'And I didn't realise you were a philanderer and a liar.'

His pulse had been even higher than it had been moments ago, pressed hard against her, his body longing for what came next. Now he'd been fuming. How could he have been so wrong about someone?

'I'm not cheating. Not that you'd believe me.'

She'd placed her face in her hands and turned away as he'd reached for his clothes. 'I think you should leave.'

'That's what I was trying to do,' he'd mumbled. How could she think that of him, after all they'd shared the night before?

He'd pulled his pants up with force and winced.

How dare she insinuate all men were the same? How dare she insinuate he was a cheater? A selfish bastard?

Meg Granger was clearly some sort of man-hater and he'd had no desire to get caught up in her hatred. He'd had enough of misunderstandings like this in his marriage. He'd been foolish to fall headlong into another relationship so quickly.

'This was a mistake,' he'd said.

'You think?' she'd snapped back.

He'd let himself glance back at the bed where Meg had still sat, clutching the sheets to her body and looking more terrified than angry. She hadn't been just a woman he'd met at a bar, she'd been a colleague. They'd still had to work together.

'Look, how about we just try to forget this, write it off as the result of too much wine?'

'You're asking me to just forget you lied to me?'

'I didn't lie to you,' he'd groaned.

'You weren't truthful.'

There had been more. More words he had blocked out as soon as he'd said them, his mind red with rage. Details hadn't mattered—they'd both understood the situation perfectly.

Surely Meg's feelings, whatever they might have been at the beginning of that night, had faded entirely after that exchange? The way she'd spoken to him afterwards had suggested that anything she might have felt for him had evaporated the instant she'd decided he was a cheater. She hadn't cared for him as he'd stormed out of her house, and she certainly didn't care for him now.

That Night.

Wow. What a mess. What a misjudgement.

What a lucky escape.

Then there was the strange encounter they'd had last night in the lift. The way she'd looked at him. She'd appraised him. Her blue eyes had flicked up and down his body, taking every inch of him in.

Oh, my goodness.

George was right.

Meg liked him!

'Door open or closed?' George asked, knocking Dan out of his reverie, but he couldn't answer, still remembering the sound of Meg's front door slamming behind him as he'd left her house all those years ago. His body twitched.

'Closed,' George decided and shut the office door very gently behind him.

All these years. Meg had been hiding what she'd felt. Not just hiding, but disguising it with distaste, jibes and sarcasm.

Of course she has. What choice did she have when you've been so rude to her?

The office. The launch.

Every day for the past fifteen years?

He'd been rude to her because she'd been rude to him. Because she'd rejected his designs, disagreed with his ideas. Not just because of That Night. No, if he'd been rude it had been because professionally she'd thwarted and suppressed him. Rejected his plans, not been willing to make them work. And she'd got George to agree with her.

No, he told himself, That Night was almost forgotten and had played an insignificant part in their relationship and even less as the years had gone on. So the fact that Meg still held a torch for him didn't change anything at all.

CHAPTER FOUR

THE SMALL PLANE was full of couples. Honeymooners.

Great. Just what this situation with her and Dan needed was for them to be surrounded by loved-up couples.

Meg hadn't had to interact much with Dan on the flight from Sydney to Papeete—the aisle separating their business-class seats had provided just enough of a barrier. Certainly more than she had now, the pair of them squeezed into adjoining seats on the twenty-seater plane. She pushed her shoulders as far into the aisle as she could but their bodies still kept accidentally brushing against one another's and the resulting frisson she felt each time was putting her body on high alert.

He'd offered her the window, but she'd declined. It would have felt like being trapped. But she realised now it was a mistake. Dan was tall, well over six feet, and even though she got perverse pleasure in watching him try to fold his tall frame into the tiny seat, he did keep rocking their seats, reminding her constantly that he was next to her. Close.

As a rule, she did not get close to Dan. It was best for everyone's sanity that they kept their physical distance.

It was even more important now.

Dan likes you.

She bit back a groan. She'd tried to compartmentalise George's revelations. She had to, as a coping mechanism. Each time she remembered it was like being pinched. A small, painful recollection.

You don't have to do anything about it, you know. It's his problem, don't make it yours.

That was true, but she couldn't shake the discomfort. Especially now when he was centimetres away from her, his knees constantly knocking the tray table his drink was balanced on.

Without asking, Meg took his drink, placed it on her stable tray table and hooked his back up.

Dan glanced at her, his eyebrow raised for a second and nodded.

Meg's chest felt tight and sweat spread over her skin. What was this sensation?

Horror.

She'd done something kind for him and he hadn't snapped back at her.

That was almost more upsetting than him telling her how uptight she was. Or how pedantic.

Meg looked straight ahead for the rest of the short trip. She tapped a fingertip against her other hand and counted off the issues.

He's attractive. Flat stomach, most of his hair. Yes, and he smelt good.

His staff like him. Which was true and had always been true.

He likes you.

Which was still something she was struggling to get her head around.

He's not a horrible person.

She stopped. That one was tricky. Not a horrible person? He did have some good points, his desire to save the world was a pretty big one, but did it outweigh everything else? The years of scowling? Pettiness?

How he called her Megan, even though everyone else called her Meg. How he grumbled and huffed and grimaced almost every time she spoke to him. Secret crush or not, he'd been rude to her every day for the last fifteen years. He'd hated every single idea she'd ever brought to him, avoided her whenever he could.

Meg stilled her hand. All those things looked different in light of the new information. What if he scowled because it was painful for him to see her? What if he was short with her to put some distance between them?

If he'd liked her all this time, then maybe his actions were *not* exactly as she'd thought. No. That was all ridiculous. The whole thing was ridiculous.

And not her problem! Knowing about Dan's feelings made things awkward for her, perhaps made her a little more sympathetic towards him, but that was all. His feelings were his problem, and he had to find a way to manage them appropriately.

The small plane flew low enough that the turquoise waters and coral reefs could be glimpsed from the window of the plane. Dan must have noticed her watching because he said, 'Are you sure you don't want the window?'

'Perfectly sure.' Then as an afterthought she added, 'Thank you.'

Oh, this was strange. Encounters with Dan were always unpleasant but when she'd thought their animosity was mutual they weren't so uncomfortable.

They should use the time to talk strategy and business. She had spent the past few days looking into the budgets, the cost of doing business in French Polynesia and the local rules and regulations. There were certain criteria they had to fill to ensure any hotel they established could be classified as an eco resort and she was well across these, but each country had its own rules and regulations they had to comply with, and she needed to get up to speed very quickly on them.

The site George had chosen looked suitable on the face of it, though she'd have to work out the final figures once they got there and spoke to the owner. She should focus on that. On the work.

Rather than the man squished into the small seat next to her, his warm shoulder occasionally brushing against hers sending soft sensations fizzing down her arm. If they concentrated on work then things might not be as awkward. The sooner they got the business over and done with, the sooner they could leave one another alone.

'What do you know about the owner of the site?'

'Nino Flores? Very private, reclusive even.'

'Yes, that's what I read. Did you manage to figure out why he's interested in working with us? I did some digging but couldn't find anything to suggest that he's been involved in either tourism or sustainability.'

'No, me neither. He's a local though—at least, he moved there as a child.'

Evermore's business involved partnerships with local communities and landowners, where they would design, build and develop a hotel or resort, with the community gradually taking over operation of the resort while paying back Evermore. It was a very long-term investment strategy on behalf of George but from which everyone was now starting to reap significant financial benefits.

'He could be easy to work with. If he doesn't think he's an expert he might trust a lot to us.'

'Or the opposite, if he needs significant hand-holding.'

'Yes,' she agreed.

A cold sweat broke across her body.

They were having a normal conversation. Like normal people had.

Terrifying.

'It depends why he wants to do this, what his motivations really are. Whether his financial expectations are realistic.'

'I'm sure you'll be able to negotiate something,' Dan said.

Meg tilted her head to look at him properly. He looked

earnest. She noticed the pink of his lips as the corner lifted into a gentle smile.

He's genuinely trying to pay you a compliment.

She was so shocked she wasn't sure how to respond.

'Thank you. I'm sure you'll be able to impress him with one of your designs.'

Dan's brow lowered for a second over his eyes. His smile deepened and her throat caught.

Wow. This was what being civil with Dan felt like.

She nodded and he did too. Her stomach swooped, but that also might have been because the plane was lowering its altitude as it approached the island. A small volcanic creation that rose sharply out of the sea. Emerald-green, surrounded by aquamarine.

'Ooh's and 'Ah's could be heard around the cabin.

The plane landed on the minuscule airstrip shortly afterwards. Everyone was taken the short distance from the airstrip to the hotel in shuttle buses. On one side the ocean glistened in the afternoon sun, on the other the bush stretched up to the several high peaks of the silent volcano in lush green swathes.

Meg wanted to moan, not because Dan was jostling in the bus next to her, but because the humidity was a balm on her dry winter skin. Somewhere nearby was a pool and a cocktail with her name on it and all she had to do was navigate a meeting with the owner of the site and then it would all be hers. A couple of days away from the world. Olive was right. It would be fine.

He loves you.

But there was that annoying thought again. Like a pebble in her shoe. All the other passengers were coupled up and chatting happily, pointing out the beautiful scenery to one another.

'The island's nickname is Honeymoon Island,' he mumbled.

'I can see why. Couldn't the site be on Divorce Island? Or even Leave Me Alone Atoll?'

'We can toss those around for the names of our resort,' he said.

She smiled again. A habit she was falling into far too easily.

She was being nicer to him.

Small things, like the tray table.

And speaking to him as if she was a normal person.

She is a normal person, just never to you.

Meg's behaviour towards him had changed. She had softened towards him.

Or has she been like this all along and you're only noticing it now through the lens of the knowledge that she likes you?

Maybe that was it.

He should have been kinder to her. Not because she had a crush on him, but because he simply should have been. She was his colleague and he shouldn't have let his pride about that one night all those years ago still affect the way he behaved towards her.

A small shuttle bus conveyed them slowly along the narrow road from the airstrip to the resort. Meg's usually straight blonde hair had developed a wave and her face seemed shinier, brighter. Her make-up had worn off her skin somewhere over the Pacific and she looked somehow younger.

Not that it mattered. She was attractive anywhere, in any light.

He harrumphed to himself and turned away.

You don't like her, remember?

The bus pulled up at the resort and they could finally get off and put some distance between them. Meg went to grab her carry-on bag but he instinctively reached for it and lifted it down for her. Her eyes widened but she didn't say anything else.

See, he could be considerate. He'd show her! They entered the lobby and walked to the desk.

'Hello. I have a booking for Daniel Fairweather.'

The woman looked from him to Meg, who was standing behind him.

'Yes, Mr Fairweather. You're together?' she asked, in Meg's direction.

'Yes,' he said at the same time Meg said, 'No.'

Dan turned to her but she was already explaining, 'We're together, but we need separate rooms.'

The woman behind the counter studied them. 'The booking was for a single villa, but with two bedrooms. Is that correct?'

Dan froze. This was what George had meant when he'd said the hotel couldn't know that they were on the island for business.

'Yes. We need our separate space, don't we, honey?'

He emphasised the final word hoping desperately she'd catch on.

'Honey? What...?'

Dan laughed loudly. 'I mean sweetheart, sweetheart.' He turned to the woman. Her name badge said 'Heiana'.

'Honey is what we call the dog. She gets upset when I call her that.'

Meg opened her mouth and drew breath but Dan spoke too quickly. 'Here's my credit card.' He extracted his wallet.

'The booking was made by a Marie Anders,' the woman said slowly, looking from Meg to Dan and back again.

'Yes, that's my long-suffering assistant, but you can take my credit card.'

'No—' Meg began but Dan put his hand on her arm. Her skin was soft, warm and surprising silky. She tugged her arm away but he held on tighter and rubbed her skin with his thumb, trying not to think about how lovely it felt.

'No, sweets, it's my shout. I told you. Engagement present.'

Heiana smiled. 'Oh, congratulations.'

'Thank you,' Dan said. 'It's been a long while coming but

I finally convinced her. I think it was the ring that did it. Either that or my promise to only play golf once a week.'

'Honey, may I speak with you for a moment?' Meg's voice was clipped.

'In a moment, darling.' He turned back to the desk. 'It's been a long flight. We're both very tired.'

Heiana smiled at them with a closed mouth and slid two room keys across the counter. 'Villa 202. On the other side of the resort, closest to the ocean.'

'Wonderful,' Dan said, pocketing both key cards and steering Meg away from the desk.

'Why did you tell her all of that? What kind of game are you playing?' she snapped.

'She caught me on the hop and I had to make up something.'

'What was wrong with, "we're here as friends"?'

He shook his head. 'We should have thought about this earlier. Our alibi.'

'What's wrong with being here as friends? You didn't have to tell her we're engaged.'

'Everyone on this island is a couple. She would've got suspicious.'

'She works the front desk of a hotel. She's seen it all. You didn't need to make up what was actually quite a disturbingly detailed story about an engagement.'

'When you said we aren't together I panicked.'

'We could be siblings even. Anything else.' She ground her teeth together on the last words.

Yes. Now he had time to think about it, without the woman staring him down, it was an insensitive work-around. Meg had feelings for him and he was suggesting they lie about being engaged.

'We probably should've discussed something beforehand.'

She nodded and looked away so he couldn't see her face.

Maybe she'd been right all along and he was a bit of a jerk?

On the walk to the villa, he stole glances at Meg. Her face was flushed in the warmth. He'd never really got over some of the things she'd said to him that night. Untrustworthy. Cheater. Selfish. Unreliable.

She was wrong about him being untrustworthy, but was she right about him being selfish? Unreliable? Astrid had said much the same thing, many times.

Maybe he was self-centred. It was one thing to be focused and driven but when that blinded you to everything else? Blinded him to the fact that while his feelings for Meg had ended hers had not.

No.

She'd tried to hide her feelings for him. It wasn't his fault she'd been successful. Dan found it difficult to believe that anyone their age would still entertain the fantasy of love. Surely any sensible person who made it to middle age would have figured out that love was simply a biochemical illusion that existed for the sole purpose of evolution. Nothing more.

Meg was a lot of things, but she wasn't stupid.

'What are you staring at?' she asked.

He shook himself out of his thoughts. 'Nothing, I'm just tired.'

He had to pull himself together.

Continuing to the villa, Dan looked at their surroundings properly for the first time. The resort they were staying in appeared to be well designed for the landscape and made the most of its situation, around a bay, facing north over a lagoon. It was comprised of small groups of villas dotted around, not, he was relieved to see, the over-water bungalows that were often popular in the region. A nightmare for the ocean life.

They reached the entrance to the villa and they stood, staring at one another. Probably each delaying the moment they had to go inside.

What next? It was early evening, though, according to his body clock, it was the middle of the day.

'Would you like to go over the figures again, before tomorrow?' she asked.

'Yes, that's a good idea.' The meeting with the owner was first thing in the morning. 'If you aren't too tired, maybe tonight?'

'I'm not too tired. Tonight would be good.'

'Where?'

'Over dinner? In one of the restaurants?'

She raised an eyebrow. 'You want to discuss this deal in a public place? After all that carry-on with the story about an engagement. You'll need to get me a ring, by the way.'

'You'll say it's getting resized.'

'You've thought of everything. It's like you've done this fake relationship thing before.'

He resisted the urge to roll his eyes. 'I'm a bit out of practice with the fake dating caper. You'll have to excuse me.'

He was out of practice with dating full stop. He hadn't dated—fake or otherwise—for…a while anyway. It wasn't a conscious decision. It had just happened. Work had been busy. And finding someone who shared his expectations—or lack of them—about relationships was fraught.

Meg narrowed her eyes and studied him, a crinkle of a smile crossing her pink lips, prompting the sudden thought that it might be nice to kiss them.

Ridiculous.

She was right. Something was wrong with him. Why had his brain turned to mush lately? He was out of his time zone and probably hungry.

You know exactly why you're floundering. The conversation with George. The little bombshell he dropped on you a few days ago. The fact that Meg likes you.

'I think it'll have to be in our room,' he said. Of course it would, they were sharing a villa, but in Dan's mind that had involved him keeping to his bedroom, Meg being in hers and the common area as a kind of no-man's-land.

Meg pursed her lips together.

'Unless you can think of anything better?'

She shook her head.

'Will you be okay with that?' he asked. He didn't want her to feel uncomfortable.

'What would make you most comfortable?' she asked in return.

What's the etiquette when doing business in secret with a colleague who has a crush on you?

That was not in the 'Frequently Asked Questions' section of any HR manual he'd ever read. When in doubt, just ask. Wasn't that always the rule?

'You tell me, what would make you feel most comfortable?'

Meg's eyes narrowed once more, a look that until the past few days had been unfamiliar to him, but one she was throwing at him a lot lately. The myriad of blues in her eyes darkened and deepened under lowered lids and a crinkle appeared between her eyes. She was studying him, but with a hint of something else. Amusement. Curiosity maybe.

Finally she nodded and said, 'I'll be fine. I don't want to make you uncomfortable.'

Dan exhaled an exasperated groan. 'I'm fine. I'm not the one who…'

'What?'

'Nothing.'

Oh, no. Now he'd done it.

'No, what were you about to say?'

Think! Think! Except he couldn't…not lately. Lately it felt as though his grey cells had been replaced with a particularly sluggish type of mud.

'I'm not a female. I don't want to do anything to make you uncomfortable.'

Meg smiled then. A soft, true smile. It was strange. And beautiful. 'It's okay. Thank you for saying that, but I'll be okay.'

And then, in a gentler repeat of the way he'd touched her arm earlier, Meg placed her hand quickly and softly on his bare forearm. A gesture of reassurance more than anything else, but his body didn't know that. His blood fizzed and muscles that really should have known better tightened and tensed.

'Why don't we actually see what this villa is like before we get too far ahead of ourselves?' she offered.

'Good idea.'

Meg was right; there was no need to stress about the size or spaciousness of their shared villa. It had two identical bedrooms, both with king-sized beds and their own bathrooms, and the bedrooms were separated by a generous open-plan living area, comprised of a kitchen, dining room and large sitting room. In addition, there was a large outdoor patio with another dining table and some deckchairs overlooking a sparkling private pool. They would not be in one another's pockets.

'I think we should sit outside. What do you think?'

'Perfect,' Meg said. 'Just give me thirty minutes or so?'

'Good idea.'

In his own room, Dan unzipped his suitcase and decided he had time for a shower. Was Meg showering as well? And why did he care if she was?

You have to pretend that George didn't tell you anything. You have to carry on as you always have.

Except he couldn't. At the very least he had to stop being purposefully rude to her and he thought he was doing a good job at that. His politeness seemed to have prompted more civility from her.

But you also can't make her think your feelings have changed...

He pulled out all his clothes distractedly, undecided about hanging them in the closet or leaving them in the suitcase. He couldn't make his mind up. Probably because he was over-thinking everything else.

So, you forget that Meg likes you and you forget, as always, that you once spent an amazing night together and you just pretend she's your competent colleague. Nothing more. Or less. But you are civil. You are polite. As you would be with any other colleague.

He repeated the words over and over as he showered and dressed and as he walked out to the deck.

Competent colleague. Civil colleague.

Nothing more.

Nothing less.

He set up his laptop, admired the view and then Meg walked out.

Competent colleague. Charming colleague...

Meg had changed out of her travel clothes and into a loose cotton dress, the type of thing he hardly ever saw her wear. Made of a soft fabric, it swished around her knees and its short sleeves exposed her bare arms. She'd pulled her hair back loosely onto her head and off her neck, which was long and smooth.

And delicious, if his memory didn't fail him.

Competent colleague. Nothing more. Nothing less.

She nodded at him as she too set up her laptop.

'Shall we compare notes of what we know about Flores and the site?'

As usual, Meg had the figures in front of her. She had a rough idea of Nino Flores's background, other investments and interests. She knew about building costs and regulations in French Polynesia.

And, as usual, Dan's computer was full of design possibilities, ideas he'd been working on, but none of which he could begin to pin down until meeting with Flores and seeing the site properly. He took in all the information Meg had and she looked over his concepts, commenting knowledgeably on them.

'That one is my favourite,' she said, pointing to the design that he thought was best as well. 'That one is probably too ambitious.' She pointed to the one that was the most beautiful, but which he knew would be a practical nightmare to build. 'But it is lovely,' she said, almost as an afterthought.

Lovely.

It was a change from 'outrageously pretentious', which was how she'd described another of his designs just last week. Dan might be different on the island, but Meg was too. Something had changed for her as well, but what was it?

It's you, you goose. She's simply reacting to the fact that you aren't being so mean to her.

'I'm going to order some room service. Do you want anything?' she asked.

His stomach rumbled. They ordered a burger for him and a club sandwich for her. The food arrived with a bottle of champagne, dripping with condensation.

'We didn't order...' Meg began.

'Compliments of the hotel. To congratulate you on your engagement,' the waiter said.

'Oh, but...' she mumbled.

Dan stepped in. 'Thank you very much. That's way too kind. Isn't it, honey?'

'Yes, sweetheart. It is.' She pronounced Sweetheart with a long 's' and he had to hide his smile.

'You have to play along with it,' he whispered once the door was closed behind the waiter. He undid the wire casing on the champagne cork.

'You're opening it?'

'Why not?'

'Because…'

'We have to drink it. For the business. For the deal.'

'I suppose so,' she said in a resigned voice as he popped the cork.

He poured the wine into the two flutes and then raised his glass to hers. 'Congratulations to us.'

'We don't have to pretend when they aren't around—you do know that, don't you?'

He laughed. 'I know.' But it was fun pretending. He wasn't sure why, but it was. Something about the ridiculousness of it, he supposed. But Meg had feelings for him so she wouldn't find it funny.

'I'm sorry, I shouldn't joke about it,' he said.

Meg narrowed her eyes at him over her glass.

She continued to tap at her computer while she ate, but Dan shut the lid of his laptop.

'You're not even going to stop to eat?' he asked.

Meg tapped her fingers in turn on the table then closed her computer as well.

'Why do you tap your fingers like that?' It was a gesture she often made, as though she were playing a piano, or typing something.

'I just do.' She shrugged.

'Typing? Practising your keyboard skills?'

She looked up at him, her blue eyes now seemed the colour of steel.

'I'm counting.'

'You need your fingers to count?'

Her face burst red.

'I do when I'm counting the sums of money I'm going to cut from your next project.'

'Touché.' Despite himself he found himself smiling. This

wasn't how he usually fought with Meg. It was different because now he realised there was no true animosity behind her comments, only self-preservation. In turn he wasn't as sensitive to them and saw a joke as a joke.

He bit into his juicy burger.

'I know you're an accountant, but I've never met one who loves money quite so much.'

'Not money. Numbers.'

'What?'

'I don't care that much about money.' She paused. 'Except George's money. I care about that money because he pays me too. It's my job, but money in general is a means to an end.'

'But you always have all the figures in your head.'

'Yes, because that's my job.'

'And just now, as we went over everything. You knew all the figures.'

'Yes, *numbers*, not money. I like numbers. I always have. I like adding, subtracting. Counting.'

'Why?' For Dan, numbers were the nuisance part of his job. He liked lines and curves and shapes and feelings and colour and light.

'It calms me. Numbers are easy. They always do what they are meant to do. You can trust them.'

There was a lot buried in that last remark.

'Unlike people?' he wondered.

'Exactly.'

She left it at that, clearly already having said too much, hoping to avoid more questions. He decided not to pursue.

'I hate numbers,' he said.

'I know.'

'I almost didn't pass first year architecture because I couldn't do the maths component.' The words were out of his mouth before he realised what he was saying. He'd never confessed that to anyone. He'd had to re-sit the exam and even then his marks had been so bad they'd only let him into second year on the strength of his other grades. He expected Meg to laugh, but she didn't. She simply nodded calmly, sympathetically.

He looked at the champagne bottle. The last time they'd drunk this much alone together...well, the less said about that, the better.

'I don't hate all numbers,' he continued. 'I love hearing that we're able to increase the amount of energy we will save from one of my designs, and I do love hearing that one of our facilities is self-sustaining. That I'm allowed to build a new resort.'

'Wait. That you're allowed? Are you implying that I stop you?'

'Of course you do.'

Meg widened her eyes and his heart fell.

'George. I meant that George decides against something.'

'I don't stop you. I sometimes advise against something. George doesn't have to follow my advice, you know.'

'You're the CFO, of course he does.'

'I don't make anyone do anything. I just give advice.' Meg contorted her face into a frown. It looked painful and for some reason the idea of Meg in pain didn't bring him joy, it made him feel flat. Also because she was right. George made the big decisions. He didn't have to follow her advice. But, of course, he did because Meg was usually right.

'Good advice,' he grumbled. The champagne must be more potent than he thought.

'Pardon?' she said, though she'd heard perfectly well what he'd said.

'Good advice. It's always good advice. It's not always what I want to hear, but it's always sensible.'

Meg crossed her arms. 'Really? Because you're always complaining that I'm too risk averse. Too stingy. That I'm uptight.'

He had said all those things and could see now how, out of all context, they could have been hurtful. 'I'm talking about business,' he said. 'I don't mean that you're always uptight.'

Meg raised an eyebrow as if to ask what on earth he meant.

If only he knew.

Dan's chest tightened. This was becoming a strange conversation. Last week he would have excused himself and left the room, but now things were different.

'When you say that I'm uptight, it hurts. I don't come to work with an entirely different personality,' she said.

'Ah, but maybe I do. Did you ever think that?'

'Never. I honestly thought you were objectionable twenty-four hours a day.'

He frowned, then grinned. In one light her comment was mean, but in another, it could be seen as a joke. And that was the light in which he chose to see it now. In the fading, tropical sunset, Meg wasn't being mean, she was giving him a good-natured jibe. One that wasn't entirely undeserved.

'I'm sorry, I see that now. And I won't do it again,' he said.

Meg closed her eyes and turned her face from his so he couldn't see her expression, though he saw her shoulders rise and fall heavily. She turned back to him and said, 'Thank you for saying that. I'm sorry for calling you irresponsible, slippery and reckless.'

'Did you?' He feigned surprise. 'If you did, I don't remember.' Then he smiled broadly at her. She smiled wryly back. His chest hitched again and at the last minute he stopped himself from reaching for her hand.

His head really was muddled. It was probably the fact that the bottle was drained and they were sitting by a tropical lagoon, but it was becoming harder and harder to remember why he didn't like her.

CHAPTER FIVE

As Meg sipped the last of her champagne, her body felt as though it were rocking, but the room was perfectly still. It was her that was off kilter. Dan had apologised to her. And he seemed sincere. Stranger than that, she'd apologised to Dan.

Worse than that, she'd told him about her counting! How numbers calmed her. What had she been thinking?

You weren't thinking. The two-hundred-dollar bottle of champagne was doing all of the thinking for you.

No. It took more than half a bottle of bubbles to do this kind of thing to her.

Dan was different on the island, but Meg was too. Something had changed for her as well, but what was it?

It's you, silly. He's just reacting to the fact that you aren't being so mean to him.

He rested his elbows on the table in front of him, and rested one hand on top of the other, leaning forward attentively. His hair was messy after his shower, and the muscles in his forearms neatly defined. When he tilted his head to one side she felt her insides melting and reached quickly for her water glass.

It wasn't the pose, or even the attentiveness, but the look in his eyes. Soft, focused. She got the feeling he wouldn't have noticed if an entire troop of elephants had come dancing onto the deck behind her.

'It's getting late,' she said. The sooner she got some space from Dan and this strange evening, the better for everyone.

Thankfully he nodded and pushed his chair back.

'Thank you for a nice evening. I'm glad George sent you with me.'

The first part of Dan's speech made her chest warm, but her thoughts snagged on the final words. With me. The way he said them implied ownership.

'Dan, I'm just wondering, but…who do you think is in charge of this project?'

'Well, me, of course.'

Ah, and there it was it. What had been bugging her. She wasn't paranoid, she was correct.

'How do you figure that?' She put her laptop into its bag.

'Because I'm the architect.' His tone added the words, 'Isn't it obvious?'

'The architect, not the manager.'

'You're not the manager either, you're the CFO.'

'It's the same thing.'

He laughed. 'No, it isn't, not exactly.'

Dan might have been wrong, but he gave her pause. Dan probably didn't know about George and his planned retirement and she hardly wanted to be the one to alert him. If she contradicted Dan too strongly, she might give something away.

What if Dan *did* know and had designs on the job himself?

No. That was absurd. Dan was the ideas man, not the implementer. He left the grunt work, the *hard* work, to everyone else. Evermore would go bankrupt within a month of him taking it over. George couldn't seriously be thinking about leaving Daniel Fairweather in charge of his company.

Meg drew a breath and was about to remind Dan what an egotistical piece of work he really was but, glancing down at the table with their empty plates, she remembered their new and uneasy truce and she decided there was a better way to deal with Dan and his ego.

Just letting it go and watching smugly as it all played out. Dan would mess up eventually on his own.

She wished him goodnight and closed the door to her room behind him. She closed her eyes and let the evening wash over her. Dan had praised her, called her advice good. Then he'd apologised for the way he'd spoken to her and about her over the years.

No wonder she felt so strange and off balance.

But that conversation had been only a strange blip because then had come Dan's revelation that he thought he was leading the project. How could he possibly think he was the project lead? It was *hers*. George wasn't here, ergo she was in his place as the manager. Bloody Dan, he had a limitless capacity for deluding himself.

It was still business hours in Sydney so Meg flipped open her laptop and sent George a quick email.

Everything going well here. Arrived safely and now getting ready for the meeting tomorrow. Just so I'm clear and there are no misunderstandings, who is the project lead on this? You know how Dan can be.

Meg stared at the screen a while. George was showing up as online, but no message came through. She got ready for bed, but still no reply came.

She couldn't wait all night so eventually put her phone and laptop away. Meg got into bed and picked up a book but couldn't concentrate on the words, her body alive and alert to every strange sound in the villa. There were soft noises from outside, insects, birds and, beyond them, the ocean waves.

But her body was mostly listening out for the noises inside. Running water. Doors closing. Was he sleeping? Showering?

What was he doing? Lying in bed? Tossing and turning as she was? Images, memories, flashed across her thoughts. Of Dan lying in bed. Her bed. His head on her pillow, arm propping it up. He was looking at her, smiling. She remembered feeling that smile in her chest, thinking that, finally, things were turning around for her, that everything that had happened with Paul had been for a reason, that reason being to lead her here, to this place. To this man.

She'd been wrong. It had been the alcohol, and the fact she'd been at a vulnerable point and, of course, that Dan definitely knew how to charm someone. Philanderers knew how to fascinate others. It was their special skill. Paul was charming. Her father had been particularly so, flirting with every woman who crossed his path, like a compulsion. Her father was untrustworthy, Paul as well. She wasn't going to make that same mistake with Dan.

So when Daniel Fairweather had turned up at her desk on her first day at Evermore she should have been wise to his charming act. She should have known better.

Dan's not a philanderer.

She turned on her other side, swatting the thought away. Dan and his wife had divorced not long after That Night. And maybe they had been separated when she'd slept with him, but he'd still been married, still living with his wife and that was the sort of thing that someone ought to tell someone before they slept together. Wasn't it?

It was a question she'd asked herself on and off for years. If she should have given him the benefit of the doubt. But she kept coming back to the same conclusion—if she was going to have a serious relationship with someone, she had to trust them completely and she couldn't ever trust Dan again.

Except now she was stuck with him in this villa. In the daylight it had seem spacious, in the darkness the walls felt closer. *He* felt closer. She covered her face with a pillow and moaned into it. Life could be so perverse.

Meg woke well before the sun was up, her body not sure which time zone it was on. She had breakfast alone on the deck and checked in on things back in the office as much as the temperamental Wi-Fi connection allowed. There was still no reply from George and now she couldn't even call him as it was the middle of the night in Sydney.

Dan knocked on her door at the time they'd agreed would give them enough time to get into the small town and meet Nino Flores and his business manager. The site inspection was the most important part of this trip as it was the most difficult to do remotely. A face-to-face business meeting was a close second though. They were invaluable for getting to know a new business partner properly.

Dan walked confidently up to the front desk of the hotel. The same woman as yesterday was there, Heiana, the one who had heard the fake engagement story and who had, no doubt, facilitated the delivery of the French champagne the night before.

'Good morning,' Dan said. 'I was wondering if you could tell us the easiest way to get into town, please?'

'That all depends on why you would like to visit the town,' Heiana replied.

'My lovely fiancée and I would like to do some sightseeing.'

'In which case, may we suggest the guided tour? It leaves in about two hours.'

'My wife-to-be isn't a fan of group tours. Say we wanted to go by ourselves?'

The woman frowned. 'It would be much more pleasant with a guide to show you around. We can even arrange a private guide to take you and show you all the things you might like to see.'

Part of Meg wanted to interrupt, but it did take some delicacy. Dan had been right: no one at the hotel should find out the true purpose of their visit to the island, or the entire deal could be over before it began.

Dan shook his head. 'No, thank you, we would prefer to do it by ourselves. We're newly engaged, you see, so we'd like to be alone.'

Meg had to hand it to him, as awkward as the fake engagement story was, it did seem like the best cover.

'Then you probably should rent one of the e-bikes, unless you'd like a traditional bicycle? The road up to the town is quite steep.'

'E-bikes are perfect, exactly what we need.'

They walked up to the bikes and stopped. 'Do you know how to ride these things?' she whispered.

'I'm sure it can't be too hard.'

'In other words, you don't.'

'Do you?' he asked.

'Why don't you give it a go first?' she suggested.

'So that way if I crash, you can laugh at me?'

'Precisely,' she said, looking down to hide her smile.

Even though Meg couldn't remember the last time she'd ridden a bicycle, the e-bikes were actually easy to ride. They rode, with Dan leading the way, along the edge of a golden beach and up a hill to the main town. The address they'd been directed to for their meeting was on the other side of the town and easy to find. It looked like a residence, although slightly more upmarket than most of the houses they'd passed on the way.

He checked his phone, looked at the house again.

'I think this is it. It's not Nino's house, but his business manager's.'

'Let's do this.' Meg followed Dan along the path to the door. He held out his fist to the door, but glanced at her as though waiting for final permission before knocking, so she nodded and he knocked.

No one answered. She counted slowly and Dan shuffled around, trying to see if he could see in any of the windows.

'Knock again,' she said when she reached thirty.

'Were you counting again?' he asked.

Dan raised his hand to knock again just as the door was flung open.

A man, whose head came to about the same height as Dan's fist, stood in front of them. Dan apologised quickly. 'I'm Daniel Fairweather and this is Megan Granger. We have a meeting with Mr Flores and Mr Manea.'

'I'm sorry but they're not here.'

Dan and Meg exchanged glances.

'We have a meeting scheduled with them. We've come from Sydney.'

'I'm sorry, I don't know what to tell you.'

Meg had no idea how much this person knew about the deal and was reluctant to say anything. Dan clearly was as well.

'Do you know when they will be back?'

The man shook his head. 'I haven't seen either of them all day. I'm not sure if they are even on the island.'

Meg felt irritation rising inside her.

'We have some potential business dealings with Mr Flores. Is there any way we can contact him?'

'You have their emails?' the man asked.

'Yes,' Dan said.

'I suggest you try those. As I said, I don't know where either of them are.'

Sensing their presence was now an annoyance, Meg touched Dan's arm gently and nudged him away.

Once they were away from the house and back on the road, Dan said, 'We should call George.'

'It's five a.m. at home.'

'Okay, let's see what we can see of the site ourselves.'

It was a good idea, she thought, though didn't say that to him. Another boost to his ego was the last thing he needed. They were getting too close and she had to keep her distance. It was one thing to be polite and kind, but she couldn't have him getting the wrong idea. The last thing she needed was Daniel Fairweather thinking that she returned his feelings.

Meg directed Dan to the address they had for the development site. The map led them to a dirt road and they left the bikes and walked down the track. The path was narrow and surrounded on both sides by thick, impenetrable rainforest. 'What are we going to say if someone asks what we're doing here?' she asked.

'We'll say we're lost.'

But no one was there and when they rounded the next corner they arrived at a gate. A locked gate. A wire fence stretched off into each direction, into the tangle of bushes and tree roots.

Meg held the fence and moved it from side to side. They could slip through it.

'We can't walk through there. It's too thick and I don't fancy the idea of either of us getting bitten by whatever lives in there,' he said, reading her thoughts. 'What's plan B?'

'What if he refuses to see us tomorrow? Or the next day? What if the whole trip is a bust?'

'It won't be our fault.'

'That's beside the point. We won't have secured the deal. George wants to expand into the South Pacific and Flores is keen to develop a resort with us.'

'So keen he wasn't even at the appointment?'

'We look at other islands?'

'We can't leave the island though. What if Flores decides to meet us tomorrow?'

They couldn't just sit at the hotel sipping cocktails either. That was not the sort of attitude that would prove to the board that she'd be ready to take over the CEO role from George when he left.

'I have an idea,' he said.

Her first instinct was to say, 'Yeah, like all the rest of your brilliant and impractical ideas?' but she bit back that reflex. Dan had been surprisingly helpful already this trip. She simply said, 'Yes?'

'We can't get in by road, but we could get in by the water.'

'That's actually not a bad idea.'

'It hurt you to say that, didn't it?' He grinned.

Something in her stomach twisted at the sight of the crinkles around his eyes as they narrowed into a cheeky smile. A long dimple accentuated his cheek, his square chin raised in question.

'Not at all,' she lied. It wasn't the words that were hurting—the way her shoulders tingled when he smiled at her caused her far more discomfort.

'We could sail around,' he said.

'You can sail?'

'Not exactly. Can you?'

'Not at all.'

'Motorboat?'

'Never tried.'

'Me neither.'

Trying to access or even view the property from the water was a good idea. At the very least, they should try.

'I'm sure if we work together we should be able to figure out a way,' she said.

'Work together? Do we need that in writing?' He gave her another one of his grins, showing off the sparkle in his blue eyes, and annoyingly she felt that one in her stomach as well.

'Figuring out a way' ended up involving hiring a two-person kayak. They agreed a sailing boat was outside both their skill sets and motorboats were not allowed near the protected reef. A kayak would be the best option, as it would allow them to get close to the site, and, if they were lucky, even pull into one of the coves.

But after they'd changed out of their business clothes into shorts and T-shirts, and hired the kayak, other problems presented themselves. Dan reached down to drag the kayak to the water and as he tugged on it he groaned. Meg shook her head and tried to pull it herself but it barely budged. It was far heavier than it looked.

'On the count of three?' she suggested.

Dan nodded and began counting. On three Meg grabbed the front of the kayak and Dan pushed. It began to move but after a few metres Meg stumbled.

'Sorry,' Dan said, even though it probably wasn't his fault. 'You push, I'll pull,' he said.

They swapped ends and somehow inched the kayak closer to the water. Dan stumbled a few times and Meg felt a twinge in her back but wasn't about to admit that to Dan.

Once they reached the water Meg looked at the kayak and up at Dan. 'Now what?'

'We get in. Why don't you get in first? I can hold it still.'

This sounded like a good offer so Meg waded out into the water. She studied the kayak, now rocking in the shallow water. There was no way of doing this elegantly.

He doesn't care how graceful you are, remember? He likes you. And he still likes you even though you've been ghastly to him for so many years.

She turned her back to the kayak and lowered herself to sit in it sideways. A wave came through just as her bottom connected with the kayak and the next thing she knew, the kayak was up on one side and she had slid neck-deep into the water, her bottom landing on the sandy floor with a bump.

She squealed. 'You did that on purpose!'

'No, I swear! It was the wave.'

Meg's loose T-shirt lifted up and pooled around the surface of the water. She pushed it down, horrified, but glad she'd decided to wear a swimming costume under her clothes.

She pulled herself up, dripping wet, her clothes sticking unforgivingly to her body. Her pride aching most of all.

'I think you should try next.'

'Why? So you can watch me fall in?'

'Yes.'

He laughed but took up the challenge. Unlike Meg, Dan attempted to throw his leg over the side of the kayak before placing his weight in it, which resulted in him straddling the vessel. He winced.

'This is awkward,' he admitted as he tried again to get both legs in.

'Just be grateful you didn't fall in.'

'You're not going to tip it so I do, are you?'

'I haven't decided yet,' she said, but she held it steady while Dan got both legs in.

Dan had taken the rear seat, leaving Meg the front, which meant he now had a close-up view of her lifting herself into the small vessel. On the sand it was heavy but in the water it rocked easily as she placed weight onto it.

'Try throwing your leg over first,' he said.

'What did you say?' She turned to him.

She knew he hadn't meant it suggestively but maybe he had?

He was grinning. 'You know what I meant.'

But had she?

Getting into the kayak was just the first challenge. They floundered around for what seemed like an eternity figuring out how to paddle and then how to paddle in time with one another in a way that didn't send the kayak around and around in circles. Meg became glad that she had had the brief dip in the water because she was working up a sweat and the tropical sun was warm.

She was conscious that Dan was sitting behind her and could see her every move, though she couldn't see him. Did he plan it like that?

Probably.

No. Dan was not calculating in that way. He'd kept his distance from her since That Night, not giving the slightest suggestion that he was interested in her, and she had to give him credit for that.

They were in a good rhythm and Meg was totally lost in her thoughts of Dan and his behaviour over the past decade when she heard him say, 'It's coming up on our right.'

Meg eased off her strokes and the kayak drifted slowly to the right and towards the long, curved beach. She exhaled. It was a gorgeous spot.

Objectively, the site was pleasant, the white beach, the lush bush and the gentle slope made it an ideal place to build, but it was more than that. It was how the large mountain rose up behind it, at a good distance, somehow protecting the site in its shadow. The volcanic rock looked down at her like a face and the cliffs to each side resembled arms, reaching around, embracing the small cove.

It was the sort of perfect positioning it was difficult to find.

'I think it's beautiful, but you're the architect, you tell me.'

Dan didn't speak for a while and then he said, 'It vibrates perfectly.'

She almost laughed, last week she might have at such a

whimsical phrase, but sitting here now she knew exactly what he meant. People visiting this place would feel happy.

'Should we pull in? There's no one else around,' he asked.

'The only issue I see is getting back into this thing afterwards.'

'Nonsense, we're experts now.'

'Easy for you to say, you didn't fall in.'

'No, but I'm jealous you got a swim.'

The kayak hit the sand. Dan got out easily and then dragged the vessel further onto the beach so Meg could get out without submerging herself.

Getting out of the kayak was easier than getting in, and when she turned back to Dan it was to see him lifting his T-shirt over his head and throwing it into the back of the kayak. Meg's mouth went completely dry. Dan's body didn't seem to have aged a day since she'd last seen his bare chest, his stomach as flat and taut as it had been all those years ago.

She sucked hers in, then released it when she realised how absurd she was being. One: she exercised and took care of herself. Two: she didn't care what Daniel Fairweather thought of her. And three: it would actually be better if she looked as unattractive as possible to dampen his feelings for her.

Meg pulled off her own wet T-shirt and shorts and dropped them in the kayak. Let him think what he wanted about her black one-piece and the cellulite developing on her thighs.

She glanced back at Dan and saw him looking at her, puzzlement creasing his brow. She didn't have long to admire his torso because in three strides and one movement he had dived under the surface.

Thirsty, hot and suddenly covered in a sheen of perspiration, Meg waded slowly into the water, but in the opposite direction from Dan. This time she could properly enjoy the cool, clear salt water on her body, and let its restorative properties soothe her.

What a strange couple of days it had been. She floated on her back, let the ocean hold her. Dan liked her. Really liked her. And when she stopped hating him long enough to stop their war of attrition then he was quite pleasant to her. More than pleasant—he'd been helpful, attentive and even good company.

He can be fun, you know that. You remember that.

She let herself remember the first few weeks they had known one another, how well they had got along, how easily they had clicked. Then she thought back to moments before, how they'd paddled the kayak with one another in easy, even strokes.

They could get along, but that didn't mean her feelings matched his, it just meant they were both capable of being mature adults. Which should not have been surprising since they were adults. And colleagues.

And…?

Realising she was losing track of time, she stood up and looked around. Dan was on the beach, pulling his shirt back on over his broad shoulders and nicely flat stomach. Men his age were not meant to look like that.

He caught her eye and winked. Her body warmed again, in spite of the refreshing water. Thankfully he turned away and Meg waded in to shore, no cooler than she had been when she'd dived in.

Dan wandered along and began to investigate deeper into the scrub, but Meg stayed on the beach, walking along the shoreline, letting her body dry naturally. It was gorgeously natural unspoilt beauty. It would almost be a shame to build here and yet development was inevitable, not to mention helpful to this small island and its economy.

Meg sat on the beach and looked out across the crystal-clear water in the cove. In the distance the waves broke in gentle white horses on the edge of the reef.

Dan came and sat next to her. His long bare legs were flecked with a dusting of sand and his feet looked good. Clean, clipped nails and…oh, my goodness, what was wrong with her? Since when did she look at a man's feet? And since when did she look at *Dan's* feet? She was about to get up and walk away when he said, 'I'm thinking it would be best to place the buildings closer to the headland.' He pointed in the direction he meant. 'We want to take advantage of this bay, but without spoiling its beauty. We don't want to be able to see them from the beach, if possible.'

'Good idea.'

Dan faced away from her, musing aloud about what would and wouldn't work.

'Low-set buildings, so as not to spoil any of the views. Ideally we want the structures to be hidden.'

Rather than being annoyed, she was enjoying listening to him, seeing his mind working quickly, in all different creative directions. Meg's lips stretched into a smile.

Dan turned and caught both her expression and, she sensed, her secret warm thoughts, but before she could change her expression, he grinned back at her. Her stomach flipped.

They walked side by side along the beach. Occasionally he'd turn to her and ask what she thought and she'd answer honestly. 'Yes.' Or 'Great,' and 'No.' Or, 'You can't be serious. Are you designing an eco resort or a cathedral?'

But when they circled back to the kayak he sighed and said, 'I wish I had a pen and paper.'

Meg shrugged. 'I can remember some of it.'

He studied her, his face puzzling over a problem. Then he nodded.

What did that look mean?

Last week she'd been able to read all of his expressions: disgust, mockery, disappointment. This week, she didn't have the code.

No, she corrected herself. You could never read him. He wasn't thinking any of those things.

You've never been able to tell what he was really thinking at all.

Back at the kayak, they both reached for the same paddle at the same moment, Dan's hand landing on top of hers, secure and surprising. Bent over, their faces close, she couldn't move away quickly. Nor could Dan, his blue eyes widening in shock as his hand remained on hers. His hand wasn't heavy, but she struggled to pull hers back, enjoying the way his hand felt wrapped around hers.

'I'll get the other one,' he said finally, voice like gravel, lifting his hand off hers and reaching for the other paddle.

CHAPTER SIX

'I'm famished,' Meg said, after they returned the kayak. Her face was slightly brightened from the sun and her posture seemed looser. The guard she kept permanently up around her had started to drop away. She was no longer catching herself or watching her words around him. It was nice, but it made it impossible for him to keep up his own defences. But keep them up he must; he couldn't have her thinking that he was in any way interested in her romantically.

'We missed lunch, but what about an early dinner and a drink?' he asked.

'Sounds good,' she said easily. 'We should check out one of the restaurants,' she added, as though dinning together were something they did every other day.

Back at the villa they went their separate ways to wash and change. He showered quickly and while he waited for her, he sat on the deck and took a moment to sketch. He drew nothing in particular, but filled in the time. Drawing for pleasure was something he'd got out of the habit of doing over the years, but at the prospect of a few days' downtime, he'd pulled out his sketch pad and pencils. He packed them all up when Meg came out of her room.

Her hair was still damp, but she'd given in to the humidity and the ocean air and her blonde hair lay in gentle waves down to her shoulders. She had changed into another summer dress, this one covered in red flowers, with a high neck that cut away to reveal her shoulders and toned arms, and which fell past her knees. His mouth went dry, but he checked himself. He'd seen her in far less this afternoon, in her swimming costume.

And you've seen her in far less than that, he reminded himself.

I need a drink, he thought.

You really don't, replied another voice.

She smiled at him and for a moment all the voices in his head were silent. He simply smiled back and watched as her cheeks bloomed with pink.

'Let's go,' he said, and then cleared his throat when he heard how raspy his voice sounded.

Poor Meg. She wanted him. It was obvious. The blushing, the awkwardness. How could he have missed the fact that she still had feelings for him for so long?

You didn't want to see it.

Some part of his brain must have deliberately blocked out her feelings, but it was so clear, now he knew what he was looking for. She liked him.

She wanted him.

Dan shook open his collar to get some cooler air onto his neck and face. It was warm.

Of course it's warm, you're not far from the equator.

The memory of Meg, wet and coming out of the water, her clothes clinging to her curves, was also not far from his thoughts. The memory of Meg sitting next to him on the beach, in her swimsuit, long legs bare and strong, stretched out in front of her, was even harder to dismiss. As was the feeling in his stomach when he'd accidentally touched her hand when they both reached for the same paddle.

She looks just the same as she did when you first met. And on That Night.

Damn.

Thoughts like that were easy to ignore when he thought

she hated him, but now that he knew she liked him, they were somehow more difficult to ignore.

The fact that she had feelings for him didn't change anything. If he were to act on the desires that were suddenly, confusingly circulating through him he'd be taking advantage of her.

It's not taking advantage if you're honest with her. If you tell her it would just be a holiday thing. A tropical fling?

No. It would still be wrong.

'Ah, Mr Fairweather and Ms Granger. We didn't expect to see you. We understood you wanted privacy,' the maître d' greeted them.

Ah, that was right, they were engaged.

'We'd like a table for dinner, please.'

'In the restaurant or the bistro? Fine dining or more casual?'

They looked at one another, lost. He had no idea what Meg wanted. Luckily, the maître d' stepped in.

'May I suggest the restaurant, for your celebration?' He winked at them and Dan had to stop himself from wincing.

Fine dining it would be.

They were led to an intimate table for two, on the balcony overlooking the beach.

Their waiter offered them champagne, which Meg agreed to without a blink. The chef's degustation menu was also recommended, a veritable feast of seafood, local and French dishes. It wasn't hard to acquiesce to such treatment.

The intimate setting of the restaurant changed something. They didn't have the activities of work as a buffer. They were a man and a woman, one of whom was attracted to the other, in a romantic setting. He was walking a fine line—he needed to be kind to her, but he couldn't risk leading her on. A fact he should have thought of before agreeing to such a romantic dinner setting.

Work. Just talk about work. It is the one thing you have in common and it's safe ground.

'Do you think the site will work for a resort?' he asked, even though it was what they had discussed most of the afternoon.

'I think it's perfect, I don't think I could have imagined a more beautiful location, but we still need to see the rest of the land, figure out the access. Things like that.'

'Of course.' Dan was sure those things would be fine. 'And I was thinking of this new material they are developing in the States. Fibre cement.'

'Yes, it's gorgeous and I know how long lasting it is, but, Dan, it's exorbitant.'

'You seemed excited about it back at the beach?'

'They are all great ideas, but someone has to pay for it. I'm just being practical.'

'Do you ever do something without thinking through every possibility?'

Meg made fists with her hands then placed them in her lap.

'What's that got to do with anything?'

'Never?' he asked.

'Not any more.'

Her voice was low, like a warning, but he didn't need to be told that he'd gone too far. If even one of them had put the brakes on when they'd first met one another then perhaps they would still be friends, as they had started. If just either of them had said, 'I'm not sure it's a good idea for two colleagues to sleep with one another,' they could have avoided so much mess. So many arguments. So much tension.

Dan clenched his jaw so hard his teeth squeaked against one another.

'You don't have to be like this. I get it.'

'What are you talking about?' she asked. 'What am I *like*?'

He was about to get up and suggest they return to their

room but the sight of the maître d' smiling at them expectantly welded him to his chair. They were a happy couple. They couldn't cause a scene.

'What?' she asked again.

'Never mind.'

Her glare was everything he deserved and more. She might not bring out the best in him, but that was his problem to deal with, not hers. And right now he was the one out of line.

He had to stop talking to her like this. It was insulting to her. Meg was smart and capable and most of the time, yes, she was right. And he had to stop letting that bother him.

'I'm sorry,' he said.

'What for, exactly?'

'For being angry with you simply because you're correct, simply because you're pointing out something I don't want to see.'

Meg's eyes widened, then she closed them and dropped her head. He wished he could still look into them, see what she was thinking, feeling.

'I'm sorry I haven't always given your opinions and advice the respect they deserve,' he continued.

It felt as though something had been unblocked, unclogged. His jaw instantly relaxed, the muscles in his shoulders began to unspool.

She looked up then and faced him. He felt as though he'd been struck in the chest, almost as if he were seeing her for the first time. Fresh. Anew. With no history between them. Her beautiful blue eyes open and unguarded.

'I'm sorry too, if I ever went too far. If I ever gave you the impression that I think your ideas are bad or silly. I don't think that. I think most of them are brilliant.'

Wow. She *had* made him feel foolish. Many times. He might have deserved it, every single time, but his pride had been wounded many times by her quick remarks, blunt honesty.

'You should feel free to be honest,' he said. 'I do value it. More than I ever say. It sometimes takes me a moment to accept it, but I do appreciate it.'

'I could be more tactful.'

He shook his head. 'If you were a man I probably wouldn't react the same way. And it hurts me to admit that so, please, just let me say this. A woman's behaviour is not judged the same way as a man's. I'm sorry if that was ever the case at Evermore.'

She nodded. Her soft lips and eyes lifted into a small smile. He hadn't seen her smile like that in years. And it was beautiful.

Usually he only saw Meg's game face, the professional mask she wore at work. Now, her features were soft, her muscles relaxed, and she glowed. She was a beautiful woman. He often forgot that. Deliberately, perhaps. It was easier that way. But right now he needed to see her beauty—she deserved to be seen properly, honestly and as she was.

'Thank you for saying that,' she said.

'It's probably long overdue.'

'Better late than never.' She smiled again and his heart, his old, damaged heart, fluttered. No. Two old enemies had reached a truce, that was all.

Their meal arrived, in several beautifully presented courses: lobster, shrimp, fresh vegetables and a decadent chocolate dessert. For a while they enjoyed the food, the setting sun and the gentle breeze blowing the salty air off the water.

She made small talk about nothing much, sticking to safe topics. Things she knew they both agreed on. The weather, the state of Sydney's beaches, the best restaurants in Manly. Bland but safe.

But he found himself wanting more. He didn't want to hear about the meal she had at a new place last week. Partly because he didn't want to know who she ate it with, but mostly because he knew she had more thoughts and opinions than on the way her food was cooked.

He wanted to talk about anything with her, as they had when they'd first met. He wanted to argue with her as well, and not because he wanted to win, but because he wanted them both to be challenged. Because this polite boringness was somehow more frustrating than the bickering and arguing they did as second nature.

If they truly were to put everything behind them he owed her another apology. Not just one about how he behaved to her at work, but about the thing they never mentioned. He was surprised by how quickly and easily it came.

'And I'm sorry for that night.'

She sucked in a sharp breath.

The first rule of their relationship for the past decade and a half—the only rule of their relationship—was 'Don't talk about That Night'.

If they didn't talk about it, they could pretend it never happened, but he was sick of that approach. If they were going to have a real truce, really leave things on good terms, then they had to talk about it. At least acknowledge it.

That Night had set the pattern for their entire relationship, so he wanted to explain. He didn't know if it would make a difference, but he needed her to know he wasn't the cad she thought he was.

'I'm sorry, for how I handled myself. I should have told you about Astrid before we slept together.'

Meg stood, suddenly, her dessert still half eaten.

'We don't have to talk about it,' he said quickly.

'Too late.'

'No, it's not. We can forget I said anything at all. Please sit back down.'

Her eyes darted around the now busy restaurant where

more than a few other guests were looking on, sensing the change in the atmosphere around their table.

'Honey, why don't you finish your dessert?'

He half expected her to throw her napkin at him and storm out but instead she grimaced and sat back down.

He watched in silence as she finished her chocolate tart then he refilled her wine glass.

'Okay, then,' she said softly.

'Really?'

She nodded and took a gulp of wine for fortification.

'Astrid and I really were separated.'

Meg scrunched her eyes up as though she didn't want to hear.

'You and I were colleagues but, apart from anything else I should have told you, I should have been more forthcoming about my situation. But I wasn't cheating. I was free. But the situation was ambiguous and I can see why it was upsetting.'

And I know I should have told you, but I saw the way you looked at me and I couldn't. I remember the sparkle in your eyes, the way you leant towards me. I can still hear the music in your laughter that night. And I didn't want to say anything to ruin that. It was selfish and cowardly.

'I'm confused—are you apologising or explaining?'

'Both. I am sorry I didn't tell you.'

'Why didn't you?'

Ah, well. That was harder to explain. And telling her the truth didn't seem like the sensible thing to do, given how she felt about him.

Because I liked you so much.

'Because I didn't want to tell you anything that was going to reflect badly on me. And because, at that point, I felt the divorce was all my fault. I was afraid I was a failure. I had failed Astrid, failed my kids. I was afraid you wouldn't want me if I told you I was about to be divorced.'

It was too much to put into words then and even now it was difficult. He could only look at the remnants of their meal on the table.

In the years since, he'd moved on from this feeling of failure, but at the time everything had still been so raw. The hurt, the loss, the feeling that he'd failed at the one thing in life he was supposed to not fail at.

'I felt tricked,' she said.

'But I didn't lie.'

She raised an eyebrow and didn't have to say more. He knew she was right. Technically he had been single, but he hadn't been completely honest with her.

'Even once I knew you were separated, I still felt betrayed. My husband left me for a colleague.'

Dan's stomach dropped.

'The reason I reacted the way I did was because of my ex and what happened with him.'

'He cheated on you?'

'Yes. It was still very recent. And not long before I started at Evermore I'd found out they were expecting a baby.'

'Sheesh,' Dan said as loudly as he could with all the air knocked out of his lungs.

No wonder she'd been so upset. She hadn't been being silly or overreacting. Dan's revelation would have hurt her and upset her in ways he hadn't even imagined. Not then and not even now.

'You were my colleague, my married, though separated, workmate and I felt awful. But I also felt tricked.'

But I wasn't cheating, Dan was about to say, before he realised that wasn't the point. Meg had been betrayed by her husband and Dan had done nothing to restore her trust, only eroded it a little further. No wonder she'd been so mad. And for so long.

And instead of being civil to her after that he'd been the opposite.

He'd been belligerent and inconsiderate. He'd waged a petty one-man war against her for years.

And he'd done all of that to a woman he'd once cared about.

He'd hurt Meg, just as he'd hurt Astrid.

It was a damn good thing he didn't believe in love or relationships because clearly he was hopeless at both.

'I just don't get it, Dan. Before that night I actually thought we were friends. And not once did you mention a wife and kids. We spoke every day for weeks and you never said anything. All you said was that you were single. A wife and two sons is a pretty big thing to leave out.'

She was right, as usual.

'I was afraid you wouldn't want me if you knew.'

It was perhaps the most honest thing he'd ever said to her. To anyone. It was as if he'd shed a heavy coat he'd been suffering under for way too long, but he didn't feel exposed, he only felt unburdened.

Meg's mouth curled into a frown. Her face wasn't triumphant, it was sad. 'Well, turns out that not telling me was the bigger problem.'

'Yes, I do see the irony.'

With that, her expression changed and she let out a wry chuckle and then a long sigh.

Was it forgiveness? No, but it was understanding.

'Let's get going,' she said and stood.

He was grateful for the silence on the walk back to the villa. He didn't think he had more honesty left in him that evening. Besides, something else worried him: now they had reached this understanding, would Meg think that something more was on the cards? It hadn't been his intention to give her any hope. He only wanted to ease the tension between them, be a little kinder. Would she be hoping for friendship? Or for something more?

He had to find a way to let her know that even though he was sorry, and that while he respected her, they were colleagues—and friends—only. He had to figure out a way to let her down easily.

In this new spirit of honesty, it was only fair.

They made their way along the path to the corner of the resort to their villa. The sun was low on the horizon and the pale pinks and purples were gathering across the sky. It would have been a supremely romantic moment—with the right person.

She thinks you're the right person.

When George had first told Dan about Meg having feelings for him, he'd struggled to believe that, after everything that had happened over the years, the feelings she'd had for him when they'd first met hadn't been extinguished by his poor behaviour. But after spending two days together it didn't seem so unbelievable. Here, removed from the rest of the world, they had settled into an easy peace. They'd had their moments, last night's disagreement about who was leading the project was a case in point, but it was just a blip. Not only were they getting along, he was also having a good time. For a few hours out on the beach he'd half forgotten that she was Megan Granger, his CFO and nemesis. She was simply Meg. Colleague and friend. Attractive friend. Very attractive friend.

She walked a few steps ahead of him on the narrow path and the skirt of her dress swished around her legs with the hypnotic side-to-side motion of her hips and bottom as she made her way along the path in the moonlight.

Beautiful.

Not watching the ground, he stumbled on something and Meg turned.

'Are you okay?'

'Fine, yes,' he said, even though his hands were suddenly filled with pins and needles.

Pay attention to where you're going!

He'd even apologised to her about not being honest about Astrid, something that a week ago he couldn't have ever seen himself doing. He understood Meg better now and knew he should have been honest with her about Astrid from the beginning.

If he had been upfront, who knew what might have happened? Instead of having years of bickering they might have had years of something else.

Friendship. That was all. Because only a fool would want a relationship.

He liked Meg. He respected her. As a colleague. As a friend.

It's more than that, don't kid yourself again. Your body temperature rises each time you think of her. You can't stop looking at her. Hoping for a smile. Hoping to see that conspiratorial look in her eyes. Searching for signs that she likes you.

He was addicted to the search. He still wanted proof that Meg felt some sort of longing for him. Proof that George really was right.

They reached their villa far too quickly. They'd discussed a lot that evening but it still didn't feel like enough. He still had questions, or maybe answers, he wasn't sure. They stood outside the villa and Meg reached for her key card and said, 'Goodnight.'

'Wait,' he said before he'd even realised what he was going to say.

Do you want another drink? Do you want to sit on the deck?

No. All of those things were very bad ideas.

If Meg had feelings for him, he couldn't lead her on or give her any reason to think that his feelings were the same. Particularly when his feelings were an explosive mix of regret, shame and desire.

'Should we discuss a plan for tomorrow?' she asked.

Tomorrow was the last thing on his mind. This moment, right now, the only thing he was capable of thinking about.

Her eyes were a kaleidoscope of blues, gorgeous and mesmerising.

And how had he not noticed?

Because she was hiding her true feelings behind snark for self-preservation. She didn't really dislike him. Meg looked up, expectantly, waiting for something of sense to leave his mouth.

You don't really dislike her either.

It was true.

They had their difficulties, but beneath all that was a deep respect.

And attraction.

Which he had been trying all day to ignore. Honestly, he'd been trying for fifteen years to ignore. And when he'd been certain she despised him, it had been easy. But now?

Now it was going to be more difficult than ever, but he had to. Her feelings for him were obviously much more intense than his and he couldn't lead her on. Not ever, but especially not now.

His heart dropped and the earth shook.

A noise, like a train approaching, made him look up the path they had come.

But of course there were no trains on the island. Meg's eyes were wide and he grabbed her arms, steadying her. But the noise became louder and the ground more unstable and he pulled her to him. Even as he did so, he wasn't sure what he was protecting her from, or even how he proposed to do it, only that it made perfect logical sense for her to be in his arms. And when she didn't object he didn't think too deeply on it, he held her close, placed a hand gently on her head and looked around for what was coming.

But it was nothing.

The noise and the shaking subsided and Meg tugged herself gently away from where her face was tucked into his chest. She looked up at him and his heart swooped. Her skin was still pale but her eyes were bright and alert.

'Earth tremor,' she said, giving a name to the danger he couldn't place.

'Of course.' Neither of them had been in any particular danger, at least not standing in the open as they were, and certainly not now it had passed, yet she didn't pull away and Dan had to admit that her warm frame, pressed against his, felt good. It felt like what had been missing all day. All evening.

He should have pulled back—after all, he was the one who needed to remain strong and sensible—but he didn't. He was caught in her gaze. Her eyes were mesmerising. His eyes flicked away from them, only to land on her lips. Pink, full and her bottom lip hanging ever so slightly open. Soft, plump. It would taste so wonderful between his own.

Meg looked down and pushed gently but definitively back from him.

'I think it's passed now. We should be fine to go into our rooms.'

'Yes, of course.'

Should he apologise? But what for? She didn't seem upset or annoyed. *Of course she's not annoyed, she still likes you. In spite of everything.*

But he didn't have to decide because Meg simply said, 'See you tomorrow,' and she opened the villa door and disappeared into her room as quickly as a magician.

Leaving Dan standing there alone to worry about the aftershocks.

Meg tossed and turned. Dan's words went round in her head in a loop.

'I was afraid you wouldn't like me if you knew.'

So raw, so bare.

So honest.

But a single moment of raw honesty, lubricated by wine, didn't mean she could trust him. Not after everything else that had passed between them over the years. It had been a strange day, followed by an unsettling evening. And the less said about the earth tremor the better. She should have thought faster than she had, she shouldn't have let him hold her like that, tender, protective, his hand over the back of her head as though he actually planned on stopping something from hitting her. It was obviously what he'd needed at that moment, to feel close to her, but what if he got the wrong idea?

And what is the wrong idea, Meg? You liked being held. You liked that there was someone there to grab you in a moment of confusion, you liked the way his chest felt against your cheek and you liked the way he smelt of ocean and chocolate.

She had liked all those things and that caused her to roll over in bed for the millionth time, trying to find rest that never seemed to come.

She must have fallen asleep eventually because when she finally woke, the sun was well above the horizon. She showered and dressed and emerged slowly from her room. As soon as she walked out, though, she could tell the villa was empty. The door to Dan's room was wide open and there was no sign of him. She exhaled.

That was nice of him to give you some space, wasn't it? said the voice she was starting to think of as a bad angel.

Yes, it was considerate. And yes, maybe Dan wasn't as much of an arse as she'd believed this time last week, but what of it?

She ordered breakfast and happily ate tropical fruits and drank good coffee on the deck overlooking the lush green bush and the sea beyond. She caught up on emails, but there was, frustratingly, still no word from Nino Flores or George.

Dan didn't appear and she was grateful for the space. She was very grateful not to have to see him again so soon after last night's... What even had that been? It wasn't about to be a kiss, she was almost, nearly, certain. Mostly because she wouldn't have let it happen.

Though that Dan had wanted to kiss her, she'd been absolutely certain. His eyes had been dark, focused, full of desire.

And full of something else. He had looked at her—more than that, he had *seen* her. And she had let herself be seen. For a moment she had looked into his face and her guard had dropped away. His barriers had as well. His whole expression had been different. Softer. New.

Or was she reading way too much into it all? It had been a strange evening, a strange couple of days, and then there was the earth tremor. If she needed further proof that things weren't exactly normal, then that was it.

The knock on the front door was soft, but it still made her jump, as though she'd been poked. She got out of her chair to see Dan letting himself back into the villa. He was wearing a green polo shirt and shorts. He didn't look rested and his hair was slightly askew, which made her slightly pleased.

Dan walked out to the deck and said, 'George wants to speak to us.' He held up his phone, pressed the speaker function and placed his phone on the table between them.

After making some small talk about whether they were having a good time and the shaky Internet connection, George said, 'I got a message from Flores and I'm sorry about the mix-up in dates. The fault was at my end. He can meet with you in four days.'

They were stuck here for four more days.

'Sorry about it, but I assume you won't mind. Being in paradise and all. And, Meg, you did say you wanted a break.'

Dan looked at her, eyes wide. She shook her head. She

didn't want George giving Dan the wrong idea about anything.

Four more days!

George continued, 'I guess there's nothing we can do. But it's a good opportunity when you think about it. I want you to get out there together, get to know the place. Get to know the people, but, remember, discretion is paramount. You can't tell them who you are or what you're doing there until we get Flores on board. Go diving, swimming, hiking. Or eat and drink as much as you can. It's all on me. You've both been working too hard.'

An employer-ordered and all-expenses-paid holiday. On a tropical island. For most people that would be heaven, for Meg, it would have been too, except for the man still standing next to her, slipping his phone into his pocket and looking…gorgeous.

A lock of his hair curled at the front over his forehead and she wanted to slip her fingers into it and brush it back. A memory, a long-forgotten one, resurfaced of wanting and then doing exactly that.

She wanted him.

The realisation was staggering at first, discombobulating, but, she realised with a faint horror, it was true.

No. No.

In a few moments she'd be mortified by the thoughts she was having. Of asking Dan to go snorkelling. Or swimming… or…any other activity that involved both of them taking their clothes off.

He likes you. He wants you. He probably won't object.
No.

Something wasn't quite right. It must be the beautiful tropical setting, or the fact she'd just been told to have a few days off. It would pass, because this was Dan. Sooner or later he'd say something ridiculous or annoying and this tightness in her chest would disappear.

'It's not like George to get dates wrong.' Even as the founder and CEO of a company as large as Evermore, he still didn't get small details wrong.

'No, it's not. But he hasn't been well,' Dan said.

'Yes, that must be it.'

Did George plan this? Do it on purpose? No. Surely not. He knew she didn't get along with Dan and forcing them to spend a week alone together was not the ideal way to make her relax. If George had wanted to force her to take a break there were better ways of going about it.

'So,' Dan said, 'what are you going to do today?'

You. Singular. He wasn't pressuring her, he was giving her an opportunity to do something on her own, which she appreciated.

'I'd like to get to know the island better. George is right—if we're going to be developing here, I'd like to get a better feel for it and the people.'

'On your own?'

She would like to go on her own, but...

'George did say we should go together,' she said, to make it clear it wasn't her idea or even her choice.

'And if we don't, people might get suspicious about what we're doing here.'

'I guess we're going to have to be the newly engaged couple again?'

'I guess so,' he replied.

It was okay for him. He was probably loving this 'pretend couple' caper, but the longer it went on, the more nervous she became.

CHAPTER SEVEN

IT WAS OKAY for Meg, she was probably loving the fake relationship ruse they had to perform, but Dan was not. The last thing he needed was Meg getting the wrong idea about his feelings for her and pretending to be a couple was the surest way to get everyone's emotions muddled.

He had to find a way to let her down easily, if only he could figure out what that was. He didn't want to come right out and say, 'I don't have feelings for you.' Because she'd want to know why he felt the need to say it and he didn't want to drop George in it and embarrass her in the process, so he had to be subtle. But if fifteen years of complaining about her hadn't sent a clear message that he didn't return her feelings, then he wasn't sure what on earth he could possibly do.

They walked to the resort lobby. Heiana was behind the front desk and beamed when she saw them.

'What can I help you both with today?'

'We're looking to do some sightseeing.'

'Wonderful.' Heiana pointed them to a display of pamphlets advertising activities. 'There's snorkelling, or diving.'

No. Definitely not anything that involved either of them taking off their clothes and getting wet.

Meg shook her head. 'Anything more cultural?'

'There's a cooking class. We run it here, at the hotel.'

'That sounds great,' Meg said, and took the pamphlet from Heiana.

'No,' Dan said.

'It'll be fun,' Meg said.

He shook his head and steered her away from the front desk and Heiana's ears.

'What's up? Can you not cook?'

'I can cook perfectly fine. I don't need a class.'

'You cook French Polynesian food like an expert?'

'I didn't say that. Maybe I just don't want to show you up.'

'You think you can cook better than I can?'

'I've been cooking for myself every night for the past fifteen years.'

Meg's eyes widened. He'd given more away than he'd wanted to.

For himself. Every night. Fifteen years.

The fact that he'd never re-partnered after his divorce was now clear to Meg, if it hadn't been already. It wasn't something he hid. He wasn't ashamed of his single status.

It was a fact of his life. But it was something he wished he hadn't inadvertently blurted out to the woman he was meant to be letting down easily.

'I tend to cook alone.'

He could cook. Very well, he thought. His sons always ate his food, which was a pretty good sign. He didn't not want to do the class because he couldn't cook, but because he knew how these things worked. They would both have to work together. Cook together. The kitchen and their different cooking styles had been a constant source of friction between him and Astrid. She'd hated the way he chopped things and had told him so frequently. He'd hated the way she didn't clean up as she went and left a pile of dirty dishes and pans from one end of the kitchen to the other even after cooking a simple meal.

Well, one thing was for sure. Once she cooked with him, Meg would be sure to be put off him for ever.

After agreeing to take the class, they were directed to a

minibus that would take the group to the nearby market for shopping and a tour before they headed for the hotel's kitchen. There were four other couples waiting on the bus already. Dan indicated that Meg should climb in first and she did. When he climbed in his heart fell. There was, of course, only one seat left, and it was the one next to Meg. The bus, which was a generous description for the vehicle, was not large. Even when Meg pushed herself as far as possible against the window, their thighs still touched. More than touched, they brushed and rubbed and pushed against one another until he decided it was better to just let his body sit flush against hers to avoid all friction down that side of his body. What must she be thinking? He couldn't tell, as she looked steadfastly out of the window.

'Welcome, everyone! I'm Raina,' announced their guide. 'Let's introduce ourselves and share where we are from.'

Dan's heart fell. It already felt like corporate bonding.

The first couple were from California. 'We're on our honeymoon,' they said in unison.

'So are we,' chimed the remaining couples. Dan wanted to grind his teeth together and jump right off the bus but instead he smiled at Meg. 'I'm Dan and this is Meg. We're from Australia and we've just got engaged.'

'Ahh...' replied everyone and Dan smiled and thought about how in a few hours he could sit alone in his room and have a real holiday. The only consolation was that beside him Meg's leg felt just as tense.

'Can I see your ring?' asked one nosey woman.

'It's getting resized,' said Meg.

'Have you set a date?' another of the honeymooners asked them.

Dan wished for another earth tremor.

'Not yet, it's still new and we're taking our time,' Meg said through a tight jaw.

'Oh? Doesn't look like you two have much time to waste,' laughed a young-looking man from the back seat with an obvious jibe about the fact that Dan and Meg were at least twenty years older than everyone else on the bus. Dan decided he hated him.

'Yes, well, we don't want to rush into anything. We've both been married before. We understand that while things look great now, they don't always stay that way. As you all know, most marriages end in divorce,' Meg said.

The bus fell silent. Dan looked at Meg and didn't bother to hide his smile. It would have looked strange if he'd high-fived her. Instead he leant slightly closer and whispered, 'Love your work.' Next to his lips, Meg's cheeks bloomed with colour.

Raina took them to the bustling local market, where she showed them around and explained what everything was. Dan had thought he had a good handle on tropical fruits, but the trip to the market showed him otherwise. They tried the fresh pineapple and mango as well as starfruit, rambutan and breadfruit.

The seafood was also stunning: fresh tuna, shellfish, squids. For such a small island, there was an amazing amount of fresh produce. They purchased some fresh fish and then all piled back into the minibus to return to the hotel.

One of the hotel kitchens was set up with five cooking stations and each couple chose one.

Raina showed them how to make poisson cru, a dish of chopped raw tuna, marinated in lime and coconut juice. Dan expertly used the knife to chop the fish. He glanced at the other participants and compared his perfect cubes to the mush in front of them.

They were also taught to make poulet fafa—chicken fried with onion, garlic and ginger and then sautéed in coconut milk. Meg took the lead on that dish and he salivated as it cooked. She also tidied as she went, he noticed with warmth in his chest. They worked together to make po'e, a pudding made of pureed taro, flavoured with fruit and sugar.

Meg's and Dan's dishes were not only the first finished, but they looked the best. The obnoxious man looked to theirs and back to the burnt mess in front of him. His new wife crossed her arms and frowned.

Everyone got to eat the food they had prepared. The honeymooners took seats around the large communal table, but Meg pointed her head to the deck outside, and Dan followed her away from the young couples.

'You really can cook. I'm sorry I suggested otherwise,' she said.

'Thanks. You, too.'

He smiled at her and she smiled back. His chest warmed. Though that also could have been the ginger and garlic in the chicken.

'They're all so bright and optimistic. They have no idea what's coming for them,' Dan said.

Meg sighed. 'Yes. I almost want to go up to the women and say—watch out! Or get out while you still can!'

'Really? You wish you hadn't married Paul? You'd give up Olive?'

'No. Of course not. But they have no idea how hard it's going to be. How much it's possible for a heart to break.'

Dan glanced at Meg. She was eating as though she hadn't just said something so devastating. He was still reeling and wasn't sure how to respond.

'I'd like to tell the men that no matter how hard they work it won't make a difference,' he said.

'That's not true,' she said. 'Hard work is fine, it's the cheating that's the real deal-breaker.'

'I worked as hard as I could. I tried as hard as I could, and it wasn't enough.'

Meg put her fork down.

'When Paul left me, I asked myself over and over what I did wrong, what I could have done differently. Was I too fat, too ugly?'

'Stop right there,' Dan said, but Meg waved him back to silence.

'Was I too boring? Was I doing something wrong? And it took me ages, years in fact, to realise it wasn't about me. It was about him. His choices. His weaknesses. It was never about me not being enough. It was about him being unfaithful. Disloyal.'

Meg was right. But look at her, she was beautiful, attractive, clever, fun. Paul was the idiot for leaving her.

But it was different with him and Astrid.

'After we broke up, she married a doctor. He works half the hours I do and gets paid twice as much. She had two more kids. They're still together.'

Meg shook her head. 'But that also wasn't about you, that's just about her and her expectations. You got together when you were young?'

'Fifteen.'

'People grow apart. And you were together, what, over twenty years?'

'Nearly twenty-five.'

'That's a long time.'

But it wasn't for ever.

'Yes, and I still managed to mess it up.'

'You don't need to answer this but...did you cheat on her?'

'Of course not.'

'And she?'

He shook his head. He was pretty sure about that at least. Unlike Meg, he hadn't had to deal with a betrayal of that kind. He wasn't sure how he'd handle something like that at all. So it was just as well he didn't believe in love. Or relationships.

'That doesn't mean it was anything you did. People do

just grow apart. Their priorities change. Especially when kids come along. You were just kids when you got together.'

'No, our love wasn't strong enough. And if ours wasn't… well, I don't think love can ever last for ever.'

'Wow. That really is cynical.'

'You know me,' he said. He wasn't saying something he hadn't said a hundred times before, probably even in her presence.

'I'm not sure I do.'

Meg studied him closely and his throat closed over. She was looking for answers, things he didn't want to tell her. Things he didn't even know.

He saw more dancing across her sparkling blue eyes. Curiosity. Affection. Even love.

He had to shut it down. Now!

'Meg, the one thing you need to know about me is that I don't do relationships.'

'You—' she began.

'You're going to contradict me, because that's what you do. But you know I'm right about this. I wasn't good enough to make my marriage work. I messed up with you at the very first hurdle. Relationships are my kryptonite.'

She laughed. And hard.

'What? I've just shared one of my most personal fears and deepest weaknesses with you and you're laughing!'

'And you compared yourself to Superman in the process.' She wiped a tear from her eye. Once she'd caught her breath she said, 'No one is perfect.'

'You still haven't forgiven me for That Night.'

'I'm not sure what that has got to do with you and your Superman fantasy, but it hurt me. But that was just as much to do with where I was in my life as it was to do with you and what you did.'

Dan blinked. 'Are you saying you forgive me?'

'Ah, look, is there any point going over what happened? We seem to have reached a truce in the last few days. Isn't that enough?'

A truce. That was enough. It was all he wanted.

He didn't need her forgiveness and shouldn't have asked for it. And yet, it would have been nice to know he had it.

A truce. She was right, that was all either of them needed. He certainly didn't want her thinking he wanted anything more.

Meg put her fork down. The meal they had cooked together had been delicious. She wasn't sure why she'd had Dan pegged as incompetent in the kitchen. He wasn't at all. He sliced and diced as well as Raina.

But the way they had shown up the younger couples was the most thrilling of all. The look on their faces when they'd seen the way Dan had cut his fish. The look of disappointment on the faces of some of the young women when they'd realised that the men they'd just married couldn't make a basic dish would have been funny if it hadn't been so sad.

A truce. This new easiness between them made her feel lighter.

However, Meg wasn't sure how she felt about Dan continuing to want to talk about That Night. Now she knew Dan had a crush on her, the night they had spent together was something she was trying her best not to think about at all. Yet, stranger still, even as Dan kept bringing it up, he seemed almost at pains to stress he didn't want a relationship. It didn't make sense.

'I was thinking,' Dan said, 'and there's no pressure, but if you like we could paddle out to the reef this afternoon. It's not too far offshore.'

'I'd love to,' she said, but her chest constricted. She wanted to see the reef with Dan, but she also didn't want to give him the wrong idea. They might have reached an uneasy truce, but she didn't want him to think they could be anything more than colleagues and friends.

She just had to figure out a way to let him down gently, let him know that, while she respected him, they could only ever be friends.

This time they handled the large kayak like pros, getting it easily into the water and paddling in synchronised unison out to the reef.

The coral reef off Isle St Jean was one of the most unspoilt in the region, thanks partly to the relative isolation of the island and the lack of development in the area. If they did develop a resort here one of the priorities would be to contribute to marine rejuvenation programmes. They padded over some of the clearest, most crystalline water she'd ever seen.

The vibrant colours of the coral shifted as they floated across it, greens turned to purples, pinks turned to blues. The rest shimmered.

They moved the kayak as if they were one, stopping instinctively at the same times, steering in unison. She pointed out the angel fish and he pointed out an octopus hidden in the colourful coral.

'Shh...' Dan said at one point and they both lifted their paddles as a shark glided by silently to the left of the kayak. It was as large as a big dog and swam away from them quickly, but her heart was still in her throat, more from the awe of seeing such a creature so close as anything else.

'Other people get to see dolphins,' Dan said from behind her. 'Only we can handle the sharks.'

She smiled.

Dan had also had the foresight to order a small picnic basket from the hotel, which fitted neatly onto the back of the kayak and contained cold drinks, fresh fruit, and the ubiquitous bottle of champagne. Lest the hotel let these lovebirds go without.

Past the reef was a small uninhabited islet, only accessible by boat and on which they were the only people. Dan carried the basket up to the small amount of shade offered by the few trees on the low coral island, and motioned for Meg to make herself comfortable.

'Champagne or cold water?' he asked.

'Can I have both?'

'Of course.'

You're literally on a desert island with Dan. Meg of a month ago would have been horrified, but now, as she bit into a piece of sweet melon, she felt only contentment.

'I don't think it gets much more beautiful than this,' she said.

'Being somewhere like this reminds me why we do what we do. If we can let people experience something like this, without spoiling it for everyone else still to come, then we've done a good job.'

'I agree.' Meg lifted her glass gently to his.

The sun was low behind them, so the water in front of them was lit up with dramatic streaks of pink, orange and purple.

They chatted about what they had seen over the reef then the conversation returned to the cooking class and they debated which marriages would make it and which ones wouldn't.

'Let's face it, they're all young and this is all new to them. I doubt any of them got married thinking it wouldn't last,' Dan said.

She was silent.

'What is it?'

'I thought my marriage would last. I was prepared to do anything for it. But he wasn't.'

It was Dan's turn to be silent.

'I know it's been fifteen years, and everyone thinks it's old news, but seeing them all today, so hopeful and innocent, I don't know. It did remind me of the me twenty years ago.' And it hadn't been comfortable, it had been confronting. She wasn't even sure why, considering she didn't think about Paul day to day any more. He didn't cause the wrenching feeling in her gut as he once had, but there was no denying that the wound he'd caused her still ran deep.

'Anyway, what am I telling you this for? What happened to my marriage just proves your point that love doesn't exist.'

But love did exist. She knew it, she'd felt it. And she still felt the pain of its loss and the betrayal of the man she had once loved. If she hadn't loved Paul, he couldn't have hurt her as he had.

'Meg, my friend, this is what I've been saying. Forget love. It only leads to pain. There are so many other things to enjoy. Like now, this beautiful place, this champagne.'

She'd never admit that Dan might be right, but in this case she could admit to herself that he wasn't entirely wrong. This was a beautiful moment and life was full of them when you just stopped being resentful about the past and looked around you.

'We'd better get back before it gets dark,' Dan said and they both stood.

The kayak hit the sand as the light was beginning to fade. Dan got out, waded through the shallow water. Meg went to climb out and saw that Dan was extending a hand in help, which she took without thinking. His hand large and firm around her and she felt his strength throughout her body.

'Thank you. That was amazing.' Meg was short of breath. Probably from the paddling. It couldn't possibly be because Dan was still holding her hand.

'I see what they mean about the reef being spectacular,' he said.

He didn't release her hand.

You're not letting go either.

She had to though, let go and find the words to tell him that they could only ever be friends. But the words didn't come. All she could think to say was, 'It was a good idea of yours to go.'

He grinned. 'I do have them.'

'I never said you didn't.'

He took the final step to her. There was now less than a foot between them. Water lapped around their ankles. 'Can I get that in writing?'

'That's as much of a compliment as you're about to get.'

Her feet sank lower in the sand. Dan picked up her other hand and held it between both of his as though he were making a pledge. She stared down at their hands, entwined. It was as if she were watching someone else, because Dan Fairweather couldn't be standing here on this beach holding her hand in his. He couldn't be turning it over and over in his own as though he was searching for something. He pressed both her palms between both of his and, slowly, the heat started to move up her fingers, across her palm, into her wrists. The warmth spread up her arms and into her chest.

You have to step away. You have to be the strong one. For both your sakes.

'We should return the kayak,' he said, but he made no move. The longer this went on, the more accustomed she became to holding his hands and the more comfortable she became. And the more both their feet would sink into the wet sand.

She looked up at him and found him looking down at her. He pressed his lips together for a moment and something in Meg's stomach shifted. She had to say something, to tell him that she didn't feel the same way about him, but the words didn't come. The air around her was thick and at that moment her vocabulary shrank to one word only. Yes.

She tugged one hand free, meant to use it to push him away, but somehow when she lifted it, it came to rest flat against Dan's chest. And stayed there. His chest was firmer than she'd thought it would be, though, to be honest, she made a point never to think about any part of Dan's anatomy and how hard it might be.

Because that would remind her of That Night. The first half, not the ending. And if she thought too much about how that night had begun, and about bringing him home to her place, and about all the things he'd done to her in bed that night…then she wouldn't have the resolve to push him away.

You have to let go of her hand. Let go, step away.

But he couldn't. It was as though the damp sand were quick-setting concrete, capturing his feet.

She'd been staring at him. Running her hands through her hair a lot. A dead giveaway for attraction. Each time she did it he was reminded that this wasn't just Meg, his old nemesis and his new tentative friend. This was Meg, who liked him, who hadn't got over him after their disastrous one-night stand all those years ago.

He *had* to think of something to say or do to let her down gently. It was the kind thing to do. He'd even thought that was what he was doing now, picking up her hands to tell her that even though he liked her, it was as a friend and a colleague only.

Only then she'd thanked him for the trip to the reef, and once her hands were in his it felt so…right. He couldn't pull his away. His brain would not connect with the muscles in his arms. They'd shared such a nice day, talking, laughing. They had just fitted together and it had been the nicest day he could remember having in years.

Meg had been the first to extract her hands, but now one hand was pressed against his chest, as though she'd also meant to push him away but, like him, found her hand somehow stuck fast. She must be able to feel his heart pounding. It was barely contained in his chest cavity as it was. He still held her other hand between his two and felt a soft pulse beating in his palm. Though that might also be his own. His heart rate wasn't within his control at this moment because he was standing on a tropical beach, surrounded by a lagoon that captured all the colours of a setting sun, holding Meg Granger's hand and wondering if she was about to kiss him.

When her hand had found his chest their eyes had locked in some sort of mind game. How long was it possible to look at someone without breaking eye contact? Or appearing as if you were deranged? They seemed to be able to do it, look at one another, blinking occasionally, but not breaking the stare. As if she was challenging him to look away, but she should know by now that he didn't resile from a challenge, especially where she was concerned.

She loves you...she always has.

Surely that was a good reason *not* to kiss her. This wasn't just a game for her. He might not believe in love but he knew others still entertained the fantasy. He should step back, go back to his room. Alone.

She's not going to hurt you.

That was also not a reason to kiss her. He would never get hurt because he wasn't going to fall in love. But Meg did believe, and she might. As much as he used to like teasing and tricking her, he never actually wanted to hurt her. He'd naively assumed that Meg was never actually hurt by their feuding. And she still had the prettiest blue eyes he'd ever seen. Eyes with which she was still looking at him.

He shifted his feet from side to side in the sand and she did the same. Her hand felt good in his, anchoring him to the present. The hand against his chest steadied him as his heart ricocheted around his chest.

One kiss couldn't hurt, could it? It couldn't undo years of pettiness. But it could be a sorry kiss, a truce kiss?

'I don't think we could work,' she said softly.

'I agree.'

'You do? Then why are you holding my hand?'

He couldn't tell her the truth: *Because I'm trying to let you down easily and this is the only way I know how.*

She shifted closer; their bodies were still a foot away, but, he realised, it was the closest they'd ever been in years.

Since That Night.

Her tongue slipped out between her lips for a fraction of a second, and when it disappeared, her lips stayed slightly apart. He imagined his lips fitting perfectly against them. She'd taste of fruit and the ocean. He smiled and noticed her brow dip. She wasn't moving. Of course she wasn't, she was waiting for him to. He was waiting for her. He lowered his head.

At the same moment she lifted hers and their lips came to rest gently touching each other's. Touching, but not moving. Or pressing. He couldn't taste her, though he could smell her and the hint of gardenia that was always in her perfume. The one she'd always worn, the one that made his head spin and his inhibitions dissolve like a spell, as they were doing now.

He'd known her for years, but the last few minutes had felt like a decade. The kiss unfolded in slow motion.

His lips parted and hers mirrored his, their mouths both opened slightly as though they were both about to say something, and yet both lost for words. They paused, getting used to the sensation of soft lips lightly touching soft lips. It was as though she was giving him time to pull away, and he considered taking it.

But then his lips moved to start the conversation properly and she moved hers in reply. He tasted the champagne they had shared on the island and the world swirled around him, the stars appearing in the darkening South Pacific sky spun. When her tongue slid against his something inside him began to unravel. He was melting, slipping, even though their mouths were hardly moving.

You're kissing Meg! It was simultaneously a great idea and a very bad idea.

I'm kissing a woman who loves me.

He was meant to be letting her down easily but his blood was fizzing through his veins. He slid his arm around her waist and pulled her to him and her pelvis lifted to his. Meg noticed how he felt and he knew it. The kiss had turned from a friendly goodbye kiss to *Your-room-or-mine?* in a matter of seconds.

Meg did what he couldn't and pulled away.

'Um…that was…' She panted for breath and words and stumbled back, her shock blazingly apparent in the bright sunshine. Dan was breathing deeply, his body still pumping with blood in capillaries he hadn't even known he had.

'I'm sorry,' she gasped.

'Don't be.' His voice was as raspy as hers. 'I'm the one who's sorry.'

'No, I am. I shouldn't…have…'

'It's really okay.' He couldn't look her in the eyes. He'd messed up. Badly. 'These things take two people. It was as much to do with me as it was to do with you.'

Meg's brow furrowed and for the briefest of seconds he thought she looked slightly annoyed.

Of course she's annoyed, she likes you and you've just led her on. You just kissed her, gave her an unambiguously passionate kiss. It was clear to anyone nearby that you wanted her, and badly. What was she supposed to think?

Meg looked around the beach, anywhere but at him.

Blood was still pounding through his chest and neck, rushing past his ears. The kiss kept replaying in his head and his thoughts spun in confusion. It had felt so right. And yet...

'We should get the kayak back,' he mumbled, and he tried to lift it, his limbs heavy and useless with shame.

This was no good at all. He'd really messed up. He was sending Meg all sorts of mixed messages. He had to figure out a way to tell her that it was all just an innocent mistake and it could never happen again. Only how could he do that when every cell in his body was, not only against the idea, but actively fighting against it?

No. The idea of him and Meg was impossible. No matter how much his body might want to reach for her hand and pull her back to their villa, she was his colleague. They had a history, and she clearly had stronger feelings for him than he did for her. It wouldn't be fair to her to continue the kiss and see where it took them.

And it wouldn't be fair to you.

Dan might have been hopeless at relationships, but that didn't mean his heart was made of stone. It had taken him years to be able to look at Meg without his heart pounding in his throat after the night they had shared, and he had no wish to go back there.

He'd disappointed her once before, and he was not going to do it again. He'd changed and he'd show her he wasn't the person he was fifteen years ago. If only he hadn't just demonstrated the opposite.

CHAPTER EIGHT

THE LOUD KNOCK at her bedroom door startled Meg. It was a knock from someone on a mission and could only be one person.

They'd retreated to their own rooms after returning from the long day of cooking and kayaking. A beautiful day had been ruined because she'd let herself get swept up in the moment and in the swirl of Dan's way too tempting pheromones. It had felt so good standing next to him, having him look adoringly at her. It had been so long since she'd kissed anyone, let alone been kissed by someone who cared about her. As Dan did.

As soon as their breath had begun to mingle, even before their lips actually touched, she'd known it was going to be next to impossible to pull away. And she'd been right.

Their mouths had barely moved before she'd begun to tighten inside. He'd taken the kiss so slowly, as though making sure she truly wanted it, giving her every chance to pull away, but the longer he'd hesitated, the more she'd wanted it. Once his soft lips had brushed hers she'd been lost, the touch making her long for more. More friction, more movement, the push and pull, and not just between their lips, but against all of him.

The force of her desire had shocked her into pushing him back and thank goodness, or she might have pulled their clothes off right there on the beach.

Dan knocked again at her door. He loved her. That thought was more exhilarating than she liked to admit.

No.

So what if he liked her? It was flattering, but beside the point: what mattered most of all was how *she* felt about him. And the reason she didn't want to think about that was because that was the hard part. The confusing, conflicting, complicating part.

She was attracted to him, she could admit as much. Age-appropriate men who still looked as good as Dan did were few and far between. A man who made bubbles of excitement rise in her stomach like a teenager was even rarer. She also made a mental tick next to 'attractiveness'.

Good company? He was that as well. When he wasn't complaining that she was an uptight penny pincher he could be fun and entertaining. She'd been having a lovely day with him today until the kiss had changed everything.

Trustworthy? Ah, that was the kicker. The big red stop sign. She didn't think she could trust him as far as the next woman's bedroom.

He had explained about his wife and his divorce and while his excuse about wanting Meg to want him had been feeble, it had been heartfelt. But it still couldn't make up for That Night and all the years afterwards.

On Meg's count, that was two in the positive column and one in the negative, and there wasn't time for more calculations because Dan was not going to give up and walk away from her door.

Was he coming to confront her? To ask for explanations, or perhaps to offer them, which would be worse. What if he was going to tell her that he had feelings for her? Her stomach churned.

Oh, no. Please not that.

She wasn't sure what she wanted him to say, all she knew

was that she couldn't let herself get too close to him, lest she get wrapped up in the same whirl of desire that had caught her at the beach. She just had to stay strong and let him down as easily as possible.

That was it. Let him down gently. Tell him she didn't feel the same way about him. Simple.

Or not.

Meg hadn't had any experience in letting people down gently or ending relationships. Paul had been the sole instigator of the unilateral end to her marriage. She'd also been on the wrong side of all the other break-ups she'd had before her marriage.

It's not you, it's me.

Wasn't that what people said? She'd heard that several times.

Without knowing exactly what she was going to say or how she was going to say it, she took a deep breath and opened the door.

Dan was there, as she'd known he would be. He'd changed since earlier and showered—the hint of soap and shampoo announced his arrival. She stepped back, to give her senses space.

Dan frowned and glanced behind her into her room, then at the floor.

Oh, no, he's nervous. He really has come to declare his love!

A pit opened up in her stomach.

'I shouldn't have kissed you,' he said.

She exhaled. 'It's okay. We can chalk it up to the sunset, the champagne, this whole crazy situation.'

She hoped that would be the end of the conversation, but Dan continued to stand in her doorway.

He took a deep breath. 'Thank you for being so understanding. I don't want to pressure you. Or give you the wrong idea.'

She partly appreciated the sentiment, but was also miffed that he thought she wasn't all right. She wasn't the one with feelings for him!

But what was a little bit of annoyance when he'd come to say all the things she didn't feel brave enough to do so? She should be relieved! Grateful!

'I'm fine, really, I am.'

'Good, that's good.'

But Dan still didn't budge, still looking as though there was something more he wanted to say. And she couldn't have that.

'Okay, then.' She motioned towards the door, his exit and the end of this conversation.

'You're sure you're okay?'

She waved a hand dismissively. 'I'm perfectly fine. You can leave now.'

Still, he didn't budge, his brow deepened into a V.

Ah, Meg realised. It was a ruse. This was just an excuse to come and see her again.

'Are *you* all right?' she asked.

'Of course, why wouldn't I be?'

She smiled, tried not to look as though she pitied him.

'Meg, I came to tell you that I think you're wonderful.'

Oh, no. He really was going to declare his love and she couldn't have that!

'Dan, stop.'

'No, Meg, I think you're exceptional. And beautiful. And I'm very attracted to you.'

'Dan, please.' She grabbed his upper arm, hoping to silence him. And the gesture did, but it silenced her as well. His arm was firm, strong and her fingers melted against it. 'Please don't say it.'

'No, Meg. I need you to know. I really like you—'

'I said stop! Please don't say it, there's no need.'

Dan stepped back, as startled by the volume of her voice

as she was. Yes, she'd been forceful, but she didn't want him to go on. It would embarrass them both if he told her how he really felt about her. It would be even more awkward for their relationship than all the years of mock hatred had been.

'Dan.' She stepped back up to him. She had to let him down easily. 'The last few days have been nice, but there's so much history between us.'

'Yes, I know. Which is why I need you to know—'

'Dan, I think you're great too. You're talented and charming and, when you want to be, great company. And that kiss was great…'

Don't mention the kiss or he really will get the wrong idea! But it was too late and the next thing she knew he was next to her again, holding her elbow gently and when he did she was hopeless. Because kissing Dan was so good and even though she'd blocked out the memory of That Night, just a few hours ago she'd been reminded anew about how good a kisser he was. How good he tasted. How good his body felt pushed against hers.

'Meg, you know we shouldn't.'

'I know.' She knew all right.

But why not? She wanted him, he really wanted her and it wasn't as though it would be their first time. As long as she was clear with him that from her side it was physical and nothing more. They were both adults, so as long as everyone had clear expectations, would it really be so bad?

Who knew what feelings she might develop over time? Not everyone started with identical feelings, did they? Would it really be so very wrong to kiss him again?

There was only one way to find out. She leant closer and lifted her heels ever so slightly off the floor, pressing her lips to his. As soon as her mouth tasted his she realised her mistake. He smelt so good, better than was fair or reasonable.

She needed to keep breathing him in. He was the only air that would sustain her lungs.

This kiss was a different speed again. Neither fast nor slow, but deep and deliberate. He slipped his arms around her, pulled her closer.

Despite their history, despite everything, when he held her she felt safe. She felt loved.

That's because he cares about you.

The thought didn't scare her, but emboldened her. To feel cared for, to feel loved, was powerful and the sexiest feeling of all.

Meg nudged Dan towards her bed and made him sit on the edge. She stood between his legs and looked down at him. Surrendering herself to her fantasies, she slid her fingers into his hair, ran her sensitive fingertips through it and pushed that annoyingly gorgeous lock of hair off his forehead. Dan closed his eyes, submitting in turn. He wrapped his arms around her waist and pulled her closer to him as she continued to twirl her fingers through his hair, continued to let things unfold slowly, but surely, towards their inevitable conclusion.

'Meg.' His voice was hoarse. 'You know how things are between us. I can't make any promises.'

'No promises,' she said. 'I agree.'

He opened his eyes and took her face in his hands. 'You do?'

'Dan, of course. No promises. This is physical only.'

She understood this. It was all she wanted. No promises, no emotion. And if he understood as well, then how complicated could it be?

'Are you sure? Are you sure you're all right?' he asked.

'I know what I'm doing.'

Could she believe him? Yes, she decided, this time she could, because he stood to lose much more than she did. Meg lifted one knee to the bed and then the next, straddling Dan and bringing their faces nearly level.

Meg lowered her head and Dan lifted his and their lips found one another again, sending waves of want rippling through her entire body. If this was what one kiss would do, how would she cope with what came next? Dan cupped her chin and tilted her mouth to his at exactly the perfect angle. His other hand slid into her hair and gently held her head, his kisses soft, tender and yet exhilarating.

This was what it was like to kiss someone who loved you. This was what it was like to be loved. Amazing. Any thought that this could be a mistake evaporated with her inhibitions and then their clothes.

She unbuttoned his shirt as she kissed her way down his throat and chest, while Dan's hands slid up her skirt, along her thighs and higher, unhooking her bra, releasing her breasts with a moan from both of them. In no time her dress was around her waist and Dan's shirt thrown away.

'This has been a long time coming,' he said.

She didn't quite understand why he felt the need to say that, but that was probably because she was distracted by his lips and how agonisingly close they were to her nipples. 'Yes.'

'I want to make sure it's perfect,' he said as he wriggled out of his shorts.

'It will be,' she reassured him.

'For both of us.'

'I'll do everything I can.' She laughed, her lips tasting the skin on his bare shoulder.

Dan pulled back and looked at her quizzically.

'I'm talking about me doing everything for you,' he said. 'You can trust me. I know what this means to you.'

Meg pressed her mouth against his again. His kisses were addictive. This whole thing was so crazy, so unexpected. She could hardly believe that a few days ago she'd thought he hated her. That a few days ago she'd thought she hated him.

But Meg froze. Something didn't add up. And Meg knew numbers.

She pushed Dan back.

'Wait, what are you talking about?'

'What?'

'Why did you say that you know what this means to me?'

She held him at arm's length, even though her body was still pounding, wanting him on top of her. Inside her.

'Meg, I *know*.'

The way he placed the emphasis on the final word made Meg's stomach heavy with a creeping dread. Things didn't add up, and she shouldn't have ignored her suspicion that her calculations were out.

'Know what?' she asked.

'And it's okay.' Dan's eyes were wide, his mouth—that ridiculously kissable mouth—open and earnest.

Oh, no.

She grabbed the closest piece of clothing, which, unfortunately, was Dan's discarded shirt. It smelt like him but, as distracting as that was, it was worse sitting topless in front of him.

'Dan, what do you know?'

'Meg, it's okay.'

'How do I know what's okay if you won't tell me what you're talking about?' She spoke quickly, head spinning.

Oh, no. Oh, no.

'George told me. And please know that if I had known I wouldn't have been so vile to you over the years.'

What did Dan know…or what did Dan think he knew? Suddenly Meg knew exactly what it was that didn't add up about this whole situation. Her calculations hadn't been wrong, but the figures she'd been given had been very incorrect.

'Dan…listen to me. It's very important that you tell me exactly what George told you. About me.'

'I'm trying to be as sensitive as I can be.' He dragged his hand through his gorgeous hair. Still shirtless. She saw the muscles in his side and under his arms flexed. Why couldn't he be unattractive? If he hadn't been so kissable, so strokable, they wouldn't be here now in this monumental mess.

'Believe me. I can handle whatever you're about to say.' She'd handle it all right. She'd handle George. And Dan. And whoever else had been involved in what she now suspected was an elaborate conspiracy.

Dan edged closer to her on the bed but she drew back, her stomach tight with anxiety.

'George told me you have feelings for me,' Dan said.

Meg groaned and put her face in her hands. Over the sound of her groans she could make out some of his words.

'…don't be embarrassed…meant well…just trying to make sure I wasn't an ass to you… I should've been kinder. I didn't know. I'm a fool.'

Meg uncovered her face. 'Yes, you are a fool! I don't have feelings for you. He was tricking you!'

Dan's face fell.

Then he shook his head. 'No, Meg. It's okay.'

'No, I do not have feelings for you. George made it up. He told me the same thing about you.'

She saw the exact moment Dan understood when his expression turned from blank confusion to livid anger.

'George told you that I like you?'

Meg nodded.

'Yes, he told me you've been in love with me for years.'

'Years!' Dan's voice was a roar. 'And you believed him?'

'Why wouldn't I? I trust him.' Meg groaned again. 'Well, *trusted* him.'

'But after everything…after all these years? The way I've treated you?' Dan asked.

'He said your behaviour was due to self-preservation.' *And the fact was that once upon a time you did like me. A lot.* 'Don't put this on me, you believed him too.'

'Of course I believed him! He's my boss, my mentor. Why wouldn't I believe him?'

'Because me loving you is such an absurdly ridiculous idea that you should have realised it was a joke!'

Meg's heart beat in her throat, blocking her airways. Her head felt light but her limbs felt like stone.

'Is it?' he asked.

Her stomach swooped. Dan leant across the bed towards her, eyes challenging her. She pulled back as far as she could without falling off the bed, acutely aware that both of them were half naked and not ten minutes ago she'd been practically begging him to kiss her breasts until she came. The fires he'd stoked inside her were no longer a conflagration, but they were still smouldering.

So what if a part of her was attracted to him? It was physical only. She knew they were physically compatible and it had been a while between drinks, for her, so to speak. She was vulnerable to suggestion. That was all.

'I think you wanted it to be true,' she said.

'I could say the same thing to you.'

She winced.

'You don't have feelings for me? Not even a little bit?' he asked, grinning and looking pointedly at the state of disarray they were both in. Him, shirtless, sitting there in his boxers. Her covering her chest with his shirt. Hardly the poses of two people who despised one another.

'Not a bit!'

'And yet, here we are. Both nearly naked. Moments away

from having what we both know was going to be very satisfying sex.'

She shivered. *Very satisfying sex.*

'We were tricked.'

Dan closed his eyes and took a few deep breaths.

'I've never known you to be tricked into anything you didn't want to do.'

He was right. Just a little. Not that she could admit that.

'And you couldn't wait to get into bed with me,' she said.

'Excuse me! I've been the model of gentlemanly restraint.'

She barked a laugh. 'We've been here two days! Two days you've managed to keep your hands off me. It's almost like you were just waiting for an excuse.'

'You can talk! You've been giving me looks since before we even left Sydney.'

'I have not!'

Dan blinked a few times and then said, 'It was the day after the launch, wasn't it?'

Meg's cheeks felt as though she were standing in front of a massive bonfire. She knew what he was talking about but she still said, 'I don't know what you mean.'

'George told you I liked you the day after the launch.'

There was no point denying it. He was right.

'Maybe.'

'You changed from that day. You were polite to me in the lift.'

'Of course I changed. I was trying to be kind.'

'By kissing me, undressing me? Begging me to make you come? That was very kind of you.'

'You know what I mean. We were both fooled. Neither of us can win this argument.'

'Is this an argument?' He smiled again and she had to look away because Dan's smile was almost as potent as his kisses.

'You know it is.'

She wasn't sure what this was. Or what she was going to do about it.

Call George and confront him? Resign? No. This was such a mess. She had no idea how to even begin to unravel it.

Meg tugged on the sheet, tugging it loose and wrapping it around herself. She threw Dan his shirt.

'For goodness' sake, put that on so we can figure out what we're going to do.'

Dan caught his shirt in one hand, but then dropped it onto the floor. He stayed sitting on the bed, still grinning.

'What?' she demanded, but he didn't answer.

It wasn't just her behaviour that had changed, his had as well. He'd been polite too, less of an ass. The plane, the kayak. How long had Dan been labouring under the misapprehension that she had feelings for him?

The launch. Caught together in the corner. Dan next to her. Inhaling the smell of her hair.

'George told you before the launch, didn't he?'

Dan grinned. 'Wrong.' He looked as though he'd just won a quiz show.

'You smelt my hair. That night. When we were stuck in the corner.'

Dan's brow furrowed. 'Why does it matter when he told us?'

'Because it does.'

He raised an eyebrow and her stomach swooped again.

Maybe he was right, that the timing wasn't the most important thing at the moment.

'Either way, you need to get dressed and get out of here and we need to never speak of this again.'

He didn't move. Just stood there in his boxers. Looking as though she'd just bet her life savings but he was holding a winning hand.

Oh, he was irritating! She shook with frustration.

'Knowing this does change everything, but not in the way you think,' he said.

'Oh, pray tell, how does knowing change things?'

'Because you were just about to sleep with me. You wanted me.'

'And you were about to sleep with me.'

'I don't dispute that. The point is, we were about to sleep together. We both wanted it.'

'But under false pretences.'

He shrugged.

'You can't just shrug like that. It does make a difference.'

'Yes, but not in the way you think it does.'

His certainty was almost arrogant.

'And what difference do you think knowing that we were tricked makes?'

'I think it makes things *less* complicated, not more.'

'How?' As far as Meg was concerned the entire thing was a complete and utter mess and doing in her head. Dan didn't love her after all. It made so much more sense…and yet, it didn't at the same time.

'I was feeling guilty that your feelings were stronger than mine, that I might be leading you on. Sound familiar?'

She tried to keep her expression neutral but knew it was hopeless. He was right.

'Maybe.'

'And now we both know there are no feelings involved. It's just physical, for both of us. Neither of us have to feel guilty.'

He did have a good point.

'Because neither of us have real feelings for one another, we only want something physical. I'd say things just got much simpler.'

She was attracted to Dan physically, and he was to her. Neither of them were in love, nor—given their history—was there any danger either of them would be.

'As much as I hate to say it, I think you're right.'

Dan smiled and her limbs turned to jelly.

'We're just friends, having a good time,' he added and stepped towards the bed.

'And we did do it once before so...' she said, loosening her grip on the sheet.

'Now you're talking.' Dan edged even closer and this time she didn't pull back.

He reached the bed and rested a knee on it. Then both. Then he crawled across the mattress towards her. 'We have three more days. Just you and me. No past, no future, just here in this hotel where we can forget the people we were. We forget the people we are going to be and we just enjoy ourselves.'

She was about to make a list, checking off the pros and cons, but then stopped because, really, how often did she get the chance to have string-free sex on a tropical island with a man who made her heart race, and her knees weak?

Finally, everything added up.

When Meg began to move across the bed towards him, Dan's heart leapt. When she smiled at him in that knowing way of hers it practically somersaulted. And when she let go of the sheet covering her beautiful body he pretty much unravelled.

He wanted her. He wanted her as he wanted his next breath.

All the worries and concerns he'd had over the past few days evaporated because they were both consenting adults who desperately wanted to have sex. Two people who knew they were physically compatible. And, most of all, two people who knew they would never develop feelings for one another.

It couldn't be more perfect.

He reached for her and pulled her next to him, back to where they were before. Meg wrapped her legs around him and pulled herself against him with a happy sigh. He was happy to be the cause of her sighs and ran his thumb over her erect nipple so he could hear some more of her soft moans. Meg was enjoying herself as much as he was. And he was enjoying the fact that she was enjoying herself.

He brushed his lips gently over her bare shoulder and felt her shiver. Her hands explored his chest and he could feel each groove of her fingertips, each whorl stroking a different piece of his heart. Her breath was warm, sweet with the wine and the tropical air, and he wanted to bask in it.

He pressed his nose into his neck and smelt her properly. Something familiar tweaked inside him. His body remembered her scent and tightened in anticipation. He slid his hand down her bare arm to her hand and entwined his fingers with hers. He opened his mouth and planted a deep kiss just below Meg's ear and felt her body melt against his.

He could feel the emotion rippling beneath her skin. Dan's free hand wound its way up her back and into her hair. He felt her muscles melting as he caressed her scalp.

The taste of the skin of her neck wasn't enough so his lips went searching for more along her jawbone, her cheek and finally, slowly, so slowly in case either of them changed their minds, to her lips. A rough pant escaped her mouth, as though she was struggling to breathe.

He felt the same way. He was out of oxygen but the one thing his mouth needed were the lips now tantalisingly close to his. So close the kiss was now a technicality only.

When she opened her lips and pressed them hard against his something inside him clicked.

Like a light going on.

Dan let go of her fingers and slid both his arms around her and rolled her on top of him. As their lips kissed, their tongues entwined, their bodies melded and melted.

This. This was everything.

His lips craved the next kiss, even as he was still relishing the current one. So slow, his body felt tired, yet on fire. Time was slow, but days could have passed.

Her fingers explored the waistline of his boxers, slipping in and out, driving him crazy as he waited for her to finally slip all the way under. He played the same game with her, tracing the hem of her pants, then exploring under, over. Everywhere. The fact that they were still wearing underpants was a technicality and all were shed.

'I want… I want…you,' she gasped. More. 'Do you have any protection?'

Yes. But not here.

He didn't need to say the words and she rolled away.

'It's okay, I do,' she said.

Moments later she was back on the bed, triumphantly holding the packet. He ripped open the package and she took the condom from his trembling hands. Taking him in her hands, she used long firm strokes, judging by the lowering of his lids and the shortness of his breath what he liked and what he loved.

'Please, Meg, please.'

He nudged her on top of him, where he could feel his entire body against hers. She guided him into her and they both paused. He wanted to move, his body wanted to feel every part of her, everything that was possible, but their eyes locked. Checked. Waited until their bodies could wait no more. Meg closed her eyes and groaned and he began to move. Slowly at first then fast at all the right moments, soft and hard, her body smooth, his breath ragged. Why hadn't they been doing this for ever? It was so right, and in the end so simple.

Afterwards, they lay there, too hot for sheets, too relaxed to move. Limbs sprawled over one another.

All complications had vanished. They finally understood one another. They'd finally found their way back to the place they had been That Night.

Except…

What if one day soon he was her boss? Dan went cold.

That was a bridge to cross later. Right now, his body was spent, and he fell into a boneless sleep.

It was only later, in the middle of the night, after they had made love again and slept some more, that Dan's mind reached some sort of clarity.

It was worrying to know he'd been so easily tricked by George, but also comforting that his instincts about Meg had been correct to begin with. He'd been right to be suspicious about her true feelings for him.

And yet you're spooning with her, holding her warm, naked body against yours, listening to the cicadas singing outside and wondering how long she will sleep and when you can make love again.

Have sex. They were not in love, ergo they would not be making love. But sex? String-free sex for a few days. That was all it was.

George wasn't wrong about he and Meg being physically attracted to one another. But he was wrong about the rest. Problem solved, Dan fell back to sleep.

When he woke, hours later, the sun was up and Meg's side of the bed was cold. He found her on the deck, clutching a cup of coffee and looking thoughtfully at the ocean. He cleared his throat and she turned. His chest clenched. She was wearing a white T-shirt, her hair was loose and she looked gorgeous. But wary. He stayed standing at the distance he was.

'Good morning.' He almost added the word 'lovely', but stopped himself.

'Good morning. How are you feeling?'

Relaxed, excited. A little floaty. Surprised. But apprehensive.

'Good,' he simply said. 'And you?'

'Good,' was her tight reply.

Ah, the morning-after awkwardness. Still apparently a thing when you were in your fifties.

'I had a good time last night,' he said.

'I did as well.'

'Should we talk about it?' he asked.

'I'm not worried. If anything, I'm relieved.'

'Relieved?' He could see by the look of panic on her face she was anything but.

'Yes, because we were honest with one another. I'm not worried any longer that you have feelings for me I can't reciprocate.'

'I'm happy that we're friends again.'

She looked at him blankly and his heart skipped.

'We are, aren't we? Friends?' he asked.

She nodded and patted the seat next to her.

'Yes, though I reserve the right to call you insufferable.'

'And I reserve the right to call you…' He faltered. He didn't want to call her uptight, or a penny pincher or any of the insults that had fallen thoughtlessly from his lips over the years. Beautiful. Intelligent. Funny. Those were the only words that came to mind. Instead he settled on, 'Insufferable.'

Meg raised a single eyebrow, but didn't say more. He sat and poured himself a coffee. That would make his synapses engage again.

They drank coffee, enjoyed the view, Meg tapped away on her keyboard, he scrolled through his phone.

That was all? His heart rate increased.

This is all you need and want, remember?

What mattered was that he and Meg were alone for a few days of sunshine and no promises. And they should get started.

'I was thinking of having a swim. Would you like to join me?'

'At the beach?'

'I was thinking of our pool.'

'Oh?'

'There's more privacy. Just in case…'

Meg watched him, blinked and then her face was lit by one of her beautiful smiles. 'I think that is a very good idea.'

They talked lazily about leaving the villa and exploring the island, but each time one of them made to get dressed, the other soon removed their clothes. They lay by the pool. In his bed. In hers.

Neither of them broached the subject of George again and each time she remembered what had led to this, she wished she hadn't because it only confused her more.

What had George actually said to her? Meg couldn't remember her exact words, only the sensations that had skipped through her body during the conversation. Panic. Confusion.

Delight.

No. She hadn't been happy to hear the news that Dan liked her. She'd been surprised and that wasn't the same thing.

We all know Dan likes you? Or, *I think Dan likes you?* Or had it been a question? *Does Dan like you?*

It didn't matter who had said what because George was mistaken. She and Dan didn't have *feelings* for one another.

That night they shared a dinner of seafood and more champagne on the deck, watching the sunset. Work was a no-go topic of conversation but their discussion skipped easily over everything else.

He asked after Olive and Meg asked about his sons. All their children were now in their twenties and forging independent lives, which brought them both satisfaction and contentment. Dan told her that even though he spoke to his sons at least once a week he missed them now they lived overseas.

'Their childhood flew and I missed more of that time than I wanted. There are many things I'd do differently,' he sighed.

When Dan opened up about his sons Meg felt comfortable sharing her sadness that it wouldn't be long until Olive moved out.

'What about your parents?' Dan asked.

'Gone,' she said simply. It was easier to speak about it now, though short answers were best.

'Both of them?'

'Mum just last year.'

'I'm so sorry,' he said. 'I should have known.'

She shook her head. 'I didn't broadcast it.'

'No, but I'm still sorry.'

'It's okay. I mean it was. It was reasonably quick with Mum—she had a brief illness and we got to say our goodbyes. She had enough time to get her affairs in order and she lived at home until the end. It was a good ending.'

'Still, she was your mother. I'm so sorry.'

Meg shrugged. She missed her mother terribly, wished she'd had more years, but it wasn't to be. Instead of dwelling on that, Meg was dreading the next question.

'And your father?'

'Not as good. But we were estranged for many years. He wasn't a nice man.'

She tried not to think about her father. It was a habit she'd had many years to perfect.

'Do you want to talk about it?'

'Not usually,' she said.

Dan didn't press, but it might have been his calm accepting silence that allowed her to take a deep breath and say, 'He was a charmer, my father. He charmed Mum and then, it turns out, countless other women.'

At some point in her early childhood her father had stopped turning the charm onto her and Meg had felt bereft. She'd longed for the kind of attention he'd seemed to always be able to give others and hadn't understood why her previously loving father had turned cold. As she'd got older, she'd finally recognised the pain on her mother's face for what it was. And it had hardened her. Still, Paul had managed to slip past and break her heart.

'Their marriage was over long before Mum kicked him out. I was eleven. From then on, I saw through him.'

Meg didn't give Dan the chance to ask further questions. 'What about your parents?'

'Dad left early on, leaving my mum to raise and support us on her own. He died a while ago. Mum's good though. She's getting old, but getting by. She's in an assisted living facility.'

'In Sydney?'

Dan nodded. 'And my brother and sister are close as well.'

Not every conversation they had over the next couple of days was as heavy.

Some made her laugh so hard the muscles in her chest ached. Sometimes he'd turn to her and smile or even wink, and she'd know that they'd just seen or thought exactly the same thing.

By day they played tourist, by night they lay tangled together, bodies sated. They tried the other restaurants at the resort but always left before dessert.

Meg had to keep reminding herself that this was a work trip. That they still had to visit the site and meet with their prospective partner. A voice in the back of her head kept insisting it would all be all right, but the voice telling her that she had to get serious about things began to get louder.

She wanted to seal this deal. It was the one way of proving to the board that she was CEO material.

And when you're CEO, what about Dan?

She'd be his boss. How on earth would he cope then?

He'll cope fine. Things between you are different now. He won't be as unpleasant as he was in the past.

The day before the meeting, they were eating breakfast

on the deck overlooking the water when, almost as though he were reading her thoughts, he said, 'We need a plan for when we get back.'

'What sort of plan?'

'You know. What are we going to tell people? What happens between us when we get home? What happens at work?'

Nothing, nothing and nothing, were her answers to all those things. But she wasn't yet ready to say that to Dan. She was enjoying this time, savouring it, and confirming that it would be over when they got home would ruin this easy, relaxed mood they had now. So, those were conversations for another day.

'I'm thinking George might want to know how his little experiment went,' he said.

'I say we keep him guessing. I don't want to give him the satisfaction of thinking his trick actually worked.'

He nodded. 'Agreed.'

Yes, that was sensible. It was no one's business. Dan was making this far more complicated than it needed to be.

Dan turned to her, thoughtfully. 'You want to get back at him?'

She shook her head. 'Not at all, though I'm still annoyed with him.' But also partly grateful, though she could hardly say that aloud. If George hadn't done what he'd done then she and Dan would still be bickering and the trip would have been much less fun than it had been.

'I'm not annoyed. Okay. Maybe a little,' he confessed.

She stood. This conversation was a mistake. It would open a door she wanted to keep closed until after they were ready to return home. They weren't meant to be thinking about the future right now.

'I think I'd like a walk.'

'Do you want me to come?'

Yes.

'No, it's okay, I'd like to be on my own.'

Dan was distracting her from her real mission on the island, to make the deal and get the CEO job. She hadn't even opened her laptop in a whole day.

Dan stood. 'Is everything okay?'

'Yes, yes. I just want to clear my head.' She reached over and touched his hand. 'Honestly, everything's fine.'

And it was. They both understood what the deal was. And it was exactly what she wanted. A little time away from Dan was all she needed to clear her head and restore her equilibrium. Meg slipped her laptop discreetly into her handbag when she went to her room to put on her shoes. Then she set off to find a quiet corner of the hotel where she could work without being disturbed.

CHAPTER NINE

Dan watched Meg walk out of the villa on her own and the place suddenly felt empty.

To recap: he was sharing a villa with a colleague, with whom he was pretending to be engaged. This was because their boss had tricked them both into believing that they had crushes on one another. Which was, as they had realised, not in fact true. Even though they had for the past two days been enjoying hours and hours of wonderfully string-free sex.

This was the sort of thing that made the HR types wake up in a cold sweat.

Except Meg was technically also the head of the HR department.

He rubbed his temples. Did that mean he had to be the sensible one? He didn't excel at the corporate stuff, Meg knew that. Everyone knew that. He was great at grand visions and big ideas, but he needed people like Meg to help execute them.

He had to concede she was right a lot of the time. The business would not be what it was without her firm—albeit sometimes cold—hand.

Meg.

He'd liked her from the first moment he'd laid eyes on her. He'd even liked her from the moment George started talking about her, before he'd even met her. George's enthusiasm had been contagious as he'd told Dan all about this fabulous woman he'd managed to poach from another firm.

'She's smart, brilliant and she's also fun. I think you'll like her,' George had said. 'It took quite an effort to get her, so don't blow it with her.'

Dan had liked Meg more and more as he'd got to know her in those first few weeks. At some point the fact that they would sleep together had shifted from possible to probable to inevitable.

But then he'd messed it up. He should have told her about Astrid. He hadn't meant not to. In an attempt not to risk what he'd had with her, he'd actually ruined it all.

Because it was just as he'd always thought. He was terrible at relationships. First Astrid, then Meg. Then every other woman since. His relationships always fell apart. As far as he was concerned, love was an illusion.

Meg returned a couple of hours later, her face flushed but bright. He probably should have been on the deck or in his room, but somehow he'd remained sitting on the sofa, with his sketch pad, with a view of the door.

'Hey,' he said.

'Hey.' She smiled.

'How was the walk?'

'Good. I just went down to the beach.'

'Good idea. I think we've been cooped up in here too much for the past few days.'

A knowing smile crept over her face. 'Probably. I was asking around. There are some good walks, longer than the one I just did. There's one up the mountain to a waterfall.'

'Oh, are you going to do that?'

'I'd like to, but it's a long way to go on my own.'

'You'd like company?' His heart pounded.

'If you want to come?'

'I'd love to,' he said, meaning every word.

* * *

Heiana gave them a map and pointed them in the direction of the nearby mountain. They strolled through lush green bush, the incline gradual at first, but soon becoming steeper as they pressed further and further into the rainforest.

At one point the peak of the mountain came into view high above their heads and Dan groaned. 'Please tell me we aren't going to the top.'

'I don't think so. According to the map, it isn't that much further.'

Luckily Meg was right, because as they climbed higher and higher, the more often he had to wipe the sweat off his face, lest it get in his eyes. Finally the roar of rushing water could be heard in the distance, becoming louder as they got closer. They rounded a corner and the forest opened up before them, revealing a glassy blue-green pool and, at its far end, a picturesque waterfall. Crystal-clear waters tumbled down over a granite ledge into the small pool.

Meg gasped. 'It looks like it's from a storybook.'

She wasn't wrong. If someone had told him to imagine a waterfall in a rainforest, this was what he would have pictured. Even more remarkably, they were the only people there. It was late in the afternoon, so presumably most of the visitors had left for the day, but if he'd known about this place earlier, they would have walked up here every day, despite the distance.

'I'm going in,' he said.

'You brought swimmers?'

'Nope.' That was hardly going to stop him. Besides, it was just him and Meg, and they had seen too much of one another's bodies in the past few days to worry about modesty. He slipped off his shoes, shirt and shorts, leaving just his boxers. He went in carefully, uncertain of the depth, but once satisfied it was deep enough he dived right under.

Meg also stripped off to her underwear, simple black briefs and a black sports bra, and she entered the pool as he lay on his back in the refreshing water, watching her.

'It's colder than the sea.' She grimaced as she waded deeper.

'It's perfect once you're in.'

She closed her eyes and submerged herself with a whimper. Dan moved towards her and they swam with long lazy strokes, side by side, around the pool, towards the rushing water. Up close, the noise was deafening, but he motioned behind the waterfall. He wasn't sure what they would find, but they were able to swim around the waterfall and scramble onto the rocks behind. A large flat rock made a shelf and he held out his hand to help Meg up onto it. Side by side they looked through the waterfall back to the pond. The view was obscured by the rushing water and countless rainbows, the refracting light bouncing off the droplets in the spray.

'It's an amazing perspective,' he said but behind the noise it was difficult to hear. She mouthed something back, but he couldn't hear what it was.

Instead, he reached for her and placed a hand on her chin, tilting it towards him, seeing more rainbows reflected in her eyes. She smiled at him, sending his insides crashing as hard as the waterfall. He closed his eyes and pressed his lips against hers. Meg melted against him and he held her tight. This moment, this place, it seemed impossibly beautiful, impossibly perfect. As Meg had said, it looked like a picture in a storybook. For a brief moment he believed the fairy tale because places like this really did exist, feelings like this did too.

With Meg in his arms his body felt powerful, his heart felt full and his thoughts were at peace. This was what love felt like, he suspected. It was perfect, secluded and they were the only two people in the world. They didn't need to speak, they couldn't have heard one another if they had, but they knew exactly what the other wanted and needed and for a few moments or an hour, he wasn't even sure, they just held one another and simply kissed.

Eventually, she pushed him gently back and they slipped into the pool.

In the fading afternoon light, the rainbows melted away and he reminded himself that, just like the rainbows bouncing off the water droplets, love was a mirage. And a fleeting, transparent one at that.

Before putting their clothes back on, they lay in the sun, side by side. Meg on her stomach, Dan on his back, head rested on his hands.

It was going to be strange enough going back to Sydney after all this, especially if he'd be promoted in the not too distant future. That would be a new challenge for both of them. Could they deal with it? Would Meg be able to cope with taking instructions from him? He'd been so excited about taking over the CEO role, but now he was finally in a position to do so, some doubts began to creep in. Could he and Meg continue like this once they were back home? Should they even try or should they leave what they had here, while it was still perfect, before the inevitable cracks began to show? But could they also negotiate a life apart after this? What would it be like to see her every day and remember the feelings he had back at the waterfall?

Back at the villa, Meg went to her room and he went out to the deck with his sketchbook. He lost track of time as he tried to render the birds and the flowers and everything he saw around him. He could sketch a perfect flower, but the picture he had of his future suddenly seemed unclear.

Meg shut her laptop. She'd checked in with the office, read her emails, put out a few fires and then George had sent her an instant message, telling her to enjoy the sunshine. If she didn't go back out to Dan he'd get suspicious. It was dark now and probably time for dinner.

Dan was out on the deck and she walked over. The table was covered in loose papers. Sketches, in charcoal and colours. Some in simple pencil, others that had been brushed over with water, blurring and shaping the colours. The water shimmered, just like the real thing. The beach, the bush, the birds, all exquisitely rendered. She gasped.

'Dan, wow. Did you do these?'

He jumped at the sound of her voice.

'Don't look. I should've cleared these away.'

'Why? They're wonderful. Is this what you've been doing when we haven't been together?'

He nodded. Sheepishly. 'You thought I was out and about partying with the locals?'

No, I thought you were doing what I was doing, working behind the scenes to get ahead on the CEO job.

'I assumed you were napping, just like me.'

He smiled. 'Maybe a bit of that as well.'

One half of his face lifted into a sheepish grin.

She inched her hand lower, slowly, so he could stop her, but he didn't. She picked up one of the sketches. It was of the waterfall.

'You did this from memory?'

He shrugged and she knew it was a yes.

'Do you mind if I look at the others?'

Dan paused, and for a moment she wondered if his guard was going to go back up, but it didn't. There were sketches of beaches, the island. And many of the site they were scoping for the resort.

She'd seen drawings of his before, of course, plans, elevation drawings, landscape drawings. Everything from rough preliminary sketches to finished detailed designs. But these were different. They weren't for the purpose of building anything, just for the purpose of rendering the beauty of things he had seen.

'Do you have more?'

'Nah, this is what I've done here.'

'I mean, at home?'

He shrugged again. She knew now the gesture was silent agreement. A yes that he didn't want to admit aloud but it irritated her, nonetheless.

She shook her head. 'Honestly, why don't you admit this? Own it? Dan, these are wonderful. But even if they weren't, who cares?'

'Ah, we don't all have time for hobbies. There's work to be done.'

It clicked. The figures aligned.

'Was it Astrid?'

'Was what Astrid?'

'Who told you to stop?'

He scrunched up his face. 'Not in as many words. It was life. There's never enough time for everything you want to do. I wanted to be there for my boys as well.'

Meg's heart clenched for him. Life raising a family was a juggle and a wrench. There was never enough time for all the things you wanted to do. She suddenly had an inkling of the sacrifices he'd made for his family over the years.

'I'm glad you managed to make time this week.'

'This week has been…' he looked at her, taking her all in, waiting to make sure she was listening to his next words '… exceptional. This week has been exceptional.'

As she got close to the bottom of the stack Dan's expression changed and he pounced, tried to snatch the bundle of papers out of her arms, crushing a few in the process.

'Hey, I was nearly done,' she said.

'You've seen all the good ones.'

'What are you hiding?'

'Nothing.'

She had to choose between tugging on the pile and seeing the last sheets and risking ripping the beautiful pictures or letting them go.

She released her grip.

Dan tidied the papers, slid them into a folder and slipped that folder into his bag.

'Why can't I see them?'

He shrugged.

'Why do you always shrug when you don't want to admit something?'

'I want to shrug now but I sense that would be wrong?' He smiled at her.

'Argh. Why can't you just be honest with me? Actually, scratch that, I don't need you to be honest with me. But can you at least be honest with yourself?'

Dan closed his eyes and took a deep breath. For a moment she thought he might storm out, but he didn't.

'I don't show them to people. I haven't for years. Not since I finished university and started working. Astrid liked them then, at least she seemed to show a cursory interest. But then life had happened. Marriage, kids, building a career and then one day I woke up and realised that even though I drew buildings every day, it had been years since I'd drawn a bird. Or a face. I'm afraid I'm out of practice. I'm afraid they aren't any good.'

He didn't meet her gaze, but she placed her hand gently on his arm.

'And I'm afraid they're foolish and I don't want to be a fool in front of you.'

She smiled. 'I don't think you're a fool. I think you're a very talented artist. And a very talented architect, for that matter.'

'Since we're being honest…' he began.

'Yes?'

'I honestly like you. I like being with you. I like this. And I think I'm going to miss it when we get back to Sydney.'

Meg stepped back.

'I'm not saying I have feelings for you—you know what I think about love.'

'Of course you don't.' Feelings, what did that even mean? When Dan said feelings, he meant love. Romantic, passionate love. When Meg used the word she meant all sorts of things: happiness, anger, frustration, excitement. She, on the other hand, had many feelings for Dan. But still, not the romantic love he was talking about. That would be ridiculous. Not to mention pointless. She definitely didn't have those sorts of feelings for Dan.

'But I've had a good time,' he said, voice low.

She didn't know what to say. She'd had a good time as well. And it confused her. What he was saying now confused her even more. She thought their tacit understanding was that they would only continue this aspect of their relationship until they got home. What happened on the island stayed on the island and all that.

But was Dan suggesting something else? To continue this back in Sydney? They couldn't do that though, because soon she'd be his boss and then everything would be much more complicated.

'Can you be honest for a moment as well?' he asked.

She nodded. 'I'm going to miss it too,' she admitted.

There, she'd said it. *When we get home, this ends.* Even though they would both miss *this*. Dan stepped back to her, but instead of pulling her straight into his arms and taking her to the bedroom, he reached out a single hand. He ran his thumb over the back of one of her hands, not even lifting it, just a single caress at a time. He let all his focus rest on that one touch, and slowly, slowly, wrapped his hand around hers, let their fingers entwine, making sure that his fingers had touched each part of her hand before moving his hand slowly up her smooth bare arm. Meg didn't move, aware of what he was doing, her eyelids lowered. She was in the moment as much as he was, surrendering herself to his touch. To him.

She didn't want it to end. She wanted to stay here. In this place, in this moment.

Impossible.

This moment was all there was, and all there had to be. Her life pivoted on this point. She didn't want to move forward, she wanted to stay here. Where everything was perfect. Where she kissed gorgeous men underneath waterfalls and nothing else mattered.

Dan moved slowly towards her and slid his other hand up her other arm to her shoulders and neck. He slid the straps of her sundress over her shoulders, let it fall to the floor as he drew a trail of kisses over her shoulders. Slowly, they both savoured each moment, luxuriating in each caress, every sweep of his tongue over hers. She kept her eyes closed and her hands at her sides, concentrating on each kiss as it happened, living each moment as it came. He didn't mind in the slightest. She opened her eyes and saw that he'd removed his clothes as well. He faced her, looked at her and then glanced at the bedroom.

She held herself here, held him there, because in a moment, life would change. Because once she lay down with him, she would be moving forward, and this perfect moment would be lost for ever. Dan looked at her expectantly. Her stomach swooped. How could she resist those eyes, pleading with her to lie with him, especially when she knew exactly what he was capable of doing to her?

She couldn't. And she didn't.

The damage was done. She might as well enjoy this because it would surely be one of their last times together. Tomorrow they would meet Nino Flores and the day after they would go home. Their lovemaking days were coming to an inevitable end.

These were her thoughts as Dan pulled her to him, as he stroked and cajoled her body into senselessness, as they breathed one another in, held and released one another over and over again, until they both unravelled.

She lay on him, catching her breath, trembling and afraid to show him her face.

Was it her imagination? Or his? What was real and what was true? Because what they had done felt a lot like making love. They had a connection, he'd hardly broken eye contact with her and she doubted that had ever happened in her life. Not with Paul. Certainly not with anyone else.

It felt real.

Or was Dan just a good actor?

What could she trust?

She pulled herself out from under his arm, grabbed a robe and slipped into the bathroom, closing the door behind her.

She sat on the toilet and held her face in her hands.

Who are you kidding? It's too late. You've fallen in love with him. It doesn't matter when it happened or why you let it happen, it has happened. George might have played the first trick, but you fooled yourself, thinking that you could handle a string-free affair with Dan Fairweather. That was the biggest lie of all.

No. It wasn't true. She'd wake up tomorrow morning and all the emotions she was feeling now would melt away when exposed to the harsh light of day. She wasn't in love with Dan. She couldn't be. Could she?

Later that night, they were lying in her bed, the fan on the high ceiling humming gently and brushing a sensuous sea breeze over their naked bodies every five seconds or so. It was hypnotic. Dan had fallen completely under the spell of this place. He couldn't wait to keep coming back to work on this new resort.

Work.

That was right. Once upon a time this was a work trip. Until it became something else.

After they'd made love, he'd ordered some dinner. They'd eaten and quickly gone back to bed and made love again. He didn't want to sleep. It felt as though they were running out of time. Which they were.

Unless he could devise some sort of excuse to allow them to stay a few more days...

'Have you heard from George? Is the meeting still on tomorrow?' Dan asked.

'I haven't heard a thing about it since we spoke the other day. You?'

'I've sent him some messages but he hasn't responded.'

'I hope he's all right,' she said.

'I do too,' he said. 'He's probably just busy.'

The next words were out of his mouth before he could think of the implications. 'Has he told you he's thinking of stepping back?'

Meg's head bobbed up and down very slowly against his chest. 'He has.'

Dan felt lighter. Not only would it not come as a shock to Meg, but he wasn't telling her a company secret that she didn't already know. It was good to clear that up between them.

'It's going to be quite a change for Evermore,' she said.

'Not if there's a smooth handover process.'

'Which hopefully there will be, particularly if it's someone who understands the business. Someone who's familiar with it.'

'I'm glad you agree with that,' he said.

'Why wouldn't I agree?' Meg pulled her warm body away from his and sat so she could look at his face. She looked ethereal. The half-light caught her hair and it flowed around her face like a halo.

'I'm not sure. I guess I wasn't sure how you'd feel about me taking over,' he said.

Meg flinched. 'Excuse me? About *you* taking over? I'm the one who'll be taking over.'

'You?' he blurted.

Meg pulled the white sheets around herself and nudged Dan, indicating he should move away. He jumped out of the bed, completely naked, as ordered. Meg pulled the sheets over her eyes, even though she'd seen all of it and more mere minutes ago.

Dan looked around for something to cover himself with and his hands grasped some fabric at the foot of the bed. He shook it out. Meg's floral robe. Too bad. He tugged it around himself and pushed his arms into the too small sleeves.

She glanced up and must have assumed he was sufficiently covered for this conversation because she demanded, 'Why not me? Why won't I be the CEO?'

Dan had learnt enough about arguing over the years to know this was one of those conversations he needed time to think carefully about. Time he didn't have.

'It's not that you couldn't do it.'

'Thanks very much,' she spat.

'It's just that I'm the obvious successor. I'm the creative mind behind the company. We build resorts.'

'And then we run and manage resorts until they can be handed back to our local partners. *That* takes management skills.'

Dan's throat began to close over. He could almost predict word for word what she was going to say about him. Irresponsible, unreasonable…

'And I suppose I don't have management skills? Is that what you're saying?' he asked.

She grimaced. 'It's not that you don't have them. Only that it's more my strength than yours.'

That wasn't untrue. But he was the chief architect! Surely that was more important than management. Besides, they were forgetting the most important thing.

'I guess the decision isn't ours though. It's ultimately up to the board,' he said.

'That's right.'

'It isn't our decision to make, so maybe we should leave it up to them and not argue about it ourselves.'

She nodded.

'I think that's right,' she said.

For a moment he thought they'd managed it. He'd defused the situation, which was awkward, but nothing they couldn't overcome. They'd learnt how to work together, how to cooperate and now they were able to resolve their differences.

But he was wrong.

'And I also think you should leave.'

'Why?'

'Because... Isn't it obvious?'

Not to Dan it wasn't.

'You don't think I can do the job. You think you're better than me.'

'I don't... I didn't say that.' He'd been at pains not to even think it, much less say it. Meg was capable of doing the job. It was just that he had been working towards this sort of thing all his life.

'No, but you thought it. And you've been thinking it all week. Or ever since George told you.'

'So?'

'So, not once did you think I might be applying for the position. You assumed it was yours.'

'And I could say the same about you.'

He knew even as the words were leaving his lips that that was the wrong thing to say.

'So now you're throwing this back on me?'

'No, I'm just saying we were both wrong. We both made assumptions and neither of us are to blame. I'm also saying that we don't need to have this argument because ultimately it will be up to the board to decide who gets the job. We shouldn't let it come between us.'

He motioned between the two of them and edged closer to her on the bed, desperately hoping she would bridge the distance between them and they could go back to how they had been, being hypnotised by the fan and the breeze and thinking about the next time they would make love.

But Meg shook her head. 'Please leave.'

'Can't we at least talk about this?' Dan might have been terrible at relationships but he knew that you were supposed to at least try to talk things through.

'I know all I need to know. I can't trust you,' she said.

'But why? Both of us made the same assumption—what's the problem?'

'The problem is that only one of us can get the job. One of us will be the other's boss. One of us will be disappointed. Disgruntled. This isn't nothing. It's not a misunderstanding. This is our future careers. Can't you see?'

She was right. It wasn't a tit-for-tat situation, where both had made the same mistake. It was their futures. The future of Evermore.

'This isn't something we can fix by talking about it. It's a fundamental problem between us and I just don't think, after everything that's happened this week, that I can trust you.'

'Of course you can trust me. I haven't done anything wrong. I haven't done anything you didn't do.'

He was right. They'd both assumed they would get the CEO role. Did the two mistakes cancel each other out? He wasn't sure but had a strong feeling that either way he was going to be wrong.

This is why you don't do this. Because you're very bad at it, remember? Not to mention the fact that love is an illusion that will fade as quickly as a rainbow.

'Well, maybe that's it,' she said and he exhaled.

It would be okay.

Meg continued, 'So clearly we can't trust one another. That's even worse. Two wrongs don't make it right.'

This time she was right. Whatever George had told them, whatever they'd tricked themselves into believing, this was the real problem between them and no amount of talking was going to solve it. She didn't trust him and he'd never really given her any reason to, from not telling her about the fact that he still lived with his ex-wife, to not being open about his career plans. The fact that both of them had been holding back didn't make it okay, it made it worse. He saw that now.

Dan got up slowly from the bed. He'd been right all along. There was no such thing as happy endings and he'd been a fool to entertain the idea. Even for a few moments.

'I guess it's over, then,' he said.

'It was never anything to begin with. We agreed it would be physical only.'

He'd said that. He'd insisted on that. He couldn't have been clearer. Because there was no such thing as love, or at least he wasn't silly enough to believe in it. Which was just as well, because if he did have feelings for Meg, romantic ones, ones that could be described as 'love', he'd be pretty devastated right now. As it was, he was disappointed, hurt. Maybe a little embarrassed and a little ashamed. That was more than enough.

But he wasn't heartbroken. No.

Then why did it feel as though he'd just been stabbed?

He turned away from her. No one needed to see his face right now, especially not Meg.

He went to his room, taking her robe with him.

You messed this up. When it comes to relationships, you, my friend, are a dunce.

And what was worse, he'd thought he'd done well. He'd thought he'd been calm and reasonable, but he hadn't. That was how clueless he was when it came to Meg. He didn't know her at all.

She was right—how could she trust him? And how could he trust her?

He couldn't, because, when it all came down to it, no one could trust anyone. Not really. Only fools, like those gormless honeymooners at the cooking class, still believed their love would last.

He'd put Meg behind him. Go back to…what? Something would have to give back at the office. One of them would get the job and the other would deal with it and life would go on and he'd forget all about this week. It would fade quickly into memory and then into dust.

He'd forget everything about her.

Dan stood in his room, still wearing her silky gown, still feeling her silkiness over his skin, her scent tickling his nose. He pulled it off, threw it onto the floor and got straight into a scalding hot shower.

CHAPTER TEN

MEG'S HANDS SHOOK as she turned on the shower. She had to wash this whole mistake away as soon as possible. She should've listened to her brain and not her libido. She shouldn't have let herself get carried away in the beauty and romance of the South Pacific and she should've known much better than to get involved with Daniel Fairweather.

Out of the shower, she opened all the windows in her room as wide as they could go and then turned the fan onto its highest setting. She called housekeeping and asked for a change of sheets. She stripped her bed, accepted the clean sheets from the housekeeper and waved away the offer to make the bed for her. She'd made this mess, she'd make her own bed. Was that the saying?

She didn't know. Her thoughts were too jumbled, her feelings too confused to have anything make sense at the moment.

The one thing she'd been right about though was clear as day: it had been a big mistake to let herself trust Dan. When he'd held her she'd felt safe. She had felt cared for, but it had all been a mirage. She might have *felt* loved, but she wasn't.

Dan had never cared for her. It had all been a trick, a big lie. None of it had been real. Not only would she never trust Dan again, she didn't think she'd be able to trust anyone at all.

She climbed gratefully in the bed with the clean, crisp sheets and tried to sleep.

You were tricked, but it wasn't Dan who tricked you. He

believed you liked him and opened up to you when he thought you didn't despise him. He's as much of a victim of this as you are.

She wasn't a victim. She could've shrugged off George's remark, but she hadn't, because she'd wanted it to be true. She wanted Dan to like her. She couldn't believe how silly she had been. She curled herself up into a ball and tried not to cry.

The next morning they hired the electric bikes again and rode back to the house they had visited on the first day. For the meeting that should have happened almost a week ago. Or did George plan this as well? She didn't suppose she'd ever get any answers from George about the mix-up with the meeting dates. Or anything for that matter.

This time Nino Flores was there to meet them and Meg went through the motions of the meeting, as if on autopilot. Since they had been on the island for nearly a week and had already seen the site, they were both able to offer more than simply first impressions. Dan had had time to think about possible designs, Meg had had time to think about the possible limitations, and Nino seemed very impressed with their initial ideas. The visit went as well as it could have done. They agreed to present a proposal to Nino in two weeks' time and, just like that, their business on the island was concluded.

They returned the bikes and stood outside the hotel lobby.

'I'll ask Marie to get us on the first flight out,' Dan said.

'I'll tell the hotel we'll be checking out today.'

Meg told Heiana they had decided to leave a day early and walked back to the villa, feet and heart heavy. Her phone buzzed with an alert from the airline notifying her of the new flight time later that day.

Dan was pacing the living room when she came back in.

He spun when the door opened. 'Is there anything you'd like to tell me?'

'I've checked us out. We just need to drop the keycards at the desk.'

'Anything else?'

'Not particularly.' She'd said everything she'd wanted to the night before and had no desire to rehash any of it. All she wanted to do was forget.

'Were you going to tell me what you've been doing all this time, behind my back?'

'What?'

'You've been emailing the office, approving things, you've been working tirelessly to secure the CEO position.'

'How do you know that?'

'Does it matter how I know? You must have been working when I was sleeping or when you said you were walking or napping.'

'Of course I've been working. I'm serious about this job, about this deal.'

'And you have the nerve to say that you can't trust *me*?'

Her face burnt. 'It's hardly the same thing.'

'How is it different? How is you telling me you've gone for a walk when really you're emailing my team about the quarterly figures any different from me not telling you I wanted the CEO role?'

Ah. That was how he knew. But what was she meant to do? Ignore her emails for a week just because Dan was?

'Maybe I'm just better at my job.'

He scoffed. 'If being CEO means being deceptive and underhanded then congratulations, you're a shoo-in. But if it means acting with integrity then you might have a bit more of a challenge.'

She gasped. Daniel Fairweather was questioning her integrity? Cheating, treacherous, untrustworthy Daniel Fairweather was calling her dishonest? There were no limits to the depths to which he'd sink.

Meg stormed into her room to pack her bag and stopped short. Housekeeping had already visited, the bed was made tightly, but spread over the tight bedspread was a love heart made of rose petals. Meg groaned loudly and swept them off the bed.

The small plane was at capacity and they found themselves, yet again, seated in the tiny seats next to one another. This time she couldn't muster any of the kind thoughts towards Dan. This time, she loathed him more than ever. A feat she would've thought impossible just over a week ago.

But no. It seemed that her loathing had no limits and there was no limit to Dan's capacity to irritate her.

'Should we discuss how things will work back in Sydney?' he asked.

'They'll work like they always have.' Couldn't he just be quiet and ignore her, just as she was trying to do with him? Ignore the fact that no matter how much she pushed herself against the window his arm still occasionally brushed against hers? That no matter how much she faced the other way and breathed as shallowly as she could, the scent of his cologne still managed to make itself known to her? Couldn't he just leave her alone to stew in her own rage?

'With us bickering, trading barbs? Is that what you really want?' Dan replied.

She almost said, 'What I really want is to never have met you,' but she stopped just short of that and wasn't sure why.

Instead she said, 'What I really want is for none of this to ever have happened.'

'Well, it did happen, so we need to deal with it. At least if one of us is going to get the job.' His tone was so patronising. As if he was lecturing her.

'Oh, I see. You want me to pretend to be polite to you so that you get the CEO gig?' She snorted. 'Not going to happen.'

'You know what I mean—'

'How do I know what you did and didn't mean? You're the king of lies. No, wait. The Superman of lies.' She smirked.

His face reddened and she was glad.

'I never lied to you.' He spoke through gritted teeth and looked straight ahead. 'Never. If anyone tricked you, it was George. Not me.'

'You led me on. You kissed me, slept with me, wined and dined me.'

'Because I thought you liked me.'

'So everything you did was out of pity?'

It was as though her brain had left her body. She couldn't stop speaking, almost didn't care what she said. She didn't mean what she was saying and she knew she was out of line. All she wanted to do was hurt him.

The way he'd hurt her. By being so annoyingly...right. She hadn't told him about sending emails, but they'd had a deal. A physical relationship only. What was she expected to do?

He can only hurt you if you care for him.

The plane left the ground at that moment and Meg's stomach contents lifted with it. For one horrible, mortifying second she thought her lunch was going to come back up. She covered her mouth. Next to her Dan was scrambling in the seat pocket. He passed her a paper bag. She grabbed it, opened it and waited for her humiliation to be complete. But someone must have taken pity on her because her stomach contents stayed where they were. She took some deep breaths and a drink of water and as the plane's altitude stabilised, so did her stomach.

'Okay?' Dan whispered.

She shrugged. No. She was not okay. She'd fallen in love with Daniel Fairweather and she had no idea what she was going to do. She couldn't trust him, so how could she love him? Wasn't life meant to get easier as you got older? Wasn't she meant to be able to see things more clearly at this age?

Wasn't she not supposed to make stupid mistakes like fall for the most untrustworthy man she knew?

She held the paper bag tightly in her hands. How had he known to give it to her? She stole a glance sideways. Dan was reading something on his phone and not looking in her direction.

He could tell just by looking at you. He hadn't laughed. He hadn't left her to fend for herself. He'd helped her. Even once she'd lashed out at him. Insulted him. Tried to make him hurt as she was hurting. He hadn't bitten back.

He didn't lie to you either.

She wanted to shush the voice.

But he didn't tell you the truth.

And she hadn't told him everything either.

Whose fault is it if you can't trust him? Dan's hardly given you reasons to trust him over the years, has he?

There was That Night. Then years and years of quarrelling and undermining. And now the mess that was this trip.

If you don't trust Dan, it's as much to do with you as it is to do with him. It takes two to build a relationship. Two can mess it up. Two wrongs don't make a right.

She glanced over at him again but he was looking resolutely the other way.

Could she be right? Could she be as much to blame as he was?

He hadn't told her the truth about his wife. Then he'd fought with her constantly for years. So why should she trust him now?

Because he was hurt, just as you were.

Because Meg had played her part too, bickering, snide remarks. Undermining him as well. Telling anyone who would listen what a pain in the neck he was.

In the past week, in a thousand tiny ways, he'd shown her a different side of him.

Holding her in the earthquake.

The cooking class.

The waterfall.

Passing her the paper bag on the plane.

And not fighting back just now when she'd been the one out of line.

No.

None of this changed anything. This island, what had happened this week, hadn't been real. It had all been an illusion created by George and his trick. She couldn't believe anything Dan did or said. She never could.

They didn't speak again on the flight after what he thought of as 'The Near-Miss'—when he'd handed her the paper bag, which thankfully she hadn't needed to use. Neither of them needed any more mess in the ruins of their relationship.

Superman of lies? She'd called him many things over the years, but *that* had hurt. Her other barbs had slid off him like water, but that remark had found a weak point in his armour and had stung.

He hadn't told her *everything*, but he hadn't lied to her. And he hadn't done anything she hadn't.

Yes, he'd flirted with her, wined and dined her, and he'd done all those things because he'd thought she liked him. It was true. But did that make it wrong? He hadn't done all those things out of pity. Or even because his ego had been stroked. He'd believed what George had told him because he'd wanted it to be true. He wanted Meg to like him. He wanted her to have forgiven him. He wanted her to love him, because he loved her.

Dan wanted a paper bag himself but he'd given his to Meg. All he could do was pretend to look at his phone and breathe deeply. The screen was a blur and there was no service. He just stared at the brightness of the screen and contemplated the realisation.

He loved her.

It was the only explanation for these feelings he was having. Longing for her even when she was next to him. Wanting her near at all times, needing to know what she thought about something and everything. Not wanting to hurt her, even when she was hurting him. The palpitating heart, the constant feeling he was forgetting what he was doing and realising he'd been thinking of Meg. And there was a great deal too much sweat. Just as was gathering on his brow right now.

Damn.

He loved her.

He loved the way she felt in his arms, loved the way she kissed. When he wasn't with her all he wanted to do was close his eyes and think of her. He loved the way she smiled, loved the way she laughed. Loved the sound of her voice. Dan doubted there was a single thing about Meg he didn't love. Even her perfectionism was perfect.

Argh!

Because along with the knowledge that he loved her came the knowledge that he'd been right all along not to fall for anyone because love wasn't fun, love was miserable. Love was painful. Love, quite frankly, sucked and the sooner he cured himself of it, the better for everyone.

Because love didn't last. The only thing love was any good at was causing pain. To him and everyone around him.

When they disembarked the small plane in Papeete they went their separate ways. He found a bar in which to sit and wait for the flight to Sydney, assuming Meg would go to the airline lounge.

He kept his distance from her when they were boarding the plane and was relieved to see their seats were at opposite ends of the cabin. He kept one eye on where she was though, mostly to make sure they didn't accidentally run into one another on the way to the bathroom. But also just to satisfy himself that she was still there. Where she was meant to be.

When they arrived in Sydney he held back, making sure she'd left the plane and cleared Customs and Border Protection while he dawdled along alone. He knew Meg and knew she'd be as quick and efficient as she could getting through the queues and out to the taxi rank. Dan spent his time in the duty-free shop and bought some whisky he knew was going to come in handy over the next few days and weeks. Until the point he managed to get Meg out of his system.

It had been years since he'd been in love so he wasn't sure what the current recovery time was. He hoped it wasn't as bad as it had been with Astrid. It couldn't be, could it? He'd loved Astrid for years and Meg for...

Years.

He wanted to cover his face with his hands and scream but he was holding his carry-on luggage and two large bottles of spirits. Instead he just muttered to himself, 'You fool, Fairweather. You damn fool.'

One week after returning from French Polynesia, Dan still hadn't discovered the cure for love and was running out of options. Drinking hadn't helped, little surprise there. Exercise hadn't either. And nor had working until two a.m. several nights in a row. Every time he tried to work he heard her voice in the back of his mind telling him what was wrong with his design. How it was too elaborate, too expensive. Too this, too that.

Finally, he realised there was one thing he hadn't tried.

Blaming someone else. Even though he and Meg had agreed they didn't want to give George the satisfaction of knowing how his trick had played out, now he and Meg weren't talking, Dan figured he didn't owe Meg anything.

He knocked on George's door. George smiled and waved him in.

'You tricked me!' Dan hissed.

George looked behind Dan into the busy corridor. 'Let's go for a drink, shall we?'

At the bar they usually frequented George ordered a beer for Dan and a mineral water for himself.

George placed his palms flat on the table. 'Let me have it.'

'You admit you tricked us both?'

'Did I? Really?'

'Yes, you told us both that we were in love with each other.'

'I was careful not to use that word.'

'Love?'

'I just said "feelings".'

Dan shook his head but wondered at the same time. What had George said? Maybe he hadn't used the L word. Did it make any difference? George had still been way out of line.

'And you think that makes it okay?'

'I don't think what I did was an HR-endorsed strategy. But I'm about to retire. And I care about you both. And I care about this business.'

That wasn't a real answer, yet Dan had suspected all along that George's motives had been benevolent. It was the only reason he hadn't stormed into George's office on his first day back.

'And you know we both want the CEO role,' Dan said.

'I suspected you both want it, and I also know that, as things stand, the one who loses will be very disappointed. It won't be good for the company. Or either of you, to be quite honest. You make an excellent team, whether you can admit it or not.'

Dan was still angry but could see George was only trying to deal with the problem of two potential CEOs in his own messed-up way.

Meg would never have managed things like this, said the

voice at the back of his mind. This time it wasn't Meg's voice though; it was his.

'Look, I wasn't trying to manipulate either of you,' George continued. 'I just wanted you to resolve your differences. Be a little bit kinder to one another.'

'Well, that backfired.'

'I know you used to be friends. I've seen you both together all these years. Mate, I've seen the sparks.'

Sparks. More like grenades.

George leant across the table. 'You obviously figured out what I'd said to you both?'

'Of course we figured it out.'

'But you wouldn't have if one of you didn't...that is, if you didn't at least discuss your feelings with one another.'

'Oh, we discussed them all right. To the point that we're not speaking right now.'

'Oh, well, I see.' George's shoulders slumped with a deep sigh. 'I guess it's all for the best.' George sipped his drink and looked out of the window at the water.

'What do you mean, for the best?'

'You know, you being afraid of relationships. Being afraid of getting hurt again.'

'I'm not afraid of being hurt. I just don't believe in love.'

'And yet...here we are.' George—his boss, his mentor, his friend—stared at Dan and smiled.

Dan gritted his teeth.

'I messed things up,' Dan admitted.

'And she behaved perfectly?'

'No.' She'd done the same things he had, made the same assumptions and the same mistakes.

'I hate to play the "I've been married fifty years" card, but I will. Sometimes the same behaviour has different consequences when it comes from a different person. From a different place or a different context.'

'What do you mean?'

'Life's more complicated than tit for tat.'

He and Meg might have both done the same thing, but it meant different things. Meg didn't trust him, that was the difference. Because of her life, because of her ex. And Dan hadn't given her a reason to trust him over the years.

'You're always going to bicker, particularly two intelligent, determined people like the pair of you.'

'Which is why we called it quits.'

George shook his head. 'You're not even going to try again?'

'There's no point. I've messed it up.'

'Look, since I've already meddled in your relationship, I'll say this—have you tried just talking to her?'

He'd tried talking and he'd stuffed that up as well. Dan nodded.

'Oh, well, it was worth a try,' George said.

Dan didn't feel vindicated after his talk with George, but nor did he feel as upset. He understood a little better why things with Meg hadn't worked. It was cold comfort, but it was the best he was going to get. It took two people to make a relationship work, though only one to ruin it.

Unfortunately, that always seemed to be him.

'Who are you going to recommend as your successor?' Meg asked.

'It isn't my choice. It's the board's—you know that,' George told her.

'I also know that your recommendation is essential. Will it be me or Dan?'

George frowned. They were in his office with the door closed and George was telling Meg about his plan to step down at the end of the financial year.

It wasn't unexpected but it was still momentous.

'I'm thinking I might abstain.'

'What? Not recommend either of us?'

'Meg, I honestly can't choose between you.'

Me! The decision should be obvious.

But it wasn't. Not to George, who knew them both better than anyone, who had seen their strengths and weaknesses. If George couldn't decide then maybe they were both suited to the role?

She knew it in her heart. She was the better manager, the better organiser and the better facilitator but Dan brought the vision and the spark and she could never do that.

'Is that what the trick was all about?'

Meg had resisted confronting George until now. At first it was because everything felt too raw. Then it was because, despite everything, she and Dan had agreed not to. But now? All bets were off.

'What trick?'

'You know what I'm talking about. George, how could you? I trusted you!'

George raised an eyebrow and she felt the sting in her use of the past tense. She had trusted George and, even after everything he'd done, she still did. This one incident wasn't enough to erase all the years they had known one another.

'I must say, I hoped the outcome would be better.'

'You hoped we'd end up together?'

'I mostly hoped you'd work out your differences.'

Nice dodging of the question. George hadn't meant to be cruel, but what he'd done had still been wrong.

'You lied to us both.'

'Did I?'

'Yes! You told us both we had feelings for one another when we didn't.' Try as she might to remain professional, Meg couldn't stop her voice rising.

'Fine, fume away. But I just told you both what I saw. You used to be friends.'

'A long time ago. A very long time ago.'

'Was I really that wrong? Did I really say anything that was completely untrue?'

Yes!

Meg didn't answer right away, her thoughts going straight to Dan. To his smile. To the way he'd silently helped her with her bags, to the look on his face when they made love. Even to the way he'd passed her the paper bag on the plane.

She did love him. But it was hard enough admitting it to herself, let alone to George.

'Have you simply tried telling him?' George asked.

'Telling him what?'

'That you're crazy about him?'

Meg's pulse raced and she swallowed, wishing a glass of water were nearby.

'And what good would that do?'

'He might tell you he loves you, too.'

Hope swelled inside her and she was powerless to shut it down with reason. She had to know. 'What do you know? What has he said to you?'

'No, this is where my meddling comes to an end.'

Meg groaned.

'Now you get all noble? George, what were you going to say?'

George shook his head. 'It doesn't matter what I tell you, you have to speak to him.'

Nothing. George knew nothing. This was more meddling, more mind games. Dan didn't love her and that was fine because Meg didn't love Dan. She didn't. She couldn't. She might desire Dan, but it wasn't love. And luckily for Meg, desire would fade. It had to. Because otherwise it would mess up everything.

CHAPTER ELEVEN

Dan sat with George, Meg and representatives from their teams in the large conference room at Evermore to present their pitch to Nino Flores in a teleconference. Flores had the proposal and they were talking him through how it could work.

Dan went through all the features, listing them as if he were ticking off a shopping list, confident the designs themselves would convince Flores that the plan was perfect.

Flores became increasingly silent throughout Dan's presentation and even though he was miles away, and on a screen, Dan could still feel the disappointment emanating from him. Dan's heart fell with each sentence he spoke. He loved this design as much as he loved the site on Isle St Jean, but it was clear that Nino Flores hated it.

'What is it that's worrying you?' Meg asked Flores even before he had a chance to speak.

'I'm not sure how to articulate it,' he replied.

'That's normal,' Meg replied. 'Let's break it down.'

Dan watched and listened as Meg went through the elements of the proposal. The number of rooms, the size of the resort, the position of the build. Then the design itself.

Dan took notes of the slight adjustments they agreed on at every step. Some small, some more substantial, but none that fundamentally changed his vision.

How had he never seen what she was doing before? George often ran these meetings and any time he asked Meg to Dan was often too incensed to pay the right kind of attention to what she was doing.

He'd never really bothered to watch what Meg was doing now, selling his design to the client, brick by brick. He'd thought she was undermining him and his design when really she'd been selling it. Convincing the client to go ahead in a way that would work for everyone. She didn't hate him. She didn't despise him. All along she'd been working for him without him noticing. Along with everything else he hadn't noticed about her.

As though he didn't already know what kind of fool he was.

Love was real, he'd just stupidly messed it up with her. And with every new word she spoke he received a further reminder.

Meg was amazing.

He'd been wrong about her. He'd been wrong about everything. And he had to keep sitting here, watching her, listening and being reminded with each word she spoke how much he loved her. He couldn't do it any more. The torture was so precise, targeted at his heart like a laser invisible to everyone else in the room. But Dan was falling apart inside.

'I agree that there are compromises that could be made—after all, we want this to work for you and the community—but a resort needs to look beautiful and feel beautiful. Visitors remember the feel of a place more than anything else. Mr Fairweather's design is beautiful. The costs are not excessive, particularly given the site of the build. We've lowered the costs as far as we possibly can without compromising the energy efficiency and the regenerative features of the build,' Meg said.

No one spoke and she continued, 'I don't think you would find a design more sympathetic to the natural surroundings, more suited to the local conditions.'

As much as he wanted to watch Meg, wanted to stare at her for ever, he had to look away, both for sanity and professionalism. The look on Flores's face had changed completely, from scepticism to delight after Meg's part of the presentation. They had won him over.

Meg had won him over. Dan had just sat there. Mute.

The Dan that left the conference room was very different from the one who had come in. George had a big smile on his face. Meg looked tired but she was also smiling. Dan should be smiling too, but couldn't manage it. He'd made a decision.

He couldn't stay. It wouldn't be fair to Meg, but also not to him. He loved Meg and, as much as staying at Evermore would give him an excuse to see her every day, that proximity was so bittersweet that he felt simultaneously joyful and heartbroken each time he saw her.

He had to do something to maintain his sanity. Staying working at Evermore wouldn't be fair to either of them and it was clear now to him that he should be the one to go.

As much as it broke his heart to leave the company he had devoted himself to, he had to do it for her, just as much as for himself. He could make at least one good decision when it came to this relationship. He could do this one thing right.

'You're very quiet, Dan,' George said.

'Can I speak to you for a moment?'

George's face fell. 'I hope there's not a problem with how the presentation went?'

Dan was only vaguely aware that the others were still standing there. The only person he was really aware of was Meg. He saw the cloud that came across her face.

She thinks you're going to complain to George about how she took over the meeting.

Meg narrowed her eyes, turned on her heel and left.

If only she knew that Dan was about to make all her dreams come true.

'Leaving?' George asked.

'I have to, and you know why.' Dan sat across from his

boss, his mentor. This had been one of the hardest things he'd ever had to tell someone but now it was out there he felt a burden lifted.

'You can't work it out with her?'

Not this time.

'It's best for her and best for the company if I leave. Meg should be the new CEO.'

'Dan, your designs have built this place into what it is. I couldn't have done it without you. Meg can't do it without you.'

'Yes, she can, and you know it. You also know that I couldn't have done my job without her.'

'You're a team. You always have been. You have always achieved more with one another. It has always taken the both of you.'

It takes two to build a relationship and two people to mess it up.

That was what she'd been trying to say. But it was too late now.

'What will you do?' George asked.

Dan smiled for the first time since the presentation had started.

Build cathedrals.

'I want to do something where I can let my imagination run to its extremes. I love our work but I want to take all the principles and ideas we've developed here into different places. Houses. Offices. All other kinds of developments. Whatever they will let me do. I believe in this work, but it's time for a change.'

He couldn't stay working with Meg, day after day, being constantly reminded how wonderful she was, how beautiful. How utterly spectacular.

George smiled at him sadly. 'It won't be the same without you.'

'Or you.'

But it would be best for Meg. She was going to run this company now and she didn't need George looking over her shoulder or Dan moping around, getting in her way.

'I'm sorry things didn't work out,' George said.

'Some things aren't meant to be.'

'Says who?'

Said the look on Meg's face when she walked away just moments ago. Said the look on Meg's face when she found out Dan wanted the CEO job.

Dan stood. 'Thanks for everything, George.'

Dan glanced into the conference room on his way back to his office.

Says who?

Said Meg when she told Dan that she could never trust him. Meg when she told him that he was insufferable.

Said Meg when she told Flores he wouldn't find a better design.

Meg when she said Dan's design was beautiful.

Dan touched the back of the chair Meg had been sitting in earlier.

But she was just saying all that to seal the deal.

Meg had said a lot of things. He had as well. He'd meant many of them, but not everything. He hadn't told her the truth.

He hadn't told her that he loved her.

Meg sat in the boardroom as the vote was held. It was unanimous, though she'd expected nothing less. She didn't have a competitor for the CEO position. Dan had resigned from Evermore two weeks ago. Today would be his last day.

He'd rather resign than work for her. It hurt, but it was the right decision for everyone. Especially her. Even so, she didn't feel nearly as good as she'd thought she would.

In fact, she felt terrible. She hadn't slept properly since

she'd found out. Her insides were a turgid soup of worry, regret and heartache.

She wanted to win the job fairly, not have it given to her.

Meg was overjoyed at winning the role and yet she felt empty. How could that be?

And apart from missing out on the satisfaction of beating Daniel Fairweather, she now had to find a new chief architect. Hiring someone to fill Dan's talented shoes would be next to impossible. She already had an inkling that being a CEO was not going to be as easy as George made it look.

And since she was counting, there was the third thing. The thing that she didn't want to think about because it hurt too much. She was going to miss him. Even if they were hardly on speaking terms, just knowing where he was and what he was doing filled her with comfort. After today she'd never see him again and that filled her chest with a kind of emptiness that was quickly filling with panic.

She walked slowly back to her office, receiving congratulations from several people she passed along the way. She sat at her desk; it was time to get on with it.

But on her desk was an envelope. White, A4 size. Addressed to her in Dan's loose, beautiful, unmistakable script. Her hands shook as she opened it. A letter? A final missive? A declaration?

It was none of those things. It was a sketch. She recognised the same off-white paper as he'd been using on the island, for the sketches she'd perused and the ones he hadn't let her see.

This was evidently one of the ones he hadn't let her see. Her throat caught. It was her, in profile, looking at something in the distance. A small smile on her lips. She looked happy. Content.

Beautiful.

This was how he saw her? She turned the paper over but

there was nothing else. Just the portrait. What did it mean? What was he trying to say?

Heart hammering in her chest, she stood and, without knowing what she was going to do, she left her office and headed to the opposite end of the building. To Dan's office. To where it had once been.

She didn't get that far. She found Dan talking to someone outside the kitchen. He was leaning against a wall but kicked himself off it and stood straight when he saw her.

He smiled and she felt the sincerity of the smile in her chest. 'Congratulations,' he said warmly.

She'd assumed he'd be avoiding her on today of all days. His last day at Evermore. She'd glanced in his office on the way to the board meeting and it had been filled with boxes and blank spaces on the walls where his prints had been.

'Does it feel like you thought it would?' he asked.

No. It feels nothing like it. Because I got it by default. And because you're leaving and I didn't expect that to hurt as much as it does.

She shook her head. 'It's going to be a challenge.'

'I know you can do it. So does the board.'

She laughed. 'Oh, I know I can do the job. The reason it's going to be hard is that my chief architect has resigned. For personal reasons.'

'Ah, yes, about that.'

This was her one shot. She had to make it work. Even if he didn't love her, she didn't want him to be gone from her life. She glanced at the person he had been speaking to and the man left with only a nod.

'Dan, you don't have to leave. We've had an awkward working relationship for years—it's the one thing we know we can do well.'

'I don't want to do that any more. I don't want to play games and I'm sick of the one-upmanship. I'm sick of the bickering. Though, I admit, the idea of some flirting with my boss could be kind of hot.'

He glanced at her sideways and her cheeks burnt. Flirting? Had he really just said that?

'Let's walk,' he said. 'It would be good to clear the air—if you want, that is?'

'Yes. Definitely.' They needed to get out of this office. She needed answers. She needed closure.

The air was fresh but warm as they walked down the street towards the water.

'You know you stopped me from winning, don't you?' Meg began.

'What? I quit! I took away your biggest challenge.'

'That's right.'

Dan smiled with understanding. 'You wanted the fight?'

'I guess so. Maybe.'

He understood her. He understood the feelings even she couldn't get into words.

'You can be perverse, you know that? Meg, look, for what it's worth, I didn't step away to let you have it. I stepped away because you're the best person for the job.'

They both could have done the job—they would have done it differently, but both could do it.

'You don't have to say that.'

'I know I don't have to say it. I'm saying it because it's true. You were right, I don't want to run a company, I want to design and build amazing things. And that's what I'm going to do.'

'You have a new job?'

He nodded.

'I've been offered a partnership at Restor Inc.'

'Wow. Okay.' It was a very prestigious architectural firm but very different from Evermore. 'Is that really what you want to do?'

'Absolutely. And, to be honest, probably what I should've done ages ago. Once I'd worked on perfecting regenerative and sustainable eco resorts, I should've moved on to other things. Houses, office buildings. Cathedrals.' He winked at her.

Meg's heart was beating in her throat. He really was leaving. For ever.

'But I was comfortable at Evermore. George is great. I travelled the world.' Dan stopped walking and turned to face her. He looked down at her and caught her gaze in his. Her stomach dropped. 'And there were other perks.'

Did he mean her?

'So it was easy to stay. But you're right, I have bigger ambitions. I felt constrained here and it wasn't because of you, no matter what I ever said. It was because of me. I was comfortable and too scared to leave.'

'Oh.'

It was really happening. He really was leaving. The sadness that expanded inside her was almost overwhelming. Losing Dan, her annoying sparring partner, would be nearly as bad as losing Dan, her lover. He couldn't just walk out on her for ever.

'Do you think, maybe, we could catch up occasionally? I'd like to hear how all goes.'

'Meg, I'm going to miss you.'

Her heart beat in her throat. She hated when people didn't give her a simple yes or no answer.

'I'm going to miss you, too. But we can still see one another, can't we?' Oh, no. She could hear the pleading in her voice. So much for maintaining her dignity.

'I don't know. I don't know if we can work as friends.'

'It's the one thing we never really tried.'

'No, we did try once or twice. Remember?'

She remembered back to the first few weeks, when they

were still getting to know one another. How easy it had been. And then how easy it had been to sleep with one another...

'The thing is, we've never been able to stay just friends, have we? Not here, not on Isle St Jean,' he said and turned away.

No. No!

'What if I don't want to stay just friends? What if we both want something more?'

Dan stopped walking and turned back. His eyes flicked back and forth, his brain ticking behind them. Meg couldn't breathe. Couldn't quite believe she'd said what she'd just said, that she'd put her heart out there for him to catch. Or drop. Or stomp on.

Dan swallowed, pressed his lips together. She didn't know what he was thinking but it was hardly a resounding 'Yes!'

It was foolish of her to suggest it. She knew he didn't believe in relationships, let alone love. But after everything that had happened with Dan, love was one thing she did know was real. She felt it in her chest, in her gut, in her head every day. Love was very real, even if it wasn't returned.

'I wish we could,' he said.

Dan didn't add 'but', though she felt it in her gut. He was saying no.

'But?'

'I don't want to stuff this up. That's what I do. I ruin relationships.'

'It takes two to do that,' she said.

'Not always.'

'Dan, yes, in this case, in our case, it was me as well. I find it difficult to trust people. Sometimes things are a little harder for me.'

'I know that. And I realise I should've known better. I thought that if we treated one another the same way things would be equal, but that isn't always the case. Two wrongs don't always make a right.'

'Dan, you *were* right, we both made the same assumptions about the CEO role. We both fell for George's trick in equal measure. And maybe we shouldn't have fallen into bed so quickly all those years ago. And maybe I was very quick to judge. It's how I am. I don't mean to and I try not to.'

'And I was too quick to dismiss. We both bring baggage with us. Our lives, our experiences, our hurts. But I'll help you carry yours.'

Her heart skipped as her memory flashed back to the way he'd picked up her suitcase when they had arrived on Isle St Jean. To all the time they had spent there. The cooking class, the kayak. The waterfall.

You can trust him. He's the real deal. He's not going to let you down.

Without realising, they had walked all the way to the water and were standing by the rowing club. The sun was low in the west over the city.

But Dan didn't believe in love or relationships.

'We can keep it light, see how we go,' she tried. She didn't want to overwhelm him. She knew he didn't believe in love. She wasn't sure how much he was prepared to give.

'I can't, Meg, because I love you. I've always loved you. And look how I messed it all up, from beginning to end.'

Love? Had he used that word? Not 'feelings' or 'care' but love?

'Love?'

'Yes, laugh all you want. I love you, Meg. From the bottom of my heart to the heights of my soul, with every cell in my body, I love you.'

Meg didn't know if her feet would stay on the ground. It felt as though she might be able to fly. To ground herself she threw herself into Dan's arms and pressed her mouth to his.

He caught her and held her, his kiss welcoming and warm. Like being home.

This was how it was meant to be.

I've always loved you.

She pulled back.

'Wait. Always?'

'Of course always. Since I first met you.'

'But...'

'And then, you know what happened. Don't make me explain it or relive it. Please, Meg, please.'

She laughed. 'I thought it was just me.'

Dan touched his forehead to hers. 'It was never just you. It takes two, isn't that what you said?'

'Or did you? I can't remember.'

'I think there are some things we shouldn't try too hard to remember. I don't think it will reflect well on either of us.'

Her limbs tingled and her next words fell out in a rush. 'I love you as well. And it's been making me crazy.'

She fell into him and the kiss and waves of happiness rippled from her lips to her toes and everywhere in between. She was home.

'I can learn. I can be better. I promise.'

'Dan, I love you as you are. We will both do our best, but *you* have to trust that I love you too.'

'I think I can do that. At least I promise to try.'

He smiled and it was as though she'd turned her body to the sun.

'You can read my thoughts,' she said.

'You know exactly how to annoy me,' he replied.

'You know exactly how to wind me up...'

'...and turn me on.'

'I trust you, I do, Dan.'

He held her close, his chin rested on the top of her head. He inhaled deeply. She pulled him closer and smiled.

EPILOGUE

They stood together, holding hands in the reception of the resort.

Meg was back on Isle St Jean to celebrate the opening of the new resort, built with Nino Flores, but, as the new place was already fully booked with paying guests, they had checked into the resort she had stayed at with Dan on their first visit.

Unable to stand the thought of Meg going to Isle St Jean without him, Dan had come as well.

Heiana saw them and did a double take.

'I thought we might see you back for your honeymoon. Congratulations.'

'Ah, no. Not yet. Life's been busy.' Good busy. Amazing busy. But also happy and fun. 'But we've set a date,' Meg admitted. In two months' time. A small wedding with their children, and George, of course.

Meg hadn't believed she'd ever marry again but Dan had been the one to gently push it. Dan might have been certain, but it turned out Meg was the one to be cautious.

'I will love you for ever and I want everyone to know. Most of all, I want *you* to know,' he'd said.

Dan had thrown himself into the relationship and his new-found romanticism with gusto even greater than he had for his new job.

'May I see the ring?' Heiana asked.

Dan picked up Meg's hand and showed her the ring, a solitaire diamond, cut just perfectly.

'It reflects light just like the waterfall,' he said, looking straight at Meg.

Heiana laughed and shook her head.

'Here's your key. The same room as last time, though I suspect you may not want separate bedrooms as much as you once did.' She winked at them both as they left.

'Sometimes, Daniel Fairweather, I'm not sure who you are.'

'What do you mean?'

'What happened to the devoted cynic who swore that love was only for fools?'

Nothing Dan had done or said in the past year had been remotely cynical. His suggestion they adopt a cat so they would have a pet that belonged to both of them. The two rescue cats he'd actually brought home so the first would have a friend.

The house they had bought and the way he wanted to remodel it so that it was just right for the two of them but also had rooms for Olive, Rufus and Jake and however many partners and children they might one day want to bring to stay. The way he offered gentle support and advice to her about the new architect she'd hired, a keen young woman with a passion for sustainable architecture that amazed both of them. She missed Dan at work, but also knew it was best for the company overall to start planning for a future in which neither of them worked at Evermore and the next generation could take over.

As they walked slowly to their room, hand in hand, Meg breathed in the tropical air and savoured the memories from the last time they had been here together. Of the kayak, the waterfall. The bed. But not the fight they'd had. They both knew that it didn't do to dwell too much on the mistakes.

'Which room should we use? Yours or mine?' she asked.

'They're both ours,' he said, pulling her into his arms. 'We can start with one and then move to the other. And the sofa.'
'And the bathroom. The pool…'
'You're always right. Did I ever tell you that?'
She laughed. 'And your ideas are inspired.'
'I know.'
'And your ego still knows no bounds.'
'But you love me anyway.'
'That I do…that I do.'

* * * * *

*If you enjoyed this story,
check out these other great reads from
Justine Lewis*

Swipe Right for Mr. Perfect
The Billionaire's Plus-One Deal
Breaking the Best Friend Rule
Beauty and the Playboy Prince

All available now!

THE BILLIONAIRE SHE LOVES TO HATE

SCARLETT CLARKE

MILLS & BOON

To Mom,
for her editing magic.

To John,
for his endless patience and plot brainstorming.

To my children,
for sleeping through the night and giving Mom
a chance to finish this book.

To Library-by-the-Sea,
for telling us a story we'll never forget.

CHAPTER ONE

Gideon

STARING DOWN THE sharp length of a spear gun was not Gideon Radcliffe's idea of a good morning. But here he was, the warmth of the Caribbean sunrise at his back and a shiny spear tip three inches from his nose. He'd walked around a tree and nearly straight into it.

"Not what I've come to expect of Cayman hospitality," he muttered to himself.

"I don't extend hospitality to trespassers."

Gideon's eyes flicked up in surprise. He'd been so fixated on not losing an eye he hadn't even registered who wielded the spear. The woman behind the weapon was unexpected. He had a flash of thick locks and an elfin face. Observations he filed away for later as his gaze returned to the most pressing point.

"I'm still on my property."

The spear wavered. "No, you're not. Who are you?"

"I'd prefer to have this conversation without wondering if I'm going to need an eye patch."

A frustrated sigh met his ears. Then, thankfully, she lowered the spear, giving Gideon an opportunity to better examine his would-be attacker.

Chocolate-colored curls tumbled over her shoulders in a riotous mass and framed a narrow face with high cheekbones and a slender jaw. Amber eyes were narrowed to slits. A chin formed into a stubborn point. She was easily a foot shorter than him, although given the way she continued to glare at him, she couldn't care less about the stark differences in height and muscle.

He'd been caught off guard by a brunette version of Tinker Bell.

"Gideon Radcliffe, at your service."

The pixie's hands tightened on the spear shaft. "I see."

The temperature might as well have dropped twenty degrees. Normally people reacted to him with respect. Owning nearly a dozen world-renowned resorts in the Caribbean, Europe and Southeast Asia had made the Radcliffe family a household name.

But this woman's lips twisted into a sneer.

"Finally decided to do your dirty work yourself?"

Irritation crawled up Gideon's spine. Thousands of miles from New York and the trial that had ruled his life for too long, and still his uncle's slander circulated. Steven Radcliffe may have appeared affable, even noble during the five-year legal battle that had caught the attention of the worldwide media. But spreading rumors that Gideon had been doing nothing but partying and spending money in the twelve years since his father had died, leaving Steven to work fervently behind the scenes to keep the company running, had been a cold, calculated move. One that the judge had ultimately seen through when he'd awarded sole control of Radcliffe Resorts to Gideon and shut dear Uncle Steven out.

The trial had finally ended last week. But the gossip

persisted, even on an island in the middle of the Caribbean Sea apparently.

"Contrary to what you may have heard in the media…" Gideon's voice trailed off. "You have me at a disadvantage, ma'am."

He used the tone he wielded in board meetings, press conferences and negotiations when he was displeased. The kind of tone that made grown men look down at their shoes.

This woman merely arched a dark brow. Reluctant admiration wormed its way through him.

"You mean the disadvantage of catching you trespassing on my land?"

He glanced toward the beach, then inwardly swore when he noted the gum tree that marked the property line. He'd been so fixated on his vision, on imagining finally bringing his father's dream to life after so many years, that he had wandered past the boundary.

An almost imperceptible nod acknowledged his mistake. "My apologies, Miss…?"

"Everett."

The puzzle pieces fell into place. John Everett, owner of just under seven acres of oceanfront property known as Crescent Point that had once been owned by the Radcliffe family, was the lone holdout who had refused to sell his land.

"Related to John Everett?"

Grief flashed across her face; the pain so acute he felt her sadness as if it was his own.

"Yes."

The woman looked away, toward the beach. "John Everett was my father."

"Was?" Gideon repeated.

She continued to stare out over the ocean. "He died four months ago. Cancer."

Gideon barely managed to keep a leash on his surprise. How had he missed this detail? He mentally reviewed his last few meetings with Peter, his executive assistant and the one person he had trusted to travel to Grand Cayman in his stead to buy up as much of the former Radcliffe property as possible. Peter had been with the company for years. He'd even worked for Gideon's father. He knew how important this acquisition was.

Although, Gideon suddenly remembered, Peter had mentioned he was pausing on negotiations for a few months due to the family experiencing a personal issue. Gideon hadn't liked it. But he'd trusted Peter, especially as he'd needed to focus his attention on the trial and the evidence being presented to the judge.

Still, it surprised him that Peter hadn't mentioned John Everett's passing.

"I'm sorry."

The urge to do something more, to reach out and offer a hand or more than a few words, surprised him. Except he had no time for grief, for regret. The past remained unchanged, a lesson Miss Everett would have to learn just as he had.

But the future... The future was limitless.

Her gaze snapped back to his, her grief evaporating in an instant. Golden-brown fire blazed in her eyes.

"Are you, Mr. Radcliffe? I imagine my father's death only makes it easier for you to go after what you want."

His hands clenched into fists at his sides. "I may be

many things, Miss Everett. But even I'm not cold enough to be happy about someone's passing."

"No, just take advantage of it."

Irritation flared into anger. "I've never met you or your father. The only thing I'm guilty of is making a very generous offer for your property."

"If you mean harassing and intimidating, then I agree with you."

"Your father bought this acreage for thirty thousand dollars forty years ago. It's now worth one point five million, and I'm offering double that." Gideon tilted his head to one side. "How is offering more than fair market value harassing or intimidating?"

She shook her head. "Just stay away from me. You and your minion."

Before he could retort, she turned and stalked away, disappearing down a well-worn path into a copse of trees.

He released a slow, pent-up breath. Miss Everett was a menace.

He turned and stalked back onto his property. The two-acre plot was the one bit of land his grandfather had managed not to gamble away in an ill-fated poker game nearly fifty years ago. Peter had managed to purchase the three acres north of his land and a few one-acre plots south of Crescent Point.

But Crescent Point was the cornerstone of what Gideon had envisioned for Radcliffe at Moonrise Bay. He wasn't pleased that Peter hadn't managed to secure the Point. But, Gideon acknowledged as he made his way down to the beach, if Peter had been squaring off against John Everett's daughter and her spear, he would give the man a reprieve. Peter had certainly earned it after his years of service. The man had worked himself so hard he was now laid up in his room at the Radcliffe Resort on the west side of the island with an aching throat and a hideous cough.

The dull roar of the ocean washed over him, soothing the hard edges of tension that had plagued him the last few months as his case had finally reached the courtroom after five years. Five years of pretrial motions, financial investigations, testimonials and coordinating with the international laws of every country Radcliffe maintained a resort in. Through it all, Peter had remained by his side, never wavering in his commitment even as other employees left, as business partners distanced themselves.

A reminder, Gideon told himself, that there were few people in this world one could trust. Including so-called family.

He stepped onto the beach, his feet sinking into the sand. Waves swept up to the tips of his shoes, then out again. Just as it had so many years ago when he'd stood on this very beach with his parents and listened to his father share his dream.

His eyes flicked to the right, to the bell-shaped peninsula that rose up from the sea. Six point four acres of grassy fields, silver thatch and fustic trees. A beach that hugged the far end of the peninsula, a crescent moon of white sand.

He could see it now. The resort would sit halfway out. A two-story building with every room featuring private balconies with ocean views and soaking tubs. The first floor would host the on-site restaurant and one of two bars, with the second on the roof. Two pools, one with a hot tub and one with an infinity ledge overlooking the sea to the north. A marina and dive shop on the property to the south.

He glanced over his shoulder, at the land that had been in his family for three generations. Forty years ago, his grandfather had owned nearly fifty acres of Grand Cayman's East End. Fifty acres reduced to two. All because of a card game gone wrong. A minor loss when compared with the totality of the Radcliffe empire. But it was a loss Gideon's father had felt intensely. He'd spent many happy years on Grand Cayman, a gift he'd passed on to Gideon as they'd spent numerous holidays at the resort on the island's famous Seven Mile Beach. Lee Radcliffe had viewed his dream as a chance to restore his family's honor, to reclaim what had been lost.

One day. His father's favorite phrase whenever he, Gideon and Gideon's mom had driven forty-five minutes to the two acres of trees and beach his grandfather had managed to hold on to. *One day, I'll get at least some of it back and build a resort unlike any other.*

Except that one day had never come. Both his parents' lives were cut short just one year apart, leaving Gideon and his uncle the last remaining heirs to the internationally renowned Radcliffe Resorts.

His chest tightened. He'd always known his father had intended for him to take over his empire. But Dad was supposed to have been there, to ease Gideon in and show him the ropes of leading a prestigious international brand known for luxury and romance.

He wasn't supposed to have passed away just a year after Mom, leaving Gideon orphaned and isolated in a sea of grief and ignorance. He'd thought asking Uncle Steven, who had been director of strategic operations, to serve as CEO while he finished college and worked his way through the ranks of Radcliffe Resorts, had been the mature thing to do. The right thing.

Wrong. He'd been terribly, horribly wrong.

Not only had Steven driven several resorts to the brink of financial ruin, but he'd blocked every attempt Gideon had made to acquire the land in Moonrise Bay. For the first few years, when he'd been acting CEO, he'd brushed Gideon off with excuses like the timing wasn't right or other resorts deserved their attention. Then, just when Gideon had been poised to take over everything, Steven had refused to give up his role. The legal battle had begun, suspending Gideon's ability to make any major acquisitions or changes as he and his uncle battled through lawyers, appeals processes and investigations.

But Gideon hadn't wasted all of that time. While Steven had accused him of frivolous spending, Gideon had actually been saving and investing. Even though he'd been all but certain he would win, he steadily built up his own wealth outside of Radcliffe Resorts. If the trial hadn't gone in his favor, he would have still had nearly $15 million to start his own company.

He'd had to move sooner than he'd expected when he'd learned that one of the tracts of land had gone up for sale just a few months before his first appearance in court. A three-acre plot just north of his. He'd quietly authorized Peter to travel down to Grand Cayman and negotiate the purchase with the money he'd saved. Once Peter had called to tell him the acreage was officially his, it had lit a fire in him. He'd authorized Peter to buy whatever $15 million could get him. He'd waited twelve long years to finally fulfill his father's wish. He was done waiting.

He closed his eyes, tilted his face up to the sun. The warmth on his skin bled the tension from his muscles. There were still challenges to overcome. He would not be deterred from his purpose again. But for the first time in years, there was a moment of peace. Contentment. Nothing but sun and sand and sea.

He opened his eyes just as a lone figure appeared on the peninsula, slim and determined as she marched toward the house. Curiosity sparked, simmered despite Gideon's best intentions. He'd simply been walking the property, savoring the quiet, envisioning the future, when warning had whispered across the back of his neck. The softest shush of a footfall a mere second before he'd had a weapon shoved in his face.

Who was the woman behind the spear? He knew a few facts about John Everett. Single father. Owner of a personal watercraft and kayak rental shop located on one of Moonrise Bay's popular beaches, less than a five-minute drive from Crescent Point. An active member of the town's chamber of commerce, well-liked and well-respected by his neighbors and peers.

Yet aside from remembering John Everett had a daughter, Gideon couldn't recall a single detail about her.

The woman stopped her march. She stared out over the sea. Even at this distance, the tension in her body was obvious, from the rigid set of her shoulders to the hands curled into fists at her sides. She looked like a woman struggling against the weight of the world on her shoulders.

Gideon followed the direction of her gaze out over

the sea. The reef that encircled the island kept the waters calm. His father had told him of the countless hours he'd spent on this beach, how many decisions he'd made on this shore that had helped the Radcliffe empire push closer to the billion-dollar mark.

An achievement his parents, Lee and Cecilia Radcliffe, hadn't lived to see. First Cecilia had passed away from a stroke during Gideon's sophomore year of college, then Lee a year later from what was officially ruled as complications from pneumonia.

Gideon knew the truth. His father had died of a broken heart. A mistake Gideon would not be repeating. If he married, it would be to someone he liked. Someone he enjoyed spending time with, who would be a loving mother to their children. A partner. No more. He wouldn't risk giving his heart away only to have it crushed.

And nor would he give it, he thought darkly, as his eyes cut back to the feisty Miss Everett, to someone who would antagonize, rile or otherwise disrupt his finally well-ordered life.

Suddenly, she turned. Too far away for him to see the details of her face, the stubborn point of her chin and the dogged lift of her upturned nose. But he knew she was looking at him across the cove. Read the challenge in her stance, feet firmly planted on the ground, her body poised to do battle.

Miss Everett certainly wasn't the kind of woman he would take on a date, let alone contemplate a relationship or marriage with. But she was intriguing, fire and fight tightly coiled inside a slender body. He could appreciate the long legs, the light caramel tan of her skin, the fierce curls that mirrored her crackling intensity.

But his appreciation would be from a distance. The glimmer of empathy he'd experienced when she'd mentioned losing her father was dangerous. Yes, the loss of her father was tragic. But it couldn't influence his next moves, didn't negate the value of what he was offering or the massive blow her refusal would deal to his plans. Too much time had been wasted. Now was the moment for action, for decision rooted in reason versus sentimentality or blind loyalty.

He bowed his head to her, an exaggerated motion to ensure she saw. He smirked when she whirled around and disappeared into the cottage. A minor victory. But after their surprise meeting earlier, he would consider this a win.

Anticipation stirred in his chest. The road to seeing Radcliffe at Moonrise Bay had taken another abrupt turn. After battling out the future of his family's company, the thought of yet another fight should have been infuriating.

There was irritation at Miss Everett getting the drop on him. There was frustration at facing down another obstacle.

But there was also a dark thread of excitement weaving through him, a savoring of this one last challenge before finally reaching the finish line. The one he'd been running toward ever since his last conversation with his father days before his death. When Lee had suddenly turned and looked at him with watery eyes and said, *Build the resort for me, son. Please.*

It had been the first time his father had spoken in over a week. He had waited until Gideon nodded before turning back to the window. He didn't speak again. Three days later, he'd passed in the night. Finally, at last, he'd been laid to rest next to his wife.

Gideon turned his back on the peninsula and walked along the beach, eyes on the horizon. There were times when anger threatened to override his dedication, when grief that his father's last words had been about a property instead of his own son nearly eclipsed his commitment.

But then he would remind himself that to his father, reclaiming the Radcliffe land and building wasn't just a business plan; it was a legacy.

So Gideon would strategize, persuade, negotiate. One way or another, Miss Everett would sell the Point. And once Gideon had possession of the last missing piece, he would ensure it never left Radcliffe hands again.

CHAPTER TWO

Cassie

CASSIE POURED A precise measure of gin into the glass. Her lips curved into a barely restrained smile. She loved her job; the freedom, the creativity, finding just the right balance of flavors to bring some of her favorite stories to life.

And after her unexpected encounter with Gideon Radcliffe this morning, she needed something positive to focus on.

"A splash of tonic water, and..." She pulled a tiny white-and-yellow flower from beneath the bar and laid it on the surface. "A daisy to finish off your cocktail."

"Oh!" The dark-haired woman sitting at the bar cupped the glass in her hands and took a sip. A delighted smile spread across her face. "That is the most delicious thing I've ever tasted."

Cassie smiled back. "I'm glad you like it."

"I love it." The woman took another sip and sighed happily. "And you came up with this?"

"I did. I love to read, so finding a job where I get paid to read and come up with recipes is a dream come true."

The sigh that escaped this time was markedly different: quieter, deeper. Melancholy.

"A dream coming true sounds nice."

Cassie leaned one hip against the bar. "It can happen."

"Sure." The woman made a sound like a grunt and a snort rolled into one. "And someday I might finally meet Prince Charming."

Ah. A broken heart. The most common malady of those who chose to confide in Cassie.

"I take it the last prince turned out to be a toad?"

"The largest toad you've ever seen." The woman gestured to the empty seat next to her. "He was supposed to be here with me. On our honeymoon." She held up her left hand and waggled her bare fingers. "Catching him with my maid of honor in the closet at the rehearsal dinner derailed that."

Ouch. "Wow."

"Yeah." She tapped the daisy, watched the ripples spread out from the petals. "But I wasn't going to waste a trip that was already paid for."

"That says a lot about you. Truly," Cassie insisted when the woman arched a brow. "You're making the most of a horrible situation, and you're doing it for yourself."

"I guess." Another sigh, deeper than the last. "The worst part is I knew he wasn't the right one for me. I just wanted to be married so badly, move on to the next step in my life, that I tried to make him fit." She gave Cassie a sad half smile. "Ever fall for the wrong guy?"

Gideon Radcliffe's too-handsome face flashed in Cassie's mind. Hard blue eyes, a straight blade of a nose, chiseled jaw and a determined chin with an actual cleft in it. The man looked like a superhero who had just stepped off the pages of a comic book.

More like a villain.

"I don't date much. But," she added as a traitorous shiver moved down her spine, "I've made my share of mistakes."

"Well, in my current mood, I'd recommend staying far away from the male species."

"We're not all bad."

Cold flooded Cassie's chest even as warmth whispered over her skin. Slowly, she turned her head, her eyes narrowing as the object of her duplicitous thoughts walked up to the bar. A navy blue polo clung to his broad shoulders. His thick, dark brown hair had been combed to the side, but a few wayward strands fell over his forehead. Tan slacks were fitted perfectly to his muscular thighs.

The woman with the gin cocktail blinked as her mouth formed an O.

"Well…no, of course not. I just—"

"Had your heart broken by an idiot." Gideon sat on the stool next to her. "I agree with Cassandra, though. A lot to be said for making the most of a bad situation, Miss…"

"Ashley. Ashley Simmons."

Gideon held out his hand. "Gideon Radcliffe."

Ashley's eyelashes fluttered as she placed her fingers in his. "A pleasure, Mr. Radcliffe."

Gideon flashed a brilliant smile at Ashley. Cassie rolled her eyes even as something heavy settled like a stone in the pit of her stomach. Not jealousy. No, more like disgust that he would flirt with a woman who'd just been cheated on by her ex-fiancé.

Confirmation that despite his protests of innocence this morning, the man wasn't as innocuous as he made out.

Or any less of a saboteur.

The shiver that crept down her spine this time was anything but pleasant. She couldn't picture Mr. Custom Tailored Suit personally executing the little acts of sabotage that had been plaguing her the last two weeks, ever since she'd turned down Radcliffe Resorts' fourth offer. But the man had a personal fortune valued at well over a billion dollars. More than enough to hire someone to do his dirty work. Someone like his increasingly persistent representative Peter Zam, who had let his mask slip on his last visit and essentially threatened her before he'd left in a huff.

If she had any doubts about Gideon's capacity for ruthlessness, all she had to do was remember the recent lawsuit that had been in the news. Gideon had taken his own uncle to court, an uncle who by all accounts had kept Radcliffe Resorts running in the wake of Gideon's father's unexpected passing.

But Gideon hadn't been content sharing the wealth. He'd wanted it all.

Gideon's eyes cut away from Ashley, his gaze sharpening as he turned to Cassie.

"Good to see you again, Miss Everett."

Cassie reached under the bar and pulled out a bowl of carrots. "Good evening, Mr. Radcliffe." She pulled a knife out of a drawer, laid one of the carrots on a wooden cutting board and expertly sliced it halfway down the middle. "Can I have a drink sent out to you? Perhaps a table on the terrace would be more to your liking."

"I'd prefer to dine at the bar tonight."

"It gets pretty busy. The terrace—"

"Here." He shot her a cold smile. "Unless you would personally prefer I sit elsewhere?"

She narrowed her eyes at him. Oh, he was a slippery devil.

Ashley's gaze flitted between the two of them. "Um, I think I'm going to go out on the balcony." She stood, then paused. A flush crept up her neck. "It was nice to meet you, Gideon."

Cassie's shoulders dropped. The last thing she wanted was to make a customer uncomfortable, especially one who had been through the hell Ashley had.

"Sorry." She forced what she hoped was more of a smile than a grimace. "Mr. Radcliffe and I can continue our conversation later. Please stay."

"I actually wanted to see the sunset." Ashley's smile was kind. "But thank you." She held up her glass. "For everything." She nodded once more to Gideon, then disappeared behind the gauzy emerald curtains fluttering in the breeze.

Cassie resumed slicing, focusing on the rhythmic thud of the knife hitting the cutting board. She could feel Gideon's eyes on her, hated that her pulse kicked up. "Can I get you a drink?"

"What do you recommend?"

She nodded toward a red velvet book lying on the bar. "We have twelve specialty cocktails, an extensive wine list and a mix of local and imported beers."

"Do you have a favorite?"

She gritted her teeth. "All of them."

His low, husky chuckle rolled through her as he reached for the book. "I'll settle for one."

It was odd seeing his tan hands cradle the project she'd invested so much time into. The closest she'd come to achieving her true dream of writing her own story. As

Gideon turned the pages, long fingers tracing over the linen pages and embossed writing, Cassie forced herself to look away.

Get. A. Grip.

Yes, the man was handsome. But he wanted to take away the one thing she had left of her father. The only place that had ever been a true home. Turn it into a resort that would cater to the clientele he was used to—wealthy investors and entrepreneurs and corporate lawyers—instead of the people who enjoyed Moonrise Bay's farmers market, art shops, cozy restaurants and quiet beaches. A man like Gideon Radcliffe would bulldoze his way through the town she'd come to call home, building not only his own resort but changing the landscape of the Bay to fit his own narrow vision.

He was, she realized with a jolt, similar to her mother in that regard. Her mother had developed a reputation in her nearly thirty years as a corporate consultant. Kacey Smith always turned a profit for her clients, even if that meant altering the landscape of everything from a company's structure to an entire town. She'd enjoyed her profits, evidenced by the custom-designed mansion she had built in the Castle Pines neighborhood just outside Denver. But it had been prestige that had always driven her to take on more clients, to travel longer and farther even as she left her only daughter behind to be raised by a private nanny and tutor.

A daughter who had simply wanted her mother home to read her a story.

"I'll have what Miss Simmons was having."

Cassie started. "The Gatsby?"

He nodded, then cocked his head to one side when her eyebrows shot up.

"What?"

"Just surprised by your choice." She nodded toward the book. "I would have figured you more for The deVille or The Moriarty."

One thick brow arched up. "Villainous cocktails."

She pulled an emerald-colored glass down from the shelf. "I'm good at sizing up my customers, Mr. Radcliffe."

When she turned back around, she had to tighten her fingers around the stem so she didn't drop it. Gideon stared at her, his eyes blue chips of ice.

"You assume a lot of your customers."

She straightened her shoulders as she set the glass down carefully. "Assumptions based on observation and experience."

"It's a wonder any of them come back." He tilted his head to one side. "I don't have to be the villain in your story, Miss Everett."

Yeah, right.

After their tense conversation this morning, she had no doubt he'd do anything to get her property and move his plans forward.

Or at least instruct someone to do anything to get it.

She swallowed hard. The headlights flashing into her bedroom window at two in the morning. A hose being turned on and left running while she was at work. Flowerpots knocked over on her front porch. Mundane incidents, but ones that had never happened before until she'd rejected the last offer from Radcliffe Resorts.

The hose and the flowerpots had been frustrating. Except the headlights...

She ducked down behind the bar to pull the bottle of rose extract off a shelf and champagne out of the fridge, taking advantage of her position to suck in a shuddering breath. The headlights had frightened her. The cottage sat a quarter of a mile away from the main road. Someone had intentionally driven onto her property in the dead of night.

One quick breath in to steady herself. Then she stood, avoiding looking in Gideon's direction as she lined up her ingredients. If she kept moving, stayed busy, she didn't relive those awful moments when bright lights yanked her out of sleep, when her heart beat so hard she thought it would pound out of her chest as the driver had flashed the lights three times before gunning the engine and speeding back toward the road.

It had made her keenly aware of how alone she truly was out on the Point.

The worst part was none of it was enough to file a formal complaint. She was all but certain Peter Zam was behind it. In all the years she'd been visiting her father, and in the last six years of living here, they'd never had any issues with vandalism. The accidents had started two days after she'd rejected Peter's last offer, a rejection he had not taken well. That was more than just coincidence. She just couldn't prove it. Neither could she prove Gideon Radcliffe had orchestrated the whole campaign.

But I will. She had a security camera on order. Another good shift at Prose & Tide would give her enough money for another. One way or another, she would catch them.

Don't let him get to you.

She focused on the drink, the ingredients that created something magical.

"The Jazz Age." She pulled a bottle of gin down from the glass shelf behind her. "A time of joy, innovation and rebellion. One of the most well-known novels was written during this era—*The Great Gatsby*. Two of its main characters, Jay Gatsby and Daisy Buchanan, are the inspiration behind your drink."

As she talked, Cassie let herself drift into the past, into the world she had imagined as she had spent hours crafting the recipe. She took the bottle, the glass tinged a faint pink, and measured out a spoonful of syrup before pouring it into the bottom of the glass.

"A pinch of rose extract in honor of the bouquet Gatsby sent to Daisy, followed by gin to represent Jay." The faint scent of juniper drifted on the air as she uncorked the gin bottle. "A dominant flavor, yet also the most common alcohol produced during the nineteen twenties. Common like Jay Gatsby, who, even when he had everything—a mansion, riches—was never enough for the one person he wanted."

She inwardly cursed at the small hitch in her voice, at how she could feel Gideon's eyes shift from the glass to her.

"Our gin was distilled in Kansas City, known as the Paris of the Plains during Prohibition." She grabbed the wine bottle. "Sparkling white wine to represent Daisy—delicate, soft. Sourced from a vineyard in New York where the story takes place. A dash of lemonade, a summer ritual and a favorite luxury of Gatsby's." She plucked another daisy from the small bouquet on the bar top. "The finishing touch." She set the glass down in front of him. "Enjoy."

Gideon eyed the cocktail with a sardonic arch of one brow. "Was that lemonade or poison?"

Irritated, Cassie grabbed a shot glass, poured a splash of the cocktail into it and drank it. The complex flavors hit her tongue. She closed her eyes in appreciation and sighed. She could taste the elegance of a long-forgotten party, the sweetness of summer romance, the sharp bite of unrequited love. A story brought to life with a drink she'd created.

Not even Gideon Radcliffe would take away this pleasure from her.

Perhaps one day, she'd return to writing her own stories. Take another shot at getting published.

But for now, her second love was enough. A different kind of art, one she'd fallen in love with when she'd first arrived on the island and had taken a job bartending at a restaurant just a few miles from her father's cottage.

An art that had turned into a passion, something she could be proud of.

When she opened her eyes, she nearly choked. Gideon was staring at her, not with hard determination, but with an intimate curiosity she didn't care to examine too closely.

Their gazes held as he picked up the glass and took a sip. The intimacy of the moment, of watching surprise and pleasure brighten his eyes, had her looking away.

It had been way, way too long since she'd gone on a date.

Don't fall in lust with the pushy billionaire, Cassie.

He held the glass up, the golden lighting from the wall sconces highlighting the bubbles. "It's very good."

"Thanks."

Her reply was terse, overly so, but she didn't care. Having him trespass on her land had been violation enough. Having him here in her space, pitting her body's response against her rational mind, was too much.

"Professional mixologist."

Cassie froze.

"Online course out of New York, then a monthlong mixology course at the European Bartending School in London." He held the glass up to the light. "Head bartender and mixologist for Prose & Tide. Owner of Crescent Point and recently sold Moonrise Bay Water Sports, formerly belonging to John Everett."

"You've done your homework," she ground out even as guilt tied her chest in knots. Putting the shop up for sale had been one of the hardest decisions she'd ever made. John Everett had built his business from scratch. The shop her mother had sneeringly described as a "grungy shack on the beach" had brought her father more happiness and contentment than her mother had ever found in her high-paying, high-flying career.

But her father's medical bills had necessitated the sale of the shop, and even then the proceeds hadn't covered everything. Every time she passed by it on her way to work, to the grocery store, to anything, the sight of the familiar red-and-white awning tightened her chest with grief.

Another reason why she would cling to Crescent Point until her last breath. She wasn't going to let go of something else her father had maintained for so long until his body had turned on him. Not for easy money, and not without a damned good fight.

Gideon shrugged. "I need to know who I'm courting."

Her eyes widened as her heart fluttered. "Courting?"

"Professionally speaking. You came up with this recipe."

The sudden change in topic had her blinking like an owl. "Um...yes."

"It's good." He took another drink. "Very good."

The genuine appreciation in his tone grated on her nerves. Her mother had never once complimented her on her chosen profession. The few times they'd talked since Cassie had dropped out of the prestigious college business program her mother had essentially bullied her into, Kacey had dominated the conversation with tales of her friends' "successful" children while bemoaning Cassie's lack of initiative.

Just like your father. Lazy.

Yet, here was Gideon Radcliffe appreciating her work.

Cassie raised her chin. "You sound surprised."

"I'm surprised that someone who confronts a man with a spear when he's out for a simple walk can have such a creative and delicate touch with a drink." He glanced down at the book, traced a finger over the skillfully drawn figures dancing at the end of a dock. "Did you draw this, too?"

"A local artist." She paused, reined in her anger and the words she wanted to spit out. "You were trespassing."

"Is that how you confront all people who cross onto your property?"

She cast a quick eye over the bar. So far none of the few patrons in for the start of happy hour had noticed the byplay between her and Gideon. She tossed a towel over her shoulder and leaned forward.

"You and your minion won't take no for an answer.

Mr. Zam has been showing up on my doorstep, coming to my place of work, essentially stalking me for over four months, to get me to sell."

"Your neighbors—"

"Have their own reasons for selling." She told herself that, over and over, anytime tendrils of betrayal crept in. Moving to be closer to grandbabies, to take over a family business back in the States. Reasons she would understand far better if she didn't feel even more isolated as the land around her became a part of Gideon Radcliffe's holdings. "I have my own reasons for not."

"Not even for nine million?"

She nearly swallowed her tongue. Nine million would be more than enough to purchase land elsewhere on East End, build a stunning house and balance her schedule to allow for some time to finally sit down and write.

She'd lived in a multimillion-dollar home before. A stunning home with jaw-dropping views of the Rocky Mountains, her own private suite with a marble bathroom and a live-in maid, chef and butler who took care of her everyday needs while her mother jetted off around the world. A home that included a private classroom where tutors specializing in English, French, mathematics, science and music came to teach her everything her mother thought she'd need to know.

She'd lived in luxury for most of her life and loathed almost every second of it. None of it compared to the happiness she'd found in a seven-hundred-square-foot cottage with peeling paint and a roof that occasionally leaked during the rainier months. A place where she'd walked through a comforting, familiar door after she'd quit college, packed a few belongings and flown to Grand

Cayman with her mother's cruel insults ringing in her ears. The place where her father had wrapped her in a hug that smelled of sun and freshly cut wood as sun had streamed in through the oversize windows with views of the endlessly moving sea.

"Welcome home, Cassie."

She heard that deep, gravelly voice every time she walked through that door. After years of living in a house that felt more like a museum than a home, she wouldn't sell the first place where she'd finally felt accepted. Loved.

"No."

Gideon sat back in his chair, his hand still wrapped around the glass.

"Ten million."

"No."

"What would it take for you to sell?"

"Nothing you can offer."

"Everyone has a price, Miss Everett."

"Not everyone, Mr. Radcliffe." She leaned in. "You and Mr. Zam should remember that before you attempt another act of sabotage."

She could practically hear Gideon's spine snap as he sat straight up.

"What are you talking about?"

He almost sounded genuinely surprised. That and extremely ticked off.

"I've never had to have cameras up on my property, but I do now." A white lie, but a necessary one until she installed them. "If you, Mr. Zam or any other hired associates try anything else, I will file charges."

A group walked in, laughing and chattering as they made their way to the bar.

"I have never resorted to sabotage, Miss Everett."

Gideon's voice could have frozen hell as it whipped out, quiet enough not to attract attention but no less lethal.

"I don't care one way or the other, Mr. Radcliffe." She smiled at the advancing group as she murmured a warning out of the side of her mouth. "Leave me alone or I will contact the media and let them know my side of the story."

CHAPTER THREE

Gideon

GIDEON WATCHED AS Cassandra greeted the small crowd of college students who settled at a round table near the bar. Her smile was genuine, her voice welcoming as she passed out copies of the velvet-covered menu.

The woman was a conundrum. One he found increasingly mystifying, frustrating and intriguing.

After their encounter earlier, he'd driven back to the west end and ordered a background investigation into one Cassandra Everett. An hour later, he'd had an initial report in hand, including Cassandra's childhood spent with her mother in a small town outside Denver, her move to Grand Cayman after dropping out of college her sophomore year and the five years since that included her training as a bartender and a mixologist.

And that she now had a position at Prose & Tide, one of the highest-rated restaurants and cocktail bars on Grand Cayman. Perched on a rugged rocky cliff overlooking the waters of the West Bay, the establishment offered Caribbean dishes, soaring windows and unparalleled views of island sunsets, a terrace with flowering vines twining along the railing and the cocktail bar that served up drinks inspired by books.

An initiative, the website had noted, that was led by Cassandra when she'd been hired three years ago to oversee the new addition to Prose & Tide. A long drive by island standards—nearly forty-five minutes from Moonrise Bay to the restaurant. But Cassandra made it at least four times a week, sometimes five or six during the high tourist seasons, it seemed.

He cast a discreet eye around the room. Pale gray bookshelves lined the wall to his right, the lower shelves artfully adorned with books, seashells and flower arrangements. The upper shelves played host to bottles of wine, whiskey and other liquors. Judging by the faded labels and unique bottles, most likely rare and very expensive. Interesting choice of decor, he mused, for a woman who seemed to loathe money.

Floor-to-ceiling windows dominated the wall to his left and opened onto a balcony with tables and chairs offering views of the bay. The area behind him hosted a mix of seating, from high-tops with gleaming leather barstools to tables with deep green tufted chairs that invited customers to sit and enjoy the ambience of an old-fashioned library. And the bar itself was a work of art, the top crafted of speckled marble and topped with flickering votive candles.

Cassandra Everett had designed an impressive space—and even more impressive cocktails that had resulted in hundreds of five-star reviews online.

The profile shot on the restaurant's website had surprised him. Clad in a white, long-sleeved collared shirt, Cassandra had been pouring champagne into a tall flute dusted with what looked like sugar. Her brown curls had been pulled up into a bun on top of her head, her lips painted a subtle peachy pink.

But it had been her laughing smile, eyes sparkling and gazing right at the camera, that had punched him straight in the chest.

He'd come to Prose & Tide to scope out Cassandra in another environment, to observe the lone obstacle to his achieving his and his father's dream. Or at least that's what he'd told himself as he'd driven to the restaurant just twenty minutes north of the Radcliffe Resort at West End where he had booked the penthouse suite for the next month. This was business. Nothing more.

Except now, watching her talk about the menu, undeniable interest stirred and rippled through his body. When he'd left her this morning, he'd labeled her suspicious and aggressive at best. Yet seeing her here, listening to a woman pour out her heartaches and interacting with her customers like they were old friends, cast her in a different light.

One that didn't reconcile with the woman who'd held him at spearpoint this morning.

...remember that before you attempt another act of sabotage.

His hand tightened on the vintage glass Cassandra had poured her creative concoction into. She was lying. She had to be. That or she was attributing random acts of vandalism to his company. Either scenario was unacceptable and had to be dealt with. That and his burgeoning attraction to the woman who would be more suited to star as his sworn enemy than a potential lover.

He needed to stay focused. Keep his eye on the prize

of acquiring Crescent Point and off the intriguing Cassandra Everett. His attraction was understandable given that he hadn't been on a date in months. Since before the case went before the judge, he realized with some surprise. But his passing interest in Cassandra had no relevance to his current goal.

What did interest him was the state of her finances. She had a little in savings from the sale of her father's water sports shop. But most had gone toward paying his medical bills. The cottage, too, wasn't in the best shape. A couple of discreet inquiries had revealed that her small home with peeling paint and cracked windows wouldn't stand up to the next storm that came through.

So why, he mused, was she saying no to $10 million?

His eyes narrowed as one of the college boys gazed up and down Cassandra's svelte form. She wore the same uniform as she had in her profile picture: long-sleeved white shirt, slim black pants that hugged her legs and her hair pulled into a bun at the top of her head. Errant curls sprang free, adding a touch of whimsy to her professional appearance. Cute.

No, he grudgingly admitted. *Beautiful.*

Gideon's jaw hardened as the young man said something that made Cassandra laugh.

So different from the welcome he'd received when he arrived at the bar. From the moment she'd seen him, her anger had been swift. She'd barely managed to keep her frustration in check.

Yet, each interaction he witnessed deepened his curiosity. Every reaction, every look was sincere, genuine emotion. Even the indignation she'd leveled at him.

The smart thing to do would be to walk away. Talk to

Peter, find out his side of the story and if he knew anything of so-called sabotage, and then revise the plan. Given his reaction to Cassandra, having Peter take over again would be best.

Except every time he contemplated delegating and walking away, he resisted.

Because this is mine. He raised his glass to his lips and drank. *My father's dream. My mission.*

His choice had nothing to do with an intractable young woman with wild curls and a feisty smile. Nothing except besting a challenging puzzle.

More like a thorn in my side.

Cassandra finished her spiel to the group and walked back toward the bar, her smile evaporating as she glanced at Gideon.

"Sabotage is a serious charge, Miss Everett."

The warmth he'd glimpsed as she'd greeted her new customers was gone, replaced by a determined glint in her golden-brown eyes.

"Yes. Imagine how I felt when I woke up to headlights flashing into my window in the dead of night."

He froze. "Did someone try to break in?"

She looked away. "No."

He narrowed his eyes. "Cassandra—"

"They didn't." Her breath came out in a rush. "They flashed their lights three times, then drove off when I went to the door. It was cloudy that night, so all I could see were taillights disappearing down the drive. I sat up the rest of the night. I would have known if they had come back."

Her voice was strong, calm. Yet he could hear the fear that had clung to her that night, could almost feel the pounding of her heart. Growing up in New York City, he was used to car lights, horns honking, sirens blaring. What would it be like to be so used to nothing but the faint roar of the ocean, to be isolated away from everyone, and be awoken by something that, however seemingly harmless, made you feel unsafe in your own home?

His hand flexed against the bar as anger started to burn low in his gut.

"Did you call the police?"

"Of course I did." She turned and stretched up, pulling down several glasses from the crystal shelves behind the bar, her movements smooth and confident. "They walked around, confirmed there were tire tracks in the mud. But there was little to go on. They only had my word that the driver flashed his lights. They theorized it was a drunk tourist or someone playing a prank. Hence my recently installed cameras."

"You said the sabotage had gotten worse the last week. How so?"

"My pots of bougainvillea tipped over and broken. A hose left on all day that ruined my vegetable garden and saddled me with a huge water bill."

"Hmm." His lips curved into a slight smile. "Acts nothing but a ruthless, billion-dollar company could be behind."

Her eyes narrowed before she turned and grabbed two more glasses. "One or two is an accident. Four is either intentional or coincidental enough I should consider playing the lottery."

"I'll buy you a lottery ticket next time I'm Stateside, Miss Everett." He leaned back, secure once more on confident ground. "I don't stoop to childish pranks. Nor does anyone who works for Radcliffe Resorts. A cat or a strong wind could have knocked over your flowerpots. Hoses get left on by accident."

"I didn't imagine the headlights," she ground out.

"No." Unease slithered into his gut. Despite her prickly exterior, he didn't like the thought of her out on the Point, set back from the road and a solid half mile from her nearest neighbor. "Unruly vacationers, a teenager doing something stupid on a dare?"

She leveled a hard gaze on him. "Once or twice, maybe. But for the past two weeks, I've gone home almost every day to something wrong. My porch chair facing the other way, a bird feeder moved. Little things slowly eating away at me until I dread going home."

Her voice pitched on the final word. Either Cassandra Everett was one hell of an actress, or someone was being incredibly cruel. It went a long way toward explaining her aggressive greeting this morning.

She cleared her throat. "It got worse last week. Then the final straw—waking me up in the dead of night, reminding me that I'm alone out there." She ducked down behind the bar, reappearing moments later with several bottles. "Some might get so scared they think it's no longer worth it, especially with a multimillion-dollar offer just waiting."

Given the timeline of events, he would have probably jumped to a similar conclusion.

"I would have probably wondered the same thing. But," he stressed as she looked at him, "sabotage is not something I would resort to."

"From what I understand, Mr. Radcliffe, there isn't

much you wouldn't do. You took your own uncle to court."

Red colored his vision at the thinly veiled disgust in her voice. His empathy evaporated. "So it's not a stretch to think of you applying pressure to the lone holdout standing in your way of a resort that would completely change the environment of Moonrise Bay."

"I'm not discounting your fear." She opened her mouth to retort, but he cut her off. "But think about it, Cassandra. Truly think about it. Why would I risk such an immense project, my first after the trial, to commit a few acts of vandalism? You claim to know me based on the media coverage. Does that sound like something I'd do?"

She straightened, her gaze still hard but now with the tiniest trace of uncertainty.

"What I would do is go to the chamber of commerce and network with your community. Address their fears, identify ways I could give back. Make them want Radcliffe to become a part of Moonrise Bay so now you have not only your own mind whispering that selling is the right thing to do, but your neighbors, too." One corner of his mouth curved up. "Increase my offer until there was no way you could logically say no."

With a frustrated sigh, she resumed her work. He watched as she lined up the glasses, a mix of wine, highball and coupe glassware, then started pouring. She didn't hesitate, didn't even glance at a recipe book. Just measured and poured with precision as she moved down the line.

"Do you have every recipe memorized?"

"Yes."

"How do you come up with the recipes?"

She cast him a suspicious glance. "I read. Come up with ingredients that fit the story, a character, a setting. Then I start mixing."

One corner of his mouth twitched. He could easily picture Cassandra here late at night or early in the morning, a book on the bar as she poured various bottles into a glass trying to find the right balance.

"What do you like to read?"

"Anything." Her voice relaxed a fraction, her face softening as she sprinkled rose petals across the surface of a lavender-tinged cocktail. "Mystery, romance, science, fantasy."

"Why do you think I would change Moonrise Bay?"

Her shoulders tensed. "Trying to relax me before you interrogate me again?"

"Partially. Curiosity, too."

"The Bay gets its share of tourists. It's a nice balance of locals and vacationers. We keep the integrity of the town, enough business to support our local restaurants, galleries and shops, but not so much as to clog the streets or price our residents out of their own homes."

"Have you considered Radcliffe could enhance Moonrise Bay?"

The swift, sudden disappointment on her face surprised him.

"What?"

A heavy sigh escaped her lips. "You just remind me of someone."

For the past five months, Gideon had sat in a courtroom, one where the uncle who had sat next to him at Thanksgiving and cheered him on at football games had lied to the judge, the courtroom and the media as he'd painted Gideon as a spoiled brat who had dumped everything on Steven's shoulders while he'd partied his way through college. Each new slander had hardened Gideon's already closed-off heart. Cemented the certainty that he would never be able to fully let someone in again.

But now, one comment from a curly-haired firebrand pierced through his armor like an arrow straight to the heart of its target. He wanted to ask who, wanted to know who had put the sadness in her eyes, the disappointment in her voice. It mattered.

Which is why he stayed silent. Really, this conversation was a blessing. Cassandra might be more than he had first judged her to be. But she, too, judged quickly, not looking beyond the surface. The novelty of her resistance, of her, would fade in time. Better to acknowledge that now than to let himself be pulled in even further.

An exclamation had him turning around. A bachelorette party had entered the bar, the bride-to-be sporting a sash that proudly proclaimed her role in glittering pink letters as she fawned over the tables, the books, the brass chandeliers.

He pulled out his wallet and reached inside. "I'll leave you to your customers, Miss Everett."

She nodded towards the money in his hand. "Drink's on the house."

Her smile may have been sweet for the benefit of her customers, but her words were sharp and clear as glass. She had no interest in his money.

"A tip, then. For you and your staff."

He suppressed a grin at the thinning of her lips as he

laid the bill on the bar. He plucked the daisy from his cocktail and held it up in salute.

"Until next time, Miss Everett."

He moved past the bachelorette party, nodded in response to the giggles of some of the bridesmaids as he headed toward the door. He'd wasted five years on the lawsuit. If he hadn't been fighting his uncle in court, he would have been down in Grand Cayman himself, establishing connections and closing deals. Now it was time to wage war.

He dialed Peter's number as he walked out of Prose & Tide and into the parking lot.

"Sir?" Peter's voice still sounded raspy and slightly nasally, but much improved over last week.

"Feeling better?"

Peter sneezed. "Some, sir."

Gideon bit back a smile. His father had once described Peter as "loyal to a fault." The man lived and breathed Radcliffe Resorts, had focused on little else ever since Gideon's father had hired him. He had alerted Gideon to the money that had gone missing under Steven's leadership, had gathered evidence of all of Steven's misdeeds.

Radcliffe Resorts had survived because of him.

"Good. We need to meet tonight. Eight o'clock."

"Yes, sir. Your suite?"

"You're staying one floor below me, Peter. I'll come to you. No sense in making you get out while you're still ill."

"I'm not…" Peter's voice trailed off right before he let out another loud sneeze. "Perhaps that would be best, sir. Anything specific I should prepare for?"

"Any contact you've had with Cassandra Everett, for starters."

Peter sighed. "The woman is a nuisance."

Gideon smiled slightly. "I noticed."

"You've met her?"

"Twice today."

"I'm sorry, sir. Had I known you were going to see her, I would have—"

"Stayed right where you are." He glanced back over his shoulder at the white columns flanking the dark green doors of the restaurant. "Peter, she's accusing Radcliffe Resorts of sabotaging her property."

"What?"

"Minor accidents, it sounds like. Most explained by natural causes. The one that wasn't was most likely an overeager tourist or a teenager playing a stupid prank."

"Like I said, sir, she's a menace."

Gideon paused. There was something off in Peter's voice, a thread of anger Gideon had never heard before.

He shook his head. He was letting Cassandra get to him. Of course Peter was angry. He hadn't just worked for Gideon's father; he'd been a loyal friend, too.

Peter wasn't just doing his job by purchasing the land. He genuinely cared, wanted to see his old friend's wish come true almost as much as Gideon did.

But, Gideon acknowledged, even if his intentions were noble, that wouldn't excuse using nefarious means.

"Yes. But she's also recently lost her father." Gideon's voice hardened a fraction. "That wasn't included in your report."

Peter cleared his throat. "With everything you were dealing with in court—"

"That wasn't your decision to make." He let silence hang between them for a moment. He owed Peter so much. But the second someone started to hold back truth, relationships started to fracture. "I appreciate the intent. But intentions don't matter if it torpedoes the deal. We could have moved on Miss Everett from a very different angle if I had known the full circumstances of her situation."

"I'm sorry, sir."

He heard the genuine regret in Peter's voice. Yes, Peter had made a mistake. But given that it was the first mistake Gideon could remember him making in over twenty years with the company, and that Peter had been trying to protect him, he would let it go and move on.

"Thank you. I'll see you at eight o'clock."

Gideon hung up as he walked out to his rental, a gleaming red Corvette convertible. He stopped by the door, closed his eyes and lowered his head as an unexpected ache hit him square in the chest. It shouldn't have been like this. He and his uncle could have realized his father's dream together.

When his mother had been admitted to the hospital for a suspected stroke, his father had fallen apart. It had been Steven who had stayed with Gideon throughout the night, who had handled all of the details when Cecilia had finally passed. It had been Steven who walked through the door so many times over the next year to talk to Gideon's father, to try to convince him to do something, anything, besides succumb to grief.

But power had corrupted. Once Steven had tasted what it was like to be in control, he'd placed his greed above everything else.

Including his last surviving family.

Gideon breathed in, then opened his eyes. He would get Peter's update. Note down any information he was still missing as he reviewed the file his investigative team had put together on Cassandra. Then he would craft a new plan, one that would ensure Crescent Point was his before summer's end.

And bury his personal interest in Cassandra Everett once and for all.

CHAPTER FOUR

Cassie

UPBEAT GUITAR MUSIC wound its way over the small crowd gathered on the wooden balcony of Marla's Cantina, a Mexican restaurant perched on one of Moonrise Bay's picturesque beaches. Waitresses in bright yellow, blue and red shirts moved among the members of the local chamber of commerce, offering up appetizers like fried plantain chips with guacamole and shredded jerk chicken sopes.

Cassie inhaled deeply, savored the varied scents of the restaurant that almost eclipsed the lingering salt in the air. Working here first as a waitress, then as a bartender, had kick-started Cassie's love of mixology. Marla hadn't just been a great boss; she'd been an incredible friend.

"Cassie!"

Marla approached, her megawatt smile etching creases into the tanned skin by her eyes. Her silver hair hung over one shoulder in a thick plait.

"Hi, Marla."

Marla enveloped her in a warm hug. "I didn't think you'd make it."

Cassie steeled herself. "It's been a while since I've been to a chamber luncheon."

"Five months." Marla's dark brown eyes softened. "No one would blame you if you needed to take longer."

Heat stung Cassie's eyes. "I appreciate that. But I think being here will help. Although I'm not sure if I still qualify as a member since I don't own Dad's shop anymore—"

"Nonsense. You and your father were an integral part of this community. Who knows, maybe one day you'll open a bar on this side of the island."

Cassie inwardly winced. More than one person had expressed frustration that she drove over forty minutes one way to work at a restaurant on the opposite side of the island instead of opening a business in Moonrise Bay.

But no one here had offered the financial backing the owners of Prose & Tide had, or the freedom for Cassie to do whatever she wanted with the decor and, most importantly, the menu. She loved the idea of opening her own bar on this side of the island, perhaps even combining it with a bookstore for vacationers looking to relax on a beach with a well-crafted cocktail and a good book.

But the vacationers who came to Moonrise Bay preferred fun, casual cocktails. Not the intricate and expensive concoctions she created.

Have you considered Radcliffe could improve Moonrise Bay?

Guilt pricked the back of her neck. She didn't like the possibility that Gideon Radcliffe may be right. Her father had been an active member of the Bay's chamber, trying initiatives like advertising in the island's airport and offering a shuttle to bring more business to East End.

Was she holding on to Crescent Point because it was the right thing to do? Or because she was being selfish?

Marla pressed a cool glass into her hand, the rim dusted with chili powder.

"Limonada picante. Soothing with a kick." She patted Cassie on the shoulder. "If you need to step outside and take a breath, please do. We're excited to have you here, but only if it brings you happiness."

Cassie swallowed past the lump in her throat. "Thank you."

Marla moved on to greet other guests. The lump in Cassie's throat persisted, so she quietly moved to the far end of the balcony and down the spiral staircase to the beach below. Voices rose and fell. The music played on. But the small distance gave Cassie a chance to breathe, to collect herself.

The last time she had come to a chamber meeting had been an evening dinner right before her father had traveled to Texas. Five weeks, the doctor had said. Then he could come home. They'd both been hopeful. For the first time in forever, there had been color in his cheeks, excitement in his eyes. He'd still been weak, his clothes hanging off his skeletal frame, his voice still hoarse.

But he'd talked as best he could, laughed with old friends, even danced with her on the balcony just before they'd left.

One tear broke free, rolled down her cheek as she walked out onto the dock. She'd driven him to the airport the next morning. He'd kissed her cheek and told her they'd go on a trip when he got back.

"Venice," he'd said as he'd eased down into the wheelchair she'd arranged for him. "Or Paris."

She'd started to tell him after they paid off the bills, after they finally made repairs to the cottage. But one glance at his face, at the hope in eyes so much like hers it was like looking in a mirror, had stilled the words on her tongue. She'd always be grateful that she'd simply leaned down, kissed his forehead and told him Venice sounded perfect.

More tears fell as she reached the end of the dock and eased down into one of the brightly painted Adirondack chairs that looked out over the ocean, the sun-warmed wood cradling her in a gentle embrace. They'd had every summer together since she'd been eight years old, plus the last five years. Five years that had brought her more joy and contentment than she'd ever thought possible.

The sun gently caressed her skin. A sharp contrast to the frigid winters of Colorado. Perhaps, if her mother had been at home and taken Cassie out to build a snowman or go sledding, she'd have different memories of the season. But all she remembered was the cold, being stuck inside her mausoleum of a mansion with only the servants for company. On snowy days when her tutors hadn't been able to navigate the long, winding drive up to the house, she'd completed her homework as quickly as possible so she could write.

She wrote stories about a princess locked away in a tower by an evil witch. Stories of a brave warrior who ventured out into the snowy lands surrounding her kingdom.

And she wrote to her dad. A faceless man who existed solely in her imagination until her eighth birthday when her mother had finally let her meet him. It had been one of the few times reality had trumped any dream, when her father had swept her up in a hug with tears in his eyes and told her he was so sorry for missing out on the first few years of her life.

Her fingers tightened on the silky-smooth wood of the armrest. She'd asked her mother over and over about her dad, why he wasn't a part of their life. Her mother had always deflected. Sometimes it had been that her father lived far away. Other times it was that he wasn't suitable to be a father.

To this day, Cassie didn't know why her mother had changed her mind and finally told John their brief romance had resulted in a child. But Cassie would always remember the way her father had stared at her, tears in his eyes, when he'd come to their house in Colorado. How he'd held her so tightly against his chest and kissed her hair.

She remembered, too, creeping out of her bedroom that night and hearing them arguing in the living room downstairs. How her mother had accused him of not being suitable enough to be a father, and her father had replied that her mother's expectations were too high for anyone to reach.

How he'd demanded summers with his daughter.

Cassie's lips curved into a smile even as she sucked in a shuddering breath. Her mother had agreed to summers. And so had begun some of the happiest times of her life. She'd lived for summer, for those blissful two and a half months when she'd run wild over the Point, help her dad out at the shop, learn to snorkel and then eventually dive beneath the waves. Every time she'd gone back to Colorado, it had felt like leaving a part of her soul behind.

And when she'd finally accepted that it didn't matter how many honors courses she took or internships she completed, that her mother would always demand more, it had been her father who had supported her and loved her. Who had made a tiny house into more than her mother's mansion had ever offered.

Her eyes fluttered open. How could she give up Crescent Point? Relinquish one of the few places in the world where she had belonged?

As her tears slowed, she became aware of a prickling sensation between her shoulder blades. She reached up and brushed them away before abruptly turning around.

Gideon Radcliffe stood on the balcony, staring down at her. Heat suffused her cheeks before creeping down her neck. God, why did she react like this? She'd dated a bit in college, gone on a few dates here on the island. But no one had made her feel like this: unsettled, distracted, feverish. Certainly not someone she should hate. Did hate.

Humiliation burned a slow trail in her stomach as she glanced back out toward the sea. Had he seen her crying? Did he think it was over him, over the pressure he and his crony Peter had placed on her? The man already had a fortune at his fingertips and a relentless determination to claim her land for himself. She didn't need to give him any more ammo. The man had the tenacity of a bull shark. As soon as he scented any type of weakness, he would strike.

Although, she thought as more guilt settled in her stomach like a heavy stone, she'd hurt him yesterday. The flash of pain when she'd mentioned the trial had been so quick she'd almost missed it.

But it had been there. And, she was forced to admit, what did she really know? When she'd gone digging for information on Gideon, she'd gravitated toward the negative news that had surrounded him for the past few years. Every article had confirmed her own bias, made her feel justified in telling Peter Zam to take his offers and jump off the end of a dock. She'd compared him to her mother, likened his need to bring a resort to her mother's insatiable desire for prestige and profit.

But what if you're wrong?

She couldn't be wrong. If she was, it would open the door to more doubt, would shake the foundation of her resolve.

Steadying herself, she stood and faced the shore. Gideon was still at the railing. He raised his glass of lemonade. She gritted her teeth even as she nodded in case anyone else was watching. The people she talked with before her father had passed had wanted nothing to do with Radcliffe Resorts. There were a few business owners who disagreed, who had made their frustration with her refusal to sell more than clear. But most had seemed to agree Moonrise Bay was not the sort of place that needed a luxury resort.

Had that changed?

...now you have not only your own mind whispering that selling is the right thing to do, but your neighbors, too...

She managed to keep her face calm as she walked back down the dock, her eyes fixed on the lower level of the restaurant and off Gideon. Was that why he was here? To make good on his threat and use other methods to pressure her into selling? Chamber luncheons were only open to members and invited guests. Had Gideon simply shown up and pressured his way in?

Or worse, Cassie thought as her stomach dropped, had someone invited him?

As she neared the beach, she knew the moment he looked away, felt his eyes leave her like a physical snapping inside her chest. Irritated, she took the stairs quicker than normal and sought out Marla. It took several minutes, and a few conversations with people she hadn't seen in a while, before she finally tracked the chamber president down inside the upper level of the restaurant where lunch and the day's program would be held.

Arched windows let in natural light that made the terra-cotta tiles gleam. Each table had been draped in a white tablecloth, a stark contrast to the azure-colored chairs and booths. Glass vases overflowed with red-and-white hibiscus blooms. Marla stood at the back, uncovering chafing dishes filled with coconut rice, Caribbean roasted sweet potatoes, Mexican street corn salad and shredded jerk pork. She smiled at Cassie.

"Did you enjoy the lemonade?"

"I did. Marla, why is Gideon Radcliff here?"

Marla bobbed her eyebrows up and down. "Handsome, isn't he?"

"Nice on the outside doesn't mean nice on the inside."

The humor vanished from Marla's face. "He contacted me this morning and asked if he could speak right after lunch today."

Cassie's mouth dropped open. *What?*

She waited for the punch line. Except it didn't come. Of all the people who knew Cassie, and her father's wishes about Crescent Point, Marla had been nothing but supportive of her decision not to sell.

Shocked, betrayed, Cassie tried to formulate her words. "How could you?"

"Cassie, this is bigger than you. Bigger than the Point."

Marla rubbed absently at her temple. "Regardless of whether you sell or not, Mr. Radcliffe will build something here in Moonrise Bay."

Cassie thought of the property next to hers, just under three acres of woodland with its own white sandy beach. She could hear the loud music, envisioning the drunken guests that would stumble onto her property. And knew she had no recourse.

"Do you really think this is what's best?"

The usual sparkle that was present in Marla's eyes dimmed a fraction. "I don't know. I do know land on East End has surged in value. I know in ten years the island is not going to look the way we know it now."

Cassie looked out one of the windows. Beyond the people milling around the balcony, the calm waves of the Caribbean caressed the shore. Just a few years ago, she had dreamed of change, craved it. But now the thought of it made her want to crawl into bed and pull the covers over her head.

There was far too much change occurring, change that was out of her control. Change that catapulted her back to the little girl she had been, one who had spent at least two-thirds of her time at home with a private nanny as her mother had jetted off around the world. She had never known when her mother would be home next, if she would leave right before a band concert or a dance recital or any of the other numerous activities her mother had pushed her into.

The only things she'd been able to depend on for twelve years were her summers at Crescent Point and her father. She'd already lost one. And now, with each passing day, she felt dangerously close to losing the second. A gentle hand on her arm made her head snap up.

"I will always support your choice, Cassie." Marla gave her a gentle squeeze. "However, I do like Gideon far more than that associate of his, Mr. Zam. I've done some digging into his other properties. I've heard nothing but good things."

The words were meant to reassure. But they landed with the force of a blow to her chest. Deepened the fear that she was judging the man because it was easier than to truly evaluate Gideon Radcliffe and his offer.

"I'm... I'm lost, Marla. I don't know what to do. I know what I want to do," she amended quietly, "but I don't know what the right choice is."

"You have some time. Listen to him today. Depending on how that goes, either listen some more or don't. At the end of the day, Crescent Point is yours and yours alone to do with what you see fit."

People started to stream in, giving Cassie a welcome reprieve from the intense conversation. She moved toward the table at the back and settled in.

She wanted to believe the worst. That alone was enough for her to know she had navigated the last twenty-four hours in a way she wasn't proud of. She'd been inside the Radcliffe Resort on the island's west end, had experienced a fraction of the luxury on a date to one of the resort's restaurants. Sleek lines, soaring ceilings, marble floors and polished coral stone walls decorated with a mix of local and international art, each painting dedicated to an ocean theme. The exterior was equally stunning, from the terraced pools to the perfectly manicured gardens. A beautiful resort. Just not the kind of place that would fit Moonrise Bay's laid-back culture.

But, Cassie resolved, she would do what she had so often accused her mother of not doing. She would at least listen.

Awareness prickled over her skin as Gideon walked into the room. His eyes immediately found hers, his gaze opaque as he stared at her. Searching, evaluating. She raised her glass to him before turning her head away and staring out the window, mentally preparing herself for whatever was to come next.

CHAPTER FIVE

Gideon

THE ROOM ERUPTED into applause. Gideon smiled and inclined his head, sweeping his gaze over the space and leaving the corner where Cassandra had sat for last. Her applause was noticeably less energetic but still polite. Dark shadows beneath her eyes spoke to her fatigue. Her shoulders were slumped, as if she couldn't bear to hold them up anymore.

His presentation had been effective. He'd asked Marla for five minutes, nothing more. He'd started it as his father had always encouraged him to: with blunt honesty. He'd apologized for moving forward with the dream that he and his father had envisioned for so many years without talking to the people it would affect the most. He'd acknowledged that most of the properties he had managed since taking the helm had been renovations of existing hotels or, in the case of some of the newer resorts, property that had been up for sale by a real estate office or business.

After apologizing for the missteps, he had concluded with a brief summary of his vision for a new resort at Moonrise Bay with an emphasis on collaborating with local businesses to elevate their hard work and blending seamlessly into the town. More than one expression had transformed from steely-eyed glare to thoughtful contemplation.

He had made significant progress in a small amount of time. But his sense of accomplishment was noticeably dim as he turned over the podium to the guest speaker for the day.

He didn't like worrying about Cassandra Everett. The woman was more than capable of taking care of herself. But the two times he'd spoken with her, there'd been a fire in her eyes, a vitality that had drawn him in even as he'd resisted.

Now, as he made his way through the maze of tables and people, all he saw was defeat.

She glanced up at him as he stopped at her table. "Well spoken, Mr. Radcliffe."

There was no malice in her voice. Only a resignation that tugged at his conscience.

He gestured to the empty chair at her table. "May I?"

Her eyes flickered to the side. He could imagine how many people were watching them out of the corners of their eyes, or even openly staring. At her reluctant nod, he pulled out a chair and sat, his back to the room. He wasn't speaking to her as a performance for the audience behind him. This conversation was for her and her alone.

For business, he told himself. *Apologize. Re-establish trust. Move toward the goal.*

"I spoke with Peter last night."

A hint of emotion crossed her face. "And?"

"He denied any sabotage, as I expected he would. But," he added, irritation creeping into his voice, "he acknowledged there were times he came across as heavy-handed or perhaps pressuring."

When he'd met with Peter the previous evening, it had only taken a few minutes of questioning for Peter to admit he'd lost his temper and even come close to verbally threatening Cassandra. A fact Peter had murmured in such a quiet voice Gideon had barely heard him.

It had taken all of Gideon's self-control not to lose his own temper. Intimidation and threats were tactics Steven had resorted to in his last few years. Still, Gideon reminded himself, Peter had been under intense pressure. Peter had worked for Gideon's father. He knew how important the Moonrise Bay development had been to Lee Radcliffe.

"Menacing or threatening is more how I would describe it," Cassandra murmured.

"I'm sorry." Gideon kept his voice low, his attention focused on Cassandra as her eyes widened. "At no time was Peter under any orders to intimidate the owners. If anyone was not interested in selling, his instructions were to communicate that to me so that I could deal with it once I was done with court. He overstepped. He broke my trust and pressured someone who should have been treated with respect."

Cassandra sighed and leaned back into her booth. "You confuse me, Mr. Radcliffe," she said after a long moment.

"Likewise."

His comment startled a chuckle from her, soft and husky, a sound that filled him with warmth. It was, he realized with a start, the first time she'd smiled at him or laughed at what he said without anger sharpening the gesture.

"I don't want to sell."

"I understand. You don't want to sell for the same reason I want to buy—family, legacy." He started to mention what his investigation had uncovered about her mounting bills. But now was not the time or place. Not when they were having their first borderline-friendly conversation.

"Allow me a couple hours of your time. To share what I envision for the Point, perhaps even discuss ways we could preserve some of what you and your father created. Find a way to support Moonrise Bay. A compromise."

Her eyes shifted again to something over his shoulder. Not something, he realized as he glanced behind him, but someone. Marla. The older woman was focused on the speaker, her elegant profile framed by the low lighting in the restaurant.

"She said I should hear you out."

Gideon turned back to Cassandra. "You're close?"

"Very. I trust her more than my own mother."

A telling comment. But before Gideon could pursue it further, Cassandra nodded once, the gesture sharp and decisive, almost as if she were forcing herself.

"Two hours."

He barely managed to bite back a smile. "Do you work tomorrow?"

"Yes. Until six."

"I can pick you up—"

"No." She cleared her throat. "No. I can meet you somewhere."

"Six thirty, then? I know a place a few miles north of Prose & Tide. I can text you the address."

Slowly, she nodded. She inputted the phone number he rattled off into her phone before holding out her hand. Electricity crackled up his arm as his fingers wrapped around hers. Her head snapped up as her eyes widened, fixed on his. He held on to her, rooted to the spot by the need to know this woman more, by the desire to hold her hand for just a moment longer.

"Tomorrow, Miss Everett." He stood and inclined his head as if his world hadn't just been turned upside down. "Until then."

He wasn't fleeing, he assured himself. He nodded to Marla and walked out of the cool restaurant and into the warm, midday Caribbean heat.

He breathed in, then out until his pulse slowed. He'd succeeded. Turned the tide of public opinion in his favor. Secured a meeting with his nemesis.

A nemesis who had been sitting on the end of the dock, distancing herself from the crowd as she'd grieved. He hadn't missed the swipe of her hand across her cheeks, the sheen of smeared tears on her skin as she'd neared the shore.

Nor had he missed the, albeit reluctant, change in her attitude. Knowing she was trying to do what she thought was best tugged at his own resolve. It wasn't just his father's commitment to legacy. He genuinely believed a Radcliffe Resort could be a positive addition to Moonrise Bay. Certainly better than other whispers he'd heard of, ideas of development that would turn the east side of the island into a mirror of the west end's upscale atmosphere or a maze of villas and town houses that would spread, eating up the last bits of wilderness left on the island's shores.

But Cassandra's genuine grief made him question, doubt. Just as her show of strength rekindled the interest he thought he'd smothered when he'd walked out of Prose & Tide.

A natural reaction, he reassured himself. The stakes were high, emotions even higher. His last date had been over half a year ago, and it had been overshadowed by the impending trial. He hadn't even bothered calling the woman back for a second date. There had been no point, no room in his life for even a casual relationship.

His reaction to Cassandra, this attraction pulsing inside him, was natural. Controllable, he reassured himself as he climbed into his convertible.

It had to be.

CHAPTER SIX

Cassie

WHAT AM I DOING?

That had to be the seventy-eighth time Cassie had asked herself that question since Gideon had walked out of Marla's restaurant yesterday. The rest of the chamber program had barely registered as she'd sat there, shocked by both her agreement to a meeting and the lingering swirl of sensation in her hand from when she and Gideon had touched.

She glanced at her GPS and frowned. Was a new restaurant opening out here? She only knew of villas, a couple parks, and a beach with a dock. Confused, suspicious, she pulled into the parking lot.

And slammed her brakes when she saw the luxurious fifty-foot catamaran tied to the end of the dock.

Excitement flared to her life in her chest before she could squelch it.

God, this isn't a romance novel.

And how many times, she thought bitterly, had she reminded herself of that? Romance had been her preferred genre when she'd written. Even as a kid, she'd been obsessed with happily-ever-afters and true love conquering all.

But, she thought darkly as she eyed the catamaran, sometimes Prince Charming was really the villain in disguise.

Regardless of what happened with Crescent Point, Gideon would leave the island sooner rather than later. Yes, he had broken through her defenses. Happened upon the moment when she'd been in a state of inner turmoil and open to a conversation that, just forty-eight hours ago, she never could have pictured herself having.

But, as Marla had said, the choice was ultimately hers. "Mine," she said out loud.

Mine. Not his.

She pulled into a parking space, turned off the engine and glanced around. The lot was situated between two homes, both newer construction with soaring privacy fences. A beach stretched out in front of her, dotted with palm trees, a couple of picnic tables and a long dock that extended out into the bay. The catamaran bobbed up and down at the far end of the dock, its hull painted a gleaming white.

Her phone buzzed. She glanced down at the screen, ignoring the slight uptick in her pulse at the message that flashed on her screen.

I'll meet you at the end of the dock.

Was the man spying on her with binoculars? Irritated, she got out, locked her car and struck out down the beach.

The catamaran might as well have had a sash draped over the mast that said *I'm very expensive.* From the large gleaming cabin windows and sleek lines to the elevated flybridge and underwater lights glowing a pale shade of lavender just beneath the water's surface, the price of the boat could have paid for her to renovate the entire cottage, if not just buy a new one and have it plunked down on the Point.

Cassie smoothed a hand over the skirt of her dress. She'd imagined dinner would be something at least moderately fancy, if not expensive. It had taken four tries before she'd finally settled on a spaghetti-strapped dress with a straight bodice and full skirt. Nice enough for any of the exclusive restaurants in west end, but not over the top.

No, she thought irritably, that would be the silver sandals and delicate matching hoops she'd grabbed on her way out. Vanity had trounced pride, a fact that still ate at her as she neared the end of the dock.

Gideon stood at the helm talking with a man in a crisp white uniform. Probably the captain. Gideon glanced in her direction, then did a double take. A slow smile spread across his face as she drew near that had blood rushing to her cheeks. He murmured something else to the captain before descending the stairs. Her skin grew hot as she took in his outfit; a white dress shirt molded to his muscular chest and tan slacks tailored perfectly to his long legs.

She bit down on the inside of her lip.

Down, girl.

"Good evening."

"Hello, Mr. Radcliffe." There, that sounded professional and cool. She paused at the gangplank. "Permission to come aboard?"

"Granted."

He held out a hand as she stepped onto the walkway. She hesitated, her eyes seeking out his. There was challenge in the blue depths of his gaze, as well as an acknowledgment of the mutual attraction that had flared between them yesterday.

She braced herself and then placed her hand in his. The sensation of skin on skin, of warmth and the slight, surprising roughness of his palm, sent a shiver down her spine. But the lack of reaction on Gideon's part helped her rein in her response.

"Thank you." She pulled her hand back as she stepped onto the deck. "Beautiful ship. Did you rent it from Blue Sail?"

"It's mine."

Of course it is.

"I didn't realize you were a sailor."

"My father taught me."

Her irritation evaporated at the pain underlying his tone. Regardless of how much Gideon Radcliffe got under her skin, she could understand his grief. It humanized him, took the edge off the power and wealth.

"How long has he been gone?"

"Thirteen years." He stared out at the horizon, hands in his pockets, the breeze ruffling his hair. "Sometimes it feels like yesterday."

"A blessing and a curse," she murmured softly as she watched the slow creep of night crawl across the sky. "Loving someone so much they never really leave us."

She could feel his glance shift to her but kept her eyes on the sky.

"It does get better."

Emotion clogged her throat. She swallowed hard. "Does it?"

"There are plenty of moments where it feels just as painful as the second you learned they were gone. But the pain isn't as sharp. The good memories linger more than the bad." She heard the smile in his voice. "At least for me."

"My last memory of my father is a happy one." She blinked rapidly. "He was going to Texas for treatment. We thought it was going to work. We talked about traveling when he got back."

"Where to?"

"Venice." She glanced up at Gideon and gave him a small, nostalgic smile. "One day."

He stepped in closer, hands still in his pockets, as he gazed down at her. Her sadness retreated, replaced by an intense awareness of the man in front of her. Slowly, she looked up. Their gazes met, held. Her body tightened as her breath froze in her chest.

"Mr. Radcliffe? Are we ready?"

The captain's call broke the spell. Gideon stepped back as a mask dropped over his face, smoothing the emotion away and leaving the confident, distant man who had sat at her bar.

"Cast off." He held out an arm to Cassie. "Shall we?"

She shouldn't be disappointed. Shouldn't wish for another moment of camaraderie, of understanding. If she needed someone to talk to, she had Marla and her friends at Prose & Tide. Not a man who should be viewed at best as a competitor.

She tucked her hand into the crook of his elbow and allowed Gideon to lead her toward the stern.

"Unusual setting for a business dinner."

"Guarantees privacy," Gideon countered. "Relaxing scenery to offset potential conflict or disagreement."

He led her up a short flight of stairs. Her mouth dropped open at the sight of the table draped in a crisp white tablecloth and topped with two flickering votives and a small vase of luscious blooms.

"Well... This is nice."

Not relaxing. Not relaxing at all. It looked like a date. She hadn't been on a date since the doctor's diagnosis had ripped hers and her father's world apart.

But it's not a date, she reminded herself firmly even as Gideon pulled out her chair. *Business meeting. Negotiations.*

Gideon sat across from her. Candlelight flickered across his face, accentuating the sharp planes of his jaw, the elegant hollows of his cheeks. He signaled and seconds later a waiter appeared, setting two wineglasses on the table before holding out a bottle of local pinot grigio.

Business, Cassie repeated to herself. *Just business.*

Maybe if she said it enough times throughout the evening, she'd keep herself on track and off any ridiculous fantasies regarding Gideon Radcliffe.

Gideon

Everything had been planned down to the last detail. The crisp wine to take the edge off the midsummer heat. The succulent fish cooked in a simmering butter sauce and topped with fresh cilantro. The sailing route that took them past Rum Point and the glittering lights of seaside villas while staying just far enough away to enhance the sensation of privacy. What he hadn't planned, however, was how much he would enjoy Cassandra's company. The few women he dated before the trial had consumed his life had treated exquisite meals and luxurious vacations as an expectation. But with each dish that had been brought out, from stuffed mushrooms to a creamy soup topped with dill, Cassandra's eyes had grown wider, her smile bigger.

The stiffness that had returned following their mutual confessions of grief had slowly dissipated. It hadn't been just the food. Gideon had skillfully steered the conversation toward the island, something they both loved that would put them on good footing before shifting the conversation to Crescent Point. Except, he'd realized as she'd talked to him about her favorite beaches for snorkeling with turtles and how much she missed horseback riding, that it had been a long time since he'd truly enjoyed the island. Savored what it had to offer instead of buying it as a business opportunity.

The memories were tinged with grief. It hurt to remember the happy moments with his parents, hurt even more to revisit the times Uncle Steven had joined them for a week on the beach or a long weekend spent aboard a sailboat cruising between Grand Cayman and Cayman Brac.

But there were good memories beneath the ache. Memories that made him smile.

Gradually, the conversation had shifted to her work. By design, he slowly eased the discussion toward business while still keeping the topic safe, comfortable. He hadn't anticipated being caught up in how she created her cocktails, the planning, creativity and even chemistry that went into her work.

"I read your biography on the restaurant's website." Gideon nodded to the waiter as she refilled his wineglass. "You wanted to be an author yourself."

Pale pink stole into Cassandra's cheeks. "Yes. Something else I hope to achieve one day."

"What stories do you like to write?"

She hesitated. "Romance. It's been years since I've written anything decent, though. Just doodles."

He remembered the descriptions in the menu, the lyrical phrasing and dreamlike descriptions.

"You're more talented than you give yourself credit for." At her sudden jerk, he cocked his head to one side. "Are you all right?"

Slowly, she nodded. "I'm not used to talking about my writing. My father was really the only one who was ever interested." She paused, shook her head slightly. "That's not fair. I haven't shared much with anyone except my father. Not since I left the States."

"Why not?"

Her blush deepened. "Are you really sure you want to hear this?"

It was clear she wasn't sure she wanted to tell it.

"I do now." He meant it. The woman was a mystery. Fierce and loyal, creative and kind. Standing up to him when it would have been so easy to give in and walk away with literally millions in the bank.

"I grew up with my mother, a corporate consultant who advised companies wanting to expand their operations."

Cassandra held her wineglass up, turning it this way and that, watching the last rays of the setting sun stream through the pale gold liquid. Gideon waited silently, patiently, for her to continue.

"Success to her meant money, promotions, power."

"How did you fit into that?"

One side of Cassandra's mouth worked up. "I didn't. I spent a lot of time with nannies while she traveled around the country, sometimes around the world. She thought having her child with her would reduce her professionalism."

"Yet she fell in love with your father?"

Cassandra let out a half laugh. "More like lust. She came to Grand Cayman for work. From what little she said, she met my father in a bar and thought she'd have a quick fling. Brief, efficient." The last word dripped with condescension. "When she got pregnant, she saw an opportunity for a different kind of legacy."

Anger simmered low in Gideon's gut. "And your father?"

"My mother didn't tell him about me until I was eight. Not because it was the right thing to do, but because she got tired of me asking."

Gideon's horror must have shown on his face, because Cassandra shrugged.

"She said she wanted the best for me, and that wasn't a former corporate real estate agent who had given up everything to move to an island in what she described as 'the middle of nowhere' to own a water sports shop. She thought the best for me was a stable existence in a small town just outside Denver with the finest nannies, tutors and eventually the best private school her money could buy. I spent a lot of time reading, and eventually started to write my own stories, to keep myself from being…" Her voice trailed off, and she shook her head. "Sorry, this is very heavy conversation for such a nice evening."

"Still listening."

Her eyes flew to his. Luminous, amber orbs assessing, evaluating him, much the way he appraised others. He realized with a jolt how disconcerting it was to be on the receiving end of such evaluation.

"My mother wanted me to go into something prestigious, something that would keep me financially stable. She pushed me toward business. The few times I tried to share my writing with her, she was more interested in my advanced placement classes' grades than she was in my short stories." Her casual shrug did little to offset the bleakness in her eyes. "It got to me. I had wanted an English degree, had plans to add a teaching certificate or a marketing minor, something to make money off my writing while working on my own projects. I know it's not something that most people just jump into and start making a fortune off of. But even that wasn't good enough. Nothing was."

"And now you are the head bartender and primary mixologist at one of the most successful cocktail bars on Grand Cayman."

Cassandra's smile spread until it lit up her entire face. Maybe it was the wine, maybe it was the atmosphere or maybe it was simply enjoying dinner with a woman he found so interesting. Whatever it was, he savored the smile, committed it to memory.

"Thank you. For putting it like that."

The genuineness in her voice rocked him. A simple compliment, yet she received it with the same pleasure as if he'd just given her a diamond necklace.

"You're welcome."

"Quitting college and moving down here was the best

thing I ever did. I wish I'd had more time with my dad, but this was still the best thing that ever happened to me."

As if a bucket of icy cold water had been dumped on both of them, the air chilled. The conflict that had lingered at the edges for the past hour now reared its head, striking with devastating accuracy in erasing the camaraderie they had just shared. Cassandra sat up a little straighter, squaring her shoulders as her smile disappeared. Readying herself for whatever was about to come next, she asked, "So, what else did you have to say?"

Gideon watched her, regrets forming in his gut. Another time, another place, and things might have been different. But they weren't. He had known Cassandra for a matter of days. He would not allow any developing feelings he had for her to interfere with the promise he had made to his father. It was a promise he intended to keep. To soothe his few remaining misgivings, he reminded himself that the circumstances of this particular acquisition were very different from the others Peter had achieved for him. Cassandra could barely afford to repair and maintain her own home, let alone pay off the mountain of medical bills she had been left with.

"Your primary reason for not selling the Point is because it's your home."

"Yes."

"Is it the cottage, the land itself?"

Cassandra looked away. "You wouldn't understand."

Frustration trickled in. "Oh?"

"How many homes do you own?"

"Homes?"

"Yes. Penthouses, lofts, vacation homes?"

Gideon's jaw tightened. "How is that relevant?"

"Let me guess. A penthouse in New York. A villa in southern France. A ranch in Montana. How am I doing so far?"

The feisty woman who had confronted him on the beach was back, and judging by the fire in her eyes, she was more than ready to do battle. His muscles coiled in anticipation.

"Your point, Miss Everett?"

"You don't know what home is. How can you possibly understand my reasons for not wanting to sell?"

The barb struck him square in the chest. "I had a home once. But for me, home wasn't a place. It was the people."

Cassandra's face softened. She knew she'd pushed things a little too far. "I'm sorry—"

"I can understand being attached to a place," he continued, not wanting her pity. "What I can't understand is being so attached that it blinds you to the reality of your situation."

Cassandra went still. "What are you talking about?"

"Your father's medical bills. The repairs on the cottage."

Her fingers tightened on the stem of her wineglass. The blush that had so entranced him disappeared as her cheeks went white. "You looked into my finances?"

He steeled himself against the wave of guilt. "Standard operations."

"An operation." Her laugh was harsh, dry. "Of course you would see this whole thing as an operation. You didn't come to the chamber luncheon to actually connect with anyone in Moonrise Bay. You didn't bring me out here to talk about finding common ground or a compromise. This was all just some manipulative tactic to finally get what you want." She shook her head. "Take me back."

How, Gideon wondered, *had things gotten out of control so quickly?* "Cassandra—"

"Please."

It was the slight catch in her voice that stilled the words on his tongue. He wanted to push, to fight. He knew there was an answer, one that would eventually satisfy both of them.

But he wasn't his uncle. It wasn't power he wanted. He wasn't going to bully or manipulate.

When Gideon conducted his deals, he did so honestly. He started to stand when the captain walked up on deck.

"Apologies, Mr. Radcliffe. A storm has shifted and is now heading this way. I recommend we return to the dock to allow ourselves plenty of time."

"Thank you."

Gideon waited until the captain had disappeared before he turned to Cassandra. "Probably for the best. Should you need me, I'll be in one of the cabins below deck."

Cassandra didn't answer. She simply nodded and kept her eyes trained on the horizon.

Gideon walked down the stairs, keeping his eyes facing forward and resisting the temptation to look back. Forward, he reminded himself as he settled in at the teak desk he had had installed in the main suite. Always forward.

Yet his mantra didn't rally him as it usually did. Instead, he slipped back, back toward a woman who had forgone a life of wealth and committed instead to one she enjoyed, one that offered hardship and happiness in equal measure. Damn it if he didn't respect her for that, even like her.

And therein lay a problem he had been denying for days. His attraction to Cassandra couldn't simply be ignored. It was growing. Little things like her heartfelt gratitude were thawing his frozen heart. Her creativity and passion intrigued him. Her fire entranced him.

He pinched the bridge of his nose, his breath a sharp exhale in the small room. He couldn't give up on his mission. Not now, not when he was so close. Not when he genuinely believed selling would be the best thing for Cassandra and her future, too.

But that certainty was no longer black-and-white. Yes, it would be the best thing for her financially. But now that he understood her motivations, her reasons, he saw a woman caught between reality and loyalty, between her past and a daunting future.

A woman who was quickly becoming more than just business.

Although after what had just happened topside, that particular loose thread may have resolved itself.

The thought should have been a relief, fate handing him a solution. Yet as he pulled out his laptop, there was no relief, only a deep-seated ache that he had missed something significant.

Thirty minutes later, the engines slowed. Gideon closed his laptop. Reviewing financial reports and emails connected to some of the properties his uncle had overseen and nearly driven into the ground had given him something else to focus on instead of the tangled mess of emotions inside his chest. Not the happiest of projects, but one that needed to be done.

With determined steps, he walked back up to the fly deck. Cassandra had moved away from the table to one of the circular couches on the perimeter. She was seated with one arm across the plush cushions, the other around her nearly empty glass of wine as she gazed out at flickers of lightning illuminating where the sky met the sea.

"We've arrived."

Cassandra slowly turned to look at him. "Thank you." Her voice was flat, her expression devoid of any emotion. It was manners, not desire, that had Gideon offering his hand to help her up. She glared at his fingers as if they were a snake about to bite. Then, grudgingly, she placed her hand in his.

He pulled her to her feet. He realized too late that he had miscalculated. Miscalculated how close she would be when she stood, how they would be standing almost chest to chest, the top of her head coming to just below his chin. Startled, she raised her eyes to meet his. And then her gaze dropped down to his mouth.

Fool. I'm a damned fool.

Foolish enough to give in to temptation and lower his head. His lips brushed hers, the touch light and gentle. Her sigh feather-soft across his skin. He slid one arm around her back, pulled her closer, leaning deeper into the kiss—

Thunder cracked, jolting them apart. Cassandra stumbled back, sitting down hard on the cushions. Gideon's head whipped around as he stared at the horizon. Lightning flashed again, highlighting massive thunderclouds barreling across the sky toward the island.

"We need to get you to your car."

Cassandra stood. "We've had plenty of storms here before. We'll have more again."

"I've been through a few storms on the island myself," he said as he plucked the wineglass from her hand and set it on the table, "and I would prefer that you are off the boat and on land."

Cassie pressed her lips together in a tight line and brushed past Gideon. He followed her down the steps to the main deck. "Tell me, Mr. Radcliffe," she said over her shoulder, "was seduction always a part of your strategy?"

Gideon's hands curled into fists. Peter had been right all along. The woman was a menace. She'd experienced hardship and loss, yes. But like so many, she was willing to believe the worst of him without even getting to know him. She had made assumptions based on his wealth and the media reports rather than looking past the surface.

And whose fault is that?

The thought stopped him short. The last time he'd been vulnerable with anyone had been twelve years ago. The day after the will reading. He'd been raw, grieving, yet determined to do right by his father, by the company. So he'd gone to his uncle, confessed his deepest fear of not being ready to lead. He'd asked for Steven's help, for his guidance and mentorship.

Your father would have been proud of you.

He'd steeled himself after that, closed himself off from his own emotions as he'd thrown himself into college, into working every role he could so that no one would ever dare question if he had earned the right to lead. It had been the only way to move forward, to not sink into the grief that had claimed his father. Over time, the walls became second nature. They'd kept him whole when he'd realized the extent of Steven's betrayal. They'd staved off the worst of the media's hounding throughout the trial.

But now, as Cassandra stopped by the gangplank and stared at him, waiting for a reply, he felt the first strain of keeping himself so contained. He'd created the image of aloof billionaire, leaned into it until there were times he wasn't even sure where the farce ended and he truly began.

What would it be like to be like Cassandra? To wear one's heart on their sleeve and risk getting hurt over and over again?

He started to reply with something abrupt and cutting. Then stopped. He didn't want to play his role. Not with her. But he wasn't ready to let her fully in either. So he opted for simplicity.

"Good night, Miss Everett."

A frown appeared between her brows. Her lips parted, then closed again. Finally, she turned and walked down the gangplank and onto the dock. He stayed there, watched until he saw her get into her car and drive out of the parking lot. As he moved toward the cockpit, a light rain started to fall. It was a sharp contrast to the heat still curling inside him. He needed to step back, get himself under control and strategize how to approach the purchase of Crescent Point. And, he thought morosely, as thunder boomed overhead, get Cassandra Everett off his mind once and for all.

CHAPTER SEVEN

Cassie

TODAY, CASSIE THOUGHT irritably as she dumped shards of a wineglass into a trash can, might be one of the worst days she'd had in months. Little mistakes here and there because she wasn't paying attention. Because if she wasn't thinking about how arrogant and condescending Gideon Radcliffe was, she was thinking about that incredible, barely there kiss. A kiss so light, so fleeting and, oh, so memorable. It was easily one of the top three kisses she'd ever had in her life.

Oh, come on, she irritably told herself as she shoved the trash can back under the bar. But her disloyal mind continued.

Best. Kiss. Ever.

She should be grateful for the crack of thunder that had separated them. Emotionally and physically, however, were very different matters. Logically, she understood his need to investigate her. But to dig into her finances, especially her father's medical bills, was a violation, one that confirmed her original opinion. Gideon might have finer points than she had initially given him credit for, but he was a mercenary. An opportunist.

And a great kisser.

Damn it!

Never mind that he had created an incredible evening for her, one that far exceeded her expectations for a business dinner.

Because he wanted to wine and dine you.

That made the most sense of all. But it didn't explain the warmth in his voice when he'd complimented her, when he'd talked about her work like it mattered. He'd made her feel...seen.

She closed her eyes and released a pent-up breath. Was it all a lie? Just a clever ruse to manipulate her?

And if not, where did that leave her and her growing attraction to the man?

"Good afternoon."

Cassie's eyes flew open as she nearly knocked over her wineglass at the sound of Gideon's deep voice. A voice that was becoming all too familiar. One that now not only stirred those embers of attraction, but also fanned them with the memories of his hand at her back, his lips on hers.

Slowly, she looked up.

Why, she thought crossly, *does the man have to look good in everything?*

Today's outfit was a dark gray suit, white dress shirt and a vivid red tie. Confident, bold, masculine.

Jerk.

"Hello, Mr. Radcliffe." She forced a small, polite smile onto her face. "What can I get you?"

"Hopefully, your forgiveness."

She didn't bat an eye. "I don't seem to recall adding that to my menu. Is there a particular book you're thinking of that I could potentially base the future recipe on?"

His lips twitched. "I haven't read a good book in a very long time. I'm trying to think of one where forgiveness figures in. Not *The Great Gatsby*, if I recall."

Cassie huffed. "Not exactly. Actually, it's the opposite. It exemplifies what happens when selfish people think only of themselves."

His eyes flickered, his hands curling into fists on the bar top. "Point taken. Then what would you recommend?"

When he stared at her with those deep blue eyes, sincerity and genuine apology shining out, he made it very difficult for her to hold on to her anger. "The Pemberley."

She pulled a chilled bottle of champagne and a container of elderberry syrup out of the fridge beneath the bar, and a bottle of elderflower liqueur from the shelf behind her. A quick tug on the small rosebush growing in the arched window yielded three ruby rose petals.

"This cocktail represents the elegance and grandeur of Pemberley, Fitzwilliam Darcy's estate in *Pride and Prejudice*." She popped the cork with ease and poured the sparkling liquid into the glass. "Elderflower liqueur, a nod to the use of elderflowers in the Regency era for anything from herbal remedies to flavor cakes and jellies, and elderflower syrup to add a touch of sweetness. Rose water in honor of the roses that appear throughout the novel. And champagne from the Montagne de Reims region in France, symbolizing the luxury of Pemberley."

As she handed the drink to Gideon, their fingers brushed. By sheer will, she managed not to drop the glass even as her heart pitched into her throat.

Gideon accepted the drink and took a sip. "Even better than The Gatsby."

He set it down, then looked at her with a frankness that made her feel as if he could see right through her. The inner battle that waged inside her chest every time she opened yet another bill and thought longingly of accepting Gideon's offer. Her grief at having her world turned upside down.

The desire that pulsed through her veins despite her best efforts.

She forced herself to hold his gaze.

"I would be lying," he said softly, "if I said I had not made similar mistakes in the past when trying to secure a deal. This is the first time, though, that I've come face-to-face with the consequences of procuring such intimate information. I'm sorry."

Cassie sighed. "You know, I could have handled most of your investigation. I do get it. Sometimes business is business. But my dad's bills…" Her voice trailed off. "That one hurt."

"I know how I would feel if someone utilized my parents' death to pressure me into making a choice I wasn't confident in. I would appreciate your forgiveness, but you certainly don't owe it to me."

Cassie's lips parted in surprise. Of all the things she had expected, this genuine apology was at the bottom of her list. Heck, it hadn't even been on her list. "You apologizing doesn't change my mind about the Point."

"It's not meant to. If I want to change your mind, we still need to have the conversation I intended for us to have last night." Gideon's phone rang. He pulled a sleek new model out of his pants pocket and glanced at the screen with a frown. "Excuse me."

He stepped off to the side, leaving Cassie standing in

a state of confusion behind the bar. An apology was the last thing she had expected. But like his compliment last night, it seemed real.

Which now placed the ball back in her court. He'd insinuated he wanted to talk again. Did she take him up on it? Or did she put her foot down and tell him no more conversations, no more sunset sails or negotiations?

Except, she thought as she absently wiped at a spot on the bar top, that would also mean not seeing Gideon again. A thought that made her chest unexpectedly tighten.

"You're doing what?"

Gideon's elevated voice made Cassie glance over. He had turned slightly so she could see his profile backlit against the window. One hand was clenched around his phone, the other shoved into his pocket. His shoulders were tense, his jaw tight. His pulse thumped in his neck.

"Yes, and the new bartender is starting tonight. The rest of the staff is slated for the Humphrey-Wittington wedding. We can't operate on the current staffing we have." His voice was brisk, firm, a sharp contrast to the tension she could practically see radiating off his powerful frame. He raised his chin up a fraction. "Do this and you will never receive a recommendation from Radcliffe Resorts ever again."

The ice in his voice easily brought the temperature of the room down by ten degrees. Cassie suppressed a shiver as he tapped his screen and shoved his phone back in his pocket.

"Trouble?" she asked as he drew near.

"My head bartender at my west end resort has decided to run away with one of our guests."

"Seriously?"

"She said it was true love and worth far more than her position or a future recommendation from me."

"So what does that mean for you?"

Gideon's lips twisted into a frown. "We'll be able to open the restaurant as usual. But we'll have to operate at a reduced capacity, nix our cocktails and offer wine and beer at reduced prices. We hired two new bartenders who were supposed to start training today. The rest of the bar staff are needed for a high-profile wedding."

"I'm surprised she called you directly to quit."

"My events manager is on maternity leave." He thumped his phone against his thigh, his eyes distant. "I'm working with her assistant given that it's our first event since the trial and our bride and groom are from a prominent family." He started to tap on his screen again. "There's a temp agency that may provide some help."

Cassie hesitated for a split second. Then she spoke. It was the right thing to do, she told herself.

"What about me?"

Gideon's hand froze over the screen as his head snapped up, and he met her gaze. "You?"

"Me."

His eyes narrowed. "Why?"

She drummed her fingers on the bar top. "Because if it was anyone else on the island, that's what I would do."

"How flattering." His tone was dry, but his expression was thoughtful. "What time do you get off?"

"Four o'clock."

"Be at the Radcliffe at west end at five. You'll work the main bar until eight if the new bartenders do well, later if they need additional guidance and training. Unless," he added as he picked up his drink, "you decide you're too afraid to help out the competition."

Now it was Cassie's turn to arch a brow. "The Radcliffe Lounge has a very different vibe than Prose & Tide. The Lounge is elegant, glamorous. We have our own version of glamour here, but it's more relaxed, eclectic. And," she added as she nodded toward his drink, "you may have some of the finest wines and rums available, but I make better drinks."

He stared at her for a second before surprising her with a boisterous laugh. The uninhibited huskiness made her skin pebble into goose bumps.

"You'll have a chance tonight to prove it."

Gideon

Cassandra hadn't been lying, Gideon thought as he watched her behind the mirrored bar of the lounge. She'd simply been stating fact. She wasn't just a professional mixologist. She was an artist who loved her craft.

She'd been early, arriving in the lobby of the Radcliffe at ten minutes to five. Gideon had escorted her to The Lounge, a long, thin room painted navy blue and trimmed in gold. The matching dark blue couches and gold tables glimmered beneath flickering wall sconces. The Lounge offered an atmosphere of intimacy, a place to relax away from the brightness of the sun and beaches. Or, when the night rolled in, a place to enjoy a Caribbean evening as the floor-to-ceiling windows were thrown open to the darkness. A far cry from Prose & Tide's cozy, upscale-library feel.

The Lounge was never empty, its elegant chairs and gleaming barstools filled with resort guests and visiting tourists. One of the daytime bartenders had recognized Cassie, going so far as to gush over Prose & Tide's menu before becoming aware of Gideon's presence. Under his observant eye, she quickly returned to restocking the bar.

He'd taken a seat at one of the corner tables and ordered dinner. He didn't think Cassie was the kind of person who would offer to help while secretly planning to poison his drinks. But he also hadn't thought the man who had been by his side through the darkest year of his life was capable of betrayal.

But every time he looked over, Cassandra was doing exactly as she had promised: teaching his new hires and taking the pressure off the other bar staff as they served the patrons and prepared for the wedding later that evening. He envied how quickly she formed a bond with the staff. Not overly familiar, he observed as a waiter set a plate of shrimp scampi in front of him. There was still respect, leadership. She knew when to take charge and when to step back and let her apprentices do what she had taught them. After an hour, they were pouring glasses of wine, mixing drinks and serving with ease.

"Mr. Radcliffe?"

Gideon glanced up at the assistant event manager, Glenda. A sweet young woman who had excellent ideas. With a little more time and confidence in her own abilities, he could easily picture her as the lead manager for the future resort in Moonrise Bay.

"Yes?"

"I'm sorry to have to tell you this, sir, but another bartender has called in. She won't be here for the wedding tonight."

"And the reason?"

"Sick kid." Glenda leaned back a little at Gideon's dark frown.

Gideon felt the beginning of a headache but resisted the urge to rub at his temple. "We'll think of something."

Glenda hesitated.

"You have an idea?" Gideon prompted.

"Would Cassie be willing to stay for the wedding tonight?"

Gideon arched a brow. Had his entire staff fallen in love with Cassandra? "Miss Everett is already doing us a favor by being here and training our new bartenders."

"Of course."

But as Glenda walked away, Gideon knew asking Cassandra to stay was a logical option. He just didn't want to be the one to have to ask her, not after the tentative truce they had formed. There was also something uncomfortable about asking the woman whose land he coveted to do him yet another favor.

Cassandra approached him ten minutes later. "I hear you need more help."

Gideon frowned. "What?"

"One of the bartenders mentioned someone's out with a sick kid."

"We'll take care of it."

"How?"

"Nothing for you to be concerned about. You've already helped out enough."

Cassandra's eyes narrowed. "You don't strike me as the kind of man to let emotions override a business decision."

Gideon's voice deepened. "Excuse me?"

"Maybe you're feeling off because of last night. Maybe

you feel guilty about me helping you out given the circumstances."

The tone in her voice told him that's exactly what she thought.

"Whatever the reason, I'm here, and this is what I do. And your staff—" she gestured toward the bar "—are part of the same industry as me. We help each other out."

"Are you advocating to help me once more, Miss Everett?"

"It's what we do here, Mr. Radcliffe. Maybe, just maybe, if you come down off that ivory tower you've isolated yourself in and look around, you'd realize that there's a lot of good people here. There may be rivalries, competition, but the people in this community step up."

With his uncle's face etched in his mind along with the angry glare Steven had shot him before he'd stalked out of the courtroom, Gideon responded more gruffly than he had intended. "Not always, Miss Everett."

Cassandra leaned down. "All right. But tonight, that's exactly what this is. I don't like your plan for Moonrise Bay. I don't love the fact that you covet my land. And sometimes I think you're insufferable."

A grin tugged at the corners of Gideon's mouth. "This has to be the strangest speech I've ever heard from someone who's trying to help."

"I'm just pointing out that, even though you and I don't see eye to eye, it doesn't mean I want you or your team to fail. Your new bartenders are doing incredibly well. If they need something, I'll be just a couple rooms away."

Her face softened, her mouth curving into a small, gentle smile. As if trying to put him at ease. The realization made his heart lurch in his chest.

"Let me help, Gideon."

The sound of his name on her lips tempted him closer to the edge. Not just for tonight. But to explore those holes Cassandra had been slowly yet steadily punching through his walls.

Later. He would deal with his own emotions later. Right now, he had a decision to make. A decision solely rooted in whether or not he could trust again.

"The couple getting married tonight include the daughter of a US senator and the son of a Norwegian diplomat."

Cassandra's eyes widened. "Are you nervous?"

"I am. It's not about the money. It's that out of all of the resorts on the island, they trusted us with their wedding. They could have canceled during the trial. I offered them the option and a full refund knowing they could get caught up in the media frenzy. They chose to stay."

"And their trust means even more given the lawsuit and court battle with your uncle."

How does this woman see so much?

"Yes."

Cassandra straightened her shoulders. "I won't let you and your team down."

Gideon paused and then forced himself to leap off his ivory tower. "I believe you."

Her eyes widened. He sat, his body tense, words readied like ammo for whatever she might say next.

"Thank you, Gideon."

She walked back to the bar, leaving him at his table with the knowledge that he had just gone over the edge.

CHAPTER EIGHT

Cassie

CASSIE SWIPED A hand across her brow as she glanced at the clock. Nearly 3:00 a.m. The witching hour.

Almost done.

The wedding had been an incredible success. From the beach ceremony at sunset to the ballroom glowing with hundreds of candles and further brightened by stunning arrangements of every variety of white flower Cassie could think of filling the room. Lily of the valley and rose garlands were draped across the arched windows, multiple vases filled with lisianthus, hydrangea and roses stood in each corner, and centered on every table was a one-of-a-kind floral masterpiece. It all surpassed luxury.

At first, the sight of so much expense put Cassie on edge. It was the kind of event her mother dreamed of being invited to. Time spent socializing with the well-to-do was always more important to her than being home with her daughter. But as the evening had progressed, Cassie had been pleasantly surprised. The bride's parents had thanked her and the other waitstaff repeatedly for their service. The guests, even the tipsy ones, had been respectful.

And the bride and groom… Cassie smiled. They were in love. The bride hadn't been worried about striking the perfect pose for photos, just as the groom had been more focused on his new wife than anyone else in the room. What would it be like, Cassie wondered, to have someone love you so completely? To trust that they would see your flaws and still think that you were the most special person in their life?

Gideon flashed into her mind. As the evening had wound down, she'd spied him clearing glassware off tables, fetching a glass of water for a guest and even helping collapse some of the tables and chairs after the guests had all left. He'd disappeared a couple of hours ago. But seeing him roll up the sleeves of a shirt that probably cost as much as she'd made in tips tonight had surprised her.

Who thought seeing a man roll a table across a ballroom could be sexy?

"Why are you still here?"

Cassie's head snapped up. Gideon stood in the doorway. The sleeves of his dress shirt were still rolled up to his elbows, and he still wore those pants that fit so perfectly along the lines of his muscular thighs.

Cassie glanced down. At some point during cleanup, she had ended up with cocktail sauce on her blouse. Her curls had long since given up trying to look respectable and now fell in chaotic spirals around her face.

She huffed and blew one strand out of her eyes. "Because there was work to do."

Gideon glowered at her. "I agreed you could help, not kill yourself."

Cassie rolled her eyes. "Maybe you should think about going into writing. You certainly have a flair for the dramatic. In this industry," she added when Gideon started to retort, "late nights are a thing."

"And where is the other staff?"

"Two of them are putting away glasses in the kitchen. I sent the others home."

His eyes widened. "You what?"

"That's the way the schedule was written. They've been here since noon."

Gideon looked around the room. "It's spotless."

"Nearly. Thankfully the florist carted the flowers off to be delivered to a nearby hospital." Another point in favor of the bride and groom. "Pulling all of the glassware and tablecloths then stacking the tables and chairs took the longest."

Gideon walked over and held out an envelope. "Payment."

"You're prompt."

"I always pay my debts."

Irritated and not quite sure why, Cassie pulled a check out of the envelope. Her mouth dropped open. "This is too much."

"You trained new bartenders well enough that they were able to work with the other waitstaff and keep the lounge open tonight. That was before you jumped in and helped serve, and I suspect make, the drinks for a very important wedding. Then you stayed to help tear down. If you hadn't been here, we would have likely shut down the bar and made a bad impression on a client who will now be giving us rave reviews and no doubt bringing us more business." He arched a brow, obviously pleased with his own recitation of events. "Given all of that, I doubt I've paid you enough."

Cassie held the check between two fingers. His justification made sense. Still, she didn't like it. There was something cold about it, especially the amount. "This is more than I make in a week."

"Then you're not getting paid enough."

Cassie tilted her head to one side. "I think that's a compliment."

"It is. Go home, Cassandra."

"Wait." She held up the check. "I'm really not comfortable with accepting this much money."

Gideon's jaw tightened. "This payment is non-negotiable."

"Okay, stop right there. This isn't a negotiation. This isn't a boardroom. This is two professionals having a conversation. I understand wanting to compensate me, but…"

Gideon's lips parted, then closed again.

"What?"

"It's better left unsaid."

Her fingers tightened on the check. "If you say that I need the money, I will rip this up right in front of your eyes."

The barest glimmer of humor brightened his eyes. "It's disturbing to me, Miss Everett, how you can almost read my mind."

"On that we agree." She looked back down at the envelope, then frowned when she spied another piece of paper tucked inside. "What's this?"

"A bonus. Good night."

Cassie pulled the paper out and read it. Gideon was almost to the door when she called out.

"Gideon."

Slowly, he turned around, his face carefully blank. "Yes?"

"You bought me a horseback ride on the beach."

"I did."

She blinked rapidly as her throat tightened. "I don't know what to say."

"You earned it."

"I earned the money. Or at least some of it," she said with a slight smile. "But this... This is very kind."

He walked back toward her. Each step he took made her pulse beat just a touch faster, his presence warming her skin as his generosity thawed the last bits of ice clinging to her heart.

"I don't let people in easily." He stopped a few feet away, hands in his pockets. "But tonight, you came through for me. Not just once but twice, despite our disagreements. I wanted to do something more than just hand out money."

"Well, this is definitely more than just money." She hesitated. "Ever since Dad got sick, I haven't had time to do the things I used to enjoy doing."

"I hope you'll enjoy it."

He started to turn away. Cassie had a sudden impression of a lord sitting atop the tower she had accused him of living in earlier. Except this time she didn't see a jerk or someone who thought himself better than anyone else.

She saw someone who had been hurt. Someone who, beneath the aloofness and bravado, was lonely.

"Come with me."

He froze, then slowly turned around. "What?"

"Come with me. You said on the boat you've never

been." She held up the check. "I can even pay for your ride."

"Absolutely not."

She bit back a smile at his irritated tone. "Okay. But still, you should come."

He cocked his head to one side. "Why are you asking me?"

Because I'm starting to realize how isolated you've made yourself. Because I'm curious about you. Because you seem like you could use a friend.

She kept those thoughts to herself and instead said, "Because it'll be fun. Don't tell me you're afraid to have fun, Radcliffe."

The nudge had the desired effect. He raised his chin up. "I'm not. The certificate is good for a year."

"I'm free on Monday. Morning or afternoon?"

He waited so long to answer she wondered if he was reconsidering. Then, finally, "Morning. I'll book it and text you the time."

"Great."

"Are you okay to drive?"

She paused, touched by his thoughtfulness. "I am. I'm used to late nights."

"You're welcome to a room here. On the house, of course."

"No. But thank you," she added softly. "Have a good night."

She turned and headed toward the doors that would lead back into the hotel.

"Cassandra."

The sound of her name on his lips, the deep richness

of his voice, sent a shiver down her spine even as she turned to face him. "Yes?"

"Thank you."

"You're welcome." She hesitated. "Thank you for trusting me."

And then, before she could say anything else, she turned and hurried out of the ballroom. It wasn't until she climbed inside her car and shut the door that the full magnitude of what she'd done hit her. Had she truly just invited Gideon Radcliffe, the man she'd imagined for months as her archenemy, on a horseback ride?

Her breath rushed out as she leaned forward and rested her head on her steering wheel. Tonight had been revelatory in a way she hadn't anticipated. When Gideon had told her he believed her, it had shaken her. She didn't know the details of what he'd experienced this past year. But seeing how much the bridal couple choosing his resort had meant to him had been a small but powerful insight. A glimpse into the man she'd assumed she'd known so much about, only to realize he was nothing like the image she'd created. An image so easy to loathe, to keep at arm's length.

She sat up and pulled out the envelope, traced her fingers over her name written in his bold cursive. She wanted to believe in him the way he had believed in her tonight.

And it frightened her. It frightened her that a man she'd known less than a week had crept into her thoughts, had slipped into her dreams as if he'd been there for months or even years. A man who with every passing day was proving to be far more than she expected.

A man, she realized with equal fear and excitement, she could fall for.

CHAPTER NINE

Gideon

Gideon guided his convertible into an empty space between two trees. The designated parking area for tourists going on an ocean horseback ride was off a meandering gravel road. Instead of parking lines, there were trees staggered every ten to fifteen feet and myriad vehicles parked between them, from cars and trucks to a minivan and even a moped. As Gideon got out, a soft whinny reached his ears. He followed the sound over a dune and found half a dozen horses tethered to the trees.

A small group of people milled about, including a couple with their teenage son, and two young women. Cassie stood off to one side, chatting with a man wearing a baseball cap emblazoned with the logo of the stables.

"Good morning."

Cassandra turned her head. A smile lit up her face, one that sent a jolt through him. He'd wondered more than once over the last few days if she would cancel. If the brief camaraderie they'd experienced in the ballroom and her invitation had been rooted more in exhaustion and whimsy.

But seeing her now, actually looking excited to see him, tore down another piece of that wall.

"You made it."

He smiled slightly. "You didn't think I would?"

"I wasn't sure if you'd be able to tear yourself away from your work."

"I made a promise. I keep my promises." Gideon's eyes flickered to the young man in the baseball cap. "Hello. I'm Gideon Radcliffe."

The man held out his hand. "Anderson. Since you booked the private ride, we can leave whenever you and Cassie are ready."

Cassie's eyes widened. "Private ride?"

"It sounded more enjoyable."

That delicate, fascinating blush stole into Cassandra's cheeks once more. "I guess I just thought…"

"If you're not comfortable, I'm sure I can rearrange our reservation for a group ride."

"No." Cassandra breathed in through her nose, then out. "I'm just surprised, that's all."

Gideon turned away to hide his smile. He hadn't been horseback riding in years. Really, he hadn't done anything for a long time. He'd initially hesitated when Cassandra had invited him to join her. Judging by the surprise that had flickered across her face after she'd invited him, it had been a spontaneous invitation. But it had provided an excellent opportunity, one for Cassandra to get to know him in a different setting. She had expressed discomfort with his wealth, how it reminded her of her mother. A casual horseback ride on the beach might help change her mind about selling.

And, he admitted, it gave him more time with her.

He had finally accepted that his feelings for Cassandra had advanced far beyond anything professional. Feelings he would keep to himself. They were still at odds, foes chasing after the same bit of land, both committed to their cause. At the end of this, one of them would lose.

But he would still enjoy what little bit he could. Even something as simple and fleeting as a horseback ride on the beach.

Anderson led them off to the side where a light brown horse and a speckled gray horse waited. Their ears flicked forward as the group approached.

"Moonlight and Falcon." Anderson patted the gray one on the rump. "Gideon, I'll have you on Falcon. And Cassie, you'll ride Moonlight."

Cassie walked up and slowly laid a gentle hand on her horse's nose. "Hello." Her voice was soft, sweet.

Gideon watched as she gently rubbed the palm of her hand up and down the bridge before laying her forehead against Moonlight's cheek. The horse's eyes closed, almost as if it was enjoying the interaction as much as Cassie.

"It never gets old." She smiled over at Gideon. "Like touching velvet."

The emotions in his chest shifted, deepened. A woman who said no to $10 million but got so much joy and simple satisfaction out of petting a horse.

Where have you been all my life?

Gideon turned toward Falcon. The horse eyed him suspiciously.

"You're going to have to go easy on me, mate. It's been a while since I rode a horse."

Falcon tossed his head.

"He can be a little feisty at first." Anderson moved up and ran a comforting hand along his neck. "But he's a great horse."

Falcon leaned into and nuzzled Anderson's shoulder before giving Gideon another side-eye. Great. He wouldn't have a lot of time to talk with Cassandra if he was fighting a horse that didn't like him.

Anderson ran down the basics of their ride and a few safety rules. Five minutes later, they had mounted and were moving at a casual pace away from the grove. Gideon chose to ride behind Cassandra. If Falcon decided to pull any tricks and toss Gideon off, he wasn't going to let her see it.

They crested a hill, and all thoughts of irritable horses and potential negotiations fled. The ocean lay before them, its stunning azure a faint contrast to the morning's pale blue sky. The beach stretched out in both directions, a slender strip of gold. A few trees had taken root in the sandy soil, their branches twisting and winding up toward the sky. A mile away, one could see a few villas and seaside homes, but here, there was nothing but beach and water. The sheer peacefulness of it slipped in, soothing him in a way he hadn't even realized he needed as tension seeped from his muscles.

"It's beautiful, isn't it?"

His gaze shifted from the sea to Cassandra. She had brought her horse to a halt and was looking back at him with another small, understanding smile on her face.

"I'm glad you came."

He blinked. Before he could think of a response, she turned back around and nudged her horse into a slow walk. It took him a moment to gather himself and follow. *I'm glad you came.* He couldn't remember the last time someone had said something like that to him. Not genuinely.

He didn't want this. Didn't want this attraction to sink its roots even deeper and teeter on the verge of becoming something more. Not when he sensed that change was just on the horizon.

Cassandra only had so much time before her medical bills and repairs to the cottage caught up with her. When emotion was removed, selling Crescent Point was the best option for her. An arrangement that benefited not only her, he acknowledged, but him.

But he wasn't his uncle. He wasn't pursuing this project for his own selfish gain, purely for profit. He was doing it to fulfill a promise to his father. And after seeing Moonrise Bay, after talking with some of the other business owners he'd met at the chamber luncheon, he truly believed his resort could support the town and help it grow without altering it as drastically as Cassandra feared. Facts. Easily verifiable and documented facts.

But when Cassandra smiled at him like that, when she offered help even when they were on opposite ends of a tug-of-war, those facts disappeared. He could handle the desire that followed. It was the contentment, the whispers of happiness being with her created, he wasn't sure what to do with.

Anderson led their small group down the beach. Every now and then he would point out an interesting tree or plant, share a fun fact. Otherwise, the ride was quiet, save for the gentle hushing of waves on sand and the distant, subtle roar of waves breaking on the reef. The quietness gave him a moment to be alone with his thoughts in a way he hadn't allowed himself in a very long time. To think about all the things he had missed out on because he had focused on work, on Radcliffe Resorts, on anything but the loss of his parents, and the inevitable anger at his father that had followed.

When he thought of the time he'd spent with his parents on the island, his thoughts had fixated on that final trip before his mother's stroke. The one where his father had stood with him on the beach of their property next to Crescent Point and talked about the resort he dreamed of one day building.

What he hadn't thought of in so long were all the other summers and holidays he and his parents had spent here. The sailing, the snorkeling, the diving. His father taking him out to eat at locally owned restaurants. Exploring an art gallery or new artisan shop with his mother. His parents had always supported the local businesses near their resorts, and his father had always emphasized the importance of connecting with the people to make sure that Radcliffe Resorts' vision didn't outshine the needs of the community.

At some point, Gideon realized with a heavy heart, he had lost sight of that. East End would be the first new resort he would exclusively oversee. Almost everything he had done since joining Radcliffe's executive board had been solved, at least partially, by money. Pay increases, job benefits, renovations. He'd added plenty of zeros to Radcliffe Resorts' earnings.

But was it worth the price? Not just the price he had paid by shutting himself off from the world, the memories. But from assuming that everything could be solved with money.

"You okay?"

He smiled slightly at Cassandra as she looked over her shoulder at him, brown curls bouncing in time with Moonlight's gait. "You're supposed to be enjoying yourself, not worrying about me."

"You just looked..." Her voice trailed off. "Sad."

"I don't know if *sad* is the right word. *Contemplative. Bittersweet*, maybe. My parents used to take me to do stuff like this a lot. We never rode horses on a beach," he amended, chuckling as Falcon let out an indignant snort. "I haven't let myself remember those moments in a long time."

Cassandra slowed the pace of her horse until she was riding alongside Gideon. He focused on the reins in his hand, the sun warming his back, anything but her faint floral scent drifting on the breeze.

"Would they have liked this?" Cassandra asked.

"My mother would have." It was hard to talk about them, hard to share these pieces of his past. "My father enjoyed a lot of outdoor sports and activities, but my mother was the more adventurous one. She's the one who got me into scuba diving."

"Your mom sounds like an amazing woman. I hope I can be that kind of mother to my kids one day."

The wistfulness in Cassandra's voice tugged at him.

"Does your mother not come down to visit?"

The sharp, brittle laugh surprised him.

"No. She came down once twenty-six years ago. Once, as she often told me, was enough." Cassandra sighed. "My mom is who she is. She grew up in poverty. Swore she'd never exist in that state again. I can admire how she made her way in the world. But she saw the cottage, and both my father's and my professions, as failures." Her voice dropped so low Gideon barely heard her over the ocean. "She never understood any of this."

Nor, Gideon thought with a healthy dose of anger, had the woman bothered to try to understand her daughter.

"Your mother is a fool."

Cassandra's head whipped around. "What?"

"Wealth isn't everything. Neither is prestige." He frowned as he remembered the relentless media coverage, especially in the final days of the trial. "It's something I was born into, something I've never lived without. I enjoy what I do, and I believe in our company. But I would be lying if I said there weren't days when fame and fortune didn't carry their own burdens."

He debated over whether or not to say what lingered in his heart. Then, taking another leap, he said, "Like not being able to enjoy the little things. Watching you the last couple days, seeing how much you enjoy something like riding a horse, makes me realize I've been so fixated on the big goals and challenges in my life that I haven't truly enjoyed anything in a long time."

Cassandra stared at him, a kaleidoscope of emotions whirling in her eyes. Emotions, he realized, that mirrored his own.

Before she could say anything, Anderson turned his horse around.

"We'll dismount here and remove the saddles if you want to take a quick ride in the ocean. You up for it?"

Gideon glanced out at the ocean, then back at Falcon. "What do you say?" he asked as he rubbed his hand up and down the horse's neck the way Anderson had. "Up for a swim?" Falcon whinnied softly. "I think that was a yes."

He looked up to see Cassie watching him. "What?"

She shook her head slightly. "Nothing."

They dismounted and moved to a shaded area as Anderson took care of removing the saddles. Anderson helped them remount bareback.

"We're going to go slow but steady." Anderson gently nudged his horse forward. "Falcon and Moonlight are great swimmers, but only do what you're comfortable with."

They slowly entered the water, the waves gradually coming up to lap gently at Gideon's knees. Cassandra glanced back at him more than once.

He smirked at her. "Afraid I'll get washed away?"

She grinned. "Just checking on the city boy."

A few moments later, Moonlight began to swim. Cassandra let out a laugh of delight that echoed across the water. Falcon followed suit. It was, Gideon had to admit, one of the more incredible experiences he'd had in recent years. There was something wild about being surrounded by nothing but water, something thrilling about the way Falcon's muscles moved and bunched beneath him as the horse swam.

There was freedom, too, Gideon thought as he tilted his head back to the sky. Freedom and the first taste of true happiness he'd experienced in years.

His eyes drifted to Cassandra, to the curls hanging down her back, the confident set of her shoulders. No matter what happened next, he would hold this memory of her, playful and adventurous, kind and wild, as long as he lived.

The horses paddled for a couple of minutes before following Anderson's lead back into shallow waters.

"Oh, how I missed that." Cassie let her head drop back. "I don't know why it's so much fun, but it is."

"Definitely an experience I won't forget." And he meant it.

The horses walked back up onto the beach. They dismounted and stood off to the side as Anderson toweled the animals off before preparing the saddles.

"You should do more stuff like this."

Gideon nodded. "Yeah. I should. I'd forgotten what it was like just to take an afternoon off."

Out of the corner of his eye, he saw Cassandra glance up at him. "Because of the trial or because of your parents?"

He stiffened, started to rebut, then stopped himself. It was unfair of him to accuse her of prying given that he'd gone to great lengths to dig into her private life. She didn't want to sell, but that hadn't stopped her from helping him out not once but twice. Then she took further steps to bridge the gap between them by inviting him out today simply because she thought he could use a day off.

"I'm sorry. That was intrusive." Cassandra started to walk away.

"A little of both."

She paused.

"I loved my parents. Losing them was hard. Focusing on finishing my college degree, and then focusing on work helped. And the trial…" Anger surged inside him and stilled his tongue.

He didn't have anyone close that he could talk to about the trial. On the surface he'd come across as cold, callous.

No one knew that had been the only way to deal with the betrayal of his last living relative, a man he had looked up to, respected and depended on. Steven had not only nearly ruined several resorts for his own selfish gain, but he had thrown Gideon to the wolves to save himself.

"The trial took away years of my life. It's hard to enjoy the little moments when you might lose the last thing in the world you have."

A warm hand rested on his arm, quieted the storm inside him.

"I'm sorry for what you went through." She hesitated. "For what I said at Prose & Tide."

He wanted so badly to lay his hand over hers, to slip an arm around her waist and pull her close. To savor the feel of her against him.

"We've both said and done things the last few days we're not proud of. Me more than you."

"Please tell me you're not turning this into a contest."

He chuckled. "No, merely acknowledging my mistakes, too."

She rolled her eyes even as she grinned. His eyes focused on her smile, a gesture he felt down to his bones. He liked it when she smiled.

He liked it a lot.

Her eyes widened slightly. Her gaze drifted down to his mouth.

A second. That was all it took for the companionship to disappear, for desire to replace it with an ache that had him leaning down. Her sharp intake of breath was music to his ears. Her body swayed toward his as her eyes drifted shut.

"The horses are saddled."

Anderson's voice broke through. Gideon jerked back as Cassandra blinked like she'd woken from a dream. They stared at each other, their breaths mingling in the warm Caribbean air.

Despite every cell in his body screaming at him to stop, Gideon turned away.

"Thank you, Anderson."

"Would you like a photo before we head back?"

"Oh," Gideon said. "No, it's—"

"Sure." Cassie cleared her throat, her smile overly bright as she looked at Gideon. "Unless you're too scared of having a photo taken with the enemy."

He tried to match her mood, tried to tell himself this was for the best.

"Well, when you phrase it like that."

He handed Anderson his phone, then followed Cassie over to where their horses were tethered to a tree. Gideon thought of that moment when they'd crested the dune, that sense of utter peace, feeling Cassandra's genuine happiness that he had joined her today. He leaned in, his hand resting on her back. She tensed, then slowly relaxed into him. Her small show of trust, the warmth of her sun-kissed body leaning into his, nearly undid him.

"Smile! And..." Anderson tapped the screen. "Perfect. Great picture."

Gideon's phone vibrated.

"Oh." Anderson squinted at the screen. "Someone named Steven is calling."

Gideon froze. His entire body tense, his contentment fleeing under the onslaught of raw fury mixed with pain.

"Thank you."

Judging by Anderson's wide eyes, his anger showed

on his face. But he didn't care. He took the phone and glanced down at his screen. His uncle was indeed calling him. He declined, set the phone on silent and shoved it back in his pocket.

"Thank you, Anderson. Should we head back?"

"Sure." Anderson started to untether the horses.

Cassandra looked up at him, worry darkening her eyes. "Are you all right?"

"Yes. It was bound to happen sooner or later."

"Yeah, but you just seem—"

"I'd rather not talk about this," he replied coldly.

Cassandra jerked back.

He inwardly cursed himself. This was supposed to be a gift thanking her for her help at The Lounge, a chance for her to enjoy something she hadn't been able to in a long time. And he'd ruined it by nearly kissing her, then not being able to handle his own emotions about a man he shouldn't feel anything for anyway.

Cassandra tilted her chin up. "All right."

They rode back to the meeting point in silence.

He'd hurt Cassandra. Yet his reaction to one phone call had been a good reminder that he needed to keep his distance. Cassandra was the type of woman a man could fall head over heels for, much the same way his father had fallen for his mother. And Gideon had no interest in revealing his emotions, of opening himself up to the kind of pain he'd witnessed his father suffer through.

He'd also just proved to himself that he wasn't capable of managing strong feelings. Not now, maybe not ever.

As they rode back, the heat of the sun now beating down with a relentless power that left him sweating, he focused on the silver lining. With everything he had shared with Cassandra today, that phone call might have been one of the best things that could have happened.

Better to have one painful reminder of why alone was best before he made a mistake that would leave both him and Cassandra broken.

CHAPTER TEN

Cassie

CASSIE STARED AT the crack in the foundation. Had it been there the last time she'd walked around the cottage? But then again, she couldn't remember the last time she'd been over here.

She rubbed at the knot of tension at the base of her neck. It seemed like every time she came home, she found something else. Putting on a new roof and replacing a few windows would no longer fix things. No, she suspected the cottage needed to be completely renovated at best, if not torn down and started from scratch.

Her father had always maintained the cottage. She remembered it as a cozy haven with huge windows, creaky floorboards and hand-woven rugs a grandmother she'd never known had given her father when he first moved here.

But that had also been before her dad had started to feel sick. Before he had to start cutting hours at the water sports shop to come home and rest. Before he didn't have the energy to repair the electric box or shingle the roof.

It was days like today when she was sorely tempted to sell the cottage and move on. No more worrying about bills, repairs, the stress from not knowing what would hit next. And, she thought darkly, as she turned away from the cottage and walked across the grass, she could finally be done with Gideon Radcliffe once and for all.

It had been two days since their horseback ride. Two days since Gideon had thanked Anderson for the ride and her for the invitation before walking to his convertible and driving away. There had been no more surprise visits to Prose & Tide, no emails, no text messages. She should be happy. He was finally leaving her alone.

So why did she feel so sad? Why did she glance toward his land to the north, disappointed when she saw nothing but empty beach?

And why did a fleeting kiss, followed by a near miss of a kiss, haunt her dreams more than any other romantic interaction she'd ever had in her life?

Her feet padded softly over the grass. When they'd first started out on their ride and she glanced back to see that look of amazed shock on his face, her heart had jolted. It was as if he'd been wearing a mask ever since she met him, one that enforced the cool, collected billionaire. In that moment, though, she'd seen an entirely different side of the man who was starting to intrigue her more than she liked. A man who had focused on business not out of greed like her mother, but out of grief.

He had truly enjoyed the ride. When he'd run his hand up and down Falcon's neck and talked to the horse as if he talked to animals every day, it had shocked and pleased her. She'd never been so grateful to be so wrong about someone in her entire life.

And when he'd nearly kissed her, when he'd leaned down and she'd felt the heat from his body, she'd finally accepted that there was far more between her and Gideon than simple business.

She kicked at a stray branch. That damn phone call had changed things, catapulted them back to the beginning. She didn't know what exactly had happened between Gideon and his uncle, so she'd been tempted to revisit the news reports and reviews of the trial. But doing so felt like a betrayal after she'd gotten so angry with him for looking into her finances. Yes, the trial was a matter of public record, but so much of it had been covered by tabloids. That had forced Gideon into a spotlight he hadn't asked for as he fought against his own family for control of something he obviously cared very deeply about.

She walked down the sloping hill toward the water's edge on the north side of Crescent Point. The moon-shaped beach on the far end had given the land its name. It formed a small, picturesque cove with the land next to hers.

Gideon's land.

She glanced back over her shoulder. She had only ever known Crescent Point as an outdoor playground and nature preserve, a sanctuary for local wildlife and vegetation. It was hard to look at the green grass, the towering trees and the occasional flower or bush and imagine them replaced by a resort.

But, she thought with a resignation she felt all the way to her bones, it might be better than clinging to a dream she wouldn't be able to achieve on her own.

From here, the cottage no longer looked like a magical beachside sanctuary. It looked old, decrepit. The peeling paint and missing shingles added to the impression that the house was sagging, as if it could barely stand a moment longer.

A sigh escaped as she turned her back on the cottage and sank down onto the sand. The cottage had probably looked like this for a very long time. But now, with the sharp blade of grief dulled by time, she saw it with more realistic eyes. Recognized that she had numerous financial obstacles to overcome.

She thought briefly of contacting her mother. But aside from a text message saying she was sorry to hear of John's passing, her mother had been silent. Even if she did offer money, it would come with ties that would rebind Cassie to her mother and her lofty visions for Cassie's future.

Visions that had everything to do with what her mother wanted and nothing to do with what would make Cassie content.

Which left Cassie with a mounting pile of bills, a rotting cottage and not enough income to stave off the inevitable.

Unless she accepted Gideon's offer.

She dropped her head on to her knees. Could she live with that? Could there be another possibility, something she was missing, that would allow her to restore it and stay?

With a heavy sigh, she reached into the backpack she'd brought and pulled out her notebook and pen. It had been nearly a year since she'd written. More than that since she'd tried submitting anything to a publisher. She'd told herself she was content to write summaries of other authors' stories, to bring their works to life through her work with Prose & Tide.

But being around Gideon had stirred not just new desires but old ones, dreams she had pushed aside long ago. She put pencil to paper, let the words flow out of her. Grief and loss, desire and attraction. Everything she'd experienced over the past week, the past five months.

The words rambled, dived down with hopelessness before arcing up with hope. A story emerged, one of two people at opposite ends, slowly brought together by the realization that they had both been wrong. That beneath the misunderstandings and anger and hurt lay something more.

Awareness prickled over her skin. Her head shot up as Gideon emerged from the trees on his property. He walked down to the water's edge, hands in the pockets of his dark brown slacks, a forest green polo molded to his powerful shoulders. His feet, however, were bare.

She watched him for a moment, noted the lift of his chin and the set of his shoulders. Confident, powerful. Yet something told her he was still grappling with whatever demons his uncle's call had unleashed.

The urge to go to him, to offer comfort as she had when he confided in her just before the call, nearly propelled her forward. But the memory of how quickly he'd shut her out, how easily he'd pushed her away just moments after they'd almost kissed, stopped her. He didn't want her prying into his private life. And she had no desire to pursue someone who cut her off so easily. She had spent twenty years of her life with someone who always kept her at arm's length. It didn't matter how attractive or compelling she found Gideon. She would not get herself into another situation where she was left feeling wanting, like she wasn't enough.

Slowly, she closed her notebook, then stood and started to turn back toward the cottage.

"Cassandra."

She froze. Part of her wanted to pretend she hadn't heard him and continue on. It would be easier that way, to not have any interaction with him until she decided what to do. But another part of her, one driven by a lethal combination of heart and hormones, encouraged her to turn around.

God, when did she become a hopeless romantic?

Slowly, she turned around. Gideon was striding down the beach toward her, his shoes dangling in one hand.

Why is that sexy? she thought frantically as he drew near.

He stopped a few feet away.

"Hello." The word came out breathless.

"Hi. Do you work today?"

"Yes, the dinner and evening shift. You?"

"I actually took the rest of the day off."

She blinked in surprise. "Oh?"

"Someone recently told me I should start enjoying the little things."

She stared at him for a moment, trying to decipher if he was poking fun at her. But, she realized with some surprise, he was serious.

"So what are you doing today?"

He glanced back at his land. "Revisiting the past."

"Brave."

He made a derisive noise. "I wouldn't call it brave. It's not something I want to do."

"I think that's true bravery, though. Forcing ourselves to confront something we don't want to."

Like the state of the cottage. My finances.

She understood all too well the desire to continue moving forward and pretending like everything was okay.

Gideon looked back at her. His eyes softened, warmed just enough that it left her feeling breathless. "I hope you never lose that, Cassandra."

"What?"

"You have something I've never had. The ability to find the good amid the bad."

Blood rushed to her cheeks. "You're giving me too much credit."

"No," he said firmly, "I'm not."

His eyes flickered over her shoulder. She resisted the urge to step in front of him, to block his view of the cottage. There was no point. He was more than aware of its state.

"Have you had any more incidents?"

"No." She sighed. "I'm sorry for how I greeted you the day we met."

"Understandable after you shared what happened." His eyes roamed over the point, the cove and finally his land. "This is my first attempt at building a new resort."

"Really?" She thought back over everything she had read about Radcliffe Resorts. "Wasn't there a new one built in France? The Mediterranean?"

"Yes, but that land had been part of Radcliffe Resorts' holdings for years before my father died. The plans had already been there. This is my first time trying to purchase land for a project that isn't set in stone. And I screwed up."

She thought back to when Peter Zam had first appeared on her doorstep with a cash offer and an overly confident attitude. She remembered how quickly his bravado had turned first to incredulity, then anger when she had repeated her rejection.

"The offer was not presented well," she agreed.

"That's not how my father founded Radcliffe Resorts." Gideon looked out over the sea. "He always made sure that our resorts served the people and bettered the communities where we built." He looked back at her. "Our clients are extremely important. But the people who live in and around our resorts, who work there, deserve the same investment."

She swallowed hard. "I know many people at the chamber meeting were impressed by what you had to say."

"And I'm grateful for that. But I still haven't convinced you."

"No. Not completely."

"I'd like to have a chance to show you."

"Show me?" she repeated.

"Yes. I understand and respect that the answer may still be no. But I'd like to have an opportunity to show you why I believe a Radcliffe Resort could be beneficial to Moonrise Bay."

The roles were reversed from just a few nights ago when she had asked Gideon to trust her. Except that night, Gideon had put not just one of his businesses in her hands, but also a major event, one that could have made or broken his success following his trial. She didn't owe him anything. She knew that.

But she wanted to do this.

"All right."

Some of the tension eased from his body. "Are you able to take a few nights off?"

She grimaced. She was slated to work through Sunday. She couldn't pass up five nights' worth of tips.

"A few?"

"Three at most, although we may be able to accomplish it in two. Given that this is for the sake of business, I can reimburse you."

She put her hands on her hips. "Gideon—"

"It's an offer." One corner of his mouth tilted up. "Not a requirement."

"If we can wait until Monday morning, I'm already scheduled to be off on Monday and Tuesday, and I can probably have someone cover for me on Wednesday."

"Monday it is." His slight grin deepened. "I'm assuming your passport is an order?"

Nerves and anticipation clashed, tangled. "Yes. Why?"

"Pack light. We're going on a trip."

Before she could ask any more questions, Gideon turned and walked back down the beach.

Her mouth dropped open. "Gideon?"

"Similar climate," he called over his shoulder. "And bring at least one dress."

The hope she'd written off just moments ago reared its head. Was this trip purely for business? Or was Gideon finally giving them an opportunity to explore what had been building between them?

Her heart pounded against her ribs. She tried, and failed, to stifle her anticipation.

"Where are we going?"

He turned and walked backward a few steps, a cocky smile lighting up his handsome face. "It's a surprise." And then he disappeared into the trees.

CHAPTER ELEVEN

Gideon

HE SHOULDN'T BE EXCITED. But Gideon couldn't help the small thrill that raced through him as Cassandra parked her car in the private lot at the end of Grand Cayman National Airport. She got out of the car, dressed in white pants and a loose, flowing blue top that reminded him of the sea on their horseback ride.

He was courting fire. It was easy when they were apart to tell himself that he wasn't attracted to her, that he didn't miss her. But as she walked toward him, sunglasses obscuring her face, he knew the next few days would be the true test. Could he stay focused on his goal, enjoy her company, yet keep his feelings to himself? Spare them both the heartbreak that would inevitably follow when their individual dreams clashed?

"So," she said as she drew near, "do I get to find out where we're going now?"

He tilted his head to one side.

"Well?"

"I'm thinking."

She shook her head. "You know, I feel like this is how a lot of murder mysteries start."

"With a very handsome and wealthy businessman whisking away the heroine to an exotic, luxurious destination?" He rocked back on his heels. "Isn't that more like a Christmas movie?"

She snorted. "There's no Christmas tree farm that needs saving, no hot cocoa, and…" Her cheeks turned pink.

"What?"

"Nothing." She cleared her throat. "Maybe I should—"

"Once we're airborne, I will tell you." He reached for her suitcase.

"I can carry it myself."

"I know." He grabbed the handle. "I'm not offering because I think you can't do it. As someone once told me, people around here help others out."

She chewed on her bottom lip, a movement that drew his gaze to her mouth and sent a shock through his system.

"It's really annoying when you listen to me."

He chuckled. "I'll make sure to do less of that in the future."

He let her climb the stairs first and was rewarded with her gasp as she entered. He followed her in, watched in amusement as she took off her sunglasses and turned in a circle.

"Is this real life?"

Plush leather seats and two long couches dominated the back half of the cabin. Walnut trim accented the ivory color of the seating. An oval-shaped table with six chairs anchored around it took up the front half of the plane near the cockpit. Accent lighting cast a golden hue over the walls.

"Did you rent this?"

"It's mine."

Cassandra's head whipped around. "Yours?"

"Mine."

She trailed her fingers over one seat. His fingers clenched around the handle of her suitcase. This was the right move. Showing her what Radcliffe Resorts was like, what it could do to benefit a small community, would do far more to sway Cassandra than any sunset cruise or fancy dinner.

If it also brought her some joy, gave her a reprieve from the long hours she worked, then so be it.

A flight attendant appeared and took their drink orders. Gideon ordered black coffee while Cassandra indulged in a mimosa as they buckled their seats for takeoff. Minutes later, the plane accelerated down the runway and took to the skies. The wheels had barely come up when Cassandra turned to him. "All right. We're airborne. Where are you taking me?"

"Europe."

"Where in Europe?"

"The French Mediterranean."

Her face lit up. "Oh, wow."

"It's a smaller resort east of the more popular towns."

"Is this the one you mentioned? The one where you already owned the land?"

"No. That one is near Calais, a well-established resort town in France. Radcliffe at Falais de Vignes is a smaller resort. One of the last ones my father oversaw before passing." He said it matter-of-factly, kept his tone brisk. But judging by the way Cassandra looked at him, he didn't fool her.

"You don't have to do this for me, Gideon."

"It's time." He met her gaze head-on. "I've been hiding from the past for too long. Whenever my father wanted to start a new resort, he would go to the town, city or village where he planned to build. He would scout out the land himself, talk to the locals and visit the neighboring businesses. He didn't just instruct me to do the right thing by the communities. He lived it. Every day."

"And you feel like you let him down."

Gideon's fingers tightened on his armrest. "What makes you say that?"

"I don't know." She glanced down at her glass. "A feeling. The way you talk sometimes."

"When I realized my father wasn't going to make it, it was as if a switch flipped in me. It was my only way to deal with what I knew was coming. My mother had died from a stroke a year before." One corner of his mouth curved up into a sad smile. "They loved each other very much. Too much."

His eyes flickered to Cassandra, but she said nothing, simply sat and listened.

"When she died, my father became a shadow of himself." His throat tightened. "He gave up. It didn't matter that he still had a son who needed him or a brother who, at least at that time, cared about him. All he could think about was my mother."

"That must have been very painful."

"It was. Focusing on Radcliffe Resorts gave me a purpose."

She frowned. "Doesn't it get lonely sometimes?"

Not until you.

He had survived before Cassandra had entered his life. He would continue on long after she left.

"Loneliness is better than pain."

"But isn't loneliness a type of pain?" She laid a gentle hand on top of his, the soft touch making him ache. "A kind of loss?"

"It is."

Her fingers tightened on his. "Are you going to keep yourself closed off for the rest of your life?"

For a moment, Gideon wanted to tear down his walls. To let in the possibility of pain, yes, but also the possibility for happiness.

For love.

But he couldn't do it. Couldn't open himself up to the pain, the uncertainty, potential for loss. And that was the crux of it, the final nail in the coffin. Whether Gideon could take another risk or not, there were pieces of himself locked up so tightly he didn't know if he'd ever be able to undo the chains.

And Cassandra deserved so much more than that.

"If I ever get married, it will be to someone I like. Someone I respect." He raised his head, held her gaze. "Someone who will accept what I'm willing to give."

And not ask for more.

The unspoken words hung between them. Cassandra stared at him for a long moment. Then she gave him a small smile, squeezed his hand and sat back. Cool air hit the back of his hand.

It was better this way, he told himself. Let Cassandra know what he was and wasn't capable of before they landed. Keep the trip focused on business and not let personal temptations cloud his purpose.

So why did he feel as though he'd just let something incredible slip through his fingers?

His phone rang. He glanced down at it, kept his face expressionless as his uncle's name appeared again. He let it ring, heard the ding letting him know this time his uncle had left a voicemail.

His uncle could call every day until the day he died. Gideon would never answer.

"Mr. Radcliffe?" Katelyn, the head stewardess, came into the cabin. "Would you like for me to serve breakfast now?"

"Please."

Katelyn and another flight attendant brought out several plates and laid them on the boardroom table. A silver platter with flaky croissants, *pain au chocolat* dusted with powdered sugar. A wooden board artfully covered in thinly sliced prosciutto, slabs of goat cheese and plump strawberries.

Cassandra surveyed the food with large eyes and a smile. "This looks incredible."

And that was why he'd done it. Breakfasts on long flights normally consisted of black coffee and an energy bar. But he knew Cassandra would enjoy a French breakfast, one with luxurious touches like the soft-boiled eggs with truffle salt. In a way, it was selfish, too. Her reactions to things he took for granted brought him into the moment, made him more aware of the little joys that were to be found.

He would never be able to give Cassandra what she deserved in a relationship. But he would give her what he could. Savor the moments he had come to enjoy with the same pleasure he experienced when he'd successfully brokered a new deal, achieved a goal.

No, he acknowledged as Cassandra looked out the window, her glass cradled in her hands. The pleasure he'd experienced in Cassandra's presence had far surpassed any satisfaction he'd taken from business.

Maybe, one day a long time from now, it would once again be enough.

CHAPTER TWELVE

Cassie

IT WAS INCREDIBLE how different the beaches of the world looked. The powdery white sand of Falais de Vignes was similar to Grand Cayman, its touch like silk on her bare feet. The water close to shore was a similarly hued bright blue. The coastline, however, was a stark contrast to Cayman's soothing, gentle shores. Here the cliffs soared up to the sky, rugged and craggy. Pine trees pushed up through the rocks and added a splash of green to the landscape. Grand Cayman was relaxing, peaceful. Falais de Vignes was majestic.

The Radcliffe at Falais de Vignes was no exception. The two-story villa boasted a soaring lobby and pillars crafted of stone that mimicked the surrounding land. The simple ivory walls gave the stunning handcrafted floor tiles a chance to shine. She'd almost hated walking on them as the receptionist had greeted them with chilled glasses of champagne and a tour of the public spaces. A private library and the spa took up half of the first floor, while the other half was dedicated to the resort's restaurant, cocktail bar and café. All independently owned and operated, Gideon had pointed out, by local entrepreneurs.

The pool deck boasted lounge chairs and an infinity pool that gave jaw-dropping views of the sea. Stone paths twisted through carefully maintained gardens blooming with native flowers and plants. The ground-floor rooms included their own private soaking pools. The top floors included soaking baths on the balconies.

Yet the rooms, while luxurious, were surprisingly simple. Custom tilework, arched doorways, breezy curtains and stunning artwork. Again, Gideon had pointed out as he'd escorted her to her room, done by local artists.

Afternoon had swiftly given way to night. Gideon had taken her to dinner, answering every single question she'd posed to him, from Radcliffe Resorts' impacts on the environment to how he encouraged the hiring of local employees.

She thumped her pencil against the pad of paper balanced on her thighs. Gideon had known exactly what to say, how to strike at her deepest fears when it came to how the resort would affect Moonrise Bay. When Peter Zam had first shown up, he'd spouted off a few sentences about Radcliffe Resorts' commitments to local involvement and sustainability. Rehearsed, bland. He hadn't cared enough to put effort into his pitch. He'd thought his initial offer of $3 million would do the talking for him.

But to hear how the resort worked so much with the local community, to see it in action, was a different story. It impressed her. Along with Gideon's obvious respect for his father and how he'd run the business before his death, seeing the resort had given her much to think about.

Her chest tightened. His admission on the plane, a subtle warning that a relationship between them would never work, had helped her put a lid on her growing attraction. She wanted a family of her own one day. A husband who would love her and let himself be loved. Children she could snuggle and cheer on and serve as their anchor through the storms they would face.

Gideon would not be that man. After all these years, he still clung so tightly to his grief and wore it as a shield.

Although she admitted, as she drew a small circle in the corner of her paper, hadn't she done the same thing? She had put off writing for so long because she had hung on to her mother's derision, her own fears about trying and failing.

But that's what now was for. She reread the few sentences she'd drafted. It had been years since she'd written. Putting pencil to paper, watching her words appear on the page, had been cathartic, a release of a weight she hadn't even realized she'd been carrying.

I wish Gideon could do that, too.

She shook her head. If he was ever able to, it would be in his own time. He'd made his position clear. And really, it was the best thing for both of them. As long as they were engaged in business negotiations, removing any emotion from the equation was smart.

Even if it still left an ache in her stomach.

"What are you writing?"

Her fingers tightened around the pencil as butterflies erupted inside her.

Real tight lid on those emotions, Cass.

"I thought you were in a meeting."

Gideon sat down next to her on the sand, obviously not caring if his black suit pants got dirty. "I was. Now I'm here."

Yes, he was, and he was sitting far too close for comfort. No longer could she smell sea salt or the earthiness of the beach. No, now it was cedar, woodsy and intoxicating.

He nodded toward the pad. "Anything fun?"

She hesitated. "Writing again. Or trying to, at least." She pulled her sunglasses down. The shades gave her a feeling of protection. "Can't very well preach about moving on if I don't at least try to do it myself."

"Are you doing it to prove something or for yourself?"

She glanced at him. "That's a hell of a question." She thought for a moment, tapping her pencil against the paper. "A little of both. Part of it is I want to stand up to my mother even though I haven't talked to her since my father passed. Since moving to the island, I maybe talked with her once a year so I don't know when I'll actually be standing up to her, but the more I think about what my future may look like, the more I want to do this. For me." She smiled down at her first sentence. "Whether or not anything comes of it, I forgot how much I enjoyed this. It's cathartic."

"What's your story about?"

She kept her eyes focused on the paper. "Just a woman traveling the world trying to find herself."

"Let me guess. She meets the man of her dreams."

Gideon's amused tone teased a smile from her. "You may not believe in true love, and I may never find it myself, but plenty of people enjoy reading about it."

He was silent for a moment. "It's not that I don't believe in true love. My parents loved each other more than I've ever seen anyone care about another human being. It was the heartache that followed that soured me on the idea of committing myself so completely to someone."

"But don't you commit yourself to Radcliffe Resorts?" she asked, eyeing him steadily.

"That's different. That's business."

"Yes and no. You pour your life into it. It's doing great now, but what if tomorrow there were an economic downturn or a natural disaster?"

"An uplifting thought."

She nudged him with her shoulder. "You know what I mean. Continued success is not guaranteed. Yet you throw yourself in with your entire heart." Heat stained her cheeks, but she pushed forward. "I already glimpsed that at the Radcliffe on Seven Mile Beach. You care about your staff. You're not afraid to help out with some of the harder things. And I've seen it here, too."

He tilted his head to the side, staring at her. "I'm glad I was finally able to make a good impression on you."

She glanced back at the resort, situated a couple of hundred feet away from the beach. "It doesn't hurt that you literally flew me across the Atlantic on a private plane and gave me an ocean-side room with my own mini pool."

"That's not what changed your mind."

"No, it's not."

"Then what?" He reached up and tucked a stray curl behind her ear.

The unexpected intimate touch froze her words in her throat. "Uh…"

"I'm curious." His hand lingered, his fingertips tracing a trail down her cheek.

"It's hard to formulate thoughts when you're doing that."

"Doing what?"

Oh, God, his voice had deepened, roughened with barely restrained emotion.

"I don't understand," she said, her voice barely a whisper as she fought against the pounding of her own heart.

"I don't either." He leaned forward. "All I know is I can't stop thinking about you. And every time you gift me with your trust, it pulls me in." His lips hovered above hers. "I'm not saying that to manipulate you or seduce you. I don't allow myself to trust easily. That was true for years, mostly because I held myself back from letting anyone get close enough to trust. And then my uncle destroyed what little capacity I had left. But you, Cassandra," he said as he reached up to touch her face once more, "every time I've given you my trust, you've returned it tenfold."

She wanted to lean into his touch. Wanted to fully open herself to the feelings growing inside her. It seemed impossible that she had only known him for a week. Yet with every encounter, every conversation, she fell just a little bit harder. He was confident, sometimes arrogant, but he also remembered the names of the receptionist and the artist who had painted the watercolors hanging in her room.

She'd overheard a conversation that morning between two of the staff. They were discussing the internship program Gideon had developed for students in the nearby village and the scholarship he'd established for those wanting to continue on to university. Even though he thought he held himself back, kept himself removed, he cared far more than most people of his status did.

But less than twenty-four hours ago he'd made his position clear. She wanted to get to know him more, wanted to spend more time with him, but she couldn't allow herself to get her hopes up, to put herself out there only to be rejected and face yet another loss.

She leaned back. His hand dropped.

"I'm sorry." She blinked back tears. "I feel it, too. But you don't want to get hurt. Neither do I."

She wouldn't be someone's second choice. Wouldn't settle again for business coming before family.

She'd lived that life once. And it had nearly broken her. No matter how deeply she was coming to care for Gideon, she wouldn't surrender her own dreams to support his. Wouldn't spend any more nights by a window waiting for the one she longed for to come home, to feel for a brief moment like she mattered more than his career.

She stood, folding her arms over her chest and holding her pad of paper over her heart like a shield. And then, before she could say something ridiculous, before she made a fool of herself, she turned and walked away, leaving Gideon sitting on the beach behind her.

CHAPTER THIRTEEN

Gideon

THE DEEP BLUE waters of the Mediterranean rose and fell, the wind whipping the tips into peaks of white as a brisk wind rushed up the beach. The evening forecast called for a thunderstorm.

Fitting, Gideon thought as he raised his coffee cup to his lips.

He'd made a mistake on the beach this morning. Touching Cassandra had been foolish on his part. It had also been cruel after he'd just told her he could offer her nothing.

Perhaps he was just as selfish as his uncle after all.

His mood darkened as a large cloud scuttled across the sky and blocked out the sun. He hadn't planned on it. After his meeting with the mayor of Falais de Vignes on tourism initiatives for the remainder of the year, he'd walked back to the resort via one of the paths that connected it to many of the town's neighborhoods and businesses. He'd spied Cassandra sitting on the beach. Need had drawn him off the path and onto the sand. He'd wanted—no, needed—to see her.

That need should have frightened him. Instead, it had only pulled him deeper.

He set his coffee cup down and stood, scrubbing a hand over his face as he moved to the railing. The logical thing to do, the ethical thing, would be to stick to his original plan and keep things professional.

The thought of never getting to touch her again made his hands tighten into fists.

It was strange, he thought as the wind picked up its pace, that he'd barely thought of Radcliffe at East End since the plane had left Grand Cayman. What had once been his primary purpose, the goal he viewed as the first major achievement of his career and his life, was now barely on his radar.

He still believed in the resort and what it could do for Moonrise Bay. Still wanted to honor his father's wishes.

But it no longer carried the intensity it once had, no longer occupied so much of his thoughts.

That honor belonged to Cassandra.

His phone dinged. He glanced down at it. A text confirming the surprise he'd arranged for her tonight. He'd told himself when he'd booked the reservation that it had been as a thank-you for coming to France since she wouldn't accept any kind of reimbursement for the shift she was missing. He'd convinced himself it would make her more amenable to accepting his offer and would strengthen their working relationship.

Lies. All of them. He'd done it because he'd wanted to make her happy.

He turned away from the railing and stalked back into his suite. He'd given gifts to women before. Jewelry, trips, designer gowns—all of it had helped him maintain emotional distance while enjoying the surface-level benefits like physical pleasure or companionship.

But this wasn't just a lavish gift. There was intention behind it, an emotional investment versus just swiping his credit card or asking one of his secretaries to make a purchase. Would she even want such a gesture after he'd built that boundary between them? After he'd toyed with her feelings by saying one thing and doing another less than twenty-four hours later?

Worse, was it even right for him to offer it when he was so conflicted?

Irritated with himself and his whirling thoughts, he walked out of his suite and down the hall to the door next to his. He knocked once. A moment later the door opened. Cassandra stared out at him, her body partially hidden behind the door.

"Hi."

"I made a reservation after you agreed to come on the trip. It was supposed to be a surprise. But since it's a reservation for the two of us, I wanted to give you the choice of going given what happened earlier."

She fully opened the door and leaned against the doorframe. Her curls tumbled over her shoulders, much as they had the first day they'd met.

"What did happen, Gideon? I don't know what to think, what to do. You tell me one thing, and then you turn around and make me feel…"

"Make you feel what?" he prompted quietly.

Her amber eyes fixed on his, wide and vulnerable.

"What was the reservation for?"

He understood her rebuff. Understood it and accepted the disappointment. He had no justification to want anything more. Not after he'd told her one thing and pursued another.

"Dinner."

The tension in her face eased as she cocked her head to one side. "You've already taken me to dinner. And breakfast and lunch and—"

"Somewhere else. Off-site."

One corner of her mouth tilted up even as she eyed him suspiciously. "Where?"

"Trust me."

The words slipped out. But this time he stood his ground, willing himself to accept whatever her decision was even if it hurt. She stared at him for what seemed like forever.

Then, slowly, she nodded. Emotion stormed through him, an intense wave that rocked him to his foundation. Yet again, Cassandra offered. And yet again, he took.

This time, though, he swore he would meet her. Offer her everything he had resisted and accept the repercussions, the potential pain.

"Be ready in an hour."

"An hour?" She glanced at her watch. "It's three in the afternoon."

"It'll take a while to get there." He arched his brows playfully. "Do you have something more formal?"

She blanched. "Uh… I have the dress I wore to Marla's daughter's wedding."

"There's a boutique in town. The head chef's cousin owns it." He pulled out his phone. "I'll have her send up some samples."

"That's kind, Gideon, but I don't really have the money for a new dress."

"Camille will loan you a dress."

She rolled her eyes even as she bit back a smile. "Fine. As long as it's a loan."

"Meet you in the lobby in an hour?"

"Deal."

An hour later, Gideon stood in the lobby dressed in a tuxedo. Camille had run over herself shortly after he'd sent his text. He smiled slightly. He could easily imagine Cassandra's face when she'd seen the kinds of dresses Camille designed, could visualize her exclaiming and running her fingers over the fabric.

Movement on the stairs made him glance to his right. His lips parted as Cassandra walked down, one hand holding on to the railing as if she'd collapse without it. Her eyes found his, her face uncertain as she neared the bottom of the staircase.

The off-the-shoulder teal-colored dress clung to the slender lines of her waist, the bodice and small puffs of sleeves trimmed in gilt thread. The full skirt swirled around her ankles. Golden vines connected pale pink flowers just above the hem. Her hair had been twisted over one shoulder and pinned with a gold flower clip.

A fairy, he'd thought the first time he'd met her. Now, as she walked toward him, her hands tight on a clutch the same rosy tint as the flowers, *enchantress* seemed more apt.

"Is it..." She ran a hand over the skirt. "Do I look all right?"

He crossed to her and took her hand in his, raising it to his lips. "You look beautiful, Cassandra."

She swallowed hard. "Why do you always say my name like that?"

"Like what?" he asked as he kept hold of her hand and tugged her gently toward the door.

"Everyone else calls me Cassie."

"Would you prefer that?"

"No." She smiled as they walked out into the late afternoon sun. "I'm just curious."

"Cassie is certainly appropriate when you're running around making drinks for women with broken hearts or sitting on a beach writing stories. But," he added as a long, sleek limo pulled up, "when I first met you, even though I had serious concerns about you removing my eye, I thought you were fierce. Strong."

She gave an embarrassed laugh. "I overreacted."

He held open the door for her, joined her inside and closed the door before he responded.

"You were scared. You'd lost someone important to you just a few months before that. You were being pressured to do something you weren't comfortable with, and you had reasonable suspicion to be wary of anyone trespassing on your land."

Her eyes glistened before she looked out the window.

"What is it?"

"Just…" Her sigh arrowed straight into his chest. "Thank you." She cleared her throat. "How long of a drive is it?"

He settled back in his seat. "About ten minutes."

"Ten minutes?" She gave him a quizzical look. "Why did we leave so early, then?"

"Because we have an hour-and-a-half plane ride after that."

That smile he was coming to enjoy so much chased the shadows from her eyes as it brightened her face.

"Where to?"

"Venice."

Silence fell between them. She stared at him, her body frozen, her eyes unblinking.

"Venice?" she finally whispered.

"Yes."

"Gideon..." Her eyes drifted shut, her lips pressed tightly together. When she finally opened them, the golden brown depths glittered with tears. "I don't know what to say."

"If I was presumptuous—"

"No." She shook her head. "No. Just..." She reached for him, laid her hand on top of his and squeezed.

Emotion tightened his throat. It would have been completely understandable for her to not want to go, for it to be too soon.

But she had accepted his gift. Accepted him, even if just for a night.

As the limo sped on toward the airport, he finally accepted that some risks were worth taking.

Hopefully, he thought as Cassandra stared out the window, she would feel the same.

CHAPTER FOURTEEN

Cassie

STONE BUILDINGS STRETCHED up toward the night sky, the walls painted in varying shades of earthy color. A few had opted for vibrancy, including one eye-popping villa done in bright turquoise with gleaming white shutters. Arched windows and ornate carvings added elegance, while the stonework spoke to the history of the Floating City. Roses climbed up trellises while bougainvillea and fuchsia cascaded over the railings of wrought-iron balconies and scented the air with a delicate, floral fragrance.

Venice was, in short, more than Cassandra had ever dreamed.

Gideon guided her through the winding corridors and alleys, past street cafés and brightly lit shops, her hand clasped in his. Every now and then, she would glance at his chiseled profile. Words would rise in her throat.

But then she would look away. She didn't know what to say.

Or you're nervous.

She swallowed hard. She wasn't just nervous. She was scared.

When Gideon had told her he wasn't interested in a

relationship, part of her had breathed a little easier. The feelings she was developing for Gideon, not just the physical attraction but the respect and the admiration, were stronger than anything she'd felt before. Having Gideon be the one to cut things off before they got in too deep had been hard. But there had also been relief. For all her talk about trust and putting oneself out there, the thought of exploring how she felt on a deeper level had been intimidating.

But now it was downright terrifying. The way he had looked at her on the beach, the way he had touched her face, had lingered with her all afternoon. If he was playing games with her, she would cut him off and leave without a backward glance.

But if he had been telling the truth, if he truly wanted her and was reconsidering his stance, then she had a hard choice to make.

They crossed over a bridge that arched above one of the canals. A gondola floated by underneath, the romantic strains of a violin drifting up. Gideon stopped and pulled her over to the balustrade.

"What do you think?"

His breath feathered over her ear. Despite the warmth of the evening, a shiver teased its way down her spine.

"It's one of the most beautiful places I've ever seen."

It felt so natural to lean against him. She sucked in a breath as he wrapped an arm around her waist and pulled her closer. She turned slightly, resting one cheek against the satin lapel of his tuxedo.

"Why did you do this?"

He didn't answer right away. As she rested her head

against him, she felt the steady thump of his heartbeat against her cheek.

"I've been rich my whole life."

His voice rumbled in his chest. The sound of him relaxed her, had her leaning deeper into his embrace.

"My parents were generous. I've maintained my father's commitment to Falais de Vignes and the other communities where we have resorts. Made donations, funded scholarships."

"Bought the building and paid for the renovations for a luxurious dress boutique."

Gideon chuckled. "Camille told you?"

"She did."

The dress designer had fawned over Cassie, making her feel like a princess as she'd trotted out half a dozen dresses, each hand-sewn and more stunning than the last. She'd also shared how she'd lost everything in a divorce and moved back to Falais de Vignes penniless. How she'd worked in the resort restaurant and let it slip to Gideon that she had been saving up to open her own dress shop in Rome. And how one day, after she'd shown Gideon some drawings of her designs, he'd handed her the keys to a small shop in the seaside district.

"It was an investment."

"Given that she's opening another shop in Rome next spring, I'd agree." She nudged him with her shoulder. "But you didn't do it for that."

"No. I didn't do it for that." He slipped a finger under her chin and gently tilted her head back. "You never told me what it was that made you realize I wasn't completely self-absorbed."

She drew in a shuddering breath. Such a small detail.

But one that had tilted her world as she'd realized everything Gideon had said, everything he'd shown her, hadn't just been for show.

"The painting over my bed."

His eyebrows drew together. "The one of the *calanque*? The cove with the sailboat?"

"I asked you about it when we walked in. You said the receptionist's son had painted it last summer when he was home for a holiday." Slowly, tentatively, she reached up and cupped his face. His eyes flared as his breathing deepened.

"You bought every painting he would sell you."

"He's good."

"You knew that cove was the one his parents took him to when he was little, the one where he learned to swim. You knew that he decided to pursue a medical degree instead of going to art school."

She looked up at him then, the pressure in her chest intensifying as she stared up at the man she had once thought of as cold and ruthless. "You told him it was possible to have two dreams at once. That's when I changed my mind."

He brushed his thumb over her chin, rested it by the side of her mouth. For one heart-stopping moment, she thought he would kiss her. But then he stepped back.

Confused, and a little hurt, she allowed him to lead her off the bridge.

"It's hard to hear you describe me like that."

Surprised, she glanced up at him. "Why?"

"I always thought of myself as a fair man. That I was doing the right thing for the company, for the people who worked for me. I have no problem pushing the boundaries, especially when it comes to higher-ups in similar positions to mine. When people have wealth and prestige and use it irresponsibly, they deserve to be called out." He released a long, heavy breath. "Including myself."

"What do you mean?"

His hand tightened on hers. "As I've mentioned, the resort I've envisioned for Crescent Point would be my first new build. Everything I've done in the last twelve years has been either with existing Radcliffe resorts or buying already established properties. I prided myself on following in my father's footsteps, connecting with the communities, supporting them. But this one..." His voice trailed off. "Sometimes it almost feels too easy to receive credit for what I do. I paid attention to Henrietta's son. I bought his paintings. I could buy thousands of his paintings and still have more money than I know what to do with."

The derision in his voice, the borderline self-loathing, made her cringe.

"I had planned on visiting Grand Cayman a year ago to evaluate the properties that used to belong to my family and come up with a proposal for my team."

"So why did you send Peter to make the offer?"

"The lawsuit was the bulk of it. My uncle painted me as a selfish, greedy heir who didn't appreciate everything that he had done since my parents had passed. He accused me of overly ambitious projects that would wreck Radcliffe Resorts' bottom line. Then two of your neighbors placed their properties for sale. I was concerned that, if I approached them myself during the trial, it would draw unwanted media attention and sway public opinion to my uncle's side, possibly affecting the outcome of the trial. So, I sent Peter to serve as my representative to purchase those other properties and to start the negotiation process for Crescent Point with who I thought, at the time, would be your father."

They passed by another canal, this one crowded with more gondolas and tourists preparing to get on the sleek boats.

"After getting to know you, I'm a little surprised you sent him."

He grimaced. "Peter has been a loyal employee for a long time. He was with my father before he died. He served under my uncle. He was the one who told me about what my uncle was doing."

Cassandra's eyes widened. "Oh."

"Peter is loyal to the Radcliffe name. Telling me that my uncle was making questionable business decisions hurt him." He hesitated. "Then he took it a step further, shared evidence of my uncle's embezzlement even though it felt disloyal. Even though he was doing the right thing. Others might have fired him. But I asked him to stay. I knew I could trust him." A soft sigh escaped. "He took that trust, and his personal loyalty, too far."

Her mind went back to those lights flashing into her windows, to the tipped-over pots of bougainvillea spilling soil all over the porch. But she pushed the images away. Gideon had vouched for Peter. She still had her suspicions, but she would give Gideon a chance as he had given one to Peter.

"Everything I've done since coming to the island, meeting with the chamber, talking to you, coming up with alternatives to the original design of the resort, all of that should have been done first."

"But you were afraid of losing the land to another buyer if you waited until after the trial was over," she murmured.

"Yes. I told Peter to offer whatever it took, and I assumed that no matter what, my money would get me what I wanted." He smiled down at her. "I've rarely been told no. The few times I have, with a simple push and a little bit of money, I got everything I wanted. So, it's hard for me when you tell me you see me more positively than I see myself. I'm afraid that, if you were to look below the surface, you wouldn't like what you see. You paid the price for my overconfidence. I'm sorry."

"Thank you."

They turned a corner, and he led the way down a short flight of steps. Lanterns affixed to the stone walls illuminated the passage. It made so much more sense, knowing the reason why everything had played out the way it did. How the man she initially met had been such a stark contrast to the man at her side now.

The stairs ended at a gleaming wooden dock. On the far end, standing next to a lamppost with a brightly glowing globe at the top, was a gondolier dressed in a black-and-white-striped shirt with a red beret perched on top of his head.

"*Buona sera.* Signor Radcliffe?"

"Yes."

"Welcome." The gondolier smiled at Cassie. "And Signora Radcliffe?"

Heat infused her cheeks. "No. Just a friend."

"Well." He held out a hand. "Welcome to Venezia. My name is Vito."

They boarded the gondola and sat side by side in plush red seats.

"Music?" Gideon gestured for Cassie to answer.

"Please."

"Any requests?"

She thought back to the gondola that had floated past them just minutes before.

"Something instrumental."

A moment later, the soothing strains of a waltz drifted out from speakers beneath their seats, and Vito cast off, expertly navigating the long boat down the narrow canal. Cassie sat back and simply stared, soaking up every stained-glass window, every artfully carved emblem and dome-shaped roof. Several times she caught the scent of warm chocolate or baked bread. She turned to Gideon, slightly startled when she realized he was watching her with a small smile on his lips.

"What?"

Gideon pointed to the door of a passing house, one that featured a mighty ship facing off against huge, curling waves. "I probably wouldn't have noticed that before meeting you. Nor would I have thought to ride a horse into the ocean or to jiggle my feet in the sand. In some ways," he said as his eyes continued to move over the buildings, the people passing on the bridges overhead, "it almost feels like being reborn."

She swallowed hard. "That's beautiful."

He looked at her then, his blue eyes glowing in the dim light. "It's because of you, Cassandra."

"Almost there, Signor Radcliffe."

Cassandra blinked and looked around. Vito had steered the gondola into a massive waterway.

"The Grand Canal," Vito announced as he maneuvered the gondola amid the sea of watercraft. He guided the boat to a dock and hopped out, tethering the gondola to a post before helping Gideon and Cassandra out. "Enjoy your dinner. I shall wait for your return."

Gideon slipped him some money, enough to make Vito's eyes widen.

"Thank you, Signor Radcliffe."

Gideon offered Cassandra his arm. "Shall we?"

"You know," she said as he led her up the dock, "to you a large tip may seem meaningless. But to others, it shows that you notice us."

Gideon squeezed her hand, a simple gesture that filled her with warmth.

They approached a black podium with the Grand Canal Restaurant written in glittering gold letters on the front. The maître d', a tall woman draped in black that matched both the podium and her hair, aside from a few silver strands, smiled at them.

"Welcome to the Grand Canal Restaurant. Signor Radcliffe, I presume?"

"Yes."

"Follow me." She led them inside a stunning restaurant with round tables draped with scarlet cloth. Diners wore handcrafted suits, designer gowns and the kind of jewelry that probably required its own private security guard when not being worn by its owner.

More than one head turned in their direction. Whispers snaked like wildfire through the room. Conscious of the eyes on her, Cassie tightened her hold on Gideon's arm.

"Well, this is awkward."

"Only awkward when they realize the most beautiful woman in the room is on my arm."

His remarks startled a laugh out of her. "You really know how to lay on the charm, Mr. Radcliffe."

"I'm only sorry it took me so long to do so."

They left the gossiping diners behind them when the hostess led them into a hallway with a magnificent marble staircase. A chandelier gleamed overhead. She ushered them past the stairs and through a passage flanked by a bank of windows on one side and stunning sculptures and paintings on the other.

"Here we are." She stopped in front of glass doors, the wavy panes preventing a clear view of the outside. She opened one door and Cassie's mouth dropped open.

A square terrace waited outside, lit by dozens of glowing bulbs threaded through a pergola. The walls on either side were constructed of flowering vines, creating privacy while leaving the far side open to give dazzling views of the canal. A table sat in the middle, covered with the same scarlet cloth and topped with a flickering tapered candle. Red upholstered lounge chairs and settees were arranged around the perimeter next to overflowing pots of the same flowers Cassie had spied on the balconies as they walked through the city.

The hostess walked them to the table. Gideon pulled out Cassie's chair before taking his own. "Your waiter will be with you momentarily. Would you like to begin with a glass of wine?"

Gideon gestured to Cassie. "You're the expert."

Excitement trickled through her. "Do you have any Riserva wine labels?"

"We do. I will instruct your waiter to bring that out shortly."

Cassie stood as soon as the door closed and moved to the railing. "It's almost too much to take in," she murmured quietly.

Gideon joined her. "How so?"

"I feel as though I could look and look and still not see everything. It's so wonderful."

Before Gideon could reply, the door opened behind them.

"Oh." The waiter paused in the doorway. "Excuse me. I can come back later."

"No." Cassie smiled at the waiter as she walked back to the table. "Thank you. I'm just trying to take it all in."

The waiter, a young man with a big smile that flashed against his dark skin, nodded as he set wineglasses on the table.

"I understand. I have lived in Venice for three years, and I still feel as if I've seen only a fraction of the city." He held out the bottle for Cassie's approval. *"Signora?"*

"Yes, thank you."

No matter what happened, she thought as the waiter poured the wine, she would remember this night and all the joy this trip had brought her.

They dined on seared scallops with saffron risotto topped with nasturtiums from the Venetian Lagoon, oven-baked sea bass, rosemary-infused potatoes and grilled vegetables from a local farm. Dessert was an exquisite creamy panna cotta garnished with fresh berries and a raspberry drizzle.

At last, when all the plates were cleared away, Cassie leaned back in her chair, a chilled grappa-based cocktail in hand. "That was the most incredible meal I've ever had."

Gideon arched a brow even as his lips worked up into a teasing smile. "Even better than breakfast on the plane?" he asked as he sipped espresso.

"Yes. Even better than that. Although I will say that was the best breakfast I've ever had."

A distant boom sounded.

"What was that?"

Gideon stood and held out his hand. "Come with me."

He guided her to the railing and pointed off in the distance. "There."

Her mouth dropped open as several bright golden balls shot up into the sky before bursting into a dazzling array of red, gold and white sparks. "Fireworks?"

"One of the largest Catholic festivals is taking place this week."

She gazed, mesmerized as the fireworks colored the canal and the gondolas in a rainbow of colors. She didn't know how long they watched, but finally she turned to him.

"What are we doing, Gideon?"

He stared down at her, the distant fireworks casting flashes of colored light over his face.

"It took me a matter of hours after telling you on the plane I had no interest in a relationship to realize I was an idiot. I've kept myself locked up for so long." He reached up and touched her face. "As soon as I cut myself off from the possibility of you, of exploring the connection between us, I realized I had made a mistake. But for the first time in a long time, I wasn't sure of myself. Would

I be able to open up enough? Am I even capable of giving you what you deserve?"

She swallowed hard.

"I understand. The fear," she clarified as he gazed down at her. "For the longest time, I thought something was wrong with me, that I was the reason why my mom couldn't love me. Shh," she said, laying a finger on Gideon's lips as he opened his mouth. "Logically I know it wasn't me. And I thought, when my father, Marla and so many others showed me that I was loved and accepted for myself, that I had come to terms with my mother's disappointment in me.

"But I haven't, not entirely. Because the feelings I have for you and the desire for you to return them, revive those old insecurities, the fears that I'm not enough, not wanted."

She sucked in a shuddering breath, reliving the moment she told her mother she was dropping out of college and moving to Grand Cayman to be with her dad. How her mom, almost a mirror image of Cassie, had pursed her lips with tight disapproval.

What a waste, her mother had mumbled under her breath before turning away.

Cassandra shook off the memory. She wasn't going to let past insecurities hold her back.

"But I want to try."

She held her breath, waited for his answer with bated breath.

"You make me want to try, Cassandra. The thought of one day looking back and realizing that we might have had something and I didn't take that chance was terrifying. More than any possible heartache."

Her eyes filled with tears. "Gideon."

Gideon plucked her glass from her fingers and set it, along with his own, on one of the tables. He cradled her face once more, pressed a hand to her back and drew her close.

"I'm scared, too. I am trying to decide about Crescent Point, and I think I know what the right answer is, but I'm still trying to figure things out." She tilted her head back, looked up at him. "But I want to try, too."

Gideon's body shuddered. "Cassandra."

He leaned down and covered her mouth with his. Her entire body came alive as she kissed him back, learned the feel of him, the taste. Savoring the intimacy, he slid his hand back into her hair and cradled her head as he deepened the kiss. Fireworks boomed in the distance. But, as Gideon pulled back and gently pressed a kiss to the tip of her nose and her forehead before returning to her mouth once more, she was certain that even the fireworks had nothing on the joyful thundering of her own heart.

CHAPTER FIFTEEN

Cassie

THE ISLAND LAY on the surface of the sea, a vivid green jewel surrounded by a ring of pale blue before the reef dropped off and the water turned dark. Cassie leaned back into her seat. It had been a long time since she had left the island. Two years, in fact. She'd forgotten what it had been like every summer…that bright bubble of happiness as the island had come into view. And the sinking sensation when it had receded into the distance as she'd flown home to her mother, waiting another nine months for her life to start again.

Gideon leaned forward and brushed a light kiss across her lips. Aside from when she had slept in one of the reclined seats on the plane, not an hour had gone by when she and Gideon hadn't held hands, touched, kissed. She wished they could have had more than an evening in Venice. That they could have extended their trip long enough to explore their burgeoning relationship further. But Gideon had arranged for his plane to fly them back from Italy after their date.

She'd contemplated asking to extend their trip. But truth be told, she wasn't sure if she was quite ready to deepen the intimacy. They'd already shared so much, so many heartaches and insecurities, in just over a week. Taking additional time, getting to know each other more, before they took the next step gave her a reprieve. Time to catch her breath as she accepted how quickly they had progressed from enemies to something more.

She smiled slightly as she glanced at Gideon. *Boyfriend* seemed like a tame word for what pulsed between them. But it was the best she could come up with. They had a little more time to figure it out. Gideon planned on staying on Grand Cayman for at least another couple of weeks before he went back to New York. The thought of him leaving so soon made her nervous. But it was a challenge they would navigate as they explored what was between them.

He hadn't brought up Crescent Point. Not once. She knew what decision she was leaning toward. Just one more day, she told herself. Just a little more time in her cottage, time to walk around her land before she finally told Gideon.

"Excited to be home?"

"I am. But I think I'm going to have to negotiate more vacation time with my boss. I've caught the travel bug."

"If you manage to finagle that extra time off, I know a guy with a plane."

She laughed as the plane began its descent. The wheels touched down with a soft bump. Shyly, she turned to Gideon.

"Would you…" She cleared her throat. "Would you like to come home with me?"

Gideon grasped her hand and raised it to his mouth,

grazed his lips over her knuckles. She sucked in a breath at the naked heat in his eyes.

"I'd like that very much."

The drive to Moonrise Bay was casual, relaxed. Gideon put the top of his convertible down. Cassandra closed her eyes, savored the wind whipping her hair about, the feel of Gideon's hand wrapped around hers.

She'd been content before. Happy. But this was something else, something she had read about in her books, dreamed about in her writings.

Something she wanted to label but hesitated.

Just a little bit longer, she promised herself. *A little bit more time.*

And then she would finally be able to accept the totality of what she felt for Gideon.

Gideon turned the car down the drive that led to the cottage. The trees gave way as he navigated around the bend.

The cottage appeared. For a moment, Cassandra could only stare. The sight before her didn't make sense. Didn't mesh with the image of what she'd left behind.

Until it hit with the force of a freight train.

The cottage was a wreck. Dirt, bits of ceramic pot and shredded bougainvillea blooms were scattered across the wooden boards. Both of her rocking chairs had been tossed into the front yard, each one missing spindles, and one sporting a broken armrest. The screen had been ripped out of the screen door, the glass of the main door broken. Bright red paint had been tossed across the front of her home. Gideon wouldn't be surprised if the perpetrator had dowsed the rest of the cottage as well.

She was staring at the cottage, pale, her eyes dull.

"Cassandra."

Slowly, she turned, her eyes seeking out Gideon. He squeezed her hand. She flinched.

In that moment, she knew that whatever had happened here, whatever had occurred while she'd been across the ocean falling for her enemy, had the power to destroy the fragile foundation she and Gideon had built.

Gideon

Gideon walked out of the cottage. The interior resembled the outside: a total wreck. He'd gone from room to room, ensuring no one had stayed behind. Cassandra had remained outside, staring out over the sea as she'd waited for him.

"Cassandra."

She flinched at the sound of her name. Slowly, she turned to him. He knew exactly where Cassandra's mind had gone. Knew and couldn't help the ball of anger tightening in his gut.

Did she truly think he had spirited her away so someone could ruin the last place she'd called home? Had the last three days meant nothing? He'd thought their time in France, their night in Italy, had meant something to her. Had shown her how deeply he cared.

But if she still thought him capable of scare tactics, of manipulation and intimidation, then their growing connection had been nothing more than an illusion.

He hated that someone had done this to her, had violated her space. Every time he thought about what could have happened if she'd been home, his entire body coiled into a spring, ready to lash out at the first person who so much as looked at her wrong.

Worse, though, was knowing she suspected him. He'd felt her withdrawal like a physical ache.

Had stepping away from Grand Cayman been nothing more than a fantasy that couldn't survive the pressures of everyday life?

She started, looked away from the sea to meet his gaze. "You know he did this."

She was in shock. She had every right to be. "I understand why you may think that—"

"You don't understand what he was like." She shook her head. "You don't understand at all."

He needed to think of this as a test. An opportunity to keep his emotions under control, to stay focused on supporting Cassandra and getting through this. He'd known they would face challenges throughout the relationship. He just hadn't expected one to come so soon or strike so close.

"You don't think I had anything to do with this, do you?" He had to ask.

Cassandra glanced toward the cottage, then quickly looked away, as if she couldn't bear to see the extent of the damage. "No. I don't think so."

The pain was swift, relentless. It barreled its way in and stole every ounce of happiness he had experienced the last few days with a gleeful *I told you so*. His worst fear had been opening himself up to someone and giving them the power to break him. But he wouldn't break. It hurt. It would for some time. But at least he learned his lesson early.

"You don't think so," he repeated coldly.

Cassandra shook her head weirdly. "Gideon—no."

"Did you mean anything you said? About the man you thought I was?"

She blinked owlishly, one hand coming up and then fluttering back down to her side. "I meant it, Gideon. But I told you. I told you I thought Peter was behind those first acts of sabotage, and now..."

Her voice broke.

He started forward before he even realized what he was doing. The sorrow on her face, the slight shifting as she turned her face away, stopped him in his tracks. He curled his hands at his sides.

"I will find out who did this. But if you don't know after all we've shared the last few days that I would never do something like this, then we don't know each other at all."

Before Cassandra could reply, a car appeared on the drive. Gideon tensed.

"Who is that?"

"Marla." Cassandra's voice was barely a whisper. "I texted and asked her to come."

Moments later, it drew next to his convertible. Marla stepped out, confusion written across her face as she hurried to Cassandra's side.

"Cassie...." Marla's mouth fell open as she took in the damage. "Oh, my God, Cassie." Her gaze darted to Gideon. Suspicion darkened her face before she turned to Cassandra and held out her arms. Cassandra leaned forward, tears falling down her face as Marla folded her into a hug.

Accepting what she had rejected from Gideon.

He didn't know how long he stood there listening to the crashing of the waves and Cassandra's quiet tears. How long it took for him to overcome the pain that throbbed like an open wound in the vicinity of his heart, to make sense of his chaotic thoughts.

He'd been a fool. A fool to ever risk letting someone in again.

He walked back to his car, mentally rebuilding his wall stone by stone with each step he took. His hands closed around the handle. Hesitated.

He didn't want to leave her. Not like this. Not with her home in shambles behind her.

But judging by how she'd pulled away from him, his presence was only making it worse.

He glanced over his shoulder. "She should stay with you tonight."

At Marla's brief nod, he got in the car and pulled away, forcing himself not to look back to see if Cassandra had even noticed he'd gone.

He drove along the winding Coastal Road for at least thirty minutes before he tried getting in touch with Peter. The phone rang several times before finally directing him to voicemail.

"Call me."

Peter wouldn't do something like this. Not after Gideon had made it clear to him that intimidation was not how Radcliffe Resorts operated. Someone else had done this. They must have.

But he still needed to see Peter, to find out where his associate had been last night. He called again as he entered West End. Left another voicemail.

When he got back to his hotel, he used the private elevator to go straight to his penthouse on the top floor. He walked in and set his keys down. The penthouse had been featured in a prominent travel magazine last year. Navy blue couches and chairs created by a designer with a flair for clean lines and a modern touch. Huge windows that could turn opaque at the press of a button and still provide him with stunning views of the Caribbean Sea while giving him privacy. A marble soaking tub in the bathroom. A two-story deck with a fire table, hot tub and small infinity pool. In short, everything someone's heart could desire. And it had never felt emptier than it did now.

His phone rang. His heart jumped for a moment before he saw Peter's name on the screen. "Peter. Where are you?"

"The resort, sir."

"Then come to my penthouse. Now."

He walked into the library and grabbed a decanter off a side table. While he did not like that his employee was sick, it lessened some of the fear that had developed on his ride over. If Peter were still this sick, he had most likely not been sneaking around in the dead of night ripping screens out of doors and busting open windows. Whiskey splashed into the glass. Gideon shoved the plug back into the decanter and set it down. Glass clinked against wood. He pulled out his phone and made another call.

"This is Gideon Radcliffe. I want you to assign two of our security guards to Moonrise Bay on the east end of the island tonight, one at a private residence in town and the other fifty feet down the drive of a cottage that's recently been vandalized." He rattled off the addresses. "The house at Crescent Point was vandalized last night. The other home is where the victim is staying. Make sure nothing happens. If you see anything suspicious, call the police and only engage if necessary."

He hung up and took a sip of his whiskey. He and Cassandra may have only had a short-lived romance, but he would be damned if he was going to let anything else happen to her. His doorbell rang. When he opened the door, he frowned. Peter stood on the threshold, his skin a pasty gray and the tip of his nose bright red.

"Hello, sir—" He broke off to sneeze into a handkerchief. "I'm sorry."

Gideon frowned. "Sick again?"

"Not sick." Peter shook his head. "Allergies."

Gideon stood back and held the door open. "Allergies?"

"Yes, sir." Peter sneezed again. "Fortunately not contagious. A bougainvillea allergy of all things."

He rubbed his nose with his handkerchief. A bright red welt stretched across the back of his hand.

Gideon stared at it. His heart thumped against his ribs as he remembered the tattered magenta blooms scattered across scarred wooden planks.

"Bougainvillea?"

Peter froze. When he looked at Gideon, Gideon knew.

"Sir—" Peter broke off to sneeze again. "I was only trying to help."

"After I made it clear that intimidation was never to be used, you resorted to scaring, once again, a young woman who just lost her father! What were you thinking?" Gideon advanced toward Peter, making the shorter man scramble as he backed up. "You ruined her home. The last thing she had left."

"It was going to be razed anyway," Peter snapped back. "It wasn't any great loss."

"It was to her. That cottage meant everything."

"And it was falling apart!" Peter raised his chin, his eyes furious. "The first time you trusted me with a project of this magnitude, and that insolent young woman had the audacity to say no to three million dollars. She was the only thing standing between us and a Radcliffe resort in Moonrise Bay."

"Or you and your ego."

Peter's shoulders suddenly sank in defeat. "You and your family have given me so much. This was the first time that you trusted me with something so important. Something that honored your father. When she kept saying no, I just thought a couple of little mishaps would encourage her to sell."

"You drove up to her house in the dead of night and flashed your lights in her window. You frightened her. You made her afraid to be in her own home."

He remembered the fear that had haunted her eyes when she'd confronted him, the faint quaver in her voice when she'd told him about the accidents. It took every ounce of control not to punch Peter in the face.

"I just wanted to make her nervous. Wanted her to see that living out there alone wasn't the right thing, but that selling to us was." Gaining a little confidence, Peter switched tactics. "You know it was the right thing. That's why you've been wining and dining her, taking her on lavish trips. I thought her having no house to come back to would seal the deal. Everything I did was for you. She used you, Gideon. I was just protecting you. Protecting Radcliffe Resorts!"

Suddenly weary, Gideon shook his head. "She didn't use me, Peter."

"Maybe you don't see it, sir, but I do. I decided to give her the final push she needed to make the right decision."

"The right decision for who? For the company? Or for you?"

Peter's voice pitched up. "I did this for you. For your father. He wanted this."

"If you think this is how my father would have wanted things to play out, then you never knew him at all."

The anger that blazed across Peter's face was unexpected and fierce. "I knew him better than anyone. When you took over and I saw your ambition, I thought you would do him proud." He tilted his nose into the air. "I was wrong."

"You once told me my father gave you a chance," Gideon said quietly. "An opportunity when no one else would. Would the man who gave you that chance truly want you to terrorize a young woman and drive her from her home?"

Peter blinked. His mouth opened and closed several times before he finally fell silent.

"You're fired."

Gideon turned away and walked out onto the veranda. He heard his door close behind him. He took a long, deep drink before he pulled out his phone once more and dialed.

"Yes, I'd like to report a crime."

Nearly an hour later, Gideon lay on one of the lounge chairs by the infinity pool. The sun was sinking toward the horizon, coloring the waves a vivid orange. A few clouds moved overhead. The resort had sent a text earlier saying they were keeping an eye on a tropical storm that had been forecast to pass north of the island but was now possibly changing direction. Other than that, his phone had remained silent since he first called the Moonrise Bay police chief and then his own resort security. They hadn't even needed to track Peter down. He had turned himself in.

It hurt. He hadn't realized how much he had trusted Peter. He wasn't as insulated from others' actions as he had thought. His ego had fueled his defensive response when Cassandra had voiced her first doubts about Peter. He'd been so certain, so sure of himself.

And it may have cost him the one person he now couldn't picture his life without.

In the morning, he would contact a local contractor he knew who did excellent work. He would pay for any and all repairs for what Peter had done. Perhaps Cassandra would even let him make some of the other repairs she hadn't been able to address.

The zeal in Peter's voice, when he had said Gideon deserved this, still played in a hauntingly disturbing loop in his head. Everything about this project had gone wrong from the start, beginning first with his need to possess the property. Ambition had driven him. Grief had motivated him. Obsession had passed from father to son, infected someone else who had taken things too far.

Peter may have been the one to carry out the sabotage. But Gideon was just as responsible. If he had listened to Cassandra, had taken her concerns more seriously instead of focusing on his own goals, he could have prevented this. Could have stopped her from being hurt.

His head dropped back on the pillow. He'd pursued his father's dream not just because he'd believed in it, but because he'd needed it. Pursuing Lee's goal of reclaiming Radcliffe land, of bringing a new resort to life, had given Gideon something else to focus on besides his own loss.

Not just loss, Gideon admitted as he pinched the bridge of his nose. He'd been so angry with his father those last few months. He'd kept it leashed, but it had festered inside him. Had shortened his interactions, reduced the number of visits he paid to his father's room. Became the foundation for the wall he'd built around his heart.

And then his father had died, leaving Gideon with nothing but his anger and an underlying guilt that he hadn't been able to understand, hadn't been more empathetic or compassionate.

The more he'd learned about Moonrise Bay, about the development plans for Grand Cayman and the other businesses eyeing East End, the more he'd come to believe his plans were truly a good thing.

But that hadn't been the original reason. That had come later, when he finally did the research he should have done years ago.

His breath rushed out in a harsh exhale. Cassandra deserved far better than he could offer.

But he loved her. Loved her in a way he'd never thought he could love someone. He wanted her in his life, wanted to be a part of hers. Wanted to take her on trips and watch the wonder cross her face, see destinations he'd taken for granted through her eyes. Wanted to lie on the beach with her in his arms and watch the sun come up.

Wanted to encourage her as she picked up the pieces of old dreams and started to write her own stories.

He glanced at the clock. Just past nine. He could make it to Moonrise Bay before ten. Might have a chance to tell Cassandra everything, to beg her forgiveness.

To make things right.

Whether she accepted his love or not was another matter entirely.

CHAPTER SIXTEEN

Cassie

CASSIE SAT BY her window, her eyes trained on the horizon. Lightning darted down from the clouds, touched the horizon.

Marla had offered her the spare room in her house. It had been tempting. But with the officers stationed at the base of her drive, she wasn't afraid to be alone out on the Point.

Not when it might be the last few days of living in the cottage.

She'd cleaned up the worst of the damage. Wind still whistled through the cracks in the window. When the rains hit, drops would seep through the roof.

The beginning of the end.

She sucked in a shuddering breath. Her decision had been made for her. The cottage was no longer a home, no longer a haven for a lost young woman.

It was simply a shadow of what had been. Just like her fleeting moment with Gideon.

She blinked back tears. Shock had ruled her emotions when they'd pulled up to the cottage. Shock and betrayal. Much as she wanted to say she hadn't considered Gideon complicit in the vandalism that had left her cottage in tatters, the possibility had crossed her mind.

And instead of talking to him, she'd retreated into her own grief. Just like his father had. She'd shut him out.

Light flashed in her windows. Panic zipped through her even as she pushed herself to her feet, her phone in hand. She moved to the door. Then froze as she watched Gideon get out of his convertible and walk up the steps to her house.

Cassandra's heart pounded so hard it was a miracle she didn't pass out as he stepped onto the porch. He raised his hand to knock, but she opened the door before he could. Their eyes met, held. Her breath caught in her chest at the raw emotion in his gaze.

"What are you doing here?"

Wind whipped around the edge of the cottage. Gideon tore his eyes away and frowned at the sky.

"I could ask the same of you. I thought you were staying with Marla. I went to her house, but she said you came here."

"I just..." Her throat closed. "I wanted one more night."

He looked back at her, the hard planes of his face softening.

"Cassandra."

He said her name so gently it made her want to cry. She sucked in a deep breath as she stepped out onto the porch.

"This place has been home for so long. No," she said as his lips parted. "Please, I need to say this. After everything that's happened the last few months, all I could think about was that I was getting ready to lose something else." She threaded her fingers together and forced herself to hold his gaze. "I handled my father's diagnosis, his chemo treatments here, learning that he needed more treatment. I made the choice to sell the business that he built from the ground up when he moved down here. I did all of that and I didn't break. I felt like if I said anything, did anything, I was going to break. And I might not be able to put the pieces back together.

"I was sure Peter had done this. I know he's your friend," she rushed on to say, "and I'm not trying to call your judgment into question. But I saw that you disagreed, and in the moment it felt like a betrayal."

Gideon frowned. "Did someone from the police department contact you?"

"Not that I know of. But I put my phone on silent. I just needed a little time here by myself. I'm supposed to review the house with someone tomorrow and document everything for insurance."

Gideon stared at her. "Then you don't know?"

"What?"

He looked away from her, out to the darkening sky. Her pulse accelerated as he inhaled and then let out a long sigh before meeting her gaze once more.

"Peter confessed to me. The events that occurred before last night, all of it."

Shock rooted her to the spot. "Why?"

"Because I screwed up." Anger vibrated in his voice. "I didn't see how obsessed Peter had become. He took on my father's wish, my ambition, and made it his own."

"Wow."

Peter had made her uncomfortable from the moment he knocked on her door, from his salesman smile to the anger in his eyes when she said no. She'd known on some level that he was capable of something like this, but to hear it confirmed was hard.

"I'm so sorry, Gideon." Her fingernails dug into her hands. "Not just about Peter. I hurt you. I didn't really believe you had anything to do with it. And I didn't express that. You've shared so much with me, and I've hurt you terribly."

Gideon reached out. When she didn't pull away, he closed one hand around hers and tugged her forward. She moved with slow, halting steps. His arms came around her, gentle but firm. Her eyes drifted shut as Gideon pressed her against his chest.

"You owe me nothing. Not one single apology. You were in shock, you were hurting," he said as he leaned back and gazed down into her eyes, "and I let my own fears drive me away when you needed me."

"To be fair, I doubt Marla would have let you stay."

"She is a formidable woman." He leaned down, placed his forehead against hers. "I have no excuse, Cassandra."

She reached up, settled her fingers against his cheek, savored the faint scrape of stubble against her palm.

"It's okay."

"It's not." He leaned back, stared down at her with conviction blazing in his eyes. "Don't ever accept less than what you deserve. Not from me, not from anyone. I should have been here for you." His voice dropped as he cradled her face in one hand. "I should have been here."

"But you came back." She swallowed past the thickness in her throat. "You're here now."

"I am." He breathed in. "I love you, Cassandra."

Her world stopped. For a moment there was nothing

but the warmth of his arms, the frantic beat of her heart and the echo of his words pulsing through her.

"You love me?" she finally said.

"I know it's sudden. I understand if you need more time. But I'm here," he said fiercely, "and I will wait as long as you need—"

"I love you, too." She reached up and smoothed a lock of hair back from his face. "You're so much more of a leader than I gave you credit for. You're generous and supportive. You embody everything I've come to realize Radcliffe Resorts strives to be."

"Cassandra…"

"And you see me, Gideon. Even when we were at odds, you saw me. Trusted me." Her voice cracked. "I've never been less afraid of being myself than I am when I'm with you."

He tilted her chin up, waited a heartbeat. Then he closed his mouth over hers in a kiss so sweet it brought tears to her eyes. Her hands crept up his neck, curled into his hair.

And then the kiss deepened. Her lips parted for him as he cradled her head. Desire moved through her body, a languid warmth that had her arching into him.

Thunder rumbled. Gideon lifted his head and frowned.

"Thwarted by Mother Nature again."

Cassie chuckled. His phone buzzed in his pocket, a faint vibration against her hip. Gideon pulled it out, then frowned.

"The storm has shifted. It's poised to strike the island in about two hours."

"Oh." Cassie grimaced. "I should have kept my phone on. I thought it was supposed to go north of here." She glanced over her shoulder at the cottage. "I'll grab what I can and head for the shelter in town."

"Come back with me."

Her head whipped around. "What?"

"Come back with me to the resort." He traced a finger over her parted lips. "Stay with me tonight. I don't want to let you out of my sight."

"But…what about Marla—?"

"Is welcome to come, too. We have available rooms, enough to fit her entire family," he said with a slight smile. "Although I suspect she'll choose to stay. I know you've lived here for years and probably ridden out hurricanes far worse than this. But I'd like for you to stay here with me where I know you're safe."

His voice deepened on the last word. Cassie realized in that moment just how much her home being vandalized had affected him, too.

"All right."

An hour later, she was relaxing on a chaise lounge overlooking the roughened sea. The drive back had been quiet, similar to their drive to Moonrise Bay just a few hours ago. But beneath the warmth of their renewed relationship lay something deeper, the memory of where their kiss had been heading before the impending storm had interrupted them. Anticipation for what the night might bring.

But until then, she was determined to enjoy every moment she could. To savor this first night of being in love.

Room service had delivered savory shrimp skewers, French fries dusted with garlic seasoning and a beet and artichoke salad. After dinner, they'd moved out onto the veranda, watching the sky as the clouds thickened and the wind tossed the palm trees below back and forth.

"I've always loved storms." She sipped the glass of wine Gideon had poured for her as lightning forked down to the sea. "Colorado had some beautiful ones. But a storm over the ocean is something else entirely. The whole landscape physically changes." She sighed as she curled into his side. "Beautiful."

She felt him smile into her hair. "Is there anything you don't like?"

"Licorice. Books with typos." She chewed on her bottom lip as she thought. "I think that's it."

He chuckled. "My list is substantially longer."

She liked this casual intimacy. Falais de Vignes and Venice had offered romance, that first thrill of tumbling over the edge into something new. But simply sitting and enjoying this moment with Gideon was an equally enjoyable experience.

"Like what?"

"Eggs sunny side up. Runny yolk," he clarified when she frowned up at him. "Cold showers. Audio books."

She sat straight up. "Audio books?"

"I've never found a narrator I like."

She shook her head. "You're missing out. I play audio books whenever I'm closing down the bar or driving out to the west end."

"Why do you drive so far?"

"Having lived out in Colorado, driving thirty or forty minutes to get somewhere isn't much. I met the owner of Prose & Tide at a wedding Marla hosted. When he learned I had trained in London as a mixologist and bartender, he told me about the new restaurant he was opening and offered me a job. He offered to let me lead with everything: the menu, the decor. I wouldn't get that kind of opportunity in Moonrise Bay."

Even as she said the words, she grimaced. How unfair was it that she was willing to drive for an opportunity but turn down a potential chance for growth for her community.

"What?"

"Just thinking," she sighed. "About Crescent Point. The cottage."

Gideon leaned over and kissed her. She leaned into him. Thunder boomed overhead as rain started to fall just beyond the veranda.

"Tomorrow," Gideon murmured against her lips. "Tonight, just us."

He plucked the wineglass from her hand and then pulled her into the circle of his arms. She looped her arms around his neck and smiled against his mouth as he kissed her again. As he ran his hands up her body, cradling her against him.

"Gideon..."

Gideon leaned back, his thumbs gently stroking her hips as he held her gaze. The heat he saw there mirrored his own. "Will you stay with me tonight?"

She cocked her head to one side. "I already said yes."

"Yes." He trailed a finger up her arm, the touch slow and seductive. Her eyes followed as he caressed the skin. "But will you stay *with* me."

Her body warmed as she tilted her face up.

"I'd like that very much."

As the rain fell harder and lightning danced across the sky, Gideon stood with Cassie in his arms and carried her inside.

CHAPTER SEVENTEEN

Gideon

GIDEON SCRUNCHED HIS eyes against the bright light. He groaned and shifted. Then froze as he registered the warm body curved into his.

Slowly, he opened his eyes. Wild brown curls lay on the pillow in front of him. Cassandra's hips were pressed against him, her back to his chest. He breathed her in, pulled her just a little closer.

Cassandra murmured before she rolled over and threw one arm over his neck. Her lashes lay dark against her skin. Her lips were parted, her breathing deep and even. If he could wake up every morning like this, he wouldn't need anything else in his life.

Her eyes flickered open. As soon as she saw him, her lips curved into a smile. He pressed a soft kiss to her lips, savored her body relaxing against his.

"Good morning."

"Good morning." She glanced over her shoulder. "Sunny?"

"Maybe the storm wasn't as bad as forecast."

Her phone rang on the bedside table. Cassandra moaned as she rolled over and grabbed it. She stiffened and sat straight up.

"Marla?"

Gideon sat up and laid a hand on her shoulder as she listened. He could barely hear what Marla was saying. Judging by the way Cassandra's muscles bunched beneath his hand, though, he knew it wasn't good.

Finally, Cassandra hung up.

"What is it?"

A shudder passed through her body.

"It's the cottage. It didn't survive the storm."

For the third time in twenty-four hours, Gideon made the drive to Moonrise Bay. Cassandra's hand rested on his leg. Every now and then he would reach down and squeeze her fingers.

They would face whatever challenges lay ahead together.

This time when they turned around the bend in Cassandra's driveway, there was no ramshackle cottage. There was nothing but a pile of wood crushed beneath a cedar tree.

When they got out of the car, he took her hand and walked with her to the ruins of the cottage. Even though she clung to him, she stood tall, shoulders back, chin tilted up.

Strong. Confident. A warrior facing down yet another loss with a backbone that made him admire her as much as it made him want to push her back into the car and bundle her away to somewhere safe, somewhere he could care for her.

"It's gone." Cassandra's voice trembled. "What are the odds?"

Gideon pulled her close. "You can rebuild."

Cassandra looked up at him, then shook her head. "No. That's not the answer."

Before Gideon could say anything else, a car drove up. Marla hopped out and hurried forward. "Cassie, I'm so sorry. I meant to be here, but there was damage in town."

"It's okay." Cassandra hugged her. "Is your home okay?"

"Yes. The restaurant lost a few shingles, but that's it." Her gaze moved to Gideon. "Thank you for coming. And I'm sorry. For being suspicious."

"I'm grateful that Cassie has a friend like you."

Marla's smile was sad. "Thank you. And I'm sorry about Peter."

"Me, too."

More cars came up the lane. People wanted to help. Cassandra leaned into Gideon, her teeth biting into her lip. "I don't know what good they can do. It's a total loss."

"Take the help for now." Marla squeezed her hand.

The next few hours flew by. Gideon rolled up his sleeves and helped a group of men move a tree. Someone brought pants and steel-toed boots so Cassandra could move through the destruction and salvage what she could. Marla's husband brought food and drink for the volunteers.

Gideon grabbed a bottle of water and looked around. The number of helpers was astounding. Cassandra hadn't been exaggerating when she'd said everyone helped everyone in Moonrise Bay.

Finally, as the sun sank low in the sky, Gideon pulled Cassandra aside.

"Let's call it a day."

She nodded and pushed a stray curl out of her eyes.

Her face was streaked with dirt. Dark moons etched themselves into the delicate skin beneath her eyes. But she was still standing.

"Yeah." Her face fell. "I don't—"

"You're coming with me."

She nodded. "Okay. I can do that."

He drove her back to the resort. He managed to talk her into eating some soup before she slipped between the covers of his bed.

She was asleep before he'd even closed the door. He moved to his desk and walked out onto the veranda, hands tucked into his pockets, and gazed out over the ocean. He'd already been considering his next course of action. Now, after what he'd witnessed today, been a part of, he knew it was the right thing to do. For himself, for Cassandra and for the town she loved. He closed his eyes.

I hope one day, Dad, you can forgive me.

Cassandra

Cassandra awoke with a start. She sat up and blinked, confused by the darkness. The distant roar of the sea was familiar. But the silk sheets above and beneath her were far nicer than hers. Then it all came back to her in a nauseating rush.

The storm. Her cottage.

She lay there for a long time. Perhaps it was an unexpected blessing. She had decided to sell Crescent Point anyway. And, she thought with a ghost of a smile, she had friends. People who had shown up yesterday and supported her in her darkest hour. And she had a man who cared about her, who had rolled up his sleeves and dedicated an entire day to helping her.

There are many things to be grateful for, she thought as she threw back the sheet and got to her feet.

She padded out into the large living area. Gideon sat in a wood-trimmed leather recliner, a laptop balanced on his knees and reading glasses perched on the bridge of his nose. She stopped in her tracks.

"Whoa."

Gideon looked up at her and smiled. "Feeling better?"

"I am now that I've seen you in your glasses looking like a sexy historian."

He chuckled as he set the laptop on a nearby table. "I'm glad I could bring a smile to your face."

She walked over to him. She sat on his lap and curled into his embrace. "It's frightening, isn't it?"

"What?"

"How quickly we fell." She buried her face in the crook of his neck. "How much you already feel like home." His arms tightened around her. She continued, "You told me that, you know." She tilted her head back to look at him. "That home was about people. You were right."

"To an extent, but I've never lost my sanctuary the way you have."

"Well, if your offer is still on the table, I'd like to take you up on it. With that kind of money, I can build my own sanctuary."

He trailed his fingers up and down her cheek. "It's not."

His words had the same effect as a bucket of ice water being dumped on her head. "What?"

His hold on her tightened when she tried to wriggle off his lap. "Give me a moment?"

When she quit trying to flee, he reached for his laptop. "I'm drawing up a different agreement."

"Oh?"

"I would still like to buy your land. But I have something different in mind."

He angled the screen toward her. She read over the document, her eyes widening as she took in the enormity of what he was sharing. "You want to buy Crescent Point and build a house? For me?"

"Yes. I own the land to the north and south of the point. If you agree to let me use the back two acres along the road, I can still join the properties. I've decided to redesign the resort, try something new instead of our standard main building. This would allow us to utilize the unique rectangle shape."

"But…your father?"

"That was his dream. Not mine. It took me a while to realize that. I've come to realize," he added softly, "I want something different. Although I want the resort at East End, I want to collaborate with Moonrise Bay. But most of all, Cassandra, I want you to be happy."

Tears spilled down her cheeks. "And I appreciate that, but I don't want you to give up on something that is important to you."

"You brought me back to life, Cassandra. And I want to enjoy that life with you." He nodded toward the contract. "What do you think?"

"Yes." Her voice broke. "I'd like that very much."

He cradled her in his arms and carried her out to the veranda. He set her down but kept holding her hands. "Before you agree, you should know I added two conditions to the bottom of the contract."

"What are they?" He dropped down to one knee. Her heart shot into her throat. "Gideon."

"That you marry me. I don't have a ring yet, but I ordered one from a designer in Venice. Whether you say yes or not, it's yours."

She swallowed hard. "And the second?"

"The second is that you help me design not only the house but the resort, too. You know Moonrise Bay better than anyone else."

She gripped his hands. "Yes. And yes."

He surged to his feet and wrapped her in a tight embrace, sealing their contract with a kiss.

EPILOGUE

Cassie

Three years later

CASSIE SANK DOWN onto the sand with a grateful sigh, one hand resting on her swollen belly. The waves crawled up the sand, then receded in their endless dance with the island. She sighed, a sound of pure contentment as the late autumn sun warmed her skin.

Just one more month. One more month until they got to meet Baby Cecilia or Baby John.

"There you are."

Her head whipped around, and she smiled when she saw her husband walking toward her across the beach.

"Gideon!"

She started to get to her feet. Gideon rushed to her side and helped her up.

"Careful, darling."

She rolled her eyes even as she kissed his cheek. "I'm fine, Gideon. So's the baby."

His hand dropped down to her belly, a smile lighting up his face as the baby kicked.

"I was worried they'd decide to make an early appearance."

"We waited for you. How was France?"

She'd hated not being able to go. But at this stage of her pregnancy, all travel was off-limits.

"Good." He kissed her forehead. "I'll take you and the baby there as soon as you're cleared to travel." He smiled. "Maybe we could time it with the release of your book."

It was incredible, she thought as they walked up the beach and onto the grassy hill that led to Crescent Point's plateau, how much life had changed in just three years. The villa had been completed in eighteen months, just in time for Gideon and Cassie to exchange vows in the garden overlooking the sea. One year later, Radcliffe at East End had opened its doors, with eight luxury villas on the north end and a smaller main building toward the south with six customized rooms, a spa, restaurant and two cocktail bars. Including Prose & Tide East, under exclusive management of Cassie Radcliffe. The resort had been lauded as one of the most luxurious and sustainable vacation spots in the Caribbean. Praise that had meant a lot to her husband as he worked to rebuild his reputation following the lawsuit.

Somehow, Cassie thought as they crested the hill, she'd managed to find time to write. There had been plenty of days when she'd felt like a fool for pursuing it, when the words on the paper had seemed childish and wasteful.

But Gideon had been there through it all, encouraging her, supporting her, even reading her work and offering his critique. She'd taken a trip with him to Spain to see a newly renovated resort when she'd gotten the call from a publisher in New York. Her shriek had brought him rushing into the room, where he'd promptly picked her up and swung her in a circle when she'd shared the good news.

There had been healing, too. Gideon's uncle had called every week for nearly a year before Gideon had finally listened to one of his voicemails. He'd put it on speaker, played it for Cassie to hear, too. An apology, short and simple. A request for Gideon to call.

It had taken another six months before Gideon had finally answered. The conversation had been brief, terse. But it had led to more calls. Then, finally, a meeting in New York where Steven had shared what had happened. What had started off as good intentions to lead even as he dealt with the grief of losing his brother. How he'd covered for one financial mistake by borrowing money. Then a little more when he'd realized how easy it was. Then more still until he'd sunk so deep there'd been no way out. Holding on to Radcliffe Resorts had been his only way to stave off the discovery of his misdeeds.

There was still a distance between uncle and nephew. Still mistrust that reared its head. But the relationship Gideon had once thought damaged beyond repair was slowly being stitched back together.

Cassie squeezed Gideon's hand. For a man who had once kept the world at bay, her husband had grown so much.

The villa came into view, the stone pillars on the back terrace and ivory-colored walls mirroring the resort in Falais de Vignes.

The place where she realized she had started to fall in love.

"Welcome home, Gideon."

Gideon leaned down and kissed her.

"There's no place I'd rather be."

* * * * *

MILLS & BOON®

Coming next month

THEIR MAURITIUS WEDDING RUSE
Nina Milne

'If you agreed we would go to Mauritius and plan a small low-key ceremony, lie low somewhere on the beach.'

Images streamed her mind. Lying stretched out on golden sand, side by side with Logan. So close that if she reached out she'd be able to touch him. Long cool drinks sipped by a pool. Walks through the fabulous scenery of Mauritius, dinners for two at little local restaurants. Watching the sun set over a deep blue sea, turning to each other later in the moonlight, tipping her face upward and…

Jeez. Snap out of it. What was wrong with her? That was not a scenario that could play for her - not with Logan, not with anyone. And she understood that, was good with that. Unfortunately, her hormones clearly weren't.

Continue reading

THEIR MAURITIUS WEDDING RUSE
Nina Milne

Available next month
millsandboon.co.uk

Copyright © 2025 Nina Milne

COMING SOON!

We really hope you enjoyed reading this book. If you're looking for more romance be sure to head to the shops when new books are available on

Thursday 19th June

To see which titles are coming soon, please visit
millsandboon.co.uk/nextmonth

MILLS & BOON

afterglow BOOKS

Afterglow Books is a trend-led, trope-filled list of books with diverse, authentic and relatable characters, a wide array of voices and representations, plus real world trials and tribulations. Featuring all the tropes you could possibly want (think small-town settings, fake relationships, grumpy vs sunshine, enemies to lovers) and all with a generous dose of spice in every story.

@millsandboonuk
@millsandboonuk
afterglowbooks.co.uk

#AfterglowBooks

For all the latest book news, exclusive content and giveaways scan the QR code below to sign up to the Afterglow newsletter:

SCAN ME

afterglow BOOKS

KAREN BOOTH
NOT SO FAST
He's on track to win her heart...

Much Ado About Hating You
Sarah Echavarre Smith
They're enemies at work...but can love write their happy ending?

- Sports romance
- Enemies to lovers
- Spicy

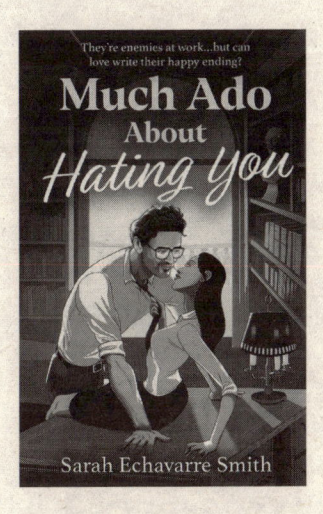

- Workplace romance
- Forbidden love
- Opposites attract

OUT NOW

Two stories published every month. Discover more at:
Afterglowbooks.co.uk

FOUR BRAND NEW BOOKS FROM
MILLS & BOON MODERN

The same great stories you love, a stylish new look!

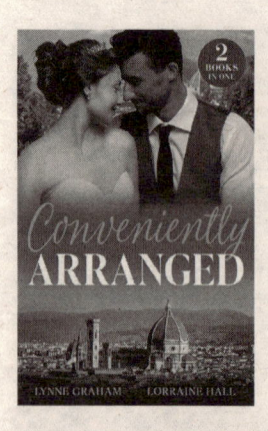

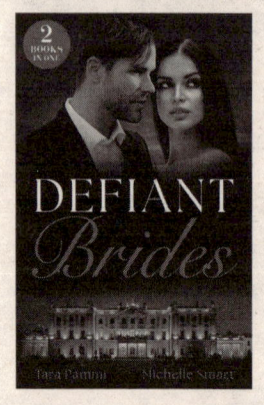

OUT NOW

Eight Modern stories published every month, find them all at:
millsandboon.co.uk

OUT NOW!

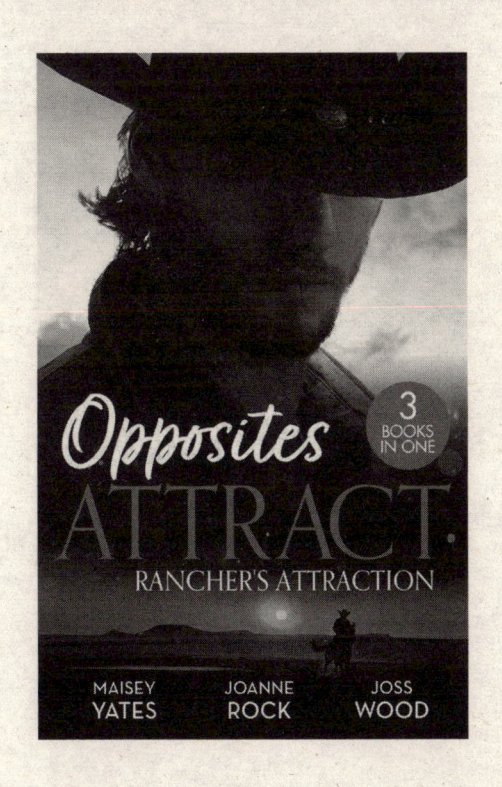

Opposites Attract: Rancher's Attraction

3 BOOKS IN ONE

MAISEY YATES · JOANNE ROCK · JOSS WOOD

Available at millsandboon.co.uk

MILLS & BOON

OUT NOW!

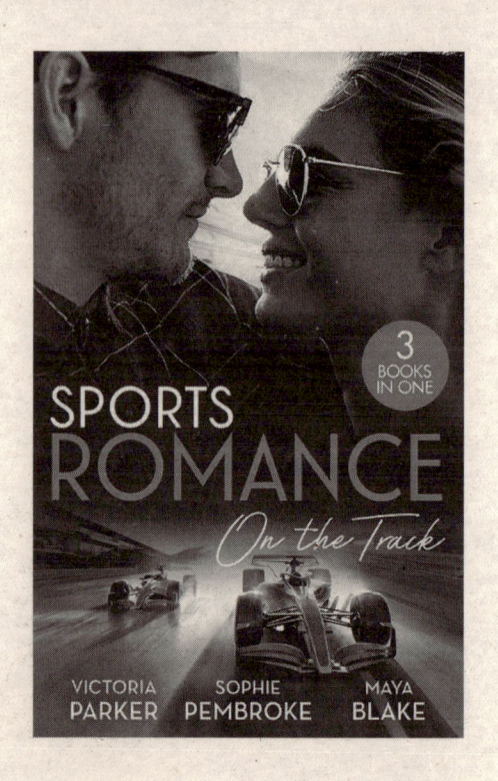

SPORTS ROMANCE
On the Track

3 BOOKS IN ONE

VICTORIA PARKER
SOPHIE PEMBROKE
MAYA BLAKE

Available at
millsandboon.co.uk

MILLS & BOON